Joan Brady was the first woman — and the only American — ever to win the prestigious Whitbread Book of the Year award. Critics hailed her winning novel, *Theory of War*, as 'a modern work of genius.' Born in California, Joan Brady now lives in Oxford.

# VENOM

Recently released from prison, David Marion didn't expect to find a hitman at his door. Warned that a powerful secret organisation is after him, David goes underground and off the radar — waiting for the perfect moment to wreak revenge . . . Physicist Helen Freyl has just accepted a job offer from a giant pharmaceutical company which is close to finding a cure for radiation poisoning. But when the mysteriously sudden death of a colleague is followed by another, Helen begins to doubt her employer's motives and realises that her own life is in danger, too.

JOAN BRADY

# VENOM

*Complete and Unabridged*

CHARNWOOD
*Leicester*

First published in Great Britain in 2010 by
Simon & Schuster UK Ltd., London

First Charnwood Edition
published 2010
by arrangement with
Simon & Schuster UK Ltd., London



British Library CIP Data

Brady, Joan.
Venom.
1. Physicists- -Crimes against- -Fiction.
2. Pharmaceutical industry- -Corrupt practices- -Fiction. 3. Suspense fiction. 4. Large type books.
I. Title
813.5′4–dc22

ISBN 978–1–44480–423–2

Published by
F. A. Thorpe (Publishing)
Anstey, Leicestershire

Set by Words & Graphics Ltd.
Anstey, Leicestershire
Printed and bound in Great Britain by
T. J. International Ltd., Padstow, Cornwall

This book is printed on acid-free paper

*For Nigel Butt and John Saddler*
*without whom nothing would have worked.*

# Acknowledgements

The Arts Council of England as well as every friend I have helped me with this book and with the troubles that ran alongside it. So did Eleanor, Alexander and Flora, who soothed, cajoled, supported, read, suggested — all this with the compassion of saints. As did my patient advisors Tim and Robert and my editor Suzanne, who knows a thing or two about trouble herself.

I am profoundly grateful.

Enemies also help you sometimes. They goad you on, make you angry enough to fight when you think the fight's gone out of you. In this spirit, I thank both the South Hams District Council and the Conker Shoe Company of Totnes, Devon.

# PART 1

# 1

## SPRINGFIELD, ILLINOIS

'David?'

'Yes.'

'You know who this is?'

'Yes.'

'You're alone?'

'Yes.'

'Get out. Now.'

There was a slight pause. David looked into the living room. The pale cotton curtains were closed across the patio doors; a light wind billowed them out towards him. 'How many guys are there?'

'One.'

'Who?'

'He's a professional, David.'

'Size? Build?'

'For God's sake, what does it matter? Just get out. Right now.'

David Marion snapped his mobile shut. When it had rung, he'd been in the kitchen of his house, folding sheets with the military precision that comes from years as a convicted man in a prison laundry. His cupboards showed the same influence: a couple of cans each of peaches, Heinz spaghetti, baked beans, spam, an aerosol of Reddi-wip. He shook out a pillowcase, tossed this whole store into it — except for the Reddi-wip — carried it to the entrance hall, set it beside the door and went back to the living room.

It was the end of March, an unexpectedly warm night in the Midwest; people had windows open all along the close where he lived. He shut the patio doors behind his curtains. Then he turned on the TV, lit a cigarette and sat down to wait.

* * *

But David was hardly a man at ease watching a TV quiz; he still had the Reddi-wip clutched in his hand when he heard a gentle knock. He balanced his cigarette on the edge of the ashtray and went into the entrance hall.

'What do you want?' he said irritably through the front door.

'I'm really sorry to disturb you' — the voice was frightened, wavery, old — 'but I saw your light. My wife — '

'I'm busy.'

'I got to get her to emergency. You *got* to help me.'

'Call an ambulance.'

'Oh, come on, mister. Please help us. *Please*.'

David sighed, more irritably than before. 'Give me a minute.' He turned the key in the lock and leaned against the door while he slid back the bolt. The abrupt pressure from the other side was all he needed to know. He yanked the door open.

Any type of aerosol — even whipped cream — is a substitute for mace. Before the guy on the other side of the door recovered his balance enough to aim the gun in his hand, the Reddi-wip blinded him. He dropped the weapon. David kicked it off to one side, grabbed the pillowcase of canned food that he'd set there half an hour before and swung hard. The man staggered, sank to his knees. Blood spurted from his nose. David swung again and kept on swinging until the pillowcase ripped apart and cans of spam and peaches rolled away across the floor. They clattered against the far wall.

He stood a moment, breathing hard, covered in blood, furious, outraged, affronted.

The guy lay spreadeagled on his floor. The face was too much of a mess to give away much, but the springy hair and the young body suggested early twenties, a big kid, almost as tall as David himself, with one of those iron-pumped prison bodies like his. A stretch inside should have taught him better than to try such a stupid trick.

David left the body where it was, and went to the garage for paint thinner and a box of Mexican Miracle-Gro for Lawns. He dumped both into a bowl with a jar of Vaseline, kneaded them into a dough and wrapped it in Saran wrap. Candles came next. He cut the wax away from a dozen of them, tied the wicks into a long string, warmed them in the oven while he ground the heads of half a box of matches, then rolled the wicks in the residue. Packing the rest of the match heads into the spring from a ballpoint pen was a delicate job; it took several toothpicks and forty minutes. He placed the entire assembly — string, spring and dough — near his front door.

There wasn't more than a couple of hours of darkness left when he emptied the kid's pockets, got out of his own blood-spattered clothes, showered, dressed. He checked over the living room, bedroom, kitchen the way tourists check out a motel where they've spent the night, except that he was checking it out in reverse: vital things such as car keys and house keys had to be left behind. His luggage was a plastic supermarket bag; he tossed a couple of spare tools into it along with the contractor's gun and pocket contents.

Then he took out his lighter, lit the string of candle wicks and left, shutting the front door behind him.

He hadn't found any keys on the man, but he knew the cars of this respectable neighbourhood, and a battered Volkswagen didn't belong here. The kid had been so sure of himself that the keys were still in the ignition. David slid into the driver's seat and started the engine; he'd reached George Washington Boulevard when the thunderclap of the explosion hit. He braked, as any ordinary driver would, and twisted around to watch the flames, white in the centre, red at the tips, licking up into the night.

Vaseline and Mexican fertilisers make as good a bomb as any terrorist might hope for. Lights in houses nearby flicked on, a few here, a few there. A second and third blast came almost together, throwing out streaks of red that scarred the sky and boiled up to join forces with an already fierce fire. A wail of sirens began in the distance, only to be drowned in further explosions.

Where David's house once stood, an inferno billowed and soared.

# 2

## DUBICZEWO, MOGILEV REGION, BELARUS

The vehicle pulled into the village of Dubiczewo every six months. It looked like a bus without windows and bore the words:

Мобильная медицинская клиника

Most of the locals were illiterate, and three years ago they'd been suspicious of this wheeled chunk of modernity. Now they all knew the words meant 'Mobile Medical Clinic'. The twin vehicle that pulled in after it said, 'Mobile Test Laboratory'; it was full of eerie-looking machinery that glowed and made clapping noises, but these days the villagers climbed the metal steps into it without a qualm. They stood in front of the chest X-ray as nonchalantly as any Westerner. They were happy to lie down in the scintillation detector that recorded the radiation in their bodies.

Consultations began at once. There were no appointments; the locals and people from outlying areas arranged a general schedule among themselves. At the front of the clinic under a wide awning, a group of the healthy waited for a check-over and the collection of blood and urine samples that would precede their visit to the test lab. At the rear, in a canvas enclosure warmed by a wood-burning stove, the ailing, the injured and the frightened waited for advice from a paramedic who would decide whether they were to see one of the nurses or the doctor.

The team included one of two doctors, Dr Tatiana or Dr Zukim, a giggly, untidy man who expected a bribe. Dr Tatiana's arrival was always cause for celebration.

She was a dumpling of a woman with cheeks so round that when she smiled, her glasses rose too high atop them for her to focus her eyes on her patient. She had only the thinnest covering of hair on her head; like most of the people who attended the clinic, she was still battling the effects of the Chernobyl meltdown nearly a quarter of a century ago. That was why the mobile clinic had come to exist: to care for Chernobyl's modern victims.

To this day nobody knows precisely how much fallout the nuclear plant released — except that it was huge. Conservative estimates put it at more than 150 Hiroshima bombs and literally millions of times more than the Three Mile Island meltdown, the worst civilian nuclear accident in US history. Parts of Mogilev had been as heavily contaminated as the exclusion zone around the power plant itself even though the region was 200 kilometres away. The official explanation was an unhappy conjunction of wind and rain. What the gossips said was that, right after the accident, Soviet chemical troops saw a black cloud travelling towards Moscow; they shot at it and turned it towards Mogilev instead.

Dr Tatiana was sceptical. Like most Belarusians, she dismissed official explanations of anything and everything no matter how convincing they sounded, but she didn't know enough about chemical troops to judge. On the other hand, what difference did it make *how* Chernobyl contaminated the region? Her problem was dealing with the human cost here and now.

She didn't have to examine the teenage boy who lay across his mother's lap. Symptoms that might puzzle an American doctor were painfully familiar to her. But she was punctilious in her record-keeping. Funds for clinics like this depended on careful documentation. She noted each of her observations in the file open in front of her. Undressed, the boy was ashen, covered in bruises, severely emaciated; he weighed less than the sacks of potatoes his mother gathered from the fields. The largest things on his body were his kneecaps.

'You are fourteen now, Boris?' Dr Tatiana asked. She spoke in Belarusian.

'He was not like this six months ago,' his mother said. Her eyes were terrified. 'He wants to play ice hockey. Now he screams when I touch him.'

Dr Tatiana took Boris's hands. 'Did you play much last winter?' He shook his head wearily. '*I* could never even stand up on skates,' she went on.

The boy smiled. 'I began really good.'

'At the beginning of the season?'

He nodded.

'What position do you play?' she said.

'Centre.' There was pride in his voice. His team was most likely a raggle-taggle of kids with home-carved hockey sticks and a potato for a puck, but ice hockey players are heroes in Belarus.

'Next winter you'll play better than ever,' she said, helping him gently off her examining table.

'I'll need to run a few tests,' she went on to his mother. 'Be of good cheer, Mrs Gres. There is a great deal we can do to make Boris more comfortable, and we hear about new approaches almost every day.'

And yet she shook her head as she watched the woman carry her son out the door of the consultation room. She knew she hadn't fooled the mother, but the young can so easily blind themselves to the obvious. She completed her notes with the words, 'Diagnosis: Acute Myeloid Leukaemia.'

The boy's only hope was the rare miracle of spontaneous remission. In the West, it would be different; there'd be extensive chemotherapy, bone marrow transplants, a good shot at recovery. The money wasn't available here. Treatment in Boris's case could consist only of palliative measures: painkillers, antibiotics and a recently introduced cocktail of antioxidants and vitamins that seemed to give a boost.

She marked him down for everything, but she would not be surprised to hear that he'd died within the week. These cases could go very fast.

It looked so peaceful here. A tractor spreading fertiliser crawled slug-like along the distant horizon — big yellow cab, tank-like wheels — a pleasant pastoral scene. And yet Dr Tatiana wasn't sure how much longer she could bear this work. There was no end in sight, not even a let-up. Three radioactive isotopes remained active in Belarusian soil — caesium-137, strontium-90, plutonium-239 — and continued to produce the poisons that cause such fearful damage to human tissue and human genes. Forecasts showed that the levels of radiation in Belarus weren't falling as the years passed; they were slowly but steadily rising as subsoil waters carried the isotopes farther and wider.

No doctor could be surprised that general health in the region was getting worse too. What so upset Dr Tatiana was the number of children who were as sick as Boris. The incidence of childhood leukaemia had remained fairly steady for almost two decades. And then, a few years ago, she'd noticed an abrupt increase. This was so puzzling and disturbing a development that the Ministry of Health issued a paper about it. Official policy blamed it on a spate of unusual reactions to common infection.

Dr Tatiana only sighed at the silliness of such an idea. On the other hand, if something like that didn't explain it, what did?

# 3

## CATON, ALABAMA

Joshua Brewster's family had been dirt poor for generations when he found a special swarm of bees and started farming them; he was only a kid then, and it's not as though he turned the Brewsters into millionaires. They lived in Wal-Mart overalls and a clapboard house with linoleum floors. They huddled around an ancient wood-burning stove for warmth in winter, while outside, hand-built hives huddled together all year around like dollhouses for the Birmingham homeless.

Joshua swore his honey had healing properties, but all beekeepers make the same claim, and Joshua's was so bitter that only a few health-food nuts would bother with it. The venom fared better. Years ago, he'd developed a special process for milking the bees; his hives produced more than most, and he supplied some eminent acupuncturists up north. Variations in its chemistry made it an interesting exercise for undergraduates, so university labs bought from him too. Recently there'd been an increase in demand — enough so that his youngest daughter could take up the scholarship that the University of Alabama had offered her. Other than that, the farm's turnover didn't put meat on the table every day of the week.

He didn't even own the farm. Helen Freyl did.

The Freyls were rich people from Springfield, Illinois, 400 miles north of here; they'd owned huge chunks of the town since Lincoln's time. Helen's title to this farm had begun as a joke of a Christmas present when she was a little girl of eight. She'd reached under the tree, grabbed the shiniest package, ripped off the ribbons and found a mahogany box with a key in a brass lock. Inside were papers that said she was now the owner of a real, live business. Then came a short treatise about the thousands of new animal species that are named every year, then an embossed certificate with gold writing that said these bees were among them. There used to be *Apis cerana, Apis dorsata, Apis florae* and *Apis mellifera*.

Now *Apis helena* had been added to the list.

Helen had let out a howl of disappointment. What does an eight-year-old care about having a species named just for her?

The gift had been her grandmother's, and to this day her grandmother took Helen's responsibility to the farm far more seriously than Helen did. Every year she sent Helen to check Joshua's accounts even though the Freyls retained expensive tax lawyers back home. Accounts and tax returns bored Helen. All business did. Her grandmother had tried again and again to kindle some interest; checking Joshua's accounts was one attempt in a long series. Not that it was an arduous job: all Helen had to do was gather up the paperwork to turn over to the lawyers.

But she loved the smell of smoke and honey that hung over the farm, and this time Joshua's sister Lillian had come along. Lillian had been housekeeper to the Freyls since Helen was born, and Helen couldn't imagine life without her. Lillian was her solace, her comfort, her sanctuary in the world. It was Lillian who'd cleaned her scraped knees when she'd fallen off her bike, and it was Lillian who'd held her tight when she'd wakened screaming from night horrors all those years ago. To this day, Springfield gossips whispered that Helen was unstable. 'Don't you pay 'em no mind, sugar,' Lillian said. 'You's just highly strung. That's a good thing. You gonna do something special with your life. They ain't gonna do *nothing*.'

Helen was twenty-nine years old, smart, well educated, pretty as well as rich. She'd inherited fine bones and a porcelain delicacy from her grandmother. She had her father's green eyes and her mother's dark hair. But her parents were dead. Both deaths had been sudden, brutal, unnecessary, and despite Lillian's faith in her, Helen woke every morning in despair and wandered through the day aimless, adrift, depressed. She envied the bees. They didn't have to live like that. Their lives had purpose and meaning, a suicide-bomber's commitment to a community.

* * *

The morning after Helen arrived at Joshua's farm, he handed her a letter on his way out to his round of the hives. She read it, shook her head and gave it to Lillian to read.

'Miss Helen, if'n I was you I wouldn't bother answering this,' Lillian said, handing it back to her. 'But it ain't my business. It's your'n — and Joshua's.'

'Who the hell do they think are they are?' Helen said.

'They's lawyers. It says so.'

'Lawyers don't do this kind of thing on their own. They're acting for somebody.' Helen glanced over the letter again. 'I guess they could've come when you guys weren't here — had a look around.'

Lillian shook her head. 'The bees woulda told Joshua.'

Joshua said the bees told him what to do and when to do it. Helen half-believed him and half didn't; he had an amused look in his eye most of the time and an impish smile to go with it. One year she'd persuaded him to let her invest in a computer-controlled venom collector, infrared cameras, ultra-modern hive design. Bees don't hibernate; they have to cluster together to keep warm. Even so, lots of them die, and more died that year than ever before. Joshua said they didn't like computers spying on them. Back came the ramshackle wood hives and the collector he'd designed and rigged himself.

The bees stopped dying.

He'd refused money from Helen after that. She'd tried to get him to let her improve the house for him and his family. He said he liked his house the way it was. A neighbour's land had come up for sale. She'd offered to buy it for him. He'd said he couldn't manage an acre more than he already had. She'd happily have put up money to subsidize his youngest daughter at the university, but he wouldn't have that either. If his daughter went at all, he'd pay for it himself. Period. No discussion. And so both the farm and his family remained at subsistence level.

And yet the letter in Helen's hands — it was addressed to Dr Helen Freyl, President, Caton Bees & Venom — was an offer of $5 million for the property and its livestock.

# 4

## SPRINGFIELD TO DC

All Springfield's tough kids knew the chasm off Route 378, a deep, narrow V-shape of stone with a smatter of trees and shrubs clinging to it: perfect for playing chicken. David drove the battered Volkswagen to the edge, got out, pushed it over. A moment of silence, a short series of crashes and a newcomer joined the corpses of chicken cars going generations back.

From Route 378, the neon lights of the town make an extravaganza of pinks and greens, stars and scintillations: McDonald's, Coca-Cola, Exxon — and off to one side, what might have been a neighbourhood bonfire that had got out of control. David walked backwards until the view disappeared behind a rise of ground, then turned and jogged to the interstate.

The highway was busy even now, even before dawn broke. A flickering neon sign on his side of the road read:

**BENNY & JANE'S**
**Full comfort for the whole family!**
**UNBELIEVABLE RATES!**
**$39.25 for Mom and Dad, and . . .**
**the kids are free!**

The place was asleep, the parking lot only half full. He scanned the cars. He liked cars. He'd restored his old Chevrolet Impala, done all the work himself, stripping it right down to the chassis and rebuilding the engine into the high-powered beauty it was intended to be. And yet the car he chose was a cheap, underpowered 1993 Toyota, parked beside the unit farthest away from the office.

He took a pick out of his plastic bag and inserted it in the Toyota's front door lock. Old cars are easier than new ones. Foreign cars are easier than American. The locks on most Japanese models have five pins, and the pick bounces up and down according to their resistance; guys like David can *feel* the pattern inside. The ignition was much the same job, and he knew that when he'd picked it a couple of times, he'd be able to start the engine almost as fast as if he had the keys. He was pleased with his choice. Papa Toyota kept the inside as neat as the outside. He'd even filled the gas tank. David eased the car out of the parking lot and onto Interstate 72.

After all, he could hardly rent a car, could he? He was a dead man — blown to bits in his own house — and by evening his face was likely to be plastered across newspapers all over the state.

Crime statistics say that if you drive along one of these highways, you pass a car that's hot almost every minute. So many get stolen that police records stop at state borders. Besides, there's not a cop anywhere who's going to do more than file a report for a patron of a beat-up joint like Benny & Jane's Motel. This is to say that about the time the Toyota's owners woke up in Illinois to find their car gone, David was crossing into Indiana in a vehicle that for practical purposes belonged to him.

He stopped outside Columbus, Ohio, for food, gas and a road atlas, then spent a couple of hours off a side road in southern Pennsylvania trying — and failing — to get some sleep. It was past midnight when he began the final leg of his journey. He'd been to DC only once before, but he'd arrived by plane, been picked up at the airport, had no sense of the baffling complexity that awaited a driver unfamiliar with the area. How can anybody negotiate the tangle of cloverleaves and flyovers — gummed up with roadworks even at night — that siphon traffic off to the south side of the Potomac? Had he doubled back this way only once? Or was it twice? About an hour before dawn, he hit the George Washington Memorial Parkway, a route lined with Americana — Arlington National Cemetery, Lady Bird's park, Lyndon's grove, even the Pentagon off to one side — but he was too weary to notice more than traffic in either direction. A pale, misty daylight was beginning to show itself when he saw the long wall he'd driven all this way to reach.

Security installations were the profession David had taken up after leaving prison; he was good at it. He'd designed and built systems for businesses from Rockford in the north of Illinois to Harrisburg in the south. He knew the system that guarded this Mount Vernon property too.

He'd studied the plans, been thinking about them ever since his drive began, and he'd found the loophole he was looking for. There was serious money on display in the mansion beyond the wall, all of it eminently saleable. The sheer amount of it gave his anticipation a queasy edge.

# 5

## WASHINGTON DC

Justice Samuel Clark woke up on the outskirts of America's capital city with thoughts of breakfast coffee. He loved the morning even when his wife was at home. Without her? Pure bliss. He stretched in his silk pyjamas — soft mattress beneath him, canopy of four poster billowing above him, view of the Potomac River through the bank of windows beyond his feet — and luxuriated his way out of bed to his marble bathroom, showered, shaved, dressed and studied his reflection in the mirror.

Whenever the media wanted to feature a Supreme Court judge, Samuel was the one they came to. He was famous for his civil rights decisions and for writing a book on prisons that had energised reform groups all over America, but that wasn't it. What pleased the people from the press — and Samuel himself — was that he looked like George Washington. He had the same square jaw, the same long nose, the same white hair brushed away from his face. His jowls radiated probity as Washington's had, and the sonority of his voice matched them; his photogenic house, down the road from Washington's Mount Vernon, added yet another touch. The staircase he descended swept outward at its base as the smell of freshly brewed coffee reached him. The solarium where he breakfasted was off the dining room, a glass-domed structure where a blue plumbago bloomed all year around.

He made his way there, opened the glass French doors — and froze in amazement.

'David Marion!' he cried. 'How in the name of God did you get in here? You damn near scared me to death. I thought you said this place was impregnable.'

David sat on the far side of a terracotta table, a cup of coffee half drunk in front of him, the *Washington Post* open in his hands. 'You lock it, I'll break it.'

'Suppose *you* lock it.'

'Even easier.'

'You still sound like Hugh, you know that?'

Hugh Freyl had been Helen's father, educated in England and never able to rid himself of English consonants. He'd taught David for the Illinois Literacy in Prisons Program and put an alien edge into his pupil's voice. He'd also introduced David to the eminent judge, his old roommate from Harvard Law School.

'What a pleasure to see you in such fine fettle,' Samuel went on, watching David take a cigarette from a pack, light it, draw on it. 'You should stop smoking. You do know that, don't you?'

'Leave me alone.'

David was mid-thirties, black hair, black eyes, tall; he'd left South Hams State Prison a couple of years back with an extension degree from the University of Chicago that had only intensified an explosive anger at the whole universe. This is not the kind of man a person like Samuel knows, much less feels in debt to. But Samuel felt very much in debt. Without *Clark on Prisons*, he probably wouldn't be sitting on the Supreme Court, and without David's inside information, the book would have been indistinguishable from hundreds of other heavy tomes published every year in the legal field.

★ ★ ★

The United States has the largest prison population in the world, larger even than China. It's a fact that Samuel had railed against in print many times; it's the reason why he decided to write his famous book even though he'd had no first-hand experience. Eight years ago, at Hugh Freyl's suggestion, he'd started up a correspondence with David. Only then did he begin to understand his own outrage at the statistic.

At the age of fifteen David had killed his foster father and foster brother. He'd shown no remorse and refused to explain why he'd done it. If he'd been a year older he'd have been strapped in a chair and injected with a lethal dose of potassium chloride. Instead they gave him a life sentence.

Samuel had expected stumbling self-justification from the letters. There was none. He'd expected claims of innocence. There wasn't any of that either. The letters switched back and forth from a ferocious intensity to absolute indifference, no middle ground, no compromise, no sense of rest. They let him glimpse day-to-day life in a brutal dictatorship, where gangs warred with each other, position in the hierarchy determined everything and a single stray glance could end in attack, rape, sexual servitude, death or all of these. Samuel was intrigued and impressed. He was eager to meet a man who wrote like this.

Hugh arranged the visit for him. On the day before it, the warden tried to put him off. He said it wasn't a good time.

Samuel insisted.

He knew South Hams State Prison from the outside. It was old. The walls were thirty feet high, topped with spirals of razor wire, interrupted by guard towers. Security was tight — CCTV, armed guards, a body search — and it wasn't until Samuel was past it that the noise hit him. Metal doors clanged. Metal staircases resounded. Men shouted, screamed, cried, sang, snored. Radios blared. The smells were rank: sweat, vomit, urine, garbage.

Samuel hadn't expected guards to lead him to the hospital ward, but that's what they did: a dishevelled bunker of a room with high, barred windows and half a dozen beds, four of them occupied.

'*This* is David Marion?' he said, staring down at a Quasimodo of a man chained to a bed.

'Yep,' said one of the guards.

Most of the man's face was purple, one eye swollen shut, the other a bare squint, the cheek sagging, mouth dragged down towards the chin, drooling at the corner. Head and chest were swathed in dirty bandages. This is what murderers look like in children's nightmares; the injuries and distortion were so extensive that Samuel couldn't connect this convict's face with the mugshots he'd seen of David.

'Are you *sure* this is the man?' he asked.

'The warden done told you it wasn't a good time.'

'What happened to him?'

'We figure he tripped and hurt hisself.'

'I see,' Samuel said grimly. 'You may go.'

The guard ruminated a moment. 'You sure about that, Judge? He ain't exactly what you'd call friendly.'

'He's chained to the bed, sir. What harm can he do me?'

When the guards left, Samuel went to the sink, filled a plastic cup with water, brought it back.

'Thirsty?' he said, reaching over the bed with the cup.

The cup flew out of his hand and his wrist was pinned to the bed itself before he even registered the rattle-clank of the chains. He found himself only inches from that disfigured, swollen face.

'Get out.' The voice was very hoarse and very weak, but Samuel knew at once from the fury in it that this was the person he'd corresponded with.

'What did they do to you, my friend?'

'Get out!'

Samuel had heard that the first rule of survival in South Hams was 'never let them see you bleed'. He did as he was told. He didn't go back either, fearing that his glimpse of David vulnerable would interrupt the flow of information. For several months it did. But he persisted, knowing also that contact with the outside world was so highly prized that the correspondence would build up again.

When the letters did start a second time, the revelations went on for months. The book that resulted came out with the dedication:

**For David, who knows**

'How long have you been sitting here in my solarium, reading my newspaper and drinking my coffee?' he said to David.

'An hour maybe.'

'You haven't smoked in all that time?' Samuel was wondering why he hadn't smelled cigarettes along with his coffee at the bottom of his stairs; he hated the smell, and he knew David knew it.

'I wanted to surprise you.'

'Well, you sure as hell succeeded in that. How'd you get past Josie? You didn't hurt her, did you?' There was worry in Samuel's voice. Josie was the maid in black and white formal dress who waited on him in the mornings. He was fond of her; she made him laugh.

There was a slight softening of the planes of David's face. 'I think she kind of likes me.'

'Not that it matters for now' — Samuel took a sip of coffee — 'but just disappearing into the night isn't going to fool anybody for long.'

'People don't leave home without their keys and stuff.'

'Come on, David, I do it when I put out the cat.'

'You don't have a cat.'

'What about when the contractor shows up. He's not going to — ' Samuel broke off. 'Christ, what have you done now? Promise me that person is still in one piece.'

David sighed irritably. 'I need papers.'

'That doesn't answer my question.'

'I need *papers*,' David repeated.

'Oh, you do, do you? What kind of papers?'

'Birth certificate. Passport. Credit cards. Driving licence.'

Samuel nodded. 'Yes. Yes, I can see that. I assume you have, er, friends who can arrange that kind of thing for you.'

'I want *legal* papers. The real thing.'

'That's quite a bit more difficult, isn't it?'

'Not for you.'

'Very funny.'

'Where's the joke?'

Samuel wasn't often taken off guard. He hated those contemptuous laughs that academics use to make opponents feel foolish, and yet he heard himself doing it. 'You're out of your wits, David. I suggested you come see me sometime. For some idiotic reason I enjoy your company, but I have no intention of supplying a felon with documents.'

David shrugged. 'I taped the call.'

'Don't even *try* to play games with me.'

David took his mobile out of his pocket, set it on the table, flipped a switch.

'*David?*' Millions of Americans knew the weight and authority of that voice.

'*Yes.*'

'*You're alone?*'

'*Yes*.'

Samuel felt a sudden constriction across his chest. For months, he'd sensed a multiple bypass on the horizon. 'Shut it off, damn you,' he said. 'David, are you actually trying to blackmail me? For an act of kindness and concern? Is this how you repay me?'

'Might sound kind of funny, don't you think? The great jurist warning an ex-con about a hit man?'

Samuel drummed his fingers on the table and stared out through the many-paned glass walls of the solarium, across the landscaped gardens of his mansion to the river where the mist was lifting off the water. 'David, I'm a judge. I don't do things like that.'

'Sure you do.'

'What do you want them for? You planning to leave the country?'

'I don't know. I might. Why not?'

'You must be out of your mind. Jesus Christ, what makes you think I could do such a thing even if I wanted to?'

David shrugged again. 'Not hard to figure. A guy who knows a hit like that is going down has better connections than I'm ever going to have.'

Samuel loved women. He truly did. He'd had many affairs, and he'd never been attracted to a man before. But David? There was something about the way the man moved. Samuel had sensed it at that first meeting in the prison hospital. The grip on his wrist had provoked what he'd told himself later was a visceral pity for a suffering fellow being. When David had got out and come to see him, he'd insisted to himself that he felt no more than an oddly oriented paternal concern; his only child had died in a hit-and-run when she was just twenty-five. Both assumptions had a good element of reality to them, but looking at David now, he knew they weren't its driving force.

Samuel was famous for his ability to plot a strategy in unfamiliar territory even when his position was weak. He got out of his chair. He paced the room, stopped to stare through the glass as he had before, then turned to David with a quizzical smile.

'So what's in it for me?'

David eyed the judge up and down, stretched his legs beneath the table, lit another cigarette from the butt of the one he'd nearly finished. 'I'll stick around for a while if you want. I'm in no hurry.'

# 6

## SPRINGFIELD, ILLINOIS

Rebecca Freyl, Helen's grandmother — Becky to her friends and family — was as frail as she was ancient, but she held herself ramrod straight. She concreted all human warmth under a layer of etiquette that belonged in the court of the Emperor Franz Joseph, and when Helen got back home to Springfield from Joshua's farm in Caton, her grandmother embraced her for a moment with a finishing school's chilly formality, gave her a peck on the cheek, then held her out with a tight smile.

'Well, well, what cream have you licked now?' Helen said. She knew that smile. Only triumph brought it on.

'Very nice cream indeed. Oh, yes. Yes, I would certainly say that.' Becky reached for a copy of the *State Journal-Register* that was lying on top of the Japanese chest in the living room.

The screamer headline ran:

**A mob hit in Springfield?**

A full-colour photograph of flames against the night sky took up most of the front page. David's mugshot was cut into the corner, the bottom edge of it beginning to curl as though it were on fire too. Helen's first thought was that the composition was more professional than the *Journal-Register* usually managed.

'The police are very happy,' her grandmother said. There were traces of Atlanta in her voice. 'If they manage to track down the man responsible, I may suggest that they apply to the Pope to have him canonised before they send him to prison.'

Some people are more alive than others. It's a quality that affects the air around them like a weather front before a storm; the leaves on the ground start swirling even though there isn't any wind. Maybe it's raw energy. All of us lust for it, and so few of us have it. Not even a mugshot could hide it in David Marion.

'Mr Marion's neighbours are very happy too,' Becky went on. 'Of course, the damage is inconvenient and ugly. There's nothing but a black hole where his house used to be. But, oh, the unadulterated joy of being rid of him. The young Hendersons — they're only two doors away — couldn't get a wink of sleep until they'd installed bars across their windows. They were afraid for their children. They were even afraid for the dog. Who knows what a criminal like that might take into his head next? Every single homeowner in Washington Close wanted to sell up and leave, but the property values! Mr Marion's presence forced them down so far that — '

'Shut up,' Helen cried, swinging around to face the old woman. 'I refuse to hear another word. Can't you ever shut up?'

Helen had always been quick-tempered,

mercurial. She'd never learned to control her tongue. Even so, Becky caught her breath — a sharp intake of surprise — and knit her brows. 'My, my, what an extraordinary reaction. Whatever could be the matter?' She put a hand on Helen's shoulder. 'Helen? My dear? Are those tears? You didn't cry even when your father died. Tears? For David Marion?'

# 7

## CATON, ALABAMA

Joshua had given up church when he was fifteen. That's when he'd started thinking about fundamental things, what was good, what was bad, what the preacher said and what the Bible said for itself. And the more he thought about it, the more it seemed to him that Christ was an ill-tempered white man. He withered a fig tree just because it didn't have a fig on it for Him to eat for breakfast. He didn't ask the money changers to leave the temple; He took a whip to them.

Mainly though, Christ was white. Joshua was growing up in a segregated Alabama, where white people had to be worshipped by law. One day he decided that he'd be damned if he'd get down on his knees for one of them when he didn't have to. He wasn't rigid about it. He married his five wives in church because they'd wanted it that way. He'd gone to baptisms and funerals in churches. But that had been an end to it.

Until Palassia appeared on the scene, that is. Palassia went regularly. She hadn't said anything about his going or not going — they barely knew each other — but everything she did interested him. The way she walked. The way she talked.

How she turned her head. So he tried church again with the idea that if she liked it, he must have misjudged it all those years ago.

He decided on the First Baptist Church in Caton — he'd married his fourth wife there — and attended regularly for a full six weeks. The singing was a pleasure he'd long forgotten, and the sermons had a rebellious force to them that would have been against the law when he was a boy. They excited him. But the prayers? Getting down on his knees for a white man still stuck in his gullet.

He talked to the preacher about it. The preacher smiled knowingly and said, 'Ah, that. I do have the answer for you. Next week, I'll make it all clear.'

And next week? The preacher got up in his pulpit, opened his Bible, pointed to it and said, 'It's all right here, my friends. Our saviour was an African just like you and me.' He said that Christ's black skin was obvious because a white man wouldn't have been able to hide out in Egypt for two years until Herod died. He said Egypt was in black Africa in Christ's time as it is today; all Egyptians were black back then, and a white man wouldn't stand a chance.

Joshua almost laughed out loud. He'd fallen in love with Queen Nefertiti when he was a kid, and the pictures he'd seen of her were as white as the pictures of Jesus. Because of her he'd gone to the library in Birmingham, where he grew up; he'd spent hours poring over pictures of Egyptian wall paintings. The people in them looked like Egyptians today, some of them light, some of them dark. There was even a green one. But a black one? Negroid black? No sir. Not anybody darker than an Arab.

Joshua glanced around at his fellow churchgoers. They were nodding in eager agreement with the preacher. What *was* the matter with them? Would they swallow any nonsense just because it made them feel better about themselves? He got up and walked out in the middle of the sermon.

A good thing too. If he hadn't, the intruder on his property would probably have died.

He was part way down the long dirt road to his farm when he heard the buzz of a swarm and the sky went black with bees, thousands and thousands of them. He stepped on the gas, spun the truck's wheels getting to the tool shed for the smoker, protective body suit and swarm-catchers that he'd had to use only a few times in a half a century of bee-keeping. Worker bees release a scent that orients forager bees and will draw them into a box; every year he synthesized one against such threats as this.

Only when he dashed out of the shed did he hear the shrieks and see the man dancing out from behind one of the hives, spinning, hopping, diving, arms flailing, body covered in bees, a cloud of them zooming in circles around him. The bees were so furious they bounced against Joshua's face mask like popcorn in a frying pan; he grabbed the man by the arm, rushed him towards the truck.

'I gonna shut the door, hear? You just kill as many as you can. Keep 'em out of your face, away from your eyes.'

Swarming bees have no home to defend, why should they be angry? These were mad as hell. Not even the smoke calmed them. But by the time Joshua got them in the catcher, he'd figured out what had happened. The principles he used for milking venom were close to standard commercial practice: an electric current provokes bees to sting through a thin sheet of material — he used polyethylene — and droplets of venom are scraped off the underside. Bees hate the process. A few die, and nests remain irritable for days afterwards. Joshua had learned early that it takes very little to make *Apis helena* sting; standard voltages madden them.

He'd set up several hives before church. Everything was ready to go: polyethylene in place, vials for collecting ready, source of electricity attached. This clumsy person must have tried to move a hive, somehow jiggled the electrical supply and sent a high current through the collector sheet.

'Joshua, that man was trying to steal your bees,' Lillian said when he told her about it.

'What for? The honey tastes like shit.'

'You talk to him?'

Joshua shrugged. 'He wasn't feeling so good. His face was all swole up, and I figured he needed oxygen. I took him to emergency in Caton. He probably didn't pay me no mind, but I told him to go find himself a nice swarm of regular honey bees. Don't seem to be nobody on earth that can control them bees but me.'

# 8

## WASHINGTON DC

'Here's what you've been waiting for,' Samuel said, handing David an envelope. They sat over coffee; the French doors were open, a warm breeze blowing through them.

David turned the envelope over in his hands, opened it, took out the contents: driver's licence, passport, birth certificate, social insurance card, all in the name of Richard François Gwendolyn.

'Sorry about the girl's name,' Samuel said. 'Nothing I could do about that.'

David shrugged. 'Marion's a girl's name too. Who is he?'

'I gather he was a young aide on the Premier's staff who blew the whistle on a politician too, er, eminent to name. The boy disappeared into Canada's Witness Protection Programme nearly a decade ago.'

'No word out of him since?'

'Not a peep.'

'No credit cards?'

'Long out of date.'

David set the documents on the table. 'You ever going to let me in on who's after me?'

Samuel frowned, as taken aback as he'd been when David had demanded papers of him in the first place. 'You don't know?'

'There are people in Springfield who'd be only too happy to have me dead, but I don't see any of them doing anything about it.'

Samuel picked up the coffee pot, held it over his cup, then realized the cup was full. 'I assumed . . . What's the matter with you? Why didn't you ask at once?'

'I'm asking now.'

'It's a little complicated. Coffee?'

'Just get on with it.'

Samuel set the pot down again. 'Who has the biggest economy in the world?'

David sighed irritably and glanced out over the Potomac.

'Most people would guess that we have,' Samuel went on. 'They'd be right. They might guess China as second biggest. They'd probably go wrong from there, but the vast majority would assume lists of big economies are rankings of countries with the odd state or city tossed in. David, my dear, of the hundred biggest economies in the world, more than half — '

'Are you going to get on with this or not?'

' — more than half are *industries*. They're businesses, David. Multinational corporations. Not countries at all. Somewhere around twentieth place, countries start giving way to Mitsubishi, General Motors, Ford. Wal-Mart is bigger than Greece. Exxon is bigger than Pakistan.'

David glanced out over the river again.

'The one that's interested in *you*,' Samuel said — David turned back with a puzzled frown — 'is right down the road from Springfield in St

Louis, Missouri: the Univers Chemical and Analytical Industries, known as UCAI. It's not up with the giants yet, but its revenues top $80 billion, and it already includes hundreds of principal companies operating in dozens of different countries.'

'Yeah, yeah. I've heard of it. What's it got to do with me?'

Everybody in Springfield knew UCAI. The corporation was the pride of the whole region, its great success story. News of it appeared regularly in the national press. Its CEOs made the covers of *Fortune, Forbes, Business Week*. It was almost as renowned for its funding of education and its charitable works as for its rapid growth and huge profits. Awed schoolchildren went on tours of its headquarters, a shiny skyscraper that towered over the Mississippi.

Samuel swallowed back his coffee. 'Look, David, I know it's hard to get an idea of how much power comes from money like that when it's combined with an inside grip on many countries. Corporations entwine the earth. They've become the financial blood supply that keeps us alive. If they cut a country off — and they can do it easily — it dies. As simple as that. No wonder everybody looks the other way while they write the very laws that are supposed to regulate them. No wonder that right here in America they elect aldermen, judges, governors. They even elect presidents.'

Samuel paused. 'But you know about that too, don't you?' he added.

* * *

Preparing to elect a president was what UCAI of St Louis was doing when David had stumbled across its plans.

It wasn't anything he'd started out to do, but as soon as the news got out that Hugh Freyl had been murdered in his own law office, the elite of Springfield started screaming for blood. Any convict in the area would have been suspect, but David was right in their midst. Hugh had educated him, helped him get out of prison, taken him under the Freyl wing. If David wanted to stay a free man, he had no choice but to find somebody else they could draw and quarter for the murder.

He did all the prescribed things, looked through the paperwork, talked to friends and colleagues. One of Hugh's old playmates caught his attention especially. But then whose attention didn't John Calder catch? Calder was Springfield's third presidential candidate, following in the footsteps of Abraham Lincoln and Barack Obama.

It didn't take long to show up a payment to the Calder campaign that Hugh was supposed to have authorized on the day *after* he died. David traced it back to UCAI. More digging revealed a hidden UCAI fund set up to ensure Calder's election. One afternoon, David faced the candidate himself with the evidence. Calder had a stroke less than an hour later. It didn't damage him severely, but it put his candidacy on hold for another four years. Thousands of man-hours of corporate strategy went on hold with him. Expansion plans had to be abandoned. Huge sums of money were lost.

* * *

David poured himself some of Samuel's coffee. 'Come on, they're a bunch of suits in a glass tower,' he said. 'Maybe they squeeze people out of business for fun, but what would they be doing with a hit man? How would they even know how to find one?'

This time it was Samuel whose sigh was irritable. 'You haven't been listening to me, David. Heart patients like me take a serious interest in their blood supply. Something interrupts it, they get rid of that something — and quick. The government is a heart patient too. That's why it subcontracts its enforcement agencies to corporations at a cut rate and backs up their fees from tax revenues. People who run these agencies are people who grew up spying in the Cold War years. The only difference these days is that treason includes damage to industry as well as to the state.' He paused. 'At a guess, I'd say they'd consider destroying a presidency a treasonable act, and treason remains a capital offence.'

'Well, well. How nice. I got the FBI after me.'

'Probably not yet. But if UCAI are sensible, that will be their next move. The various mafias are so leaky these days that we have fairly reliable information on what they're doing. If UCAI hadn't tried to run security as an internal company affair, I wouldn't have had enough inside knowledge to warn you, and you wouldn't be alive.'

David got up. 'You have any jump leads?'

'Jump leads? You mean for a car? Why?'

'That Toyota turns out to have a lousy battery.'

'Ah, I see,' Samuel said. 'You're leaving me.'

He was relieved; in a few days his wife was due home from her painting course in New Mexico, and David had finished overhauling the elaborate security system in this house. Samuel felt safer knowing he'd gone over it, but a couple of weeks of young flesh makes old flesh like his feel older and more tired.

'You'll need money,' he said to David.

'Yes.'

'I've got a couple thousand on me. That should hold you for a while. I think you'd also better be prepared to stay away from cities and people for a while.'

'Oh, yeah?'

'You can hardly go to a motel, can you? The picture of you as a dead man was in quite a number of papers. More important, blowing up your house is unlikely to hold UCAI for long. You'll need to let your beard grow or your hair or both — do something to make yourself harder to identify.' He shook his head. 'Listen, David, I have a cabin in the Smokies. Go there. Let some time pass. Then go abroad, South America, Europe. Anywhere but here or Canada.'

David looked down at his hands. He'd been putting some thought into what he should do, and he hadn't come up with much.

'The cabin is a simple place, David. No telephone. No TV. No neighbours. But it's got everything you need. You'll like it. I know you will. It'll welcome you. I always keep a fire laid in the fireplace. My daughter' — Samuel couldn't call her by name without losing control of his voice — 'always wanted a fire the moment she arrived. Her camping equipment sits in her room out there.' He'd bought her the best money could buy for her twenty-sixth birthday, including a backpack that converted to a tent, a Swiss army knife and a special titanium pot that did what only titanium does: changes its glossy colour as the angle of light shifts from morning to evening; elegant, extremely light, serviceable as both pot and bowl.

She'd never lived to see it.

# 9

## SPRINGFIELD, ILLINOIS

A few weeks after Joshua rescued the intruder on his property, he forwarded another letter to Springfield from the lawyers who'd made an offer for his farm. This time they were willing to hand over the $5 million for the patents on the venom alone.

'The venom?' Helen said to her grandmother. 'Why the venom? Isn't that about what they offered for the entire farm? What could they possibly want with it? How do you suppose they even knew it was patented?'

'The venom is *not* patented, Helen.' Becky spoke tartly. 'Synthesis of a number of its components and some of the processes involved in its extraction do, however, carry patents. I believe the vials you sell it in state the fact on the label.' The information given on a label is an important matter of business; she'd told her granddaughter so again and again.

'Why would I remember a thing like that?' Helen said, her tone as tart as Becky's.

'Perhaps you'd better find out who these people are, and whom they represent. Meantime, I strongly suggest that you write them and tell them no part of the farm is for sale, not the land or the patents.'

Traces of the beauty that Becky had handed on to her granddaughter were still visible in the bones of her face. 'Lillian tells me someone tried to steal one of Joshua's hives,' she continued. 'A crude and foolish approach. The bees are no good to anybody without the patents — or without Joshua — but we can hardly call it a coincidence, can we? I'd say it shows that these people want the venom badly for whatever reasons.' She knit her delicate brows. 'I always find it *interesting* when people want something badly.'

* * *

Great corporations touch everybody who lives in the regions where they operate. UCAI's logo flashed over gas stations on highways throughout the Midwest. It showed up on people's utility bills and pension plans. 'The caring corporation': that's what it called itself. The most prestigious enterprise that backed up this boast was a fellowship in the sciences. Applications were by invitation only, and everybody who worked in the field dreamed of getting one.

Not long after the offer for Joshua's venom had come in, Helen received an invitation to apply for one herself. She was flattered. Very flattered. Her doctorate was in physics, and she had the rare distinction of a published thesis. A title of *Collision Theory and the Absorption of Radiation in Matter* meant it was not going to make any bestseller list, but *Nature* had asked her to write an article because of it and a couple of lecture offers had come through.

Helen would have loved to think that the attention proved she was the genius she'd assumed she was when she was fourteen and better at manipulating equations than anybody else in her class. It didn't. Some crucial spark was missing, and she'd accepted an assistant professorship at the University of Illinois at Carbondale, 175 miles south of Springfield, because she couldn't think of anything better to do with her qualifications. That was why she'd come back home to live. Cutbacks in the science budget meant that the job wouldn't start for another year.

The timing of the UCAI Fellowship couldn't have been bettered.

The terms of these Fellowships were specific; what they asked for was tailored to the applicant, and it was sometimes unexpected. In Helen's article for *Nature*, she'd railed against the scientific community's failure to get the importance of their work across to the public, and the proposal to her had to have grown out of that.

The Follaton Medical Foundation in London concentrated on victims of the Chernobyl meltdown a quarter of a century ago. Its work included studies of the after-effects on people and the environment as well as on-the-ground help in the form of mobile health clinics and agricultural aid. But the science it had to get across included a good deal of physics along with the medicine. Helen was to spend a year with them, finding ways to explain the scientific complexities of their work to the public and the press.

Nothing could have been better than this Fellowship for an ego newly aware of its own limitations.

The year in London appealed to her even more.

In Springfield, people kept dying around her. They didn't just die either. They died violently. Her mother had smashed the family car head-on into a tree. Somebody had mowed her father down right in his own office. Nobody had the slightest idea why. Practically everybody she knew assumed that David Marion was the killer; the evidence just wasn't there. But what difference did it make now?

Now Springfield had killed David too.

* * *

The shock of David's death revived and redoubled her grief for her parents. It settled on her shoulder like an evil monkey and poisoned the air she breathed. Her only hope was to get out of town — at least for a while.

Her immediate problem was how to broach the subject of the Fellowship to her grandmother. Her father's death had transformed the relationship between them. Helen had become the Freyl heir. She'd taken her dead father's place as the focus of Becky's life. Becky wanted to keep her near, got frightened when she went away even for a few days. She went to Lillian for advice, as she always did when she was in trouble.

'Miss Helen,' Lillian said, 'If'n you wants to go to London, England, you gots to tell her straight out. She's a old lady. She might carry on some, but I gonna be here looking after her. Don't you worry none.'

'I have to get back to these people within the week.'

'Your grandma's setting in her office right now.'

'Oh, shit.'

'Ain't no time like the present.'

'I hate this kind of thing.'

Lillian laughed. 'Get on with you.'

Helen knocked on her grandmother's door, went in and held out the forms.

'You're not in trouble, are you?' Becky said.

Helen bristled.

Becky took the papers, put on her glasses and began to read. Helen sat in the chair opposite her desk and watched. When Becky took off her glasses, she said, 'You must accept at once.'

Helen could hardly believe what she was hearing. 'It means a year in London.'

'Helen, my dear, I love you more than life itself. But you don't really want to teach. You're too competitive to be on someone else's research team. You must do something. Maybe this is a solution. Besides, a year in London will do you good.'

Helen was too stunned to speak.

Becky gave that tight smile of triumph that David's death had brought on. 'We could have fun with this, you know,' she said.

''We'? You hate flying.'

'Oh, dear, dear, I don't mean I want to go with you.' Then without transition, 'You didn't bother to look into the buyer behind the offers for Joshua's farm.' She didn't even have to ask. Not that finding out would have been difficult. Helen's father had been a corporate lawyer. Looking into hidden buyers was one of the things his firm did as a matter of course. 'One never knows about these matters,' Becky went on. 'I hope you don't mind that I took the liberty myself.'

'Why should I?'

Becky picked up the application papers, glanced over them, put them down. 'The hidden buyer is the Scientific Research arm of UCAI.'

Helen turned away.

'Come, come,' Becky said. 'The Fellowship will look the same on your CV no matter how it came about. Use that wonderful brain of yours, Helen. Here's as good a puzzle as anything you'll find in a physics textbook. Think about it. Why does a powerful corporation offer so much for a bee farm? Why does it send some idiot to steal a hive? Why offer an outrageous sum for venom nobody really wants? Then — and this is very strange — why go to all the trouble of luring the farm's owner across the Atlantic? Teasing out what's going on should be great fun.' She picked up one of the papers. 'There is however one thing that worries me.'

'The bastards. They're using me.'

Becky chuckled. 'Of course they are. But we know it, and they don't know we know. That gives us a great advantage. And I believe they have given us a second one, whether knowingly or unknowingly.' She handed over the description of the project. 'Look at the masthead for the Follaton Foundation.'

Helen looked, then shrugged.

'No names you recognize?' Becky asked.

'No.'

'Sir Charles Hay.'

Helen checked the masthead again. 'The director?'

'I never liked that man.'

'You've met him? What is this, a coincidence or what?'

Becky shook her head. 'It might be. There's more coincidence about than people like to think, and the English upper classes are a close-knit group. On the other hand, it might be a coincidence that UCAI representatives stumbled across and decided would add to the lure. Charles Hay was your father's favourite friend at school.' She paused. 'There was something about him I didn't like.'

'You're kidding.' Helen's tone was sarcastic. Becky had never thought any of Hugh's friends was good enough for him, including Helen's mother.

'In the end, your father agreed with me,' Becky went on. 'My dislike was intuitive. I admit that. But I believe his was solidly based, although he never talked about it. He simply stopped referring to Charles in his letters. When I asked him why, he refused to fill me in on the details.'

'This Charles begins to sound intriguing.'

'He has a vein of acid in him.'

'Don't we all?'

'He's manipulative.'

'Okay, okay, what good is he to us?'

Becky explained that the Follaton Medical Foundation was essentially a charity. She'd sat on the boards of many charities in her time; she knew how they worked. She told Helen that the people who run them are never in on the management decisions of the giant corporations that give them money. Which makes sense. Charities are only glorified beggars. On the other hand, they sometimes have access to crucial information even if they don't know its importance themselves. An old family friend, who was of necessity an innocent bystander and couldn't possibly know what was at stake: what more could they ask for?

'I do not trust the man,' Becky said, 'but I believe we could make use of him. What about a little war game, Helen, my dear? Might that tickle your fancy? Lift you out of your doldrums? Just you and me: the Freyls against the mighty UCAI?'

Helen couldn't help a flare of curiosity. 'David and Goliath?'

'David won. You must always remember that: David won.'

The only David Helen cared about hadn't won at all. He'd lost, and foisted an evil monkey onto her shoulder. But if two women were willing to take on a Goliath, maybe even evil monkeys would have to back off to the sidelines.

'So,' Helen said to herself and to this new enemy, pointedly ignoring the monkey, 'you want to play, do you? I guess I do too.'

# 10

## SMOKY MOUNTAINS, WEST VIRGINIA

As a lifer, David had managed a better hold on himself than most. The day-to-day violence of prison? He actively enjoyed it. The lack of control over his surroundings had been much, much harder. A year inside, and a teenager who'd vandalised everything he could get his hands on had turned into the neat child every middle-class parent dreams of — and then some. David cleaned his cell every day. He mitred the corners of his bed. Every item had a place, mug and toothbrush to begin with, books and writing materials when he finally allowed Hugh Freyl and the Literacy in Prisons programme to begin educating him.

Guards trashing his cell every few weeks turned him from the merely neat to the puritanically neat. Eighteen years of this, and he'd ended up with a house in Springfield that had the look of a monk's quarters, furnished with little beyond the barest necessities. He'd tried pictures on the walls, then taken them down. Interruptions in the Spartan accommodation made him uneasy. Samuel's house on the Potomac was nineteenth-century plush: walls of paintings and books, heavy draperies, inlaid tables, statuary, candelabra, chandeliers, nowhere the eye could rest. For David it was a barrage of disorder. He couldn't process it. He couldn't make it *fit*. A cabin in the Smokies sounded like an oasis.

He left before dawn, the Toyota loaded with provisions. The sky clouded over around noon. Rain fell in sheets, then eased into an impenetrable fog as he reached the mountains. He couldn't see them or even a hint of the famous blue haze that hangs over them. Not even road signs were visible; the blow-up-doll voice of the satellite navigator — Samuel had insisted he take it — guided him up to the unpaved road that led to the cabin. It was almost dark by the time he parked, got out and gathered a bag of groceries.

He found the door, unlocked it, walked in.

Opposite him, a wall of glass looked out into a solid mass of fog. The fading light showed four elegant Eames chairs, covered in black leather, one at each corner of a glass table — flowered Chinese bowl in the centre — in front of a fireplace in a stone wall. A table big enough to seat ten people stood in front of a long opening to a kitchen hung with copper pots in graduated sizes.

*This* was simple?

He wandered from room to room. The place was huge, each bedroom with its own bathroom, mirrored closets and a view that would probably be mountains when the weather cleared. Quarters for cook, household help and security guard occupied a basement with washing machines, driers, rows of hiking boots in various sizes, fishing rods and tackle.

David didn't light the logs in the fireplace. Nor did he use one of the copper pots or the French crockery in the kitchen cupboards. He ate cold spaghetti out of a can and drank bourbon out of the bottle before throwing himself down fully clothed on the king-sized bed in the master bedroom. He didn't sleep. The luckier guys in prison learn to sleep away as many as sixteen hours of a day, even through the endless barrage of noise. David had gone the other direction; he hadn't slept much more than two hours at a stretch since he was fifteen.

He lay there staring up at the ceiling — the one uncluttered surface in the room — and as dawn began to break, he remembered Samuel's mention of camping equipment. He'd paid no attention at the time. Camping? Boy Scouts? Boy Scouts were the prey that street kids like David trapped and beat up for the fun of it. But that was years ago. Now? Well, now camping seemed to provide the only escape from all these *things*. He got up, sought out the equipment, squatted down to examine it.

He couldn't see how the backpack itself could turn into a tent; but there'd be plenty of time for that. The rest of it looked straightforward: something called a Pocket Rocket stove, canisters of fuel, the titanium pot that had so pleased Samuel, cup, water-purifying tablets, Swiss army knife, flashlight, local map and room for cans of food and cigarettes. When he was a kid he'd played in the forested area around Lake Springfield, made a fire and roasted potatoes on it, slept out under the trees. With a background like that, he figured he could face a rabbit if it didn't scare him to death first.

He unfolded the map, chose a route, waited for dawn. When it broke, he hoisted the backpack and shut the door on Samuel's overrich life behind him. Last night's fog held. He hiked up a long trail, crossed one burbling stream on a rustic bridge and another jumping from rock to rock. The trail grew steeper. The fog cleared. He found himself on the top of a hill that looked out over what must have been a full range of mountains. They disappeared off into the horizon in front of him, tier upon tier, each one hazier than the one in front.

He spent the afternoon in a desultory search for a campsite, and by the time it was getting dark, he'd decided on a grassy area by a pond. He set to work on the tent with barely enough daylight left for the instructions, lost patience with them, ended up bandaging the tent poles together into a tepee with a couple of socks. But he could hear birds nestling down in the trees and an occasional soft rustle in the bushes as he ate chilli heated in Samuel's beautiful pot. He unrolled the sleeping bag, crawled inside and was asleep before he'd finished making his clothes into a pillow.

The dark was absolute when he woke. The beam of his flashlight showed that his tent seemed to be more or less intact around him, but his watch said it was well past midnight. More than *three* hours? No, no. It couldn't be, and yet there was charm in the thought that a single night outdoors might have succeeded where years of pharmacology had failed. A light rain began to fall. It pattered gently on the cloth around him; a few drops forged a path down the inside near his feet.

He drifted off again, then woke abruptly.

A step? Had he heard it? Dreamed it? The rain had worked its way into his sleeping bag, but that wasn't what had startled him. There! It *was* a step, too close this time to doubt, too short in duration to be anything but a footfall. He had no idea what kind of animals go wandering around in forests, but this couldn't be a *little* animal of any variety. He eased himself silently out of the sleeping bag, Swiss army knife in hand. With the sound of another step — clearly less than a yard away — he jolted out through the tent flap, lunging at a massive form outlined against the sky as the tent collapsed around him, entangling his feet in cloth, deflecting his strike, tossing the flashlight out of his hand. When he was a child, he'd sneaked off to the zoo in Springfield whenever he could to watch the big wild animals rear up on their hind legs and shake the bars of their cages.

He lunged again as he fell to his knees, seeing nothing, knife clacking against his opponent as though he'd hit exposed bones, and juddering back all the way up through his shoulder. A flash of lightning revealed a beast so huge that he'd attacked it again before he was upright. He knew he'd managed to knock it to its knees — sheer surprise most likely — and if the collapsed tent hadn't hampered him, he might have killed it.

He grabbed the flashlight, flipped it on and stood there staring at the creature. It stared back, as terrified as he was. A moose? An elk? It had vast antlers and wet marbles for eyes that glistened in the beam of the flashlight. It clambered awkwardly to its feet and stumbled back into the undergrowth.

David was trembling so badly he could barely stay on his feet. He settled back on his haunches, holding his breath, monitoring it in and out, in and out, forcing control, trying to reason with himself.

* * *

There's an equilibrium between prisons and the streets. Not many inmates are homeless when sentenced — nor are the homeless made up of many ex-prisoners — but there's a steady trickle between the two states of being that more or less keeps a balance.

In the middle of David's years inside, one of his cellmates had been a homeless guy. He was that rare thing in prison, an educated man. He had a masters in fine art, and his conversation was sprinkled with references to Botticelli and palazzos in Florence. He was also crazy. The official diagnosis circled around terms like schizophrenia and bipolar disorder. The name he went by was Rainbow Willie. He'd explained life outside society to David and David had listened, transfixed by the freedom of people who live with only the constraints they choose themselves.

Flocks of the homeless move across America

with the seasons like migratory birds. Lots of them have no Social Security numbers or birth certificates. Willie described the life he'd lived as the life of a teenager's dream, getting drunk, getting high, smoking cigarettes, goofing off, wild and free, coming and going at will, taking up names like Wolf, Coyote, Jaguar, Gypsy, living in an intense present untouched by past or future. Guys show up one day, tell what they choose to tell — maybe true, maybe not, nobody cares — leave when they want to leave, go somewhere else, go nowhere. It doesn't matter. Just go.

While David sat on his haunches in the Smoky Mountains and struggled to get his breathing under control, it was Rainbow Willie who came to mind. By the time he was calm, he was as sure the streets were where he belonged as he'd been that the mountains were the place to hide until he'd figured out what to do with himself. No wild animals in the streets. Enough ex-prisoners to make him more or less inconspicuous. He'd drift from city to city, see the country, steal what he needed to live — or scrounge as Willie had — never stay long enough for a street group to put together too much of a picture of him.

Maybe he'd get as far as the Pacific Ocean. He'd seen oceans in movies, and Rainbow Willie had gone on and on about them. But there was something about them that made no sense to David; he wanted to see for himself.

# 11

## LONDON

The Follaton Medical Foundation occupied three buildings on Mowbray Square in London, part of a sandstone façade decorated with those ornate iron railings — a street-length balcony too — that make parts of the city look like New Orleans. But the area was sprinkled with publishers of the variety who printed poetry by minor celebrities and ate lunch at the Garrick Club — hardly the place for an organization backed by the fearsome muscle of UCAI. Who could say, though? Perhaps they felt it helped them blend into the English scene.

The introductory pack that came with Helen's Fellowship included an invitation to lunch at Mowbray Square on the day after she landed. She arrived half an hour early. She was always early, often as bad as this, and the day was too hot for wandering the streets. It was only spring, and yet the mild British climate had transformed itself into one of those steamy Mississippi Valley summers she knew so well from home. The square itself looked cool and fresh, huge trees coming into leaf and shading a lawn that ran up to flowerbeds with narcissi in bloom. But a high iron fence barred her. She tried the gate. It was locked.

She was heading away to a café she'd passed near the tube station when a girl ran up to her.

'Dr Freyl? It is Dr Freyl, isn't it?' The girl was seventeen, maybe eighteen, redhead, not particularly pretty, but the body! Those soft curves — not sloppy or fat — and the sensual ease that men will go through anything to get at no matter what the face is like.

'Oh, God,' Helen said, 'have we met somewhere? Have I forgotten?'

'They circulated your CV and your photo so we'd all know that we had a UCAI Fellow coming to the Foundation. My name's Rosemary. Do you want to look at the gardens? Hang on. You probably have to be seeing somebody terrifically important inside, don't you?'

Helen explained that she was way too early and would love to wait in the square. Rosemary opened the gate — she said that everybody who worked at the Foundation had a key — and the two of them walked across the grass to find a shaded spot under a tree.

Rosemary took out a sandwich. 'Would you like half?' she said, holding it out.

'They're going to feed me. What do you do in there?'

'Reception. I'm only a volunteer.' Rosemary took a bite of her sandwich.

'Shouldn't you be in school or something?'

'I'm taking a year off before university. It's really nice working with people who care about something. Know what I mean? It's sort of catching. I was going to do Russian and chemistry, but ten days here and I'm thinking maybe if I do an extra year of maths and physics, I could go into radiation biology. You think an extra year would be enough?'

'You *sure* you want to do that?'

'That's not my question, Dr Freyl.' She had a slightly crooked smile.

'I don't know anything about English education. Where I come from the standards are so low that a couple of weeks would do it.'

Rosemary took another bite. 'You ever been to Belarus?' Helen shook her head. 'I'd never even heard of it,' Rosemary went on. 'Now I want to go there so bad I can taste it.'

'Not me.'

'Why not? It sounds awesome.'

'I like my radiation nicely controlled in a lab. Are they pretty friendly at the Foundation?'

'Yeah. I mean, well, the cleaners, the secretaries, the kitchen staff — especially the kitchen staff — are really nice. Some of the higher-ups think too much of themselves. Mr Hardcastle is a charmer though. At least he tries to be. The charm grates a little, know what I mean? But his deputy!' Rosemary's laugh was one of those husky, come-hither ones, a perfect match for her body. 'You keep your hands off him, you hear? He's never even said 'hello' to me, and I have only the rest of this week to snag him. Gabriel Walker. Gabriel is an angel, isn't he? In the Bible, I mean.'

'An archangel, I think. They have bigger wings. How come you've only got this week?'

Rosemary chewed her sandwich. 'The moment I left school, the social cut my mum's benefits. I have to earn some money.'

'What about your lord of a director?'

Rosemary shrugged again. 'He's too grand for the likes of me. I've never even seen him. They say he speaks only to the Queen. They say he has underground connections and cuts down everything and everybody who gets in his way.' She grinned. 'They say he sold his soul to the devil. A chauffeur in a cap delivers him here in a silver Bentley.'

'I thought you hadn't seen him.'

'It's only another story.' Rosemary sighed again. 'He probably comes by tube like the rest of us.'

Rosemary finished her sandwich, and they went across to the Foundation building together. The front door opened just as she was punching in the entry code.

'Dr Freyl?' The man was small, bird-like, elfin ears, pigeon breast but a nose that belonged to a hawk. The eyes were a hawk's too.

'Oh, Mr Hardcastle,' Rosemary cried. 'Here she is.'

'You found her, did you, Rosemary? Clever girl.'

'Thanks for letting me get out of the heat,' Helen said to her. She held out her hand to the man. 'It's kind of you to come and greet me.'

'This is such a pleasure, Dr Freyl — *such* a pleasure.' The accent seemed Russian but very slight. Her information from the Foundation listed Jeffrey Hardcastle as Director of Human Resources. 'You've found a hotel, have you? Is it satisfactory? How was your flight?'

Fortunately the ceiling of the Foundation's entryway was high, and the walls of the building were thick; the air was cool inside despite the heat of the day. But the entryway itself! Helen knew that ragged disorder passes in some English circles for elegance, but this was carrying things too far. Boxes lined the walls; cobwebs connected them to plaster outcroppings on an ornate ceiling. A naked, underpowered light bulb hung from it. Halfway into the entrance, Rosemary noted her reaction and gave her a quizzical, worried smile.

'I'll put it down to British eccentricity,' Helen said.

Rosemary sat down to an ancient video console at a battered but still handsome mahogany desk. 'Maybe I can think of something,' she said, 'clear things up a bit.'

Jeffrey led Helen to a caged elevator more ancient than the video. 'It's taking us too long to settle in,' he said. The lift took them to the top floor while he explained that a belated survey had uncovered subsidence and turned a few alterations into a major overhaul; there were sounds of hammering and smells of fresh paint along the route.

The elevator opened into a hallway that brought them to the dining room. 'Gentlemen,' he announced as he ushered Helen in, 'this is our UCAI Fellow, Dr Helen Freyl.'

Four men turned and applauded: a daunting experience even though Helen had cut her teeth on groups of lawyers from her father's firm. The room was large enough to accommodate twenty; leaves had been removed from the table, and a spray of freesias decorated it along with more silverware than was strictly necessary, a linen table cloth, linen napkins.

'Perhaps, gentlemen, it would be best to sit down,' Jeffrey said. 'I'll do the introductions at the table. An aperitif, Dr Freyl? Good, good. Emilia!' he called. 'We are ready to begin.'

A bottle appeared in the hands of a squat woman, wide in the hips, strong in the arms, so placid in the face that she looked like one of those Russian dolls that fit one inside another. While the others seated themselves, Jeffrey poured.

'I propose a toast to Dr Freyl,' he said, raising his glass.

'Hear, hear,' chimed in the others.

'You know already that she's here to study how we present our work to the public. We are all too aware that we've tended to allow the science to seem so difficult that it has itself become a scapegoat. People blame it for Chernobyl, just as they blame it for other things they don't understand. This detracts from the human tragedy as well as from the simple fact that science is not the province only of scientists but of politicians and industrialists as well. Ignorance on such a scale ends up casting a shadow over our endeavours. It deflects funding. We must strive to lessen it.'

'I know we all have ideas to discuss with Dr Freyl — or we will have — but Sir Charles gave express instructions that we should not overburden her during lunch.' He turned to Helen. 'Sir Charles is our director,' he said.

She nodded. 'That's the name on your masthead.'

'He was sadly detained today, Dr Freyl. He sends his apologies. He also sends our assistant director, Joseph McGuire.'

Jeffrey indicated the rusty hair and protruding lower lip on her left. 'Let me begin by saying what a pleasure it is, Miss Freyl' — this McGuire's voice was as pompous as his face — 'to be in a position — '

'*Doctor* Freyl,' she interrupted. No bully was going to strip of her title in front of a table of men.

'Oh, yes, of course. Forgive me. But if you will allow me, I'd like to state how privileged I feel to stand in for Sir Charles in greeting you. You doubtless want to know about my duties . . . '

Helen had no interest in what this man did, at Follaton Foundation or anywhere else; he droned on through half the aperitif. The Administrative Officer followed, meaty-handed and fat-fingered. Helen stifled a yawn. Then came the Director of Technology Transfer, black-rimmed glasses resting on a sweaty nose. The cook brought on the first course as he finally wound down.

The wind changed with a man who introduced himself as Martin Goldsmith. His face showed the puffiness that comes with too much hard liquor and his breath stank of it, but his eyes were as shrewd as Jeffrey's and his manner was easy. There was a Midwestern twang in his voice.

'How come there are two Yanks in this English boardroom?' Helen asked.

'Martin flew in from St Louis this morning,' said Jeffrey. 'He's a scientist too — UCAI's Director of Science and Technology.'

'Now that *is* exciting!' Helen said, her interest alive at once. Here was her first encounter with a representative of the opposition that she and her grandmother were ready to battle before they even knew what the fight was about. 'What's your field?'

'I'm sorry to say I'm just a statistician. Very dull.'

'Oh, I don't know,' Helen said. 'My father used to have a book called *How to Lie with Statistics*. I thought I was a pretty good liar until I read that.'

He laughed. 'We're all so very pleased that you were in a position to accept our offer, Dr Freyl.'

'Me too,' she said. She wasn't sure whether she should venture the question or not. She pondered it while Emilia poured a glass of wine for her and decided it would seem unnatural if she didn't ask. 'Why me?'

'UCAI is proud of its roots.' Martin paused as she had while Emilia poured his wine. 'We're always eager to promote local talent. I'd been thinking hard for some months about Sir Charles's need of somebody to liven up material that's scientifically complex. The more I thought about what he needed, the more I found myself thinking of your article in *Nature*.'

'You're the man himself, are you? The one who put me forward?'

'The very one.'

The talk turned to the heat of the day and forecasts of the hottest summer on record. Martin Goldsmith and Helen complained that England wasn't supposed to be like this. Jeffrey described a recent summer in Moscow when the temperature was 40°C; the water supply was cut off across the entire city.

'Are you Russian?' Helen asked him. 'With a name like Hardcastle? How'd that happen?'

'You have no idea how much I've put into ridding myself of this accent,' he said. 'My parents chose the name Hardcastle because they despised their own names. Then to compound the sin, they insisted I apply for a scholarship to Winchester. Sadly, a foreign accent is not an asset in a British public school.'

'I tried to learn Russian one summer,' Helen said. 'I was hopeless. So much of it seems to rely on how you say it, not what you say at all.'

Jeffrey's smile wasn't warm, but it was intriguing and complicated. 'It's not a Russian accent that you hear, Dr Freyl.'

'Isn't it?'

'Are you very political?'

'Not me,' she said.

'My parents were. I'm sure you know the type: young, passionate, committed Russians striving to do the right thing in a Russian-occupied Belarus. They set up an underground movement to weaken Soviet ties by building links with the West for their adopted country. They changed their names, printed leaflets full of slogans and schooled their children abroad. They also refused to allow us to learn Russian. The accent is Belarusian. Politics can make people very silly.'

'I wouldn't know,' Helen said.

He smiled again. 'They ended up in the Psychiatric Prison Hospital of Kazan for their trouble, and without a knowledge of Russian, how could their children fight their case? They found out in the hardest possible way that one cannot address power unless one is fluent in its language.'

As he said this she caught the cook's eye. It was only a glance — or so it seemed — no design in it. Emilia's face remained as impassive as ever, but she moved her head very slightly left, right, left again.

Helen looked away at once.

# 12

## ST LOUIS, MISSOURI

Merlin Googe Allandale — Googie to his friends — was a happy man. He loved his wife. He loved his four children. He loved his new job, and today was his first day of work with one of his firm's important clients, UCAI of St Louis.

He drove to St Louis from his home in Springfield, Illinois, a two-hour trip south and west through cornfields that stretched from horizon to horizon, and didn't stop until he reached the Mississippi. From the far side of the river, the headquarters of the great corporation dominated the city's skyline; close up, its mirrored walls reflected the city itself.

A long ramp led to the cavernous spaces below the UCAI tower. Googie drove down it, showed his parking pass to the attendant, parked his car and took an elevator that let him out at a checkpoint manned by armed guards. One of them took his parking pass and his driving licence for examination. Another gave him a body search, X-rayed his coat, his briefcase and his shoes, then beckoned him through a metal scanner.

The first officer returned Googie's identification with a deferential smile and a visitor's pass to replace his parking pass. 'Mr Sebastian Slad himself will see you, Mr Allandale,' he said. 'Take elevator number eight to the top floor.'

The lobby beyond the checkpoint was a cathedral of muted splendour in brushed chrome and grey marble. Elevator number eight took Googie to the twentieth floor and let him out in a second lobby, modest only by the standards of the first. Full-sized trees in pots threw out shadows beneath a high, glass ceiling; a fresh-faced receptionist was waiting for him.

'Come with me, Mr Allandale. Mr Sebastian Slad is waiting for you.'

The office she led him to looked out through a window wall over the city to the St Louis Arch — the single McDonald's hoop known as the 'Gateway to the West' — but the furniture here was plain. The wooden chairs could have come from a Baptist schoolroom, the desk from the school's dining hall. The only decoration was a full-size, full-colour statue of Jesus on His knees before His God with His mother standing beside Him, her hand on His shoulder.

'*Great* to see you, Mr Allandale,' Sebastian Slad said, getting up from his desk and holding out his hand as Googie entered. 'I can't tell you how glad me and Francis are to have a man like you giving us a hand around here.' Sebastian Slad was fat. His cheeks were round. His mouth was full-lipped and red. He and his twin brother Francis had taken control of the giant corporation only months ago — a 'palace coup', the press had called it — and begun at once to conduct it according to the fundamentalist principles that ruled their lives.

'Take a seat, Mr Allandale. Take a seat.' Googie pulled up one of the school chairs and sat. He liked straight-backed chairs. There'd been sharp twinges in his lower back recently; upholstered chairs made it worse.

'I'm afraid you have a big job ahead of you, Mr A,' Sebastian went on. 'Me and Francis, we're having a heck of a time getting things straightened out here. I sent for you special, you know, but now I got me a meeting in' — he checked his watch — 'six minutes' time. I sure do hope you don't mind getting straight to the point.'

'Security downstairs looks good,' Googie said with a shrug. 'Maybe you don't need me at all.'

Sebastian gave him a rueful smile. 'That's just airport kerfuffle. It don't mean nothing — you know that better than I do — but folks expect it. Thing is, what we got us here is one administrator managing all of it, including your kind of work. No, no' — he held up a hand to silence Googie's protest — 'me and Francis was as downright shocked as you are to find that out. Mr A, we done grown like Topsy in the last five years. I ain't defending my predecessor or nothing, but one day he's taking over a promising-looking complex of factories, and the next he's operating in ninety countries. That's a heap of paperwork, Mr A. It's a *heap* of paperwork. We suspect enforcement was one of the things got lost in the scramble. Francis and me, we been talking a lot about this, and we figure we'd better start cleaning up our own backyard first. That's how come you're here.'

‘Who are your operatives?’

Sebastian gave his rueful smile again. ‘Don’t know. Freelancers, I suppose. The records ought to tell you.’

Googie shook his head, got up, went over to the window and hummed a tuneless tune while he studied the McDonald’s arch.

‘Me and Francis,’ Sebastian went on, ‘we already moved the administrator out to a subsidiary in Mumbai, ’cause we figured you’d want to use your own operatives and pick your own liaison. That’s fine by us. One thing though, we like to have a handle on the fellers working here, so we got us a dozen candidates all lined up and waiting for you on the fifteenth floor. You got my secretary at your disposal as long as you need her. Now if’n you’ll excuse me, I got to get to that meeting.’

* * *

Law enforcement was in Googie’s blood. Both his father and his grandfather had served as Sheriff of Sangamon County. Googie had gone straight from college into the Springfield Police Department. He’d been on the beat less than six months when he rescued an older officer caught in an armed robbery. The perpetrator didn’t survive the shoot-out. The day after Googie received his commendation, he tracked down a paedophile the force had been trying to find for more than a year. The paedophile didn’t survive his encounter with Googie either; Googie’s father quashed a departmental investigation into the matter before it arose by finagling his son's transfer to the internal police force of the National Security Agency in Maryland.

The National Security Agency — or NSA, as it's called — employs more people than the CIA and the FBI put together, and it's far more secret than they are. The only way outsiders can guess at the size of its operations is by its electricity bill — more than $35 million a year — which makes it the second largest user in the entire state. Googie had liked the sound of that. Its employees joke that the letters NSA stand for 'No Such Agency' and 'Never Say Anything'. He'd liked the sound of that too.

The money was good. He enjoyed the work, but since he was on the NSA's internal police force rather than its operational staff, he had to live in Maryland, and he got homesick. On trips back to Springfield, he fell in love all over again with his high school sweetheart and he knew — she didn't have to say a word — that his choice was living with her back home or staying on at NSA in Maryland. He decided to go freelance, and NSA kindly arranged his transfer to an even more secret organization attached to the CIA.

Department 4 of Domestic Wet Operations — known among insiders as 'Assassinations within the United States' — paid him $40,000 a hit. Five hits a year gave him the cash he needed to put a down payment on a real estate business, start a family, take out a mortgage on a house and watch its rooms fill up with the fruit of his own loins.

One by one all four of his kids entered the Cornerstone Christian Academy, where they learned to follow God's will. As Academy fees went up, Googie raised his kill rate to six hits a year and worked overtime at his real estate business. Twenty years of living like that, and a man realizes he doesn't have the time to enjoy what he's built. Googie began looking into Department 4's retirement plans. That's when the job of Regional Scheduler came through, a stay-at-home job that put him in charge of the Department's wet operations throughout the Midwest, paid him a salary of $800,000 a year and called for only a computer link to the head office.

Most Midwest-based multinationals had been Department 4 customers for years. The St Louis-based UCAI was far and away the most important un-signed corporation on Googie's watch. He'd made his drive to St Louis within days of their contacting him.

* * *

Sebastian Slad's secretary showed him to his new office and introduced him to a blonde called Ms Barnaby. Ms Barnaby wore heavy mascara and bright lipstick.

'How do you see your job here?' Googie said, looking her over with disapproval.

'I'm your administrative assistant, Mr Allandale.'

'What's that supposed to mean?'

She gave him an easy smile. 'Whatever you want it to mean.'

'You're fired,' he said. He turned to Sebastian's secretary. 'Let me have a look at these guys you got lined up for me.'

He settled himself behind a desk and a pile of CVs, and the interviews began. He dismissed most of the candidates in less than five minutes each, a couple of weaklings, three girls — Googie didn't approve of girls doing this kind of work — and a handful who had no manners. The ninth was Ezekiel Josephus Dowd, tall, muscular, towheaded, white eyelashes, pink cheeks, an earnest smile.

'Ezekiel Josephus, huh?' Googie said, looking over the CV in front of him.

'Yes, sir. They call me EJ, sir.'

'Know anything about files?'

'Yes, sir. I do, sir. I done filing for the US Army ground forces.'

'Oh, yeah? In Iraq?' Googie was already impressed.

EJ blushed. ' 'Fraid not, sir. I sure did want to see action, but I got me a undescended testicle, and they don't let nobody like that go to Iraq.'

'Boot camp?'

'That was the best part, sir.'

Googie glanced down at the CV. 'It says here you spent a couple of years in the Peace Corps. How'd you like that?'

EJ looked down at his feet. 'Okay, I guess, sir.'

'Come on, son. Tell daddy all about it.'

EJ kept his eyes lowered. 'They got some greedy people volunteering, know what I mean?

They made a lot of profit out of local people. That wasn't right, sir. I didn't like it.'

Googie chewed the inside of his cheek. 'You go to church?'

'Every Sunday, sir.'

'Well, lemme see now.' Googie turned to a bank of filing cabinets. 'I figure the most recent cases are in them lower right-hand drawers. You get out a pile of them, and we'll start.' EJ didn't move. 'How come you're just standing there?' Googie said.

'I got the job?'

Googie looked him up and down. 'You know, that's the first stupid thing you said. Don't make a habit of it, huh?'

The first armload EJ brought gave a shocking insight into the extent of the job he and Googie faced.

Wet operations call for work as carefully documented as a doctor's; if questions are raised about a death, accurate files are crucial. These records were a mess. Sheets that belonged in one folder had found their way into another. Forms weren't properly filled out. There'd been no system for assignments. One job seemed to have succeeded more or less by accident. A couple of others had trickled away through lack of follow-up; cold cases like these can be very dangerous to a company's security.

Googie wasn't even sure where to begin. Each sheet of paper in every file was going to call for careful scrutiny. Each would have to be entered on a master index. Googie and EJ began at once.

The following morning they hit the David Marion file.

* * *

At first glance, the Marion file looked pretty orderly if somewhat on the sketchy side. UCAI had hired the contractor, an easy job; and sure enough, Marion had disappeared off the face of the earth. This was exactly as it should be. The problem was that the records didn't show a final report or payment of the final instalment of the contractor's fee. A check with Accounts and Auditing showed that the money had never been transferred to the contractor's offshore account.

The lack of a final report certainly explained the lack of a final payment, but why was the report missing? Googie sent out a few inquiries. Word came back that nobody in the mob world had heard a word from UCAI's contractor since he'd taken the assignment.

Newspaper stories claimed that Marion's body had been incinerated beyond the reach of DNA testing. Googie didn't like that. It didn't *feel* right.

'Want to do some field work?' he said to EJ.

'Oh, yes, sir. I do, sir.'

'Find Marion's body. We have to have proof that he's dead.'

# 13

## LONDON

By the end of Rosemary's first week at the Follaton Medical Foundation she'd learned everybody's name and what they did, even down to the kitchen staff for the executive dining room on the top floor. On Monday morning of her second week, she'd begun by indexing the files on the front desk computer so she could check quickly whose office handled what aspect of the charity and put calls straight through to the right department.

She was pleased. She'd achieved a lot in a very short time, and after her sandwich with Helen in the Mowbray Square gardens, she turned her mind to the dingy, cluttered hallway. The expression on Helen's face! If the Foundation's UCAI Fellow thought the place looked bad, so would other people. Rosemary talked to her mother about it. Her mother suggested that she take a brighter light bulb from home and the Japanese lantern that hung in their lounge.

'And after all,' said her mother, 'we hardly ever turn it on.'

The next morning before office hours Rosemary installed the lantern and the bulb — and was surprised at the improvement. But she certainly hadn't expected the change to attract Gabriel Walker's attention when everything else had failed. There was a lock of hair that fell across his forehead and had begun to disturb her sleep.

'What's this?' he said. 'You trying to reveal all our secrets?'

Rosemary smiled and turned in her chair to study her handiwork; for the first time he noticed how she moved that luxurious body of hers. 'It *is* better, isn't it?' she said.

'What'd you say your name was?'

'Rosemary, Mr Walker.'

''Mr Walker', is it?'

'You're Mr Hardcastle's assistant, coffee with milk and two sugars, no biscuits.'

'The name's Gabriel,' he said. 'Anything you need, Rosemary, you let me know.'

The following day she manoeuvred him into five minutes of banter with disarmingly innocent expertise. The morning after that, mid-banter, she ventured, 'Oh, by the way, the day before yesterday you said — ' she broke off, bit her lip. 'Oh, I shouldn't really . . . it's going to seem like I'm meddling, isn't it?'

'There's something around here worth meddling in?'

'My mother says I mustn't try to mind other people's business.'

'She does?' Rosemary nodded. 'How intriguing,' he said. 'Now you've got to tell me. Come on. Give.'

'Well, I . . . it's these boxes.' She gestured at the floor-to-ceiling on both sides of the entryway.

'What about them?'

'Do they have to be here?'

'Now how would I know a thing like that?'

'What's in them?'

Gabriel shrugged. 'Personnel files, financial statements, that kind of thing. Years and years of it. Intensely boring. They've been waiting for ages for somebody to sort them. No, no' — he held up his hands — 'don't *you* offer. It's a job for some dreary professional with iron spectacles and a pinched nose.'

'Couldn't they wait someplace else?'

He chuckled, shook his head, eyed her greedily. 'You take the cake, you do. Isn't your mind ever off the job?'

'They make us look sort of, well, run-down, don't you think? Dr Freyl thinks so, and I bet she's right. I mean, couldn't we — ?' She broke off again.

'Couldn't we what? Out with it.'

'I know there's a room downstairs that's quite big enough to — ' This time she stopped because the ease in his manner had snapped shut.

'Where'd you get that idea?' he said.

What *was* that in his voice? Sarcasm? Contempt? Why? Rosemary dropped her eyes the way good children do when they've been caught out. Tomorrow was Friday, her last day at Follaton. She'd never have another chance at this guy, and she didn't even know how she'd blown this one.

By the time she looked up again, he was gone.

* * *

'What I do not understand,' Jeffrey Hardcastle said, scanning his subordinate like a predator with a rabbit in its sights, 'is what the girl was doing down there. You did not say something? Allow something to, er, slip?'

'Of course not.'

'Do you find her pretty?'

'Not really.'

'Gabriel, my friend, this would not have arisen if you had not let her think you found her so. Did you speak to her harshly?'

'She caught me off guard.' Gabriel knew better than to attempt a full evasion.

Those hawk eyes scanned him. 'To find out on her own that a room exists in a basement when there is no indication that the basement exists: this shows intelligence as well as mischievous curiosity. She will put together the room and the harshness of your voice, and she will talk.'

'So what? Tomorrow's her last day.'

'My dear Gabriel, you have great promise, but you are new to civilian work. I must impress on you the extreme importance of detail here as in the forces. You must apologize. Say that the basement belongs to our immediate neighbours, and we are not legally permitted to access it. The lift is old. The basement and the route to it constitute rights of way which the Foundation was unable to purchase with the building. Our neighbours are litigious. There has been trouble before. If she is seen, both she and Follaton Medical Foundation will be prosecuted for trespass, and *you* will be blamed for her presence here.'

Gabriel had often been amazed at the speed with which his boss could construct a story out of thin air, but this time he frowned, uncertain. 'I don't deal with volunteers.'

'She knows nothing of internal chains of command.'

'I don't see her swallowing it.'

'You must convince her. Meantime, we must 'update' the lift control panel to improve camouflage. The fire exit is inconvenient for daily use.'

'And to convince the girl?'

'Offer her a job. Give her a title and more money than she deserves.' Jeffrey turned his attention to the papers on his desk. 'And get close to her,' he added as Gabriel left.

* * *

The following morning Rosemary clapped her hands to find the boxes gone. Their absence revealed the old mouldings on the ceiling of the entryway. It looked more elegant than she could have hoped. And then Gabriel made his apology and gave his explanations, telling her his boss had called him in to see if he could persuade her to work at the Foundation full time.

She accepted the job at once. As for Gabriel's invitation to lunch, she accepted that even before he'd finished making it.

He took her to a sushi bar, where the dishes revolved on a belt, and dared her to eat the raw fish. She wrinkled up her nose but found the taste not anywhere near as unpleasant as she'd feared. He listened to her enthuse over Belarus and said he'd developed a passionate interest in the Belarusian painter Chagall. The rest of what he told her was near enough to true, mostly anyhow. He said he'd trained for the British Special Forces because he'd been teased at school, served a long stint in Afghanistan, been wounded, met Jeffrey Hardcastle, decided to give up the military, so came to work in Human Resources at Follaton.

And he seemed to find Rosemary so enchanting that she began to forget how worried he'd been about her discovery of the basement.

# 14

## LONDON

Winfield House is the biggest private residence in London apart from Buckingham Palace. It's where the American ambassador lives. It sits in twelve and a half acres of Regent's Park, a gift from Woolworth heiress Barbara Hutton to the US government. Well, not quite a gift; she charged them a dollar for it, and it's filled with fiercely expensive bribes — antique furniture, paintings, *objets d'art*, chandeliers — from alien moguls in search of US favours. A reception at the ambassador's is the highlight of many trade missions; two weeks after Helen arrived in London, she went to a party there for Illinois business people. Rebecca Freyl owned stock in several of the companies, and Helen's budding collaboration with her grandmother meant that she was happy to attend as the family representative.

Security at Winfield House was tighter than at UCAI headquarters in St Louis: two checkpoints to get in and two sets of metal detectors, body search and passport inspection. Armed police were everywhere, not even trying to be discreet. Embassy officials, business people, their guests, wives and husbands crowded into the main reception room with its oak-panelled walls hung with presidential portraits. Waiters in livery ferried platters of canapés and champagne. Helen shook the hand of Bunn & Pergamoys Bathroom Fixtures, waded through a tale from an Angus breeder, then balanced the prospects of underwear ('Mitchell's, the finest for men') against the future of Frititatas ('the taste of Mexico with the heart of Illinois') in the company of two corn-fed businessmen.

'How do you like living with a bunch of Brits?' Mr Grimes, the underwear representative, was asking her. 'You been here, what? A week now? Ten days?'

'They can take getting used to. I spent lots of vacations here when I was younger.'

'You bet your boots they take some getting used to,' said Mr Frititatas, otherwise known as Mr Roach. 'It's really nice talking to a natural, pretty American girl like you instead of one of those snippity-snippies.'

'Um,' she said, watching a man make his way through the throng towards her. Middle-aged maybe, but his eyebrows were black, and his smile — a slight gap between the front teeth — had a boyish self-consciousness to it.

'You're Helen Freyl, aren't you?' he said as soon as he reached her. He sounded British, posh.

'This is indeed Miss Freyl,' said Mr Grimes with a swing back on his heels, 'and a very smart little lady she is too.'

But the Illinois businessmen might as well not have been in the room as far as the newcomer was concerned. He took Helen's hand and bent over it without even glancing at them. 'I've been trying to reach you all day.'

'And you are . . . ?' she said.

The black eyebrows arched. 'I'm Charles Hay.'

She smiled, assuming a joke. She'd really looked forward to meeting this man; she almost always liked people her grandmother mistrusted. But Charles Hay had been conspicuously missing from her introduction to the Foundation. He'd sent that deputy of his to the lunch that was supposed to welcome her. She hadn't seen him at the Foundation buildings either. Office gossip concentrated mainly on what she already knew from Rosemary: his ruthlessness and his silver Bentley. But arrogance came into it too. She'd heard several repeats of Rosemary's report that Sir Charles spoke only to the Queen — and very occasionally to his board.

'Good try,' she said to him. 'But I'm afraid you're not old enough.'

'I am, you know.'

'You're not kidding? Really?'

'No.'

'Charles Hay, huh?'

'Cross my heart and hope to die.'

'This guy bothering you, Miss Freyl?' Mr Grimes said, pushing his face into Charles's.

'Oh, do shut up,' said Charles.

It was a flick of annoyance rather than a taunt, but Mr Grimes's mouth snapped shut. He and Mr Roach squared themselves off, pugnacious lower lips stuck out.

Helen stifled her amusement and offered a hand to each of them. 'Thank you for your concern, gentlemen. But if this guy actually is Charles Hay, he's my boss. I'd better be nice to him, don't you think?'

The Illinois businessmen drifted off towards Dairy Queen of Springfield with a suspicious backward glance.

Charles watched them go. 'I've been waiting over there' — he gestured towards the vast drinks table in the room beyond — 'working up the courage to approach you. I knew your father.'

'I know you did.'

'Should we find a place to sit down? I do dislike standing around and balancing drinks. I can never manage it properly.'

She took a glass of orange juice from a passing tray and followed Charles to a side room draped in velvet and filled with museum pieces. They sat on chairs with embroidered seats. A chinoiserie lamp towered on top of the marquetry table that separated them.

'May I call you Helen?' he said, leaning forward to see her around the lamp.

'Do I call you Charles?'

'Please.' He looked down at his hands, then leaned forward again but didn't seem quite sure what to say next.

She wasn't quite sure what to say either. 'You were at Harrow with Daddy, weren't you?'

'We roomed together at Oxford too.'

'What happened?'

'I'm sorry?'

'You had a fight or something.'

Charles searched her face as though looking

for clues to what she might mean. 'He didn't tell you about it?'

'Look, even if he had told me, I'd have forgotten. I can never remember anything like that.'

'Your grandmother never mentioned it?'

'Grandma's a jealous old woman. None of his friends was good enough for him.'

Those black brows constricted, and earnestness turned his voice into a mixture of half-shamed, half-bashful. 'I said a lot of things I didn't mean. Nasty things. I can't imagine now how I could have been so shocked when he broke off the friendship.'

'That doesn't sound like him.'

'I was exceptionally silly in those days, Helen.' Charles sat back. 'This is a very awkward place to talk. Would you like something to eat? Since I missed my last chance to make amends to my friend, at least I can try to entertain his daughter for an evening.'

'Let's get out of here,' she said.

* * *

Fifteen-foot-high gates guard the ambassador's residence along with all the police, guns and double passport checks. As Helen and Charles stepped out onto the drive beyond these barriers, a silver Bentley pulled up. A chauffeur in a visored cap got out and opened the door for her, then for him.

Helen smiled to herself. Clearly the Bentley and the chauffeur of office gossip were true.

She'd seen Charles's arrogance with the Illinois businessmen. She wondered if the ruthlessness was going to show in his choice of a place to eat.

'Where are we going?' she said to him, as the car eased its way along the drive.

'A little bistro I know.'

'Oh, God, I don't like bistros much.'

'No?'

'Full of rush and bustle. Ceilings too low: voices get amplified. Plates clatter: that gets amplified too.'

'This one might surprise you. If you don't like it, we'll leave at once.'

Helen had always had a naughty streak, and she was already wondering how far she could push somebody with a reputation as scary as his. Most of the people she knew hated the whole idea of smoking; she took out a cigarette, lit it, drew on it. 'You couldn't have met my father before Harrow, could you?'

David Marion had smoked. That's the only reason she did. But the thought of him talking with a cigarette in his mouth — smoke curling up over his face, getting in his eyes — became a sudden knot of grief in her throat, while Charles only pulled an ashtray out for her from some hidden cubbyhole in the back of the front seats. 'All those years in England,' Charles said, 'and your daddy was a Yank through and through.'

'He sounded very English to everybody in Springfield.'

'The sound was English. But the man inside? I don't think so.'

She nodded. 'Are you going to tell me what

happened? To split you up, I mean.'

Charles looked out the window, sighed, then turned back to Helen. 'My parents died when I was only a boy. I was the younger son, and the estate was one of those ancient entailments: everything went to my older brother. My brother took very good care of me, but he made certain I was grateful. Not a comfortable state of being. Then out of the blue, he died — a rich boy's overdose in a rich girl's bed — and I came into my inheritance.'

Helen was vaguely aware that they'd left the park behind and were driving through London streets that had turned foggy. Her father had gone blind when he was about thirty, just a year older than she was now. Nobody knew why it had happened. A genetic failure? Some unnoticed accident? Some unidentifiable disease? He saw dozens of doctors; none could do anything to help. He remained blind to the day he died. He'd told Helen that his visual field wasn't black the way most people imagine. He said there wasn't anything there at all. One moment there'd been sight, the next: nothing but emptiness. She'd strained to understand, but the best she could come up with — even though she knew the image was wrong — was an impenetrable fog settling in over him.

The great London fogs of old were mostly coal smoke, and this one rivalled them. It blotted out buildings, cars, people; it turned neon lights into blurs that loomed in pastels, then disappeared. Helen's sense of direction wasn't too good at best, and the fog added a tense apprehension to it. Which end of the park had they emerged from? North? South? Why hadn't she asked this guy where his bistro was?

'Are you saying your inheritance somehow came between you and my father?' she said, careful to keep her unease out of her voice.

'The old cliché about money is all too right: it causes trouble. The fault wasn't his. It was mine. I was fascinated by money, bewitched. I could think of nothing else. Your father had a puritanical streak, you know. I'm afraid my excesses — ' Charles broke off. 'Aha. We're here.'

The Bentley pulled up at a darkened entrance on a London side street. The chauffeur got out and opened the door for her.

Charles took her arm and hurried her through a door. But the sense of foggy distortion from the streets seemed to follow her inside. The hallway was long, only semi-lit, completely deserted. If this were a bistro, where were the waiters? The customers? The clash of kitchen pots? Where was the smell of garlic?

She pulled her arm out of his grip. 'Where are we?'

'Nearly there. Nearly there.'

'Nearly where, goddamnit?'

He took her arm again, more firmly this time. Now that she came to think about it, she didn't even know for sure that he was Charles Hay. That would explain why he looked so young. He'd just walked up to her and introduced himself. Nobody had contradicted him — but then the others hadn't known him either. He could be anybody. She could be anywhere.

'Money is sex and religion all rolled into one,' he was saying. 'It gives you the power to do things ordinary people wouldn't dream of doing. When my brother died I was Paul on the road to Damascus.' He pushed open a set of double doors, and light flooded into the hallway. 'And thereafter — '

'Oh, my God,' she gasped. 'So this is the 'little bistro' you know, huh?'

What lay before her was the lollapalooza opulence of the restaurant at the Ritz Hotel, its mini-orchestra starting in on the overture from *My Fair Lady*.

* * *

The Ritz has one of the most beautiful dining rooms in Europe. That's its reputation anyhow. There's gold everywhere: gold swags along the walls link full-size gold mermaids. Gold roses climb up fluted columns to an encrusted ceiling with gold chain linking chandelier to chandelier. Helen adored the place — every inch of it — for the simple reason that her father used to take her here after her mother died. Besides, the pink plush chairs were a hell of a lot more comfortable than anything the US ambassador had summoned up for her.

The champagne was better than the ambassador's too. The Ritz is as famous for its wine list as for its regal kitsch, and this one was nutty, floral, lovely in the mouth. The menu is equally famous, but food had never interested Helen much. On the other hand — her naughty streak surfacing again — nobody's as tight-fisted as a rich man, so she ordered caviar even though she hated the stuff. At £185 a head it was by far the most expensive item.

Charles wasn't fazed. 'Make that two, Lucian,' he said to the waiter. Then turning to Helen, he added, 'It's been ages since I've had caviar.'

'You going to tell me where this came from?'

'The caviar?'

'This 'little bistro' gig.'

He chuckled. 'It's good, isn't it? I have a colleague who pulled the trick on me last week at the Paris Ritz. I've always loved secret passageways that take you somewhere special. I have one in my house. You must come and see it sometime.'

'I'd like that,' Helen said with a smile. 'Is that where you were? Paris? Is that why I haven't see you around?'

'If I'd been here, I'd have introduced myself as soon as you arrived. I'd certainly have greeted you at lunch instead of the pompous McGuire. You might not believe it, but he's one of the richest men in England.'

'They say you never deign to talk to underlings like me.'

'Do they?' Charles said with a worried frown. 'But you're not an underling, you're a terrifying American intellectual who's going to tell me what I'm doing wrong.'

She tilted her champagne flute at him. 'You hardly had to go to all this trouble.'

He glanced around him. 'I used to come here with Hugh. I just wanted to bring his daughter here. For old times' sake. You don't mind, do you? You have no idea how pleased I was when I learned you were to be the fellow that UCAI deigned to give us.'

The waiter refilled Helen's glass. 'Daddy used to talk to me about the Chernobyl meltdown, you know,' she said.

'Did he?'

'He told me that there was less than a minute — 'Less than a *minute*,' he'd say — between the first warning sign and the explosions themselves. I used to have nightmares about the speed of the thing.'

Charles shook his head. 'We don't have to talk about work, Helen. Tell me how your grandmother is. I used to be scared to death of her.'

'Well, well, poor you. This whole family scares you, does it? You know, I was in high school before I realized that Daddy didn't know what he was talking about.' Helen had collected her father's failures the way some children collect stamps. They'd given her permission to blame him for her mother's death and for her own failings; they'd helped her pretend she'd loved her mother as much as she loved him.

'How very like Hugh you are,' said Charles.

'Think so?'

'Interested in so many things.'

She let out a snort of irritation. 'Nuclear energy does edge in on a physicist's field. It's the scale of it that gives me nightmares now. That library of yours at Follaton is pretty good, isn't it?' She'd been spending most of her days there, immersed in the meltdown: design flaws, missed warning signs, frightened scientists, pigheaded management, naked political ambition.

'The equivalent of 150 Hiroshima bombs,' Charles said, '16 *million* times bigger than Three Mile Island.'

'Yeah. Sure. And you can count yourself lucky that the plant was one of the crap old designs and not one of the crap new ones running on super-fuels.'

Charles pushed his champagne flute an inch or two towards her. 'Most people think the new technology is foolproof.'

'Most people are idiots.'

'How do we wake them up?'

'Just show them . . . I mean, remember the *Challenger* explosion? All the astronauts blown up because nobody realized that a simple gasket could get brittle in space? In these new designs, the cladding around the fuel rods goes brittle the same way if it's cooled quickly from high temperatures. The heat of the new super-fuels means that some of it's all too likely to crack even under normal usage. Add this to nuclear plants being prime terrorist targets and — '

'That's really good, you know,' he interrupted. 'You're as clever as UCAI says you are, aren't you?'

Helen bristled. 'Praising the 'smart little lady' for Dairy Queen of Springfield, are we?' Her voice was as sharp as Becky's.

Charles ran a hand over his face. 'Sorry. That does sound a bit condescending. It isn't meant to.' He gave her his worried frown, and she suddenly remembered that the table had been ready for them; the champagne had been resting in its cooler. She'd been so surprised — and so relieved to find herself in a familiar place — that she hadn't noticed. Had Charles planned all of this in advance? Every step?

But before she'd had a chance to pursue the thought, the waiter appeared with the caviar on ice. A flurry with two ivory spoons resulted in a tiny football of the stuff for Helen and another for Charles. She stared down at hers, forgetting his mysterious behaviour now that this alien substance sat in front of her. She'd decided years ago that caviar managed to be gooey, slimy and pebbly all at once.

Charles ate his quickly. 'Going back to the scale of the Chernobyl disaster for a minute,' he said, 'the man in charge of the clean-up claims it's far, far greater than the official estimates allow.'

'Who's he? An administrator or something?' She took a tentative half-bite of her caviar. Fortunately for her, £185 buys a mere three spoonfuls.

'No, no. A physicist. Vladimir Chernousenko, a bit before your time of course.' Helen had never heard of him; her face showed her scepticism, and Charles's voice took on an intensity she hadn't heard in it before. 'He calls what we're up against the 'Nuclear Mafia'. He says the nuclear industry will do anything — *anything* at all — to get new power stations built. Falsify fallout estimates. Falsify records showing reactors are unsafe. Falsify the numbers of people killed, maimed, diseased by radiation. Falsify the severity of their illnesses.' He searched her eyes, and she realized she was becoming fond of that worried frown. 'For five years we've recorded radiation levels in Belarusian soil, human bone and tissue — plants and animals too — as well as underground water. We absorbed the only charity whose records go right back to the beginning, and no one — I mean no one — who looks at our analyses can fail to see that they fully support the Chernousenko estimate.'

She took another half-bite of her caviar. 'I'd love to have a look at some of the actual data.'

'You'll have to take a trip to Minsk for the privilege, Helen, and that's — '

'You keep the research in *Minsk*?' she interrupted, pushing the plate away from her; the remaining four half-bites were going to go to the London homeless. 'Why? That's a dumb idea. What happens if you need to double-check something?'

'It is a dumb idea. I couldn't agree more, but the Belarusians are so paranoid about leaks — and so suspicious of outsiders — that everything has to be on paper, and all the paper has to be stored where they can watch over it. They don't make altogether easy partners. Take a look at the analyses though. I'll have them sent to the library for you.'

'What about this Russian guy . . . What's his name? Chernousenko? Think he'd talk to me?'

But Charles was shaking his head. 'Don't even think about it, Helen.'

'Oh, come on. Why not? It'd be fun.'

‘You don’t have a clue what you’re getting into, do you?’

‘So tell me.’

Charles shook his head again, took in a breath, let it out. ‘You’re intelligent, beautiful, energetic, highly trained and you have access to the media. Worst of all, you’re young. You don’t know you’re going to die. This means you’ll take foolish risks. It also makes you dangerous to the nuclear industry. The industry doesn’t like dangers on its doorstep.’ He watched her a minute. ‘You don’t believe a word I’m saying, do you?’

‘Not really,’ she said.

But she did leave the Ritz that evening with a delicious sense of threat that she embraced with all the anticipation of a fairground customer buying a ticket for a rollercoaster.

# 15

## LONDON

Helen was living at the Basil Street Hotel because it made special provisions for single women, and Becky felt safer knowing she was there. But it was modest compared to the Ritz, and Helen couldn't help a sense of comedown as Charles delivered her at the front door.

She turned to him with a resigned smile. 'Home, sweet home.'

'Only until you find somewhere to live,' he said.

'I'm not going to be in London all *that* long.'

'Helen, the Basil is a hotel. You need some rooms of your own. You need a house. You know what I mean' — he smiled his amusement at her — 'one of those places where normal people live.'

'I hate looking at houses.'

'The Foundation would be only too happy to handle that aspect of your Fellowship.'

'What's that supposed to mean? Pay for it?'

'Whatever the Fellowship doesn't cover. Find it first, though.'

'Why in hell would you do a thing like that?'

'Oh, Helen, you must know that having a UCAI fellow gives the Foundation's profile a huge boost. We want you happy.'

She studied him a moment, then shook her

head. 'Moving is a bore too. I want to get my teeth into crop rotation.'

'*Crop rotation*?'

'You seem to find it fascinating. Why shouldn't I?'

He'd just finished telling her about a long and difficult negotiation with UCAI, who'd insisted their interests lay only in health clinics; he'd reminded them that people can't be healthy when they don't have enough to eat, and equipment was so scarce in Belarus that farmers were going back to the horse and plough. He'd managed to persuade the faceless corporate leviathan to send tractors, supplies of fertiliser and pesticide, even seed potatoes. This altruism moved her — and reminded her of her father. So did Charles's almost childlike excitement over modern agricultural techniques and increasing yields.

As she got out of the car, he held her hand a moment with that worried frown knitting his brow, and she realized that she hadn't thought about David since she'd smoked a cigarette in his honour on the way to dinner. She'd enjoyed herself with Charles, got pleasure out of something for the first time since Becky had told her about David's death.

In her mind, she turned to the monkey on her shoulder. 'There!' she said to it, feeling as triumphant as Becky had been over David's death itself. 'You see? I *can* do it.'

As before, the monkey pulled back a bit.

The next morning, she went straight to the Follaton library's section on the agriculture of the Mogilev region. But the texts were agro-technical, dry, dull. They needed Charles's enthusiasm. Within half an hour, her eyes were wandering to the narcissi in Mowbray Square outside.

And her mind was back on David.

* * *

Helen had gone to Choate Rosemary Hall, JFK's old school in Connecticut, but she felt she'd grown up alongside David. Her father's letters made him into an older brother who learned quickly and wrote well, just as she did. There'd even been the usual sibling rivalries. She'd sailed through maths and felt exultant when he struggled hard with algebra. Her father couldn't understand why — he was bad at maths himself — and when the problem turned out to be that he'd failed to teach his pupil how to divide fractions, Helen had teased him mercilessly.

After David finished high school, Helen followed his progress as an extension student at the University of Chicago. She'd known his grades would be high in English and history, and she'd celebrated his failure in philosophy largely because of her competitive nature but also because the great physicist Richard Feynman had called philosophy a 'dippy subject'. Sisterly concern hadn't set in until her father told her that the failure could cost David his degree, and she'd drunk a bottle of champagne in his honour when Chicago finally allowed him to graduate.

But despite this sense of closeness, she

couldn't get a grasp of the predatory violence of the life around him. She didn't even know what he looked like. She wasn't sure she wanted to know either, and yet when her father got him released from prison on a technicality, she'd flown to Springfield from Columbia — by this time she was finishing her thesis — to be home for his first Sunday lunch with the family.

Her father brought him to the house. She'd watched the two of them walk up the long drive, her father's hand on the elbow of a tall man with an iron-pumped body and an ill-fitting suit. She remembered nothing of the introductions or of how they got to the dining room; what she did remember was that she'd found it impossible to take her eyes off him. His face was young but the engraving on it was deep; there was a scar down the left cheek and a slight swelling around his eyes like a child awakened from sleep. She caught those eyes of his several times, but what she saw in them was inexplicable. She'd expected lust, but she wouldn't have been surprised at embarrassment or curiosity or even an appeal for help.

What she saw was threat — 'Get away from me' — and it made him even more fascinating than before.

Her father had decided that a preprandial glass of wine might be too much of an ordeal for a man so new to the social conventions of the world outside prison bars. They went straight to the dining room: rare tapestry on the wall, a view out over flowerbeds full of bloom, china that had been in the family for generations. But if David was awed by what he saw, he showed no more of it than he showed welcome of Helen's gaze. The sitting down was a little awkward, as though he found a chair an unfamiliar piece of furniture. What to do with the hands was awkward too. Lillian brought in the chicken and began to carve. The table was silent. Becky's mouth was pursed.

Helen exchanged an uncertain smile with her father.

This smile, she saw, David registered as an aggressive act. Tension around the table increased.

'I expect Springfield done changed some since you seen it last,' Lillian said to him. The Freyls breathed a sigh of relief.

'Yes,' David said.

'You like it?'

'They've stopped it dying in the centre.'

'Oh, yeah, of course. All them malls had taken over back then. That was when? Lemme see. Eighteen years? Long time ago, huh?'

David nodded but didn't reply and the table fell silent again. Lillian filled the plates, passed them around and then stood against the wall in her customary place. David speared a piece of chicken, lifted his fork, looked up at her, then back at the Freyls.

'Why doesn't she sit?' he said.

'Does it bother you for her to stand there?' Hugh's voice was concerned and curious.

'Yes.'

'Perhaps you'd better go to the kitchen, Lillian. We'll ring the bell when — '

'Can't she just sit?' David interrupted.

‘She’s a servant, Mr Marion,’ Becky said, trying — and failing — to cover her irritation.

‘She has to eat.’ David’s eyes were furious.

‘So she does,’ said Hugh. ‘So she does. Please lay a place for yourself at the table, Lillian.’

‘Mr Hugh, that ain’t strictly — ’

‘Please do as I say.’

Lillian laid a place for herself and sat down to the only meal she’d ever eaten with the Freyl family.

That’s when Helen knew she was in love.

* * *

But what good did it do to remember such a scene now? She railed at herself for her weakness. Why couldn’t that memory go the way of most of her personal life? In the Follaton library, she battled hard to smother it, failed, had to use brute force to get her attention back to Belarus, not agriculture though — that was hopeless — but the radiation levels in the Mogilev region, certain that she’d find them as riveting as she’d found fertilizer and crop rotation dull.

She didn’t.

The analyses in support of the shockingly high Chernoushenko figures were triumphs of academic tedium. She began to pity the Belarusians who’d had to collate the data and make sense of it. At least Charles could rest easy in the knowledge that the material was way too boring for her to irritate the nuclear industry with it; she even lost interest in talking to Chernoushenko himself.

The most she could stir herself to do was photocopy everything with the thought of persuading somebody else to check the figures. A fellow physicist she'd met at Columbia when she was working on her doctorate had landed a lectureship at Kings College in London. She called him and flattered him a little. She needn't have bothered. He was falling all over himself to check out the figures in exchange for a drink with her. A few days later in the Basil's upstairs lounge, he told her that the figures seemed to be pretty solidly based, although he couldn't think of any way to verify them.

That might have energised her if she'd known about it at once, but by the time she did know, she'd turned to radiation's effect on humans and found it as compelling as radiation itself. Protecting a person before exposure to fallout didn't seem too outrageous an idea, but a drug to address damage after the fact? In people like the Chernobyl victims? Putting ionized cells back together and patching up damaged chromosomes sounded like thoroughly unscientific ideas. And yet the library held whole shelves devoted to journals — *Radiation Research*, the *Journal of Nuclear Medicine*, the *International Journal of Radiation Biology* — that carried reports of dozens of attempts to do precisely that. Research was ongoing into a wide array of ingredients: antibiotics, lipids, antitoxins, histamines, thiols, hormones, steroids and practically every anti-oxidant known to humankind.

One entry on the list was honey-bee venom.

* * *

Helen had told herself firmly that she wouldn't look at the Follaton research until she had enough background to make sense of it, but that mention of venom was just too intriguing. She went in search of the Foundation's reports.

The most recent ones were in untranslated Russian journals. Her abortive stab at the language meant that she could more or less make out the dates and the letters

фолатон

which looked to her like the way 'Follaton' might be spelled in the Cyrillic alphabet. None of the articles in English was less than two years old. The most recent of these — it had appeared in an obscure journal called *Radiation Biology Archive* — reported that Follaton was concentrating on a few of the usual substances, glycols, steroids, lipids. No venom, not from bees or from any other beast. The only oddity was an ingredient referred to as Yeznik (LA)-205.3.

She hadn't run across that one before, although something called WR-2721 cropped up in several of the other studies. It turned out to be a compound developed by the Walter Reed Institute for the US Army as potential protection for troops sent to a nuclear blast site. Nobody knew how or why it worked or what its long-term side effects might be, but that seemed to be true of most drugs she was encountering in this research. She got out the Russian journals again and ran her finger line by line along the unreadable text of each article with a title that featured the word that looked like it meant 'Follaton'.

In every article, the numbers appeared repeatedly in the form: яжник (ла)-205.3.

It's discoveries like this that make a scientist's heart — or a detective's — beat faster. They were certainly the numbers she was looking for, and the letters made a reasonable stab at Yeznik (LA). An intriguing piece of what she assumed had to be serendipity was the number 205. Joshua's area code was 205; she'd dialled it many times. But a trawl through the internet told her that one Lynd A. Yeznik was an organic chemist from the University of Chicago known as 'the maestro of molecules' because he could duplicate tiny particles better than anybody around.

Helen could hardly wait to talk to Becky. Becky had Joshua's patents on file at her lawyer's. They would certainly tell if a Lynd Yeznik ever worked on the venom.

But it was 12.35 in London — only 6.35 in the morning in Springfield — early to telephone an ancient woman, and in ten minutes Helen had an appointment with Charles for a light lunch in his office and her first official interview with him.

* * *

Charles met her at the door. 'You're actually punctual, aren't you? How very nice. Come in, come in.'

'It's a curse,' she said.

His office looked well settled-into despite the

unfinished state of most of the building. His desk was a clean-lined table in light oak, the chairs elegant, old bentwood and wicker, the decoration minimalist but expensive. Books lined one wall. A detailed map of the Mogilev region of Belarus covered much of another. Three tall windows went from floor to ceiling; Follaton's New-Orleans-like iron filigree balcony ran across in front of them, and the view beyond was of the trees and flowers in Mowbray Square.

'I had *such* a good time the other night, Helen,' Charles said as she sat in one of the bentwood chairs.

'Me too.'

He sat opposite her and leaned forward, elbows on his knees, chin resting in his hands. A low table separated them. 'Do you mind a personal question before we get down to business? Have you found a place to live yet?'

'Oh, Christ, Charles. There's nothing wrong with hotel life. I like not having to think about laundry or food, and it certainly beats looking at houses.'

'But you don't have to look at houses, Helen. Jeffrey knows a property finder who's certain we could turn up something you'd like, help with the move, arrange daily service. If you don't mind, that is. We'd love to see you more comfortable. Truly we would.'

Helen hadn't seen Charles since he'd dropped her off at the Basil, and as she watched his amused and mobile face, she realized that the monkey David had put on her shoulder was pulling away again, as it had that night. 'You're on,' she said with a smile.

'Good, good.' He leaned back. 'Are you still finding what you need in the library?'

'Charles, I didn't know what an awful disease radiation sickness was. Or maybe I'd put it out of mind. Jesus, some of those photographs . . . hands blown up like beach balls, eyes melted down faces . . . Even the treatment sounds terrifying. I mean, 'radioprotectant', for Christ's sake. It's as bad as chemotherapy. But look, the science itself: I don't think any of it's going to be more of a problem than comparing the flaws in reactor cladding to the *Challenger* explosion. All I need is a couple of good metaphors and a good graphic artist. It's just going to take time.'

Charles leaned forward again. 'If you can pull out another *Challenger* or two to explain some of the effects of radiation, the Foundation itself will fund you when the UCAI Fellowship runs out. Helen, I know I seemed condescending the other night. I genuinely didn't mean to be. You're exactly what we'd hoped for.'

She nodded, uncertain how to get from here to the subject she had to bring up, then decided — as she had during that boardroom lunch on her first day at Follaton — that the direct approach was probably best. 'How far along is this pharmaceutical of yours? All the recent stuff in the library is in Russian. I can't make out a word. Could Jeffrey translate it for me?'

'We have a translator who comes in regularly. I'll send him around.'

Before she had a chance to press further, a knock on the door revealed the squat cook

Emilia with a tray of sandwich quarters, a pot of tea and a jug of orange juice. 'Juice is fresh,' she said as she set it down on the table between them. Only the mouth moved in her face as she spoke, not a single other muscle, and Helen suddenly remembered the puzzling shake of her head at that boardroom lunch. 'I squeeze oranges myself.' She turned and waddled out of the room.

'She's Belarusian,' Charles said.

'She's in training to be a ventriloquist's dummy. You were going to tell me how far you'd gotten with this pharmaceutical of yours.'

Charles picked up a sandwich quarter, studied it a moment, then put it back on his plate. 'I assume you know about the American BioShield law?'

Helen nodded. The library had a folder of clippings on it. President Bush had signed the law into existence several years ago at a grand occasion in the White House rose garden; its purpose was to provide funds for research into treatments of the diseases and injuries inflicted by biological weapons.

'Then you know that the small print includes radiation sickness,' he went on. 'But here's the odd part. The BioShield law is especially generous to projects far enough off the wall to have no commercial application in sight. Not like the politicians we've come to know and love, is it?' He picked up the sandwich quarter, studied it again, again put it back. 'Politicians usually fancy results for when election time rolls around.'

'Desperation?'

'Something like that.'

'They given you anything?'

'Not a sausage.'

She got up from her chair and went to the window. The day was bright. Gardeners were planting salvias in Mowbray Square where narcissi had bloomed only this morning. 'What's the matter with them? I mean . . . look at all those other studies. Rats, mice, monkeys. Everybody tests only on animals. There were some Japanese women undergoing radiation therapy for uterine cancer, but otherwise Follaton is unique. Only you have the research on the population of Belarus, so only you can collate statistics on radiation sickness in human subjects.'

He picked up the bite of sandwich once more, studying her this time rather than the bread.

'You going to eat that thing or not?' she said.

Still watching her, he put it in his mouth and swallowed it whole.

'Oh!' she said then. 'So that's it. Wait a minute. Just wait . . . Item one: only Follaton works with human radiation victims. Item two: the US gives money only to projects that are not commercially viable, and they give you nothing. Goddammit, you've done it, haven't you?'

'Have we?'

'You've already developed a drug that does the job. You're already into clinical trials, aren't you? Jesus Christ, you've really done it!'

* * *

As soon as lunch was over, Helen dashed back to the Basil and dialled Springfield.

'Grandma?'

'I didn't expect to hear from you until — '

'Did any of Joshua's venom go to Chicago?' Helen interrupted.

'They bought for three or four years beginning about fifteen years ago, Helen. You should know these things. The farm is your — '

'Yes, yes. What about a chemist called Lynd Yeznik? Ever heard of him?'

There was a pause, then a chuckle. 'What have you found out, my dear?'

Helen explained that Follaton's formula depended on a compound known only as Yeznik (LA)-205.3, then rushed on. 'It could be only coincidence but could you check the patents?'

'Helen, my darling, I corresponded with Professor Yeznik myself — as I did with any researcher who attempted to synthesize compounds from the venom — and requested that Joshua's patents carry his area code. I wanted an easy way for him to identify them as his.' Becky paused. 'Somebody must have been careless.'

'Careless? How? You mean, just overlooked the ownership of a patent? Is that possible?'

'UCAI has grown very rapidly. I imagine many details have been lost in the scramble, and St Louis is a long way from London — from Belarus too, of course. I think I shall put out a few gentle feelers. What do you say? Perhaps we can come up with another interested party, perhaps even one with rather better manners.'

She paused. 'Are you happy at the Basil? Such a nice hotel.'

Helen explained that Charles was going to find her a house.

'I see,' Becky said. 'Is that entirely wise?'

'Oh, come on Grandma. Living in a hotel isn't normal.'

'This is Charles's idea?'

'For Christ's sake' — Helen hated it when Becky read her like this — 'what do you care?'

'I see,' Becky said again. 'My dear, as soon as you move we should start discussing sensitive issues by email only.'

'You're joking.'

'I am a great believer in better safe than sorry. I'm told there are ways to encrypt email. Please look into them at once.'

# 16

## LONDON

The property finder Jeffrey knew came for a drink at the Basil that very evening. She was a tense, dyed-blonde in her fifties, made up like a Barbie doll and dressed like a thirty-year-old on the make. She ordered a Brandy Alexander.

'Tell me what sort of living spaces you like,' she said to Helen.

Helen said she didn't care much, but she'd need to be central, near the tube, a furnished house, spacious rooms, somewhere to sit outside, daily maid service.

The Barbie doll watched her carefully as she spoke. 'I have a few properties that might suit you. I could pick you up tomorrow. We could look at them.'

'Oh, God, couldn't you choose one for me? Nobody seems to care how much it costs.'

The Barbie doll took a sip of her Brandy Alexander. 'I know which one I'd choose. It's only a short walk from the underground at Notting Hill Gate, tree-lined street, garden in the back, restaurants and coffee bars only a few streets away.'

'I'll take it,' Helen said.

She told the Basil she'd be moving out on Saturday and went to work in her room. That's how she spent most of her evenings, although she'd seen a play with friends from Kent, gone to a few trade functions like the party at Winfield House and spent a weekend in Devon with Zoya, a much-loved old friend who'd gone to kindergarten with her grandmother more than three-quarters of a century ago, then disappeared off to dance in the Russian ballet. But Helen preferred the floor of her room, where she could sit surrounded by books, journals, photographs of victims.

On the last night of her stay, she ordered a fruit salad to eat in her room and settled down to work. When the knock came on her door — she assumed it was her salad — an unfamiliar man was standing there.

'Good evening,' he said with a sharp bow of the head. 'I am Feodor Feodorovich Mussinov.'

'Room service?' Her mind was on the journal in her hand.

'I? Room service? Of course not. I am on the faculty of the Royal Naval College in Dartmouth, which I am sure is famous even in America. I teach calculus — advanced calculus — and Russian to cadets of Her Majesty's Navy. Zoya has spoken to you of me.'

'Zoya? Did she?'

'The Commander loans *me* — Feodor Feodorovich Mussinov — to Sir Charles Hay's foundation where I now do translation sometimes as often as five days in a single month.'

'Oh, yeah, sure. You're Charles's translator. Did you bring the material?' Helen vaguely remembered Zoya talking about some guy from

Dartmouth who translated occasionally for Follaton; she'd got the impression he'd given it up. Zoya adored Russians; she'd changed her own name to make herself more like them.

Feodor held out a slender folder. 'I am very quick,' he said. 'I use voice recognition software, and you are very pretty, Helen Freyl,' he said. 'This is a fact I would not expect Sir Charles to mention, but why did Zoya not tell me so? Of course, you are not *quite* so pretty as I am.'

There was enough self-deprecation in the braggadocio to take the edge off, and he *was* impressive to look at. He had high Tartar cheekbones and wide-spread eyes of an unexpected colour that reminded Helen of somebody. The dancer Nureyev? The young Stalin? Were the irises golden? Or was that some trick of the light?

'Thanks for this,' she said, taking the folder from him.

'I have come to escort you to supper. You will not need a coat. The weather is unseasonably warm.'

'I don't eat in the evenings.'

'This Zoya tells me, but I will introduce you to some old people who have first-hand experience of Chernobyl. You do not have to eat if you do not wish it.'

'Look, friend — '

'Feodor. I insist. These are only simple people I wish to introduce you to. You will know more than they do, but there are not many in England who can speak of the matter from personal experience.'

What the hell, Helen thought, he was right; primary sources aren't always easy to come by. 'Just let me put my shoes on.'

Little Moscow was below street level, a plain restaurant, plastic tablecloths, tables tightly packed, conversation animated and accompanied by expansive gestures, music in the background reminiscent of balalaikas and folk dancers in tunics. The man behind the counter was small and dour with the flat, almond-eyed features of the Mongols who thundered out of Asia in the thirteenth century. He and Feodor launched into a torrent of Russian, interspersed with bear hugs.

'This is my good friend Georgi Alexandrovich Zalenka,' Feodor said to Helen.

Georgi led the two of them to a table where an old couple and a boy sat, absorbed in conversation. They broke off as soon as they saw him, getting out of their chairs to embrace him, listen to his introductions — all in Russian — and urge him to sit down. (At least that's what Helen figured was going on.) She shook the old man's gnarled hand when he offered it; he was bald, rheumy-eyed, missing his front teeth. He told her his name. He repeated it twice, but she still had no idea even how to start pronouncing it. His wife had frazzled white hair drawn back tight in a bun; she embraced Helen as though they'd known each other for years. The boy was ten or eleven years old, in jeans and a tee shirt with 'I'm a frog' printed across it in big green letters. They gabbled with Feodor as Georgi drew up two extra chairs, set two places, then withdrew after an elaborate set of goodbyes.

'What have they been saying?' asked Helen, touching Feodor's arm to catch his attention.

'I am the only Mussinov they have met — the Mussinovs were aristocrats before the 1917 Revolution — and I have introduced them to the only American doctor they have met. They think this is an amazing coincidence. They have come here from Kursk to visit their youngest son, who married an English girl. This is the first time they have seen their grandson in four years. They feel it is a great privilege to share their table with such important people.'

'What did you tell them I'm a doctor for?'

'Are you not a doctor?' When she started to protest, he shrugged. 'To them a doctor is a doctor.'

As he spoke, Georgi set a bowl of blood red soup in front of her.

She looked down at it curiously. 'We haven't ordered yet,' she said.

'Don't you know anything?' said the boy. 'It's always borscht.'

'How come you speak Russian?'

'I lived with my nan when I was only little.'

'Aren't you eating?' The table was bare except for two bowls, one for her and one for Feodor.

The boy shook his head. 'My nan likes sitting here. She says it's like home.'

'Where is Kursk anyhow?'

The question provoked an explosion of voluble Russian, and Helen began on her soup as Feodor translated for her: Kursk is south of Moscow, northeast of Kiev, the site of the great Soviet victory over the Germans in 1943. The old man had worked as a guide in the Battle Museum there; his wife had clerked in the post office.

'Kursk must be pretty close to Chernobyl,' she said. 'Is that where you were when the power plant exploded?'

The table fell silent for a moment after Feodor translated the question. Then the old woman let out an uneven breath, shook her head sadly and began to speak.

'Her eldest son died as a result of the accident,' Feodor said when she fell silent again. 'He was one of the fire fighters called to put out the — '

'My nan says my uncle was really, really brave,' the boy interrupted, angrily protective of his grandmother. 'The fires burned for ten whole days after, and he got very ill. They saw him in hospital, and his own insides came out of his nose and his mouth. He swelled up so big they couldn't get him into his coffin. The doctors said it was radiation, but my nan doesn't understand. Nor does Grandpa. Me neither. Nobody told me radiation could do that. You're a doctor. You tell us.'

Helen gave Feodor an exasperated glance.

'A physicist studies radiation more thoroughly than a medical doctor,' he said. 'Is that not true? Speak to them as a scientist.'

'You have a strange idea of truth.'

Feodor shrugged. 'I am Russian.'

'You're also not the dope you want people to think you are.'

He shrugged again.

Only an hour before, Helen had been immersed in the symptoms of radiation poisoning, and what the boy described certainly seemed to fit the pattern. 'From what I've been reading,' she said, 'their son's exposure would qualify as 'very severe radiation poisoning'. Symptoms would start within a couple of hours of exposure — vomiting, bleeding in the mouth, under the skin, in the kidneys — last for a couple of days, stop for a bit, then start up again harder than before. That much radiation, and no human can survive.'

'But what happened to my uncle's *insides*?' the boy pressed. 'What hurt him so much?'

Helen explained as best she could that the radioactive particles spewing out of Chernobyl set off chain reactions inside human bodies much like the reactions that give nuclear bombs their power. They tear through tissue; they explode cells like Catherine wheels on the Fourth of July. Some people die at once. Others die within days, like the boy's uncle. Most people survive. Some of them become well again. Some don't.

'He was just unlucky?' There were tears in the boy's eyes.

'You could say that.'

The boy buried his head in his grandmother's neck.

Georgi took away the empty bowls, replaced them with plates of what looked to Helen like home-made ravioli, and set a plastic tray in the middle of the table: butter, pepper, a cruet of vinegar.

‘Pelmeni,’ said the woman, answering the question on Helen’s face.

‘They are meat in pastry,’ said Feodor. ‘You season them as you like.’

‘With vinegar?’

‘Butter and pepper too.’ Feodor turned his golden eyes on Helen. ‘Your father is friends with Sir Charles Hay, yes?’

‘Did Charles tell you that?’

‘It is a rumour at the Foundation.’

‘My father’s dead, Feodor.’ But to stop him launching into expressions of sympathy, she rushed on. ‘They argued over money or some damn thing when they were young. Stupid kids. They must have had so much in common even then, both of them growing up to be hopelessly rosy-spectacled do-gooders.’

‘I’m sorry?’

‘My father taught murderers how to read and write.’

Feodor nodded. ‘Deep friendships usually mend after a while.’

‘Not these two.’ Helen’s tone was clipped. She wanted no more of this discussion. There was something pushy about it, something she didn’t quite trust — as though these questions were the purpose of the supper, not the old couple.

‘Ah, well, never mind,’ Feodor said. ‘Sir Charles can be difficult.’

Helen nodded and put a pelmeni in her mouth.

‘Horashow?’ the old woman asked, eyebrows lifted. Good? The meaning was clear from the woman’s voice and Helen nodded again.

'You do not feel — shall we say? — resentful because of this break?' Feodor said.

'Between Charles and my father?' Helen knew Feodor couldn't have missed her resistance to this line of questioning. 'Why should I? What do you care anyhow? It's none of your goddamned business.'

Feodor searched her face. 'You Americans are so very secretive about the simplest things. It is a great puzzlement to Russians. Forgive me if I have been indiscreet.'

* * *

When Helen got back to the Basil that evening, she read through Feodor's translations with a growing sense of excitement. At about midnight she called Becky.

'Grandma?'

'Helen, my dear, I am about to sit down to — '

'Grandma, this business is far more important than we thought. 'Radioprotectant' isn't quite the right word for what Follaton's developing. Their formula doesn't just protect against, I think it provokes the immune system into cleaning up the mess afterwards.'

'Helen, Helen, I'm not a scientist,' Becky said. 'I have no idea what you're talking about.'

'Look, the vast majority of people who survive exposure end up with an immune system so broken down that it can't handle the cancers and all the other illnesses that came from damaged DNA. That's the part that nobody's been able to do anything about so far.'

'And for us it means what?' said Becky.

'There's something in Joshua's venom — in this Yeznik (LA)-205.3 — that . . . Suppose you own a long railway line, Grandma. Part of your job is to send out teams to find and tag the breaks, bulges, weaknesses in the tracks. Then you send out other teams to patch things up. Natural DNA repair works like that. But ionizing radiation shreds the DNA and cripples your teams. Apparently Joshua's venom shocks the immune system into making the necessary protein complexes again and fixing itself in the process.'

'Fixing itself? You think Follaton has found a species of cure?'

'Something like that.'

'How very *interesting*. How sure are you of this?'

'It's what Follaton's research says, Grandma.'

Becky chuckled again. 'This *is* rather more than we expected, isn't it?'

'A hell of a lot more.'

'Fallout victims — '

'They're only the tiniest part of the potential sales,' Helen interrupted again. 'People are so scared of dirty bombs that every government in the world is going to have to stockpile this thing.' She took in her breath, let it out. 'Grandma, this thing is going to be worth half the gold in Fort Knox.'

# 17

## ST LOUIS

UCAI's fresh new recruit, Ezekiel Josephus Dowd — known as EJ — was enchanted with his new job and proud that Googie had so quickly entrusted him with the job of looking for David Marion's body.

His began his search with a day at the Springfield Police Department. They were only too happy to help, but he wasn't impressed. The investigations team had been so certain the charred remains in Marion's house were David that — despite the newspaper reports — they hadn't bothered to check either DNA or dental records. The autopsy report did note that the corpse was six foot three, and the UCAI file said that Marion was six foot five; but both were such poor work that nobody could call the discrepancy conclusive. On the other hand, combining a discrepancy with the lack of records was enough to allow the suspicion that Marion might not have been buried under the rubble of his Springfield house.

EJ reported back to Googie for further instruction.

'Good boy,' Googie said, reading over his report. 'Yeah, good. You done good.' He read the report again. Years of tracking down men — and the occasional woman — sometimes gives a hunter a sense of his prey. 'You know, EJ, my bet is that this fellow is still alive. So the question is, where's he at?'

'Canada? Mexico?'

'Naw.' Googie explained that borders into Canada and Mexico had become increasingly tight ever since 9/11; they'd present an unnecessary risk to a man whose picture had appeared in so many newspapers. Besides, if he'd been smart enough to anticipate a professional contractor, he was smart enough to figure out that the best plan comes from the philosophy of the federal Witness Protection Program: choose a place far enough away not to be recognized, large enough to blend in but not directly away from the point of danger.

Googie thought he should probably take this one on himself. On the other hand, the kid seemed to be doing fine — enjoying the challenge — and Googie was a busy man these days. The Midwest is home to many corporations; a new Regional Scheduler has flesh to press and clients' needs to assess. Googie's desk was overflowing with printouts.

'You know, a case like this can make or break a man's career in this business,' he said to EJ. 'Use your initiative — let me see what you're made of.'

# PART 2

# 18

## TOTNES, DEVON

World weather patterns were freakish during the summer. There'd been hints of the heat to come — a very early spring full of abrupt temperature changes, heavy fogs and hailstones the size of marbles. Maybe June in London didn't rival June in Springfield, which baked and steamed like a Louisiana swamp, but tennis players collapsed at Wimbledon. Water supplies ran short. Hyde Park lawns turned brown. Trees began to die all over town. Tempers flared.

At least Helen was used to it. A lifetime of Mississippi Valley heat had taught her to hold her breath and pretend she didn't exist in the tube getting to and from work. She worked from home whenever she could because the house in Notting Hill was air-conditioned. She also made a habit of getting out of London regularly; every other Sunday she took an air-conditioned train to Devon to see her grandmother's old friend Zoya for lunch and a bottle of chilled Sauvignon at an air-conditioned restaurant.

But Zoya wasn't just Becky's old friend. She was Helen's too. Helen had spent several vacations in Devon with her, and she'd been a major attraction of a year in England. Some people suck the life out of you. Some do the precise opposite, and Zoya was one of those. Helen had tried to figure out what it was that made being with her so much fun. Zoya had always seemed ancient, obsessed with Russians and ballet and unsteady on her feet. Now she was nearly blind and too vain to wear the bottle glasses she needed to see anything at all. That didn't stop her being funny, shrewd, penetrating and yet completely impenetrable, as well as generous with her time and her strange insights.

Helen always returned to London feeling as though the world was a better place than it had seemed on the trip down.

Usually she and Zoya went to the Dart Marina Hotel in Dartmouth, but one day Zoya suggested that she come early for an event at Ways With Words, a literary festival in the nearby town of Totnes. A novelist called Gerard de Plessus was reading from his new book, and Zoya was a devoted fan.

The novelist spoke in the ancient Great Hall of what had once been a music school; stone-carved windows looked out onto tiered gardens, a full-sized jousting court, cedars of Lebanon on the skyline. The event was packed, the audience rapt; and yet within moments Helen was fidgeting. The writer let his voice swing from the middle of one sentence to the middle of the next; the passage itself kept trying — and failing — to come to an end. She checked her watch. Only two minutes since she'd checked it before. Beside her, Zoya sat pert and upright in one of her prettiest suits.

'Oh, Helen, isn't he magnificent?' she said when he finished.

Helen frowned. 'He needs an actor to read his stuff for him.'

'He's an author.'

'What makes him think he can act too? It's embarrassing.'

Outside the hall, the writer was manoeuvring himself into a chair behind piles of his novel. Despite the heat of the day, a line of fans straggled into the grand courtyard outside the ancient hall.

'I must get him to sign my book,' Zoya said, rushing to the end of the line, Helen in tow.

The foliage circling the courtyard rose and fell in subtle gradations of green-grey leaves. Helen turned to follow the colour changes and found herself face to face with the cocky smile of the man standing behind them.

'My Auntie Bess thinks he's God,' said the smile in a honeyed, Southern drawl. The hair was dark, beginning to pull back at the corners of the forehead. The regular features were probably at their best in the bathroom mirror when he shaved; without themselves to admire, they lapsed into a kitchen-utility dullness.

'Oh, you're American,' said Zoya, swinging round to face him. 'Are you here on vacation?'

The cockiness slipped easily into gallantry. 'You could call it that, ma'am.'

'Why, I do believe that's Georgia I hear in your voice.'

'You just could be right.'

'Oh, how exciting. Isn't that exciting, Helen?

All the way from Georgia. I'm Miss Bezukhova, and this is Miss Freyl. We're American too. Why did you choose to come to Devon, Mr . . . ?'

'Bloeden. Leslie Bloeden.' He made a slight bow. 'Clearly I came here to meet you and Miss Freyl.'

Zoya's eyes lit up. In private — with the help of her heavy spectacles and a special magnifying glass connected to a bright light — she would scan the Personals columns in *The Times*. Whenever she found an ad saying, 'American man seeks English wife', she would write out a stern reply: 'Don't! You'll regret it. Find yourself a nice American girl.' She had decided at once that Helen was precisely what this one needed. His suit was well tailored, and his shoes were expensive. 'My mother always said there's nothing like the manners of a Southern gentleman,' Zoya said

'Didn't I see you on the train?' Helen asked. She couldn't say why she'd noticed him. He wasn't the kind of person she usually paid attention to. 'Coming down from London this morning?'

He nodded. 'I saw you too.'

'Why don't I get the book for your aunt?' said Zoya, delighted at this evidence of a budding relationship. 'That's what you're waiting for, isn't it? A present for her?'

'Yes, ma'am.'

'Oh, listen to that, Helen. 'Yes, ma'am.' You two have coffee, and then we'll all go to lunch together.'

'Hey, wait a minute,' Helen said. 'We don't know this man.'

'Nonsense, Helen. He's from Georgia.'

⋆ ⋆ ⋆

Leslie Bloeden bought the coffees at a noisy, crowded self-service tent. 'How about we sit us down somewhere in the gardens to drink this stuff?' he said to Helen, leading her to a bench overlooking the River Dart where half a dozen swans floated as serene as bars of Ivory soap in a bathtub. 'Dr Freyl,' he went on abruptly shedding his Southern accent, 'I didn't come here to get a copy of a book.'

'Well, well. What happened to Georgia molasses?'

'I meant it when I said I'd come specifically to talk to you. I represent Galleas International.'

'Galleas?' Helen set her coffee carefully on the bench beside her. 'I see.'

UCAI looked set to blast its way into the top hundred largest economies of the world sometime this year. Galleas International was fighting hard to do the same. Its petroleum holdings were massive — 3 per cent of the world's sales — and the rumours were that it ruled whole areas of Uzbekistan, Tajikistan, Turkmenistan, as though they were subject states.

Becky had suggested a competitor for Joshua's venom that might have 'better manners' than UCAI; she'd proposed Galleas as a place to start. Helen had objected that ruling lands as though a corporation were a monarchy didn't sound all that polite. 'Fiddlesticks,' Becky had said. 'The Queen's manners are excellent. The Slad twins, on the other hand, are dictators. They have no breeding.'

And yet somebody looking over towards the river during Bloeden's talk to Helen might have thought they were a married couple, the man oppressing his wife with a lecture, the woman becoming irritated enough to throw down her cup of coffee, thrust her arms akimbo for the parting shots, then march away leaving him on his own to stare out over the Dart.

* * *

'Why do you suppose that nice Mr Bloeden didn't join us for lunch?'

Zoya and Helen sat at a table in the White Hart, a restaurant not far from the Great Hall where the novelist had spoken. Helen was glad of the wine. She was glad of the familiarity of the place — they'd been here together several times during her English vacations — of the raw wood of the tables, the square glasses, the boisterous laughter of the other diners.

'Zoya, there's something funny going on,' she said.

'It's certainly funny when a man accepts an invitation to lunch and doesn't show up.'

'I'm serious.'

'So am I. Mr Bloeden is from Georgia. He knows how to behave.'

'He warned me, Zoya.'

'Warned you? What a peculiar thing to do. What about?'

'Charles. Follaton. UCAI. Not to trust anybody there. I ended up telling him to get lost. Not that it did a lot of good. He said he'd contact me again in any case, even insisted I take his card. Zoya, he says my telephone is probably bugged.'

Becky had warned Helen that her landline couldn't be considered safe after she moved into Notting Hill; she'd also insisted that all business correspondence go by encrypted email. Which is to say that Leslie Bloeden's revelation had hardly surprised her, but her respect for her grandmother's brains had taken an upward leap.

Zoya sipped her wine. 'Mr Bloeden's eyebrows grow too close together.'

'What are you talking about?' Helen knew that without the bottle glasses on her nose, Zoya's eyes couldn't make out such a detail.

'My mother told me never to trust a man whose eyebrows grow too close together. You must go to Charles at once.'

'That sounds like a really stupid idea.'

'Helen, you must do it now. Go to Charles at once. This man may be dangerous.'

# 19

## LONDON

Helen emailed Becky for advice as soon as she got back to her house in Notting Hill.

The reply came an hour later: 'This could all be very interesting, my dear. Why not do as Zoya says and tell Charles about Mr Bloeden? Be careful though. We do not want to reveal too much.' Becky went on to suggest what Helen should concentrate on and what she should avoid saying.

Helen hadn't seen Charles in his office since he'd let her in on the news that the Follaton anti-radiation formula was already in clinical trials, although she'd run into him in the elevator several times. He'd been warm and concerned about her work — and she was finding it harder to think of him as a man her father's age. There was a youthful exuberance to him that her father had never had. She liked the arch of his eyebrows and the gap between his front teeth. She looked forward to his worried frown; she admired his commitment to what he did. She'd known from that first dinner at the Ritz that she was going to be more interested in him than she should be.

She asked to see him the following morning and couldn't help smiling when he told her to come to his office at once.

But the prospect of presenting Zoya's suspicions to him scared her. She wasn't sure why — perhaps no more than Becky's warnings to be careful about what she said — and she made no attempt to hide her fear.

'What is it, Helen?' he said, glancing up as she entered his office. 'You look quite unsettled.'

'Something weird happened,' she said.

'Sit down. Tell me about it.'

'Does the name Leslie Bloeden mean anything to you?'

'Bloeden?'

'He said he represented Galleas.'

Charles frowned. 'Hmmm,' he said. 'You met this man?'

'He was at a literary festival down in Devon. Zoya wanted to hear some guy prate on — '

'Zoya?'

'Oh, Christ. I've told her so much about you, I assumed I'd told you about her. She's an old friend.' Helen explained that she went to Devon every other Sunday to have lunch with Zoya.

'Go on.'

'Well, this Bloeden was in the audience. He was on the train from London with me too.'

'He approached you?'

'Yes.'

'Have you told anyone else about it?'

She shook her head. Becky had said she was to take responsibility for reporting the incident herself, not tell him that Zoya had insisted she see him.

'It was prudent to keep quiet,' Charles said.

'Galleas is extremely powerful.'

'I know *that* much, Charles.'

'What did you say his name was?'

'Bloeden. Leslie Bloeden.'

'Did he ask you for any information?'

She shook her head.

At one corner of Charles's desk stood a tier of mahogany in-and-out trays; he pulled a sheet of paper from one of them, glanced at it, then looked up at her with that worried frown of his.

'Corporate espionage is so pervasive — ' he began.

'Espionage?' she interrupted, truly taken aback. It hadn't crossed her mind that Bloeden was anything other than a Galleas emissary. 'Spies? At a *book* festival? What would a *spy* want with me?'

'Helen, a few years ago MI5 and MI6 — both of them — admitted they were losing the battle to protect British-based businesses from foreign agents. The FBI and the CIA say the same of US business.' Charles crossed to the window and stood there with his back towards her.

'That's what you think?' she said. 'Bloeden is some old FBI guy?'

'He was American?'

'A West Coast state, I think. When he dropped the phoney Southern accent, that is.'

'CIA more likely. And not 'old'. Currently employed by his government.'

'Really?' Helen leaned forward, startled again but fascinated too. 'Who says so?'

Charles turned back to her. ' 'The right to land

depends on the ability to defend it.' Sound familiar?'

'Thomas Paine? George Washington?'

He poured a glass of water from the bottle on his desk, handed it to her, poured another for himself. 'I'm afraid not, Helen. This was an eminent Australian industrialist by the name of Sir Roderick Carnegie. He was addressing a board meeting of Rio Tinto Zinc, and what he was talking about was Rio Tinto's control of Namibian uranium mines — not Namibia's control of them or some invading conqueror's. See what I mean? How can Rio Tinto Zinc beat Namibia away from its own investments without cooperation from MI6? Who else is in a position to bug the Namibian Embassy? Or any other foreign embassy or consulate? Or the United Nations for that matter?'

'Okay,' she said slowly. 'I know there's big money behind Follaton, but in the end Follaton is a medical research foundation, and I'm only an academic here on a year's Fellowship. What's the point of Galleas warning me?'

Charles started so abruptly that he almost dropped his glass. 'This man *warned* you? Against what?'

'He said you were dangerous.'

'Me? Personally? Not UCAI?'

The shock on his face took her by surprise. 'Oh, God, I'm sorry, Charles. I didn't mean to blurt it out like that.'

'Anything else?'

She shook her head.

'No details?'

'I wasn't feeling friendly by that time.'

'You're going to give me a heart attack one of these days,' he said, going back to his desk and sitting down.

'Are you telling me this kind of thing happened before? I mean to you? To Follaton?'

Charles nodded. 'In the wrong hands, this radiation drug of ours could make a very great deal of money for all the wrong people. We need to get it to the Chernobyl victims, and we need to get it to them at a rock bottom price.'

'Isn't that a matter of course? There must be international trade agreements that cover this kind of thing. I mean, couldn't governments — Belarus, Ukraine, the others — manufacture a non-branded supply?' She knew the answer to her own question, but Becky had counselled a ladylike ignorance until they could gauge how much Charles knew.

'This is far from an ideal world, Helen,' he said. 'Even governments must apply for permission first.'

'Sounds reasonable enough.'

'AIDS drugs still aren't available in Africa at a price that people can afford, and God only knows how many years ago the applications were made. With this much money riding on something to treat radiation exposure, legal teams can stave off permission for decades. I had to bargain hard to make that part of the deal with UCAI.'

'They finally did agree though?' This did surprise her — impressed her too — although it seemed of a piece with the man who'd also bargained so hard to get UCAI to supply fertiliser and tractors to spread it. 'Why did they agree at all? It's hardly something they had to do.'

'They needed our Belarusian contacts, information, medical infrastructure. Imagine the cost of duplicating all that, and I doubt they would have been able to in any case. Did this man Bloeden leave you any way of contacting him?'

Helen shook her head even though she carried Leslie Bloeden's card in her purse. 'He said he'd contact me.'

Charles's shoulders slumped. 'Oh, Lord, I'm so sorry about all this. You're going to have to be careful from now on. If he tries to contact you again, you must come to me right away. These people will stop at nothing.'

'I'm not sure what that means.'

'There is no Geneva Convention for industrial war, Helen. Even so, not everybody executes civilians who disrupt their plans.'

'Oh, come on, Charles,' she laughed. 'You don't have to exaggerate. I know corporations are sharks. But nobody's got anything to gain by hurting me.'

He sat down at his desk, took in his breath, then smiled. 'You're right. Of course you are. They're probably just feeling you out. But watch yourself, won't you? You're all I have left of my old friend Hugh, and I don't want to lose you.'

# 20

## LONDON

Becky's email advising caution with Charles had ended by asking Helen to call her from a safe place as soon as it was over. Helen went straight to the manager's office at the Basil.

'I couldn't have handled it better myself,' Becky said when Helen finished a detailed description of the meeting.

'What I don't see is why Galleas bothered to send that Bloeden guy at all,' Helen burst out. 'The stupid bastards. He said he wasn't authorized to make any commitments about distribution of the drug to Chernobyl victims.'

'He understood that we will not deal until that matter is settled?'

'I couldn't swear to it. He wasn't 'authorized' to guarantee a percentage of the profits either. I was furious — mad as hell. I could've killed the guy.'

'His offer for the venom was ten million?'

Helen gave a snort of contempt. 'Only *twice* UCAI's offer. It's insulting. Let's forget Galleas, Grandma — try somebody else. SmithKlineGlaxo. Ciba-Geigy. Bayer. Anybody.'

'This is just horse trading, my dear. We'd have to do something of the kind with whomever we approach, and we must give Charles time to report back to UCAI. They'll need a while to assess his information. They do appear to assume we're unaware that we are the sole owners of Professor Yeznik's work. This is an illusion we should encourage for the moment, I think. As for Galleas, perhaps they don't yet realize how important the Professor's work is. I think I might feed them another titbit. When we have them tied down, *then* we can tell UCAI a few home truths. You must remember that we are in the fortunate position of not caring which one wins.'

'So what happens? They slog it out between them?'

'All we have to do is watch,' Becky said.

* * *

The rest of the week wasn't an easy one for Helen, and her unease had nothing to do with giant corporations. Her father's birthday would have been on Thursday; it had always been a family celebration — he'd loved birthdays, especially his own — and this was the first one since he'd died.

Her mother had died long ago, a car accident when Helen was only eleven. She'd blamed her father for it as children so often do. Only when he died himself, did she realize how desperately she loved him, how much she was going to miss the sense of safety he'd carried around with him. All of this was complicated because it was her father's altruism that had brought David into her life; for that she wasn't sure whether she loved him more or hated him all over again.

Becky had always insisted that the family collect for Hugh Freyl's birthday. Every year, cousins, uncles, aunts with husbands, wives, partners flew in from all over the US. Planning took more than a month and culminated in a huge party at the Country Club. The Sunday lunch that preceded the final one was the only other time Helen had been at the Freyl dining table with David.

A dozen people there were clinking glasses and scraping chairs. They'd reached the roast beef before Helen realized that Lillian was disappearing into the kitchen between courses instead of standing at her usual place by the sideboard. Helen could barely suppress her delight: that had to be because of David. What would Becky do if he insisted *Lillian* sit down next to racist Cousin Frank of Florida or orange-haired Aunt Scary of Mississippi? But if David was aware of the embarrassment he threatened them with, he didn't show it. He remained as much on edge as he'd been at the earlier lunch. The other guests gossiped and joked while they watched him, longing for him to fall on his face — circus clown, village idiot — and justify Becky's unconcealed contempt for him.

Despite herself, Helen waited with them. The high point came when Becky was complaining in great detail about Hugh's directions to a newly opened store in the centre of town.

Hugh only laughed. 'You are making mountains out of mole-hills,' he said to her.

'On the contrary, Hugh.' She wasn't pleased. She didn't like being told things like that. 'I did as you said. Your directions misled me.'

Her voice was sharp enough to cause a momentary lull. 'You followed them too slavishly,' said David in a voice as irritable as hers.

Becky's mouth had opened, then shut. And Helen had at once added lust to the love she already felt for him, an extraordinary change for her: this was the very first man she'd ever *really* wanted to get into her bed.

* * *

On the Thursday that would have been her father's birthday, Helen left Follaton at three and walked for miles around London, so weighed down with grief and guilt that she barely noticed the heat. At about seven, she returned to the house in Notting Hill only because she couldn't think of anything better to do with herself. As she came through the door, the telephone was ringing. She almost didn't answer it.

'Helen?' It was Charles. 'I need your help. Can you come at once?'

She arrived at his office half an hour later.

'You've seen the news?' he said before she was all the way through the door. 'We have to issue some sort of statement, Helen. And we have to do it soon.'

'News?'

'I can't reach Melinda.' Melinda handled PR for the Foundation. 'You *haven't* heard, have you? Where have you been all this time?'

'Walking is good for the heart.'

He didn't seem to hear her. 'The fools have shot a dozen people, Helen. Riots. October Square. Minsk. One of them was an English student on a research project.'

President Aleksandr Lukashenko of Belarus — elected as a corruption-fighting reformer — had taken less than a decade to stifle all opposition and become, in newspaper-speak, 'the last dictator in Europe'. Police response to the riots in the capital city had been swift and brutal.

'I don't know anything about this kind of PR, Charles,' Helen began. 'Why don't you call an agency or — '

'Helen, please. If you can take problems out of physics with — how did you put it? — 'a couple of good metaphors and a good graphic artist', this ought to be a piece of cake. I wouldn't bother you if I wasn't desperate.' Then without transition, 'Have you been *walking* ever since you left here?'

'It's not all that long a time.'

'It was barely gone three when you left.'

'You got spies on me or something?'

'I do try to look after you, Helen. I feel it's rather my . . . responsibility.' He paused. 'Hang on a minute. Your father's birthday is around now, isn't it? Oh, God, I'm so sorry. No wonder you're upset. He loved his birthdays. He was always on about them. Fireworks, parties at that dreadful Country Club — ' Charles broke off. 'Is it *today*? Is that it?'

'How do you know it's dreadful?'

'He told me about it often enough.'

'Oh, Charles, how could I have misjudged him

like that? I was *so* stupid.'

'So was I, Helen. So was I. He was one of the genuinely good of this world.'

'Well, why the hell did I refuse to see it when he was alive? What was the matter with me?' But she knew she'd cry — she could feel that constriction in her throat — if the conversation continued.

He knew it too, and he shifted his focus at once. 'Well, now let's see . . . as to this press release . . . I know what we have to get across: somehow we have to make people understand that we'll find a way to work through any political turmoil, whether it results in a new government or not. I just don't know how to go about an opening . . . '

But Helen couldn't keep hold of his words. She'd forgotten that her father's moods had adapted to hers as easily and quickly as this, and the constriction rose in her throat again. She took in a sharp breath to quell it, only partially succeeded.

' . . . radiation sickness can be treated . . . *effectively* treated — we couldn't actually say 'cured', could we? — if we achieve what we have set out to despite political — ' Charles broke off again. 'Helen? Are you all right?'

She nodded, unable to speak.

He got up, went over to her, put his hand on her shoulder, squeezed it. 'Let's get away from the office, shall we?' he said. 'Why not work on this over a bottle of wine? We can have something to eat. I can start calling journalists when we've finished. What do you say?'

* * *

Charles took her to an elegant Greek restaurant called Epidaurus, treated her gently, made her laugh, eased her into the press release. By the time they got back to the Foundation, she felt human enough to start calling a few journalists herself.

She went to Epidaurus with him again twice the next week. By the week after that, dinner there was turning into as regular an event in her life as lunch in Devon with Zoya. Charles listened hard. He rarely said what she expected. And yet he was a puzzlement. He had an open physical warmth that an upper-class Englishman's schooling rarely allows to survive. He seemed to like the way women looked, moved, sounded. She once saw a photograph of him with a handsome Dutch countess in her forties; the magazine had speculated on the possibility of an announcement to come. But dinner with Helen at Epidaurus wasn't mentioned in the gossip pages, and at the office they met and parted like friendly colleagues. No more.

Becky had once said of men, 'Oh, why can't it stop with lunch?' With the exception of David, Helen agreed. Most of them disgusted her before they got so far as unzipping a fly, and not a single one had made it all the way to zipping back up again. But Charles threatened to approach Becky's ideal.

Hence the puzzle: with the exception of her father, Helen had never gone out to dinner with a man who hadn't tried to foist a hand down her blouse or up her skirt. Of course, Charles could be gay, Helen thought. That would explain his restraint. Perhaps the Dutch countess was only cover. And yet she'd decided — and was surprised that the idea didn't annoy her more — that gay or not, he was falling in love with her.

# 21

## SABRINA, COLORADO

Summer in the Middle West broke records just as it did in England. July and August blistered and boiled at temperatures and humidities that belonged in an African swamp. Dozens of people died, and that was *before* electrical power failed under demand for air conditioning. After it, without cooling or medical machinery in nursing homes and underendowed hospitals, the death toll soared up over a thousand.

Throughout it all, EJ Dowd worked the Marion case with growing excitement and a determination that hardened with every setback. Rebecca Freyl dispatched him in under five minutes. He went to DC for Samuel Clark but fared even less well there. He checked out bars where David was known, whores he'd been seen with, drug suppliers he'd bought from. Nobody seemed to know more than what the papers said. David's closest friends seemed to have died or disappeared, and apparently he'd not found new ones. His credit files and business records revealed nothing. His police files supplied names of foster parents he'd had as a child and juvenile centres where he'd been detained.

As the summer wore on, EJ interviewed as many of David's foster parents as he could

— and found nothing. He spoke to neighbours who lived in the close near David's ruined house, executives of companies that had employed him to design and install security systems, prisoners and guards at South Hams, ex-cons, visitors, relatives of prisoners. Nobody knew anything at all.

But they do say that luck favours the mind prepared, and right at the end of August, luck supplied EJ's crucial lead.

His grandparents lived in Denver, Colorado, where they published a fundamentalist weekly called *The Lord's Truth*; he'd grown fond of the paper because he was fond of them. The most recent issue concentrated on homelessness and covered an amusing story about an attempt to encourage street people into church for prayers and a bowl of mushroom soup. A scuffle had broken out, and the soup tureen had overturned to whoops of joy; EJ's grandmother had captured it on camera, and *The Lord's Truth* ran a two-page spread of her photographs.

Right in the midst of it was David Marion.

His hair was long; he was bearded and he wore a cap. But there was no mistaking the size of him even if the eyes, nose, forehead hadn't been so clear. The question was, what to do? EJ thought he should report to Googie before taking action, but it was late on a Saturday when he ran across the article, and Googie didn't like being disturbed on weekends. By Monday it might be too late. Of course, it might be too late already.

'Use your initiative': that's what Googie had said.

EJ entered what he'd discovered into his report on the case, took the first flight out of St Louis on Sunday morning and landed in Denver before noon.

* * *

For David, street life during that summer turned out to be more like prison than the absolute freedom his onetime cellmate had described. The cops are as all-powerful as they are inside. The same sense of aimlessness hangs over everybody and everything. The stretches of boredom feel as interminable — way too much time to think.

He'd headed south from the Smoky Mountains, down through Georgia, up through Tennessee, into Kentucky, walking most of the time, hitching to vary the pace, joining groups of the homeless when he needed directions or information or the sense of people around him. In late August he hit the Midwest prairies. He'd lived his whole life there, and he'd looked forward to cornfields, meadow larks, long straight roads, a sense of the familiar. He certainly hadn't expected a simple geographical closeness to Helen Freyl to destroy all that.

He'd dreaded those Sunday lunches around her grandmother's table: fish forks and cloth napkins, polite tittle-tattle about the Chicago Opera. They'd been a regular event in his life for nearly two years after he got out of prison, and he'd forced his way through them the way he'd forced his way through Philosophy 101 for his degree from Chicago: a waste of effort. He'd failed both.

The first time Helen had appeared at one of them, he hadn't known what to make of her; she was supposed to be in New York, and she was much prettier than he'd imagined. From Hugh's descriptions of her intellectual feats, he'd thought stringy hair and pimples, not porcelain skin and green eyes. Just the surprise of her was unsettling for a man who'd been out of prison only a couple of weeks after eighteen years inside, and then as soon as he'd walked through the door, she'd stared at him like he was Frankenstein's monster.

The only other time she'd been at that table, nearly two years later, she'd stared the same way.

In prison, men died for less. Hugh had spent hours drumming the rules of polite society into David; on the outside, what was an obvious insult like that might not be an insult at all. It might be humour, curiosity, self-deprecation. It might not exist all. Even if it did, punishment was at most irony, a look, a gesture. David had fought to understand — and failed yet again. That first time, he'd felt like a baited bear prancing about on its hind legs. The second time, Becky had supplied a jeering audience for his antics.

He'd hated himself both times. He hated himself now, and those memories alone justified it.

He'd barely arrived in the Midwest when he realized he had to get out of there as fast as he could. Go to California. Maybe seeing an ocean would change everything; maybe his old cellmate had been right about that if nothing else. He hitched through Illinois and Kansas, made Denver at the end of August and joined a group of the homeless there who were in the Rockies to escape the heat. He had no intention of staying, but he got a kick out of the assault on the soup tureen. When some of his fellow assaulters decided to go to the town of Sabrina — a hundred miles south — to celebrate their victory at the Sabrina Mushroom Fest, he went with them.

* * *

The Mushroom Fest had started out as a business venture and expanded quickly into an alternative festival and tourist attraction. In the mountains, magic mushrooms are ready to harvest in late summer, much earlier than anywhere else. The bearded, the beaded and the ohm-sayers flocked from as far away as New York. White river rafters — Sabrina was right on the banks of Yellowback Creek — made it a regular stop, and busloads of hikers and sightseers from Aspen and Vail came to gawk and dare each other to take a nibble.

The great party at the end of the week-long festival took place in a barn with ear-splitting live music and a sweaty crush of people. Mushrooms were everywhere: raw mushrooms, fried mushrooms, broiled mushrooms, stewed mushrooms, mushroom cakes, mushroom juice. In prison, David had been force-fed enough haloperidol to make him uninterested in psychedelic experiences; but there was plenty of beer, and plenty of people drinking it.

The party was still going strong at three in the morning when he went down to the cellar to fetch more liquor and smoke a cigarette in peace. There was only a single bare bulb for light and a long flight of stairs that wound down into the darkness below. He'd just picked up a crate of beer when he saw one of the alternative lifers crouched in a corner, shoulder-length hair secured with a headband, stud in the lower lip, shark's teeth around his neck.

'What are you doing down here?' David said. 'All the mushrooms are upstairs.'

The alternative lifer kept his gaze on David and brought out a hunting knife.

'What's that for?' David said. 'Oh, come on, you don't want to — '

The alternative guy lunged.

The simple speed of the attack took David by surprise. A dull thud of pain meant that the knife had caught him in the side. The attacker drew back, crouching again, feet wide apart, arms spread, knife poised. From upstairs came the clapping of hands, stamping of feet, loud bellowing:

*Mushrooms, mushrooms, keep them in the dark*
*'Mushrooms, mushrooms,' I heard the boss remark,*
*'You feed them bits of bullshit . . . '*

State of mind is everything in an attack. There can be no doubt, no stray thought: absolute concentration. David balanced himself, feet wide apart like the other guy's, keeping hold of the crate as a shield to deflect the next blow, which clattered against it, jolting the attacker's arm. He drew back to attack again. David didn't move, not a breath, not a flicker, eyes seemingly unfocused as though he were dead already, just hadn't yet fallen down. The attacker lowered his knife in puzzlement. As soon as he did, David heaved the crate of beer at him, then followed through with a chop to the throat.

The alternative lifer lay on the floor beneath the crate, glass broken, beer foaming, hunting knife still clutched in his hand, stunned but not out, headbanded wig slipping at a tilt over his forehead. David kept him pinned down with the beer crate, searched him, found a few coins, a set of keys in his pockets and US Army dog tags in his shoe that read:

Dowd<br>
Ezekiel J<br>
066-03-6731<br>
A POS<br>
Baptist

# 22

## ST MARY MAGDALENE HOSPITAL, ELLISTON, COLORADO

'Open your eyes, Paul. Paul? Can you hear me? Paul?'

'Urg.'

'You've taken an overdose of something?' The nurse was dark-haired. Paul figured almond-shaped eyes, cute. Was that a pony tail? Or some kind of a headband?

'Gimme my glasses,' he said.

'You *broke* glasses, Paul.' His mother's voice was precisely the combination of heavily accented whine that he'd hated all his life. 'Paul be *good* Catholic boy. *Nice* boy.'

'Eighteen Tylanol,' Paul said.

'Okay,' said the nurse, 'when did you do that?'

'Dunno. About 4.30.'

'Did you have any alcohol?'

'Yeah, lots.'

'Have you been depressed?'

'Who the fuck isn't depressed?'

'Paul!' cried his mother, 'Speak *nice*. Another word so and you never see me again.' Paul knew he'd never be that lucky. It wasn't in his stars any more than it'd been in his father's. He felt sick and dizzy. How much *had* he drunk? A quart of gin? More?

The nurse disappeared for a few minutes, returned, took hold of his arm. 'Just a slight prick now,' she said. He watched her slip the needle of an IV into his vein, tape it in place, hook it up to a bag and hang the bag from the aluminium rack behind him. The bag had a yellow fluid in it. 'I got to take a piss,' he said. The nurse took a urinal out of a cabinet and handed it to him. 'In *there*?'

'You can't go to the men's room with a line in your arm, Paul.'

He stared at her in disbelief. Then with the abrupt illogic of the drunk, he was outraged, raging, off the bed, tearing the line out of his arm, blood spurting, stumbling out of the ER and into the cold of the night beyond, thinking that all he'd wanted was to be dead. Maybe the attempt he'd made an hour ago was half-assed, but now he was going to do it right. Yellowback Creek met the Arkansas River only a block or two away from the hospital. The whitewater of the join boiled into whirlpools and falls that crashed through boulders and threw up spray higher than a man's head.

He lurched against trees to get there, swayed on the banks a moment, then blinked, staggered — and drew back aghast.

Somehow he'd already done it. Somehow it'd already happened. There he was, Paul himself, lying dead and tormented by the water. He couldn't make out any features without his glasses, but there was his pale blond hair across a rock and his strong shoulders, legacy of his father. He bent down. There were his white eyelashes around his staring eyes, his chest caught between rocks, his legs bouncing with the river.

And yet here was Paul, squatting down over his own body, watching it.

His mother was right. He was a good Catholic. He'd sinned, and he knew it. Was this purgatory? Was it hell? Was he damned? He fought his way back to the hospital chapel to beg forgiveness from his God.

* * *

Whitewater rafters showed up dead along river banks from time to time in the mountains. Not long ago one of them had been a movie star, and a tiny town called Never Die had been all over press, TV, radio, internet. Whitewater rafting companies were still scrambling to set up offices. New restaurants and motels were still opening. Local commerce was booming.

Every town in Colorado prayed for a repeat performance. Only moments after Paul babbled out his story to a nun arranging flowers in the hospital chapel, police squad cars screamed out of the station to look at the body he'd found.

# 23

## LONDON

By the end of August, Helen and Charles were welcomed as regulars at Epidaurus, the elegant Greek restaurant they'd started going to in July; every Monday and Thursday the chef came out of his kitchen on the far side of an open fire to lead them to a table, pour out some Retsina and discuss the merits of brizoles as against kokoresti.

Helen enjoyed the dinners for themselves. She enjoyed Charles for himself. She also enjoyed the novelty of being with a man who seemed in love with her but didn't keep grabbing at her. But what she really looked forward to was the game of Joshua's venom that she assumed was behind the entire façade. With Becky's encouragement she was still acting as though she'd made no connections between the synthetic compound Yeznik (LA)-205.3 and the venom, much less between UCAI's attempt to buy Joshua's farm, steal his bees and lure her across the Atlantic with a fellowship. Whether Charles believed in her ignorance she couldn't tell, but both she and Becky were quite certain he knew more about UCAI's desperation to get hold of the patents than he let on; they were also certain that a part of his brief was to woo the patents out of her.

Becky had warned her that a business negotiation involving a disputed patent and a secret formula could take the better part of a year — maybe longer. But Helen had a sense at the end of August that something definite was in the air. She was aglow with anticipation as September began, and yet a scratch began in her throat shortly after noon on Monday of the first Epidaurus dinner of the month.

An hour later her nose clogged, and her head started to throb. She pleaded with a pharmacist to give her enough of something — anything — to get her through this evening. When she promised faithfully that she'd spend the next two days in bed, he pulled out a codeine syrup from under the counter and sold her that along with an amphetamine decongestant and some ibuprofen. By the time Charles was at her door in Notting Hill, she was feeling much better if a little drunk and overexcited.

'You're getting a cold, aren't you?' he said as he opened the door of the Bentley for her.

'You're not supposed to notice.'

'You should be in bed.'

'I'm going to give it to everybody at Epidaurus — you included.'

'Rubbish. I never get colds on a Monday. Let's go to the Ritz tonight, Helen. It would be a shame to infect the whole of Epidaurus. They're not anywhere near so deserving.'

This time there was no trek through semi-lit passages; Helen and Charles went through the front door into all that gilded Louis XVI splendour. A honeyed champagne was waiting in a cooler by the table.

'You planned this *again*, damn you,' she said as she sat down. 'Don't you ever consult your friends?'

'Not when they have colds.'

The sommelier opened the bottle and poured frothing glasses for them both. A pâté de foie gras followed, then roast duck with a burgundy. Usually their talk at least touched on work, but the conversation at the Ritz remained firmly on life in London, a play he'd seen, another trade function she'd attended on Becky's behalf, an opening at the Victoria and Albert Museum. Helen finished her duck, knowing that she had to get home to bed soon or go to sleep at the table. She was debating with herself on the virtues of another decongestant when Charles said something she was sure she must have misinterpreted.

'What?' she said.

'Helen, would you consider marrying me?'

'That's what I *thought* you said.' She set her glass down. 'This is a hypothetical question?'

'Not entirely.' His smile was sad. 'I'd have asked you the first time we sat at this table if I'd dared. It's not just my age — although I'd say I was forty-two if I thought I could get away with it — it's that I can . . . ' He took in his breath. 'There's somebody else, isn't there? I can feel him there.'

The jolt of pain she felt was as abrupt as it was unexpected. 'He's dead.'

'Could you tell me about him?'

'Why?'

'I want to know everything I can about

somebody who was — who is — so important to you.'

She rearranged the silverware in front of her, trying to resist the desire to talk about David. She failed. 'The only reason I smoke is because he did,' she said. 'I don't like the taste much, but it brings him back to me a little. I don't even know what my relationship was with him. I'm not sure I had one. What do you think, Charles? Think I made him up? Could I be that unstable? To have made him up? People say I'm unstable. You do know that, don't you?'

'You must have loved him very much.' Charles put his hand over hers.

'He didn't love me.'

'Silly fool.'

Helen pulled her hand away. '*Exactly* what I thought. How could anybody not love such a 'smart little lady'? Right?'

'Oh, Helen, Helen, you're so prickly sometimes that finding a way to approach you isn't all that easy. Perhaps he didn't know how to get through to you.' Now that she came to think of it, the hand that had been over hers wasn't unlike David's. The fingers were long. The palm was broad. 'Tell me about him.'

'I don't know anything worth telling.'

'Yes, you do.'

* * *

Helen had sleepwalked through the period after her father's death, not sure what was real and what wasn't. She meant what she'd said to

Charles: she couldn't be absolutely sure if she'd managed to get David in her bed — or just imagined it. What had happened between them kept sliding sideways in her memory, interspersed with a fierce revival of the night horrors she'd suffered as a child that seemed as real — or as unreal — as he did himself. And yet she remembered the way the muscles of his back fed into the muscles of his waist and hip. She remembered prison tattoos on his arms: a flower — a chrysanthemum, she thought — and a revolver tied together with a ribbon.

When her mind cleared a little, she'd decided that was her clue. She could have made up the musculature, but the details of a tattoo like that? She'd searched prison tattoos on the net and been half-shocked, half-relieved to find this one on a prison website. The site told her that the Northside Mob of Chicago, origin of the South Hams Prison gang the Insiders, had been the only one to present Al Capone with serious competition. Deanie O'Banion, its founding father, had owned a florists; he'd been in his store arranging $2,000 worth of chrysanthemums for the funeral of another mobster when he'd been gunned down, not with the tommy guns that the era was famous for but with revolvers.

She hadn't seen David for weeks after this discovery, and the hurt of his absence deepened the grief for her father that was already threatening to overwhelm her. Then one night there'd been pebbles against her bedroom window. She'd opened it and looked out.

David stood in the rain below, his coat billowing out around him.

'David?' she said.

'I wanted to see you.'

'Oh, David, I've wanted to see you too. Where have you been?'

'Are you all right?'

'Okay. Okay. Better now that you're here.'

'That's what I needed to hear.' He turned, stumbled, took a step, turned back, paused. 'I thought you'd have stringy hair.'

'Why?'

'And pimples.'

'Are you drunk or something?'

'Little bit. Maybe.'

'Would you . . . I mean, *could* you spare a moment? Maybe come up? I'd love to talk to you.'

He hesitated. 'No. Best not.' But he took a step towards her, hesitated again. 'Best not,' he repeated, then turned once more and sprinted off into the trees that surrounded the Freyls' house.

* * *

The sommelier at the Ritz poured out the last of the burgundy. 'You wear hardly any jewellery,' Charles said. 'Don't you like it?'

'I don't dislike it. It doesn't interest me very much, that's all.'

'May I show you something?' He took a small brown envelope from his waistcoat pocket and shook out a ring.

Rose diamonds are cut to resemble the petals of a bud in spring; the crown of the stone is a dome with facets meeting at the centre. 'This *is* different,' she said, turning it to catch the light. 'I've never seen anything like it. Absolutely beautiful.' She looked up at him. 'It must be very old.'

'I'd say it has been waiting nearly three hundred years just for you.'

She glanced down at it, then back at him. 'Charles, why in God's name would you want to mess up your life with marriage to me? I'd make you a lousy wife. You and your Dutch countess are a fine-looking couple, and there must be dozens of other women who'd leap at the chance.' But she hadn't expected the pain on his face.

'You mustn't mock me, Helen.'

'Mock you? That's a weird thing to say.'

'I'm fully aware you're not in love with me, but maybe it will come. I can wait. I'd be happy for the opportunity to do no more than that. We have so much in common. We both love the work we do. We believe in it. Very few people are lucky that way. We're unlucky in the same way too. We have no brothers or sisters — not even cousins. Our parents are dead. We could be family to each other. I don't mean I'd try to take Hugh's place even though — ' He broke off, frowned. 'It isn't that I don't want to be a father to you.' He frowned again. 'But Helen, I wouldn't dream of pressing you into anything you didn't want. I'd be more than satisfied just to share a home with you, knowing you'll be under the same roof when I wake in the night.'

Helen scanned his face. His brows were slightly constricted with the intensity of what he was saying. 'That's quite a speech,' she said softly.

This time his smile was sheepish. 'I've been practising it for days.'

'We don't have to get married, you know.'

But even as she said the words, she realized that UCAI wouldn't like the idea of Follaton's director living with a woman half his age. Since the Slad brothers had taken over, a display of Christian values was mandatory in all staff who wanted to keep their jobs. They'd replace Charles without another thought if the London gossip pages reported an out-of-wedlock liaison.

Helen thought she could probably put up with a month married to Charles, but no longer than that. The problem was sex. Maybe he was gay. Maybe he wasn't. Neither appealed to her. If he wasn't, his body would disgust her before the month was up. If he was, it meant he was too scared of the Slads' evangelism to tell her, and cowardice like that disgusted her too. In either case, there'd be the mess and expense of a divorce. It hardly seemed worth it just to find out how UCAI stood on Joshua's venom.

But then, of course, the threat was minor. 'I'm sorry, Charles,' she said. 'Grandma would never allow it.'

'I'm not asking to marry her, Helen. I want to marry you.'

Helen shook her head and explained that Becky had cut off her own son when he married

— a breach that had lasted several years. After Helen's mother died, Becky stepped in to prevent a second marriage. Now that Hugh was dead, Helen had taken his place in Becky's life. On top of that, Becky was grooming her to take over the Freyl estate. If Charles had been David . . . But he wasn't David, and she explained to him — as gently as she could — that she loved her grandmother more than she loved him.

He frowned once more. 'Your grandmother finally accepted your mother?'

'Very grudgingly.'

'What happened to the other woman?'

'She couldn't take the pressure. Another irony in all this is that if she'd stayed around, my father would probably still be alive.'

The waiter stood beside the table. 'Coffee, madam? Sir?'

'Not for me,' Helen said. 'Charles, I hate to tell you this, but I feel absolutely dreadful. I have to — '

'She will not refuse to cooperate a third time,' Charles interrupted. Then to the waiter, 'Not for me either.'

'Charles — '

'I'm sorry, Helen. The pieces don't fit. Twice, yes. I can see it. But three times? No. She's a highly intelligent person. Her intelligence will move in and overrule the jealousy. What she did was wrong — horribly wrong — and it ended in destroying exactly what she wanted to preserve. She must know that. She'll agree to the marriage.'

'You don't know her.'

'I think I do.'

'Look, Charles, there's not a cat's chance in hell.'

Charles swirled the last of his wine in his glass, then clinked it against hers. 'Would you like to place a bet on that, young Dr Freyl?'

# 24

## SPRINGFIELD, ILLINOIS

'He says his name is *what*?' Becky said to Lillian.

'Sir Charles Hay, ma'am.'

'He knocked on the door? Just like that?'

'Yes, ma'am.'

'What does he want?'

'Said he wanted to talk to you.'

'Interesting. *Interesting*. Show him in.'

She sat behind her black desk and surveyed Charles as he entered her study in Lillian's wake.

'How many years has it been?' Becky said before he could open his mouth. 'Thirty-five? Forty? Please stay with us, Lillian.'

'Nearer to thirty-five,' Charles said, 'although probably on the wrong side of it. You haven't changed a bit.'

'Don't you try to flatter *me*, young man.'

'I wouldn't dream of it. But how are you? You look tired.'

'How would you expect an old woman to look? What are you doing here after all this time? You always refused to spend vacations in Springfield. I do not like European snobberies. We are not your colony. You are *ours*.'

Charles laughed. He'd been only a teenager when he'd realized that a vein of humour lurked behind Becky's acerbity; it amused her — just as it did Helen — to see how far she could push a person. He knew he'd been a thorn in her side for most of Hugh's schooling; she'd flown to England twice a year to visit her son, and much of the time the visits had been with Charles as much as with Hugh. She hadn't been displeased that Charles had shown so little interest in coming to Springfield.

'Never mind all that,' she said. 'You have helped give Helen a purpose in life. I'm deeply grateful to you for it, perhaps more so than you'll ever know. On the other hand, I know perfectly well that you would not visit the relatives of every person who spends time at your Foundation — especially when you have to fly across the Atlantic to do so. I do not give grants to foreign-based organizations, and despite my gratitude, I will not change my policy. I'm afraid you have wasted your time.'

'How very like your granddaughter you sound,' Charles said, smiling. 'May I sit down, Mrs Freyl?' She gave a delicate shrug, and when he'd settled himself in a sleek art nouveau chair opposite her desk, he said, 'I have come to ask your permission to marry Helen.'

Becky started. 'You *what*? How dare — ' She broke off and clutched her hand to her breast. Lillian was at her side at once with a silver box, pressing a tiny pill to her lips. 'Under your tongue, ma'am. Open just a little wider. Calm yourself now. You gonna be okay, hear me?'

'A glass of water,' Becky whispered a few moments later.

As Lillian hurried out of the room, Becky used what strength she had to turn her chair away from her desk and hide her face from Charles. As the pain diminished, her mind raced. A marriage could mean only that he knew UCAI had failed to secure the patents to Joshua's venom. Either he was here as UCAI's emissary or he wanted the patents for himself. In either case, he was more dangerous than she'd feared, and she had no idea what he'd done to Helen — or threatened to do — to get her to agree to a marriage.

Most frightening of all was the lack of word from Helen. All Becky could be certain of was that she was going to have to handle this extremely carefully.

Lillian returned with the glass of water, stroked Becky's back while she sipped it, stood beside her as she turned to face Charles again.

'Age does terrible things,' she said to him. 'This is not what I expected, not what I expected at all.'

'I can't imagine it was.'

'You were Hugh's best friend for years, but I don't think I like you any better now than I did when you were young. Helen is all I have, and you are way too old for her.'

'Old enough to be her father.'

'You are, however, unusually well preserved.' The colour was returning to Becky's cheeks. 'This indicates good genes, and good genes are important in a marriage. You should be rich too. Are you?'

'Very.'

'You are also well educated. Do you love my granddaughter?'

'I do. Very much.'

'Does she love you? She has not mentioned any of this to me. Not a word. Not a peep.'

'She's lonely. I think I can change that. She thinks so too.'

Becky took another sip from the glass of water. 'All she wants is a father. Girls do that, especially when they've recently lost one.'

'I don't mind what she wants as long as I'm part of it.'

'When she recovers from her grief, she'll find a younger man.'

'A short marriage is better than no marriage at all.'

Becky harrumphed. 'What happened between you and my son?'

'Oh, dear' — Charles ran his hand over his face — 'I was afraid you'd ask about that. I've thought and thought, and the trouble is I'm not entirely certain.' He shrugged, shook his head. 'I came into my inheritance, and for a while it acted on me like a huge jolt of amphetamines. I made an absolute and total ass of myself. I bought a Bugatti and a Monet. I ordered caviar by the kilo. I held wild parties at Gstaad. Hugh didn't like it. He didn't like it at all.'

'Didn't he? That does surprise me. He was overly fond of girls in those days and feckless with money. He always overspent on his allowance.'

'Things sometimes blow up over what seems to be a trifle, then leave a person stranded with no way back to where life was before. Perhaps by the time I came to my senses, Hugh had simply moved on. I can't say I blame him, although I was very cut up about it at the time.'

But there had been something more. Becky knew that from the way Hugh had behaved. Whatever it was had so upset him that he refused to talk about it. He'd died without ever mentioning Charles's name again. On the other hand, Charles was very credible — quite good-looking too — and he was probably right about Helen being lonely. Perhaps she actually did want to marry him.

'Helen has agreed to marry you?' Becky said.

'With your permission.'

'I intend to speak to her first.'

'Of course. I know she wants to talk to you too. There are many plans to make. We could marry here in Springfield if you like.'

Becky drummed her fingers on the desk again. 'You may go, Lillian,' she said.

'You want me to get you some more water first?'

'Just go.'

'Yes, ma'am.'

When Lillian had closed the door behind her, Becky said to Charles, 'You probably already know that I stood in the way of Hugh's wife, whom he loved. After she died, I stood in the way of the only woman he'd loved since then.'

Charles nodded. 'I gathered something of the kind,' he said.

'It is, er, *disagreeable* when one's best intentions turn out so very badly. Especially given the magnitude of the consequences, twice is enough to make the same mistake.'

She glanced out the window, sighed, then turned back to Charles. 'The marriage will take place here at the First Presbyterian Church. That was Lincoln's church. Bishop Banning will conduct the service. We will hold the reception in the Governor's Mansion.'

'That sounds like an excellent plan.'

'You think so?'

'I do.'

She drummed her fingers on her desk as she had before. 'As I say, I do not trust you. You will draw up a prenuptial contract. I will need to see a draft before Helen signs it.'

'So you shall.'

'I will also need a full statement of your financial position.'

'But of course,' Charles said with a slight bow of his head.

* * *

'Helen? My dear? Are you all right?' Becky's voice was frightened, quavery.

'What is it Grandma?' The telephone had wakened Helen out of a deep sleep. She lay huddled in bed — still wearing the clothes she'd had on last night — shivering and boiling both, her head throbbing. 'Oh, God, I feel awful. You don't sound so good either. Are you okay? You're not alone, are you? Where's Lillian?'

'I've just had your . . . fiancé here.'

Helen yanked herself upright. 'My *what*?'

'Sir Charles Hay.'

'Oh, Jesus, he didn't!' Helen laughed despite herself.

Becky heaved an inward sigh of relief. Helen clearly had a bad cold, but she was safe. 'He says you don't love him,' Becky said, 'but he thinks you'll come to it. Why didn't you tell me this was happening? You might have warned me.'

'He never said a word until last night. Don't worry, Grandma. It's okay. *Please* don't worry.'

There was a pause. 'What did you plan to do? Email me when you felt like it? Is this *all* I'm to expect?'

Becky's voice was bitterly sarcastic, but she was heaving another inward sigh of relief. She knew her granddaughter's self-defensive temper, and so far there'd been no angry defiance, no righteous indignation, even though she knew perfectly well that Becky would disapprove the match vigorously. All of which was likely to mean that this twist in the relationship with Charles was professional rather than emotional.

For months now, both women had acted on the basis that Helen's phone was tapped. The warning from the Galleas representative, Leslie Bloeden, had made them more cautious still; they'd grown used to making a game of what they said, giving out signals that only the other could penetrate.

'Grandma, dearest' — Helen's tone showed nothing but amusement, fond indulgence and a stuffed-up nose — 'it never occurred to me that he'd fly to Springfield at once. The poor man must have spent the entire night on a plane. It's *so* sweet, don't you think? It didn't occur to me that you'd agree either. I'll call you as soon as — '

'The wedding is to take place at the First Presbyterian,' Becky interrupted. She knew herself quite well too, and she knew what she'd say if she thought that the situation was real. 'I will speak to Bishop Banning tomorrow. This is non-negotiable. Do you understand?'

# 25

## ST LOUIS, MISSOURI

Googie felt like Pontius Pilate. He should have known better. He *had* known better. Barely days in the water, and the kid's body was badly decomposed. If it hadn't been for the Colorado police's happy insistence that it belonged to a Hollywood star, identification might have taken months. As it was, every US agency started at once to scour their files, hoping to uncover a match for Leonardo di Caprio or Daniel Craig. The army and the Peace Corps found — within hours of each other and to their great disappointment — that the DNA belonged only to one Ezekiel Josephus Dowd.

Their disappointment upset Googie all the more because EJ had shown promise. He'd had a future ahead of him. He'd been careful, orderly, systematic about his work. The latest entries in his report — he'd logged onto the UCAI site before he'd left for Denver — had stated his belief that David was hiding among the homeless in the Rocky Mountains; he'd included scans of *The Lord's Truth* with its photographs of David and the mushroom soup tureen.

Googie printed out the entirety of EJ's file and took it home with him; he started in on David Marion's past while his children watched westerns on TV in the living room.

David's birth had gone unrecorded, a difficult feat in America. He'd appeared officially in Springfield when he was about six years old and living with a drug-addict of a grandmother called Clotilde Marion, who'd apparently forgotten to feed him if not to beat him regularly. Social Services had removed him from her. The next chapters were not unexpected: removal from foster homes and detention in juvenile centres for shoplifting, drug dealing, felonious assault. Then came murder and a life sentence without the possibility of parole.

The Illinois Education in Prisons Program had done its best to rehabilitate the boy. Its eminent volunteer teacher, Hugh Freyl, had taken an illiterate, foul-mouthed 15-year-old, cleaned up his language, given him a slight English accent and turned him into that prison rarity, an educated man. The rest of him though? Prison documentation suggested no change; records showed attacks on other prisoners, guards, prison property — as well as psychotic episodes, many months in solitary confinement and too much time in the prison hospital with stab wounds and concussions.

Despite this evidence of his protegé's dysfunctional personality, Hugh Freyl had put all his considerable legal talents into a campaign to free David. He'd demonstrated that since the boy couldn't write until after he'd been sent to prison, the signature on his confession could not be his; he'd also presented medical evidence showing that the confession itself had been beaten out of him over the course of several days. After eighteen years behind bars, David Marion had walked out of prison without even the restraint of a parole.

The warden of South Hams had been furious. He'd written an angry letter to the judge describing David's suspected illegal activities, including the death of another prisoner.

The prisoner's name? Robin Mercy Allandale.

* * *

Googie's distress turned to an abrupt nausea. He bolted for the bathroom, threw up his wife's Irish stew, spent the next twenty minutes on his knees gagging and trembling.

Robin Mercy Allandale was his little brother.

It took Googie almost an hour to control the turmoil in his mind enough to go back to the file on the teenage Marion's arrest for the murders that had put him away in the first place. He already knew what he'd find there. *Robin* had been in charge of the investigation. *Robin* had been the interrogator who beat that confession out of David Marion, probably signed it too.

Googie checked the warden's letter again. Among the illegal activities the warden had suspected was David's membership of the Insiders, the prison gang named after the infamous Northside Mob of Al Capone's Chicago. Even more significant: the warden felt sure — although he'd never been able to prove it — that David had been promoted to the rank of lieutenant when he was only eighteen. Eighteen!

Most lieutenants are old men of twenty-five. And when did the warden believe this astonishingly early elevation had taken place?

The week after Robin died. The very week. It had to be payback. It just plain had to be.

Googie had been grandfathered into the police force, both father and grandfather before him; he'd joined the Springfield department right out of college. Robin had followed him there, stayed on after Googie left, made a reputation for himself as a cop's cop and risen as quickly as Marion himself to the rank of lieutenant.

Googie had been proud of him, and his fall from grace had come as a complete shock.

'Justice at last: Springfield's police torture ring feels the lash'. That was the headline. Beneath it, the story began:

> Lieutenant Robin Allandale, son of the Sheriff of Sangamon County, has been sentenced to 10 years in prison for mistreating eight prisoners in his charge. The proven facts are grave. They include shattered cheekbones and kneecaps, broken jaws, ribs, fingers, cigarette burns and electrical burns, internal injuries.

They'd sent Robin to South Hams State Prison. Googie's last memory of his brother was an orange uniform and leg irons.

At best prison is a bad place for a cop. They put Robin in protective custody, which is where they put all convicted cops. But a man has to eat, and an inmate working in the kitchens can easily slip a boiled tomato leaf into his dinner. Off the cop goes to the prison hospital with symptoms of acute appendicitis because the prison hospital is where *every* sick inmate goes. Like most such installations, South Hams' hospital was staffed by inmates from the prison population. There's not a prisoner anywhere who doesn't have his price. And for a cop? Cut rates are not only the rule, they're a privilege.

A week after the gates of South Hams State Prison closed on Robin Allandale, he was as dead as Ezekiel Josephus Dowd.

* * *

Googie's remorse weighed so heavily on him he could hardly breathe. Both Robin and EJ had been younger than he was, less experienced, more vulnerable. Both had needed his protection, and both were dead because they hadn't had it. Googie's enquiries took on the intensity of a crusade.

He needed a new approach to the case, something EJ hadn't tried. He called Hugh Freyl's old law offices and made a dinner date with Jimmy Zemanski, who'd taken over the firm of Herndon & Freyl when Hugh died and changed its name to Herndon Freyl & Zemanski.

# 26

## SPRINGFIELD, ILLINOIS

'What do I have against David Marion?' Jimmy Zemanski said. 'Jesus, is it all that obvious?'

'Yep,' said Googie.

'That motherfucker. He stole my girl.'

The two of them sat over fried chicken at Springfield's Sangamo Club, where the power brokers of the town took clients to dine. Googie had chosen the Grill Room because large-screen television monitors — and the opening of the football season — removed any threat of an overzealous listener recording a conversation. This caution impressed Jimmy. Googie's extraction of an unguarded response to David Marion impressed him even more.

'Marion stole your girl, huh?' Googie said to him.

'Fuck it all, man,' Jimmy said. 'Can't you see it? It'd have been perfect: the best legal mind in Springfield married to the daughter of the town's oldest and most prestigious law firm. If the guy wasn't dead, I'd kill him myself.'

'How about Miss Freyl? She like him?'

Jimmy was an all-American boy, tanned, square-jawed, smooth-skinned, cowlick in the hair and boyish still even though he was several years past forty. He *was* good at his job too — if not quite as good as he thought. He had a sense of pattern, a sense of detail and a cold, unsentimental eye that he wasn't afraid to turn on himself. He picked up a leg of chicken, took a bite, thought a moment. 'You know, I'd say those two could hardly wait to get at each other. Funny thing is, neither one of them knew what to do about it. Now he's dead, I got a second chance. I got to bide my time — I kind of rushed her before — but with him out of the way, I have a good shot at it.'

'Hasn't she got herself engaged to some English lord?'

Jimmy shrugged. 'Yeah, sure, but he's *old*. I mean, Jesus, what's she going to *do* with him? I've already arranged to spend the winter in London. How come you're so interested?'

'You sure Marion wanted her?'

'Oh, yeah.' Jimmy laughed. 'A guy can't very well hide that kind of thing, can he?'

Googie hadn't expected this information, but he could see exactly how to use it. 'Okay,' he said. 'Suppose I tell you he isn't dead?'

Jimmy almost choked on his chicken. 'Don't kid about stuff like that.'

Googie explained that David had been sighted only ten days ago in the Rockies, that he'd probably blown up his own house and wandered around the country ever since, pretending to be homeless.

Veins stood out on Jimmy's forehead as he listened. 'Anybody else know about it?' he asked when he could bring himself to speak again.

'Only you.'

'You're Department 4, right? Wet operations?'

Googie nodded. 'Regional Scheduler for the Midwest.'

'You plan to, er, *rectify* the situation?'

Googie nodded again. 'I'm going to do just that.'

'You'll let me know when it's done?'

Googie nodded once more. 'You wouldn't by any chance still have Mr Freyl's files on the case, would you?'

'Come back with me to the office. They're yours.'

* * *

Hugh Freyl had collected a great deal of material that had gone missing from the police files on David Marion and a great deal more that had never appeared in them. Googie kept running across references to Clotilde Marion, David's grandmother. He decided to start by following them up.

The case worker who'd removed David from her home had found syringes and a couple of packages of suspicious-looking powder that turned out to be heroin. The court had sentenced Clotilde to an indeterminate sentence for possession and dealing. Hugh's file on her included details of an agonising cold turkey that had practically killed her and left a gaping hole where her memory of David should have been. Prison psychiatrists noted that she seemed not even to know she had a grandson, much less that she'd treated him badly. She'd stared aghast at the picture they showed her of a dirty, angry little boy. She swore she'd never seen the child, but she seemed pleased to know he was alive and grateful for the copy they gave her of his photograph. Meantime, they diagnosed drug-induced amnesia, psychogenic disassociation, schizophrenia, old-fashioned hysteria and of course simple lying.

Mugshots showed her ageing from a handsome if dishevelled woman into a crone who looked as angry as the little boy himself.

David had been in South Hams for several years by the time she got out on parole. She tried to see him. He refused. She wrote him several times. The letters came back unopened. She took the rejection hard. She'd cut her thighs with razors, stubbed out cigarettes on her arms; there'd been several suicide attempts. All this had stopped only when she contracted a particularly painful form of rheumatoid arthritis that satisfied her need for revenge on herself for the damage she'd done to him.

Hugh had located her — only days before he died — in a Springfield nursing home called The Beacon.

* * *

Googie took Saturday morning off from his family to seek her out.

The Beacon was a single-storey, flat-roofed prefab on a desolate piece of ground outside Springfield. It was an oven inside. Smells of stale urine and rotting flesh greeted him at the door along with the heat; they followed him down a hallway to a door that said, 'Office'. He opened it to a small room where a teenage girl — wodge of pink flesh showing under a tee-shirt top with a fringe on it — sat glued to a TV with the sound booming. Two fans took the edge off the heat. Googie tapped her on the shoulder.

'Clotilde Marion?' he shouted.

The girl looked up at him and stopped chewing her gum. 'Who?'

'Clotilde Marion!'

The girl hauled herself out of her chair, went over to the desk and glanced down a ledger. 'We don't got a Clara here.'

'Not Clara. Clotilde. C, L, O, T, I — '

'Yeah, yeah. I got you now. Down the hall. Take a right. It's number, uh' — she checked it again — 'seven.'

The stench of urine was stronger in number seven. A tattered curtain hung unmoving at a small, high window. Iron bedsteads stood in a row, three of them occupied by unmoving bodies. The temperature was well over 100°. A fourth person, a woman, sat hunched in a broken-down wheelchair.

'Clotilde Marion?' Googie asked her.

'Who wants to know?'

'I do.'

'Go away.'

Two photographs stood on the table beside her, one of them a girl about twelve years old, the other was the photograph Googie recognized from the case worker's file as the six-year-old David.

'It is Mrs Marion, isn't it?' Googie said.

'*Miss* Marion. I never married nobody.'

David's grandmother was a big woman, not fat, but if she'd got out of her wheelchair, she'd have been close to six feet tall. The skin of her face was streaked with sweat and crumpled by years of pain.

'I'm here to help, Miss Marion,' Googie said.

'Ain't nobody can help me. Get the fuck out of my sight.'

'I've come about Hugh Freyl's estate.'

'Ain't got nothing to do with me.'

Googie squatted down beside her wheelchair. 'Your grandson?' he said, gesturing at the picture of David.

'You leave my David rest in peace, hear me?'

'Miss Marion, your grandson is not dead. I know this for a fact.'

The wrinkles of her face all jumped together, then fell apart, then repeated the performance. He got up, left the room, gave her some time to compose herself.

'I believe I can help you see your grandson in person,' he said to her then.

Jimmy and Googie had worked out the approach together. 'I represent the American Bank of Chicago,' Googie said. He could switch back and forth between the macho image of semi-literacy he cultivated in his work and an educated voice that would be far more convincing to someone like Clotilde Marion. 'I'm sure law isn't your field, Miss Marion,' he went on, 'but a year or so ago the government passed a law saying banks are legally responsible for tracking down ownership of trust funds.' This didn't happen to be true, but Clotilde was hardly in a position to know about it. 'One of these funds had been set up by Hugh Freyl in your name.'

'Why'd he do a thing like that, huh?'

'He got your boy out of prison and — '

'I know that.'

' — I'd say he wanted to look after the whole family.' She turned away. 'The papers *were* sent to you.' He brought out a document Jimmy had drawn up the day before. 'We have your signature.' He showed her the signature he'd filled in himself.

'That don't look like my writing.'

'I can assure you that it is. Who else would have signed it? I can also assure you that Mr Freyl would be very unhappy to find you here. I mean, really, he understood David as nobody else did. They were friends, close friends.' Googie was good in sympathetic mode, and nobody had been nice to Clotilde in a long time. 'Would you let me help?'

The tear that joined the sweat rolling down her face was all the answer he needed.

The Allandale/Zemanski plan was to draw up a will naming David and Helen Freyl as joint beneficiaries. As Googie explained it to Clotilde, David was in love with Helen Freyl. He'd have to be curious — perhaps worried — as to why Helen was named alongside him.

'How's he supposed to find out about it?' Clotilde said.

Googie had asked Jimmy the same question.

‘A person may make public anything she wishes to, Miss Marion,’ Googie explained to her. ‘All we have to do is place advertisements in the national press with a current photograph, state the terms of the will and offer a reward for information. Since David appears to have become homeless, we will get a story about his good fortune into homeless journals and send posters to homeless shelters. He will hear about it one way or another, I assure you of this. In the meantime, we’ll transfer you to a much more agreeable place. You do not belong here, Miss Marion. You deserve better.’

# 27

## LONDON

A couple of weeks after the engagement of Sir Charles Hay and Miss Helen Freyl appeared in *The Times*, Helen was rushing, head bowed, through a morning downpour that belonged in the tropics, sheets of rain so heavy that she took cover under a Starbucks awning to escape. She didn't even see the person she bumped into.

'Shit!' she said. 'Why don't you look where you're going?'

'Hi, Helen. Are you caught too?'

She looked up to see Rosemary. 'I hate rain,' Helen said.

Rosemary nodded. 'I'm meant to be meeting someone.' She started to say something, stopped, pulled her tiny pink raincoat further over her head even though she didn't need it under the awning and then seemed unable to think of anything at all to say. Helen was puzzled. Their meetings in the Follaton library had led to a bantering friendship that included ionization processes inside living cells alongside tales of Rosemary's conquest of Gabriel Walker.

Over the summer, Gabriel had developed into her secret boyfriend — 'secret' because his boss Jeffrey Hardcastle wouldn't approve. Or at least that's what Gabriel had told Rosemary right back at the beginning when he took her to eat raw fish at a sushi bar. By now, Helen knew more than she wanted to about his apartment with its windows overlooking the Thames and his vast double bed in which he made a fairly experienced Rosemary feel things she'd never felt before.

Helen had met Gabriel in hallways and at the coffee machine. She'd looked at him more carefully because of Rosemary's stories and decided that she rather liked the harshness around his eyes and mouth for the simple reason that they didn't seem to fit in with the functions of a Human Resources Department.

'You haven't had a fight with your sex god, have you?' she said to Rosemary.

Rosemary shrugged. 'It just . . . well, you know. Maybe this job turned into more than I really wanted.'

'Come on, Rosemary, give. What's going on?'

'There are things . . . ' Rosemary shrugged again.

'Things? What kind of things?'

'Look, you wouldn't want a coffee or something, would you? I'd really like to talk to you.'

Helen had an appointment with her hairdresser — she was fond of her hairdresser — but she was early as usual and, as usual, trying to figure out how to waste half an hour. She and Rosemary pushed through the glass doors into Starbucks, picked up lattes, found a table.

'Helen — ' Rosemary began as soon as they sat down, then stopped short. Helen waited.

Rosemary took in a breath, then went on. 'What do you think about the Follaton Foundation?'

'As against what?'

Rosemary stared down into her latte. 'I've never worked for a charity before.'

Helen cocked her head. 'They haven't fired you or something, have they? That would be seriously stupid.'

The doors burst open and a group of dripping teenagers filled the entrance area with smells of rain. They piled over one another, peeking at the pastries on display, bubbling with the delights of something to drink, something to eat, an hour of gossip and giggling. They were about Rosemary's age — their ebullience was precisely what Helen associated with her — but she watched them as though they'd come from another planet.

'It's going to sound silly,' Rosemary said.

'I kind of like silly.'

'They keep peculiar secrets.'

'Who does? The Foundation? Do they? Like what?' Helen leaned forward, her interest abruptly focused.

'I went down to the basement, and they didn't like it. They said the basement doesn't — '

'There isn't any basement there, Rosemary.'

'Oh, yes, there is. Gabriel told me off for going down there. That's how we got together. One minute he was chatting me up, and the next — I just mentioned the basement — he went all cold and sarcastic. Half an hour later, he came downstairs to say sorry. He was really sweet about it. He told me the basement didn't belong to Follaton and that I'd get him into trouble if I did it again. He said I'd been trespassing. Then he asked me out.'

'Was there anything interesting down there?'

'Not that I could see.' Rosemary seemed close to tears.

'That part of the building could easily belong to the guys next door,' Helen said. 'Or to somebody else entirely.'

But Rosemary was shaking her head. 'Last summer I worked at an estate agents, and rights of way came up all the time. If I was actually trespassing down there, all the owners had to do was ask me to leave. There wasn't any sign saying 'Keep Out' or 'Private Property' or 'No Trespassing' or anything like that. How could I have got Gabriel into any trouble over it?'

'Some special stipulation in the deeds? What were you doing in this basement that isn't there?'

Rosemary gave her a crooked smile. 'Trying to find a place to store all those boxes. Remember them? I'll never forget your face when you saw that entryway. I mean, I thought it was pretty bad but . . . all I had to do was take one of those clip-on things off the control panel in the lift and push the button beneath it. The lift went straight down.'

'It doesn't sound as though anybody was exactly encouraging you to go there.'

Rosemary glanced around nervously. 'Helen, could you — ' Her smile turned sheepish. 'Could you come to east London with me?'

'East London? Why?'

'Just to . . . Could you come?'

'You mean now?'

'Could you? Please.'

'And you don't want to tell me why?'

Rosemary shook her head. Helen explained that she had to get her hair cut, but Rosemary seemed so crestfallen that she said, 'Why don't we get together later? I'll be finished by one. You going to tell me what this is all about?'

'Meet me here' — Rosemary took out a piece of paper and scribbled an address — 'whenever you're finished. Okay?'

⋆ ⋆ ⋆

The torrential rains had cleared by the time Helen and Rosemary left Starbucks. They held off while Helen had her hair cut, but the streets were steaming and the sky started growling again as she left the tube at the east London station of Stratford. The clouds were so dark that the orange lights of Charwell Lane were lit, and the only pretty sight around was their haze halos. A huge crane loomed across the skyline, spotlights from it lit up the construction site on one side of the street. Even though it was Saturday, workmen were milling around. Pneumatic drills buzzed. Trucks backed and beeped. As Helen passed the site itself she saw a wrecking ball take its first swing at an intact building.

Despite the noise levels, she could hear music from inside number 273, an alien mix of heavy rock and punk. The names on the motley collection of buzzers were in the Cyrillic alphabet, and her one summer of learning Russian allowed her to make out no more than the name Igor. Not promising: she didn't know anybody called Igor. She began a systematic ringing of the buzzers, top to bottom.

The door flew open before she'd reached the last one.

'Emilia!' she said in surprise, looking into the placid face of the cook from Follaton. The expression would have been welcoming if it had life to it, but it seemed carved into the woman's face.

'Oh, goddammit, I've ended up at the wrong address somehow, haven't I?' Helen said. 'I'm supposed to be meeting Rosemary Figgis somewhere around here. I don't suppose you've . . . '

But Emilia had turned and started up the stairs.

'What do you expect me to do? Follow you?'

Emilia continued plodding up the stairs.

Helen followed, abruptly curious. As she climbed she realized that the rock lyrics weren't in English. Russian? Belarusian? 'Is Rosemary here?' she called.

No reply.

'Emilia! Answer me!'

Still no reply. When they reached the top floor, Emilia turned, that smile as fixed as ever.

'Is secret,' she said.

'What's secret?'

'You speak: I cut out your tongue.'

Helen almost giggled, and yet the calm of the voice commanded respect.

'You come into my house knowing this?' Emilia pressed.

Helen paused. She had no idea what the woman was talking about. But this was beginning to sound like fun. She nodded.

'Say it!' Emilia demanded.

'Say what?'

' 'I swear on my grandmother's grave.' '

Helen decided this was not the time to point out that her grandmother was very much alive. 'I swear on my grandmother's grave.'

'Goot.'

She followed meekly as Emilia ushered her inside. The moment they were across the threshold, Emilia's doll-like expression dropped away; she smiled, suddenly a cheery warmth of a person, pulled Helen into her arms, kissed her on both cheeks.

'Welcome. Welcome to my house.'

And the room! Three mobiles hung from the ceiling, as delicate and airy as spun glass, one a rectangle filled with an elaborate geometry of smaller rectangles; another, a pyramid of triangles with tassels. A plumed unicorn at least two feet high stood beside a tea urn. On the floor was a tapestry carpet of green leaves on arching branches with cherries hanging from them.

'What *are* they made of?' Helen cried, delighted.

'Please?'

'That unicorn. Those beautiful — I don't know what to call them — hanging from the ceiling. What are they made of?'

'Straw.'

'You're kidding. Who made them?'

'I make.'

'Did you? You're brilliant.'

'Hi, Helen,' Rosemary said, bouncing up out of a chair with the ebullience that had been missing at Starbucks. 'You know Feodor? Kastus?' She gestured at the two men in the room.

'Ah, my dear friend,' Feodor said, getting up to kiss Helen's cheeks as Emilia had. 'It has been too long.' She'd never met Feodor before he'd arrived at her door to take her to dinner at Little Moscow, and she hadn't seen him since. She'd forgotten how beautiful he was — even that his eyes were yellow — and she was as surprised to see him here as she'd been to see Emilia.

'We did go to a restaurant together once,' Helen said with a wry smile.

'It was enough, Helen Freyl. You are engraved upon my soul.'

'This is Kastus,' Rosemary said. 'He's Emilia's nephew.'

Kastus shook Helen's hand. He was young: crew-cut brown hair, designer stubble. 'Unremarkable,' she thought, and then he smiled. He had steel-plated teeth like that arch-villain in the James Bond movie. Helen had never seen anything like it. Dentistry in the East European states was crude; she'd read about it without giving any thought to what it might mean.

'I'm all the way from Pripyat,' he said, flashing that steel, but the tyre-screech vowels were pure Nebraska.

'How does a voice like that get to be Emilia's nephew?' Helen said.

'My mother's people are all in Omaha,' he

said. 'They don't like my father much. They don't like me much either.' He shrugged. 'They don't like *any* foreigners.'

Emilia urged her guests towards a dining table set for five with a dish of sausages and a great round loaf of bread on a platter. 'Rosemary, you sit here. Kastus, pour vodka. And you, Dr Freyl, sit here.'

'Helen,' Helen said. 'Please call me Helen.'

The sausages came with horseradish. As soon as they were finished, Emilia brought on a soup made of lamb and potatoes. The talk centred on an ice hockey match while Rosemary gazed at light glinting off steel teeth, and Kastus tried to tear his attention away from that sensual body of hers. Helen was more or less deciding that Rosemary's secret was no more than that Kastus had become Gabriel's replacement when Kastus turned to Helen and said, 'I'm a journalist.'

'He's just got a job on the *Sunday Times*,' said Rosemary. 'He wants to do a story on the Foundation, don't you, Kastus?'

'Oh, God,' Helen said. 'Don't tell me I've been enticed here in some kind of official capacity.'

He shook his head. 'They're not going to want to paste this one in the scrapbook. Look, Rosemary tells me you act suspicious of them yourself.'

'Does she?' Helen was taken aback. 'Do I? Suspicious? Of what? Whatever makes you say a thing like that?'

Rosemary picked up her spoon, set it down. 'I see what you work on in the library. I know you're meant to be helping Follaton with the scientific stuff it writes up for blokes like Kastus. But you do spend an awful lot of time looking into what *doesn't* get written up.'

Helen gave her an appraising glance. 'I'm going to have to watch myself when you're around.'

'We both think Follaton's up to something,' Kastus said. 'We just don't know what it is, and I'm too junior on the staff to go to my editor with nothing more than suspicions and rumours. What I'm hoping is that you — '

'Rumours?' Emilia interrupted angrily. 'Farmer smells metal. Mechanic says air *taste* like after Chernobyl. This is *rumours*?'

'A chemical leak from a factory could explain it,' said Kastus.

'Bad headaches? Bad cough? Dry throat? It's same cough, same headache, same throat as after Chernobyl. This is nothing also?'

'They blame it all on the Chernousenko figures.'

'Blame *what* on Chernousenko?' Helen said irritably. She'd been so bored by the Belarusian analyses that she'd put the Russian physicist out of her mind. 'He's the guy who says Chernobyl belched out much more than official estimates, isn't he? You guys think there's been another massive meltdown or something? Is that it? What could the Foundation have to do with that?'

Kastus shook his head and poured out more vodka. 'Aunt Emilia was living outside Pripyat when Chernobyl exploded, and now people are reporting the same kinds of things that happened back then: strange smells, coughs and headaches, no worms or May bugs.'

'I still don't see — '

'They tell me I cannot see radiation,' Emilia interrupted again. 'But I see it. It lies in field: ink-black in colour, size of kerchief. I run home. In garden: another piece: blue. In neighbour's garden: another piece: red. Women come together. We ask soldier. He say, 'This is caesium. This is how it look.''

'Caesium?' Feodor asked.

'Element in radioactive fallout,' Helen said.

'In maybe two hectares we find four big pieces,' Emilia went on. 'Next day: early rain. By lunchtime, everything gone.'

'Who's going to believe you, Aunt?' Kastus sighed. 'All kinds of scientists say that the idea of seeing caesium is nuts.' He turned back to Helen, who agreed wholly with the scientists, but knew that she'd hear nothing more if she said so and couldn't help being intrigued. 'When my aunt went back to Belarus last year, she was so proud to be working for a foundation that set up medical clinics and somehow finagled UCAI into supplying fertiliser for the lousy Belarusian — '

'They spread fertiliser in spring,' Emilia interrupted once more. 'They make farmers — all people from village — go into shelter kilometres away. 'Fumes bad for you,' they say. But I leave dog behind. I go to look for him. Only little dog. And again I see them: pieces of caesium.' She took her flowered kerchief from around her neck and held it out. 'Like this in size: except blue.'

‘Look, you do seem to be assuming another vast nuclear accident,’ Helen said, shaking her head, ‘but nobody could keep something like that secret for any length of time. Besides, why would the Foundation bother to try? I mean, it’s got to be to their advantage to *publicise* another meltdown, not cover it up.’

‘What we’re saying,’ said Kastus, ‘is that they’re spreading radioactive substances when they spread the fertilizer.’

⋆ ⋆ ⋆

‘Spreading radioactive . . . On the ground?’ Helen shook her head with one of those dismissive laughs that academics are so well known for. ‘That’s ridiculous, Kastus. What would they want to do a thing like that for?’

Feodor leaned forward. ‘I do not understand their precautions, Helen Freyl. In the Soviet days tractor drivers sometimes wore full fire-fighting uniforms with face masks and oxygen supply. They had lead-lined cabs because they were spreading radioactive substances as a pesticide. I think there was also some effect on the germination of crops. A week ago I translated discussions about supplies needed: replacement tractors with lead-lined cabs. Fire-fighting uniforms. Oxygen masks. They told Emilia that fertiliser fumes are dangerous. I am sure this is true. The most likely explanation is that the Foundation is especially cautious about protecting people.’ He sighed. ‘And yet I am uneasy in my soul.’

'You'd hardly need lead-lined cabs for standard fertiliser,' Helen said. 'If they're ordering lead-lined cabs there must be something radioactive. But why would they spread stuff like that? What could the point possibly be?'

Kastus shook his head. 'If we had some solid evidence, some way of explaining what Emilia's seen and heard, maybe we could figure it out. She's not alone, you know. Lots of people over there are talking like this.'

'What *sort* of evidence?' Rosemary said. 'You mean maybe stuff they could store in a basement?'

'Oh, Christ,' said Helen, 'I'm sure there's a simple explanation for this famous basement.'

'Helen, I don't want to be rude,' Rosemary said, 'but you don't understand rights of way any better than you understand lift control panels.'

'Why on earth would Follaton Medical Foundation pretend they didn't own a basement that they did own?'

'Haven't a clue,' Rosemary said. 'They changed the control panel the very next day after I went there. They must have done it for a reason.'

'To keep out snoops,' said Kastus.

'You can both go to hell.' Rosemary's cheeks flushed with anger. 'I've never seen so many filing cases in my life. They cover all the walls. They must have something in them. I mean, what do you keep in a room full of filing cabinets that you pretend isn't — '

'The room's full of filing cabinets?' Kastus

interrupted. 'Are you sure? Why didn't you say this before?'

Rosemary gave him an irritated glance. 'It might take me a while to suss out the new control panel, but I'll go down in that lift. I bet I'll find you something to shut you *both* up.'

# 28

## GUILDFORD, SURREY

Helen was furious that Becky had been stupid enough to agree to this marriage. It left her trying to figure out how to negotiate the physical side of the thing right up until they could strike a deal with UCAI or Galleas.

It wasn't that there was anything *wrong* with Charles. If he wasn't gay — or even if he was — she was sure most women wouldn't mind crawling into bed with him. But no part of it appealed to her: humiliating positions, grotesque noises, absurd movements. She hated the loss of control and ended up hating whatever man provoked it. It's true that David's body had fascinated her, but even now she couldn't convince herself that sex with him was more than imagination, despite the tattoos. Maybe her father had said something about them. Or maybe they'd played some part in a newspaper story that she'd read and forgotten. As for the other guys — hairy backs and a meaty smell — the very thought of them made her queasy.

Nor was it as though Charles had pressed anything. He'd said he wouldn't and he hadn't, but when he suggested she go down with him to see the Hay family estate near Guildford, she was afraid the time had come. She considered options: she was an old-fashioned girl who didn't believe in sex outside marriage; it was her period; or worse, the truth: she wanted no part of it with anybody but David and David was dead.

On the car trip from London to Guildford, Charles worked on the Foundation's Annual Report while she tried to find a metaphor for the assault radiation makes on the human body. Her work at the Foundation had turned out to be fun. She'd quickly caught the attention of a number of journalists and managed to place stories in most of the national papers: how a nuclear reactor can go wrong, why nuclear waste lasts so long, how the new super-fuels are manufactured.

She was completely absorbed when the Bentley turned into a long drive, and Charles said, 'You're going to have to meet the relatives, you know.'

'Oh, God,' she said, looking up from her work. 'Now? Today?'

He laughed. 'No, no. This weekend's just for us. Well, mainly for us. Martin Goldsmith is coming for dinner. Do you mind? Remember him? The UCAI statistician at that board lunch I couldn't make?'

'I could hardly forget the drunk who got me my Fellowship.'

He patted her hand. 'Martin always comes to see me when he's in the country, but he'll pass out before we get to the table. I'll have a taxi waiting for him half an hour after he arrives.' Charles touched her shoulder, pointed. '*Now* you can see the house. What do you think?'

The Hay family estate occupied fifteen acres north of Guildford in Surrey. The house had been burned down twice in its long history. The last time — in the early 1920s — was complete devastation. The family called in the young Swiss architect Lescaze, who designed them a granite and buff limestone building with flat roofs on its several levels and bands of windows on its upper floors. The ground floor was walled in glass.

'Was your father around when all this was built?' Helen asked as they made their way through the rain towards the broad porch in front of the building, the chauffeur trotting behind them, umbrella held over their heads.

'He was the one who demanded that Lescaze build a secret passageway into Trust land.' Charles waved an arm at rolling woods and distant ridges, barely visible through the rain. 'That's all National Trust land over there. Miles and miles of it. He was an imperious small boy.'

'You have lots of — ' Helen stopped short, realizing that even though she thought Rosemary's secret basement at the Foundation was unlikely to say the least, she would be wiser not to tease Charles about it until she was certain.

'I have lots of what?'

'Can I see this passageway?' she said, overriding his question. 'Or is it too secret for that?'

'I'd be only too happy to, but I'm afraid it turns into a sewer in weather like this.' He opened the heavy front door for her. 'It's not all that secret either. Busloads of architectural students examine it every year. I'll show you as soon as the rain eases off. Come in, come in. This is Mrs Paskevitch. Another Belarusian, I'm afraid.'

Mrs Paskevitch was tall and thin. Her feet were tiny, and she seemed to sway atop them as she stood at the door. 'Is good to see you,' she said to Helen with a toothy smile. 'I show her room, Sir Charles? Dr Freyl may want little bit freshen, yes?'

To Helen's dismay, the room Mrs Paskevitch showed her to was clearly large enough for two; a vast, raw-looking bed stood against an even rawer-looking wall; Lescaze's designs had called for walls of two-inch-thick solid plaster, and to Helen the room looked more like a factory floor than a place to sleep. A horizontal strip of window showed only grey sky.

'This is *my* room?' Helen said, emphasizing the 'my' in the hopes of clarification as to whether or not she was supposed to be sharing it.

'Yes.'

'It's kind of big for one person.'

'Yes.'

'Where does Sir Charles sleep?'

Mrs Paskevitch gave her an indulgent smile. 'He sleep where he want to sleep. Sometimes here. Sometimes there.'

'Is he sleeping *here* tonight?'

'Here? I do not know. As I say, he sometimes sleep here, sometimes — '

'Yes, yes,' Helen said irritably.

* * *

Martin Goldsmith arrived at the house at eight. 'You look tired, Martin,' Charles said, taking his raincoat and handing it to Mrs Paskevitch. The puffiness that had marked his face in the spring had worsened, and some of the shrewdness seemed to have gone out of the eyes. He looked to Helen like a worried man, maybe even a frightened one.

'Hey, it's the brilliant Dr Freyl,' he said, taking Helen's hand and shaking it. 'Congratulations are in order, right? I've already congratulated the groom here. When's the wedding?'

'No date yet,' she said.

'Well, you make a damn good-looking couple, understand me? Extra bonus? The holy Slad twins are pleased. All of UCAI beams over you. You've raised the Foundation's profile yet again. Who could want more than that? You know what, I'd be happier sitting down. That okay, Charles?'

The walls of the living room were the same solid plaster as the bedrooms above. The fireplace consisted of two openings in the wall, one above the other; it was lit, and it burned on both levels, but there was little sense of warmth here. Lescaze had designed the furniture too; lamps and tables appeared regularly in books on design. Helen wasn't much interested in furnishings, but these looked bleak even to her.

Martin manoeuvred himself to a chaise longue and half fell into it. 'Charles, you got the goddamndest most uncomfortable chairs in all of England, know that?'

'Your usual, Martin?' said Charles, sliding open the door to a tall drinks cabinet.

'Them holy twins is going to can me, Charles.'

'Oh, Martin, don't be silly.'

'Nothing silly about it.'

'They couldn't afford to lose you.' Charles handed him a glass half full of neat Scotch. 'You're the only man on the board who actually understands their business.'

Martin took a deep swallow. 'They don't drink. They don't smoke. They don't swear. They say grace and kneel beside the bed before they go to sleep. The only thing God allows them to do is fuck and make money. You see them hanging onto an old souse like me?' He tossed back the rest of his drink, got up unsteadily and refilled his glass himself.

Charles attempted reassurance while Helen's mind wandered from how to get out of the sex to come — without compromising the Freyl interests — to whether Martin would throw up on the edge of the carpet. Over dinner, talk stagnated into an elaborate comparison of American football and soccer; she waited for his face to drop into his mashed potatoes. That didn't happen either. He stayed awake all the way back to the living room, accepted a glass of armagnac, then slipped mid-sentence into a drunken stupor.

'Well, thank God for that,' Helen said.

Charles rang for the chauffeur, who carried the inert Martin out of the room to the taxi that had been waiting there for nearly two hours.

'You should be flattered,' Charles said. 'I'm sure you're the only reason for his making it as far as the dinner table.' He ran a hand over his face, a gesture she'd grown familiar with. 'Helen, I'm so sorry, but I'm exhausted. Do you mind? I always find the country air does that to me, and God knows babysitting Martin doesn't help.'

He took her arm, and they walked up the wide stairs together. As they reached the landing at the top, Helen said, 'Charles . . . er, awkward moment.'

' 'Awkward moment'?'

'The sleeping arrangements.'

He let out his breath and ran his hand over his face again. 'Oh, my dear Helen. Forgive me. I won't ask to share your bed without an invitation. I meant what I said. We can be family to each other, brother and sister, if you like. If at some point that changes, wonderful. If not, well, I can't say that's wonderful, but I'll settle for just being with you.'

'I thought you might be gay.'

'Did you? Because I didn't make a move on you? I'm too much in love with you, Helen. Sometimes . . . sometimes it seriously upsets my sense of balance in the world. I know you don't feel the same way, and the thought of losing you by some clumsy . . . But gay? No chance.' He touched her arm, gave her a reassuring smile. 'Good night.'

'Where will you sleep?'

'There are always several rooms made up.' He touched her arm again. 'Rest well, my sweet.'

'Good night, Charles.'

She watched him walk away down the hall. He walked well, handled himself well. Now she came to think of it, she rather liked his being single-minded enough to prostitute himself and his family's ancient name, even toss in the 300-year-old ring she wore on her finger, just to get hold of Yeznik (LA)-205.3 — and without even the promise of getting fucked for his trouble. Single-mindedness at this level shows passion. She hadn't realized before this very moment that passion was what she'd seen in David. So here was a man whose hands resembled David's and whose intensities did too. She began to think that one day she might find herself interested in Charles Hay after all.

# 29

## FORT COLLINS, COLORADO

David had hoisted Ezekiel Josephus Dowd's semi-conscious body onto a shoulder and carried it up the stairs from the cellar below the barn. The crush on the main floor of the mushroom festival had been so great — and by then so zonked-out — that only one celebrant noticed him pressing his way through the crowd towards the doors.

'What happened to *him*?' this girl asked, struggling — and failing — to focus her eyes on EJ. Her hair was layered colours, red, blue, green.

'Same as you,' David said.

'Good party, huh?'

'Right.'

'Want a taste?' She held out a fried mushroom.

'Take care of him first.'

She hadn't even noticed the blood that was spreading out over David's chest and soaking his clothes.

He'd stumbled towards the edge of Yellowback Creek, fallen twice under EJ's weight before he reached its banks, finished the job by holding EJ's head under water, pushed the body into the rapids. He watched it bound away long enough to make sure it didn't catch on rocks, then threw the dog tags in after it. Back at the festival barn, he broke into one of the cars parked in front and drove it down the mountains towards Denver.

After that he remembered only Helen.

* * *

David hadn't been any virgin when he'd gone to prison as a teenager, and he'd learned within hours of arriving that sex was a very different commodity inside, a weapon of power and control, a way to establish territory. Release of tension and frustration was secondary. Desire and pleasure played almost no part at all.

When he'd got out, the softness of a woman's body had come as a shock to him all over again, as it had when he was a boy. So had the emotional minefields. There'd been a tumultuous experience shortly after he was released; it had ended badly, and he'd sworn to limit himself to whores chosen at random so it wouldn't happen again. But he'd broken his vow with Helen, unable to hold himself back from the skin that was almost transparent and the flesh so delicate that he was afraid it would bruise when he touched her. If he gave into her a second time, he'd be lost. He knew it.

Then one day she'd come running after him in the street, touched his arm, an electric shock of contact that had told him who she was even before he'd had a chance to swing around and face her.

'Go away,' he'd said.

'Why?'

'We can't do this.'

'Oh, David, why not?'

'Because — ' He'd broken off, knowing his confusion showed in his face. 'Just go away. Leave me alone.' There'd been a pause. 'Please,' he'd added.

⋆ ⋆ ⋆

There was pain when he breathed, and the face hovering over his was bearded like his but grizzled, the hair on the head straggly enough to blend into the beard. A knitted cap came down over the ears.

'Hey,' said Grizzle-beard. 'Hey! You awake?'

'Yeah,' David said. Or at least he tried to say it. Perhaps he succeeded. Perhaps he didn't.

'You been so fucking sick, man. You got no idea. I was scared you'd die on me.'

'What day is it?'

'You've made it all the way to the third week in September. Up, down, up, down. But you've made serious progress in the last twenty-four hours. Am I pleased with you? I am. Pleased? I'm enchanted.'

The mushroom festival had been right at the beginning of the month. If the beard was right, David had lost at least two weeks.

'How'd I get here? Where is 'here'?'

'What were you doing wandering along the road like that? This is my crash spot. You looked like you could use some help so I — Hey! Leave that alone.'

David felt something damp that was stuck to his side with Scotch tape. He looked down at a grey patch, touched it with his fingertips, looked back at the beard.

Grizzle-beard chuckled. 'Shit, you should have seen the pus. Vinegar wouldn't touch it. Hydrogen peroxide: useless. I met this guy whose mom and dad used to board cats. I told him I had a cat with an infected wound, and he said, 'Get a bottle of silver colloid. Clean the wound with your peroxide, dab it with the colloidal silver, change the bandage every eight hours. A couple of days at the most, and your kitty's going to be at the Whiskas again.' I always wanted to be a doctor. Know something? It's an incredible experience watching somebody get better. Inspiring. But when I was a freshman at college, I put off anatomy because . . . '

David slept.

When he woke again, the sunshine was bright, the air crisp, the pain in his side no more than an ache. He lay in a clearing with scrub pine trees around him and a makeshift tent over his head. Beyond him Grizzle-beard squatted beside a small fire, heating a can of soup; he heard David getting up behind him.

'How you feeling?'

'Weak.'

'As a kitten, huh?'

'As a kitten.'

'Have some soup.'

As David was finishing, Grizzle-beard said, 'You're David Marion, aren't you?' David almost dropped the can. He'd chosen the street name Canada, and nobody had called him anything but that for months. The beard watched him carefully. 'I figure you're going to give me lots of money. Not that I'd know what to do with it.

Maybe you'd better keep it. You ought to go and see your old grandma though. I wish I had an old grandma.'

'I don't have one either.'

'Better look at this.' Grizzle-beard took a piece of paper out of his pocket, unfolded it, brushed it off and handed it to David. 'I found it at the Mission in Fort Collins. Sure as hell surprised me to find out I'd been taking care of a man soon to be rich.'

A picture of David dominated the small poster.

**HAVE YOU SEEN DAVID MARION?**

**David Marion's grandmother is dying. She wishes him to know that she has named him her joint heir along with Dr Helen Freyl of Springfield, Illinois.**

**She also wishes him to know that she is deeply sorry for the pain she has caused him.**

**Any information concerning his whereabouts will be greatly appreciated and amply rewarded.**

**Please contact:**

**Ms Clotilde Marion**
**Heaven's Acre Nursing Home**
**Springfield, Illinois**
**217 546 3624**

**info.heavensacre@aol.com**

# 30

## LONDON

Early one morning right at the end of September, Helen received a letter, plain envelope, no stamp; delivered by hand.

She slit open the envelope:

*Dear Helen*
*I must see you. It is urgent. I will visit your house at three this afternoon.*
*Please tell no one about this letter.*
*Your loving friend,*
*Feodor*

She assumed whatever was on his mind must have grown out of Emilia's party, and she was intrigued even though she thought most of what she'd heard there was outright nonsense — and the rest of it was conspiracy theory rather than fact. But as Becky had told her way back at the beginning, sometimes people hear useful things and don't know what they mean.

Helen stayed at home that day in air-conditioned comfort, and at a few minutes to three, Feodor knocked on the door of her Notting Hill house.

'Helen! Thank God,' he said as she opened the door. The golden eyes were tired, harassed, clouded into a brown-grey. He took her by the shoulders and kissed her on the cheeks.

'Sit down, Feodor,' she said. 'What's with all the cloak-and-dagger?'

'I do not wish to sit,' he said. 'I wish to walk outside with you.' He gazed around at the furnishings. 'I am not comfortable here. You have a cold taste in domestic matters, Helen. I am sorry to tell you this, but it is so. We will walk in the street.'

Helen's house was spacious and high-ceilinged; a bank of windows looked out into a pretty garden at the back. It had been designed, like her grandmother's house in Springfield, for opulence, and the interior was the work of professionals. She glanced around at it, knowing that it lacked the personal touch that rented properties like it tend to lack but deciding that it wasn't anywhere near as chilly in feel as Charles's Lescaze house.

'I have heard some very strange things, Helen Freyl,' Feodor went on, 'and I hope I do not make the right sense of them. You will need a raincoat and an umbrella.'

'What kind of strange things?'

Feodor's gestures and expressions were theatrical, ebullient — very Russian — but both times she'd seen him before he'd been in complete control of them. Not today though. Today he paced nervously back and forth across the room while she got her things together. A bead of sweat worked its way down his cheek.

'Your family owns a bee farm, does it not?' he

said, stopping mid-pace.

Helen was startled. 'That's what the trouble is?' she said cautiously. 'Bees?'

'Your family *does* own such a farm?'

She shook her head. '*I* own it. My grandmother gave it to me when I was eight years old. Caton Bees & Venom of Alabama. It's a joke of a business, a little girl's fancy.'

He took in his breath. He let it out. 'I *must* be certain. Something is special about your bees? They have — ?' He broke off. 'I need to be outside.'

The sticky, monsoon-like weather of the last two weeks had turned blustery enough to blow umbrellas inside out. Feodor walked so fast that Helen took hold of his arm to slow him down. 'What is this Feodor?'

'I do not wish to frighten you for nothing.'

'Frighten me? Goddammit, what *are* you talking about?'

'The bees, Helen. Tell me about the — ' But this time he'd caught sight of a small café. 'I must have tea to drink. I am very thirsty. I am disturbed in my soul, Helen. I have not eaten since yesterday.' He grabbed her arm and rushed her across the street, threw open the doors of the café, collected a tray with trembling hands — tea, soup, bread — and was biting into a roll as they sat down at a table. He followed with three or four spoonfuls of soup in quick succession.

Then he leaned forward and said in a whisper, 'Honeybee venom has radioprotective action.'

'That's hardly earth-shaking news, Feodor.'

She watched him carefully as she spoke. 'There must be hundreds of studies involving it.'

'There is more.' Feodor mopped up the last of his soup with the remains of his first roll. 'Yesterday I was translating for Mr Goldsmith and some men — '

'Martin Goldsmith? UCAI's statistician?'

Feodor nodded. 'The men were from Belarus. I am not sure who they were — maybe secret service. Mr Goldsmith was explaining about patents for a bee venom from Alabama. You see? You see? In *Alabama*.'

'There are lots of bee farms in Alabama, especially around Caton.' This was entirely true; at least half a dozen of Joshua's relatives owned bee farms.

'They talked about the venom from *special* honey bees. Very rare. It has properties that are found in no other venom — crucial to the formula. Mr Goldsmith said law wasn't his field, but he'd been informed of some technicalities that were slowing the patent process. He also said he'd been assured they would be entirely clarified by the end of the year.'

'Did he indeed?' Helen was careful to keep her smile less than exultant. This was the very confirmation she and Becky had been waiting for: UCAI was ready to negotiate.

'You tell me this,' he went on. 'Someone wants to buy your farm?'

'I got an offer. I turned it down.'

'You cannot be forced to sell?'

She shook her head. 'My grandmother decided I was too young to handle stockholders.'

'Stockholders? I do not understand. They are nobody.'

'If they get together, they can sue me for not selling at such an outrageously high price.'

He swallowed what remained of his second roll. 'Ah. I see. The bid was too high? Then it is as I thought. All they lack is the patents for your venom.'

'Look, Feodor' — she and Becky had worked out a cover story for just such a contingency as this — 'UCAI is developing lots of pharmaceuticals. An early version of one of them did involve my venom. I sold them a batch. It didn't do what they wanted it to, and I imagine they're trying to fob it off on the Belarusians. But as for the Foundation's radioprotectant, you translated the material yourself. They're not working with venom from any animal, and certainly not venom from my bees.'

Feodor waved a hand in dismissal. 'There is a strange compound mentioned many times.'

'The Yeznik synthetic? It's a glycol, Feodor.' After all, that's what Martin himself had told her when she'd queried it; he'd even supplied an elaborate molecular diagram of its structure.

'Not a venom?'

'No.'

He waved dismissal again. 'Do you not find it strange that UCAI wants your bees? Then offers you a Fellowship in London? At a foundation UCAI supports?'

'Charles wasn't a part of this conversation with Goldsmith and the Belarusians, was he?'

'Only to say, 'Hello, how are you, goodbye.'

But, Helen, you must not trust him either. You must trust nobody there. Nobody.' Before she could comment, he rushed on. 'I have a confession to make.'

'What *now*?'

'Sir Charles asked me to speak to you. This is why I had to take you to Little Moscow.'

'Really? You said Zoya suggested it.'

'This is, in fact, not exactly so. Perhaps you will recall that I explained Zoya had suggested I make contact. I did so. But it was Sir Charles who suggested that I take you to supper. He questioned me afterwards. 'How did she look?' 'What did she say then?''

'Oh, Feodor.' Helen shook her head. 'He was just worried that I might harbour doubt of him on my father's behalf.'

'This I know. It is on this subject that he wished me to question you.'

'I knew there was something funny about all that. You were pushing too hard. But now I come to think of it, what's more natural? They had their break-up. He had to know if it was going to get in the way of my working with him.'

'He tells me you are a very good liar. I am to study you as you talk.'

'He didn't!' Helen was delighted, flattered. She'd always been proud of her talent as a liar.

'I fear this is so. I however told him that you spoke the truth.'

Helen looked down at the rose diamond on her finger. The more she thought about Charles walking away from her down the hall, the more she thought he might be able to push David into the shadows at the back of her mind. This cat-and-mouse game with him was giving her a zest for life unlike anything she'd experienced before.

'Stop worrying,' she said to Feodor. 'I know what's going on.'

But doubt still clouded the yellow eyes. 'Since you refuse to sell your farm to UCAI, I think they plan to take it away from you by force.' He glanced around the café nervously. 'I am afraid, Helen. I am afraid for you, and I am afraid for me. I cannot deny that. I am *very* afraid.'

'Don't be.' She patted his hand. 'Everything's going to be okay. I promise.'

# 31

## LONDON

That evening, Rosemary made her trip down to the Foundation's basement.

The old control panel in the lift had been polished, antique brass with buttons in an arc. The way she'd seen it, the clip-on plate over the button to the basement had been begging for somebody to pry it off. The new panel was a harder proposition: simple and modern, a vertical row of buttons for ground floor to top floor, a horizontal row for open doors, shut doors, alarm. A small logo at the bottom said, 'Smedley'.

She'd spent a couple of hours Googling 'control panel + lift', then she'd called Smedley Building Equipment and explained in a breathlessly dim-witted manner that her boss had told her to buy a panel with easy access to the hidden administration buttons — 'whatever they are,' as she'd put it with a helpless giggle. The Smedley man had been wonderfully helpful. He'd said he had just the model for her: it had an inconspicuous release on the underside like a CD rewriter on a computer. All she had to do was press it and off the panel would come. He'd emailed her a diagram explaining the entire design. A lunchtime test had showed her that the control panel came off as easily as he said. His diagram identified all the buttons but one.

But that was weeks ago. She'd decided it wasn't a good idea to risk a trip down during normal working hours, and no matter how many times she'd offered, nobody had seemed to need any overtime from her. When at last Jeffrey Hardcastle asked her if she might be able to do some extra transcribing for him, she jumped at the chance, got through the work as quickly as she could, then raced to the lift.

It went down as soon as she pressed the button.

The room wasn't exactly as she remembered it. The strips of neon that lit it from above had been there. So had the rank upon rank of dark blue cabinets lining the walls, floor to ceiling, their white labels reflecting the light like a grid of polka dots against a theatre backdrop. But a glassed-in computer cubicle now took up the middle of the room; it glowed a faint blue colour, processor and memory bank at one end of a narrow desk with a couple of computer screens and keyboards. A smattering of lights indicated that the machinery was powered up, and the background hum was probably air conditioning.

She tried the first drawer of the filing cabinets. Locked. The next drawer was locked too. She decided on a systematic approach, top left to bottom right. No luck on the first wall. She was halfway across the second when a drawer finally did give. She slid it open. The files were labelled by country and contained studies of what seemed to be recent soil samples. But the countries were all western European — France, Germany, Belgium, Switzerland — no references to anything like Belarus or Ukraine or any of that part of the world. She continued her search. No other drawer had escaped the central locking system.

It wasn't until the middle of the night that she woke with the sudden realization that several of the pages had been stamped, 'Follaton Medical Foundation'.

So the basement *did* belong to the Foundation after all.

She hadn't even noticed the CCTV camera that had watched her every move.

* * *

'This now turns into something different,' Jeffrey said to Gabriel the following morning.

'The bitch played me.' Gabriel could hardly get over the shock of it. 'Me!'

'It would appear so. However, some of your failure is my misjudgement. You are too old.'

'Christ, I'm barely thirty.'

'Just so. Puppy fat covers a multitude of sins. The file drawer she found was uninteresting, but what is it that made her decide to look again? She has been talking to somebody. Galleas International is, of course, the most likely. They have been distinctly tiresome of late. However, our sources show up nothing, and she is very young to be approached directly. Hence she is doing a favour for someone. Who? The translator

Mussinov? His visit to Dr Freyl yesterday is more than worrisome, and there is clearly a spark between him and your girl that was lacking before.'

'He's *ancient*.' Gabriel was shocked all over again.

'He has human warmth,' said Jeffrey, who had no more himself than Gabriel but knew it when he saw it — and recognized its power. 'We must consider his work for the Foundation to be complete.'

Gabriel nodded. 'What about the girl? We ought to keep London for an emergency.'

'You managed very well in Norway, did you not?'

'What do you want me to do? Shove her in a fjord?'

'Two English incidents in quick succession might attract the press. She wants to go to Belarus, does she not?'

'She's desperate to.'

'Grant her wish. At once. We are suddenly short of a volunteer. Does she have a passport?'

Gabriel nodded. 'She's boring on the subject of her holiday in Paris.'

'We will arrange visas and all the paperwork. She should be ready to leave before the week is out.' Jeffrey turned to the papers on the desk in front of him. 'We must henceforward regard the files as vulnerable. Arrange to tie the basement into a high security system with a rapid response team.'

'As for the girl?'

'I want *positive* publicity to come of this.'

'Not easy.'

'But not difficult. A little delicate timing perhaps.'

* * *

Why do mothers cling so? Rosemary sat in the bustle of the vast airport: Dior bags and Hugo Boss ties to her left, display of Clinique soaps and face creams to her right, people milling about, mobiles ringing, babble of languages. All this excitement — and even so, her mother's voice kept whining on in her ear.

'If anything seems to go wrong — *anything* makes my dearest girl unhappy — you're to ring me at once.'

'Mm.'

'Not 'mm'. Please, Rosemary, *promise* me.'

'I promise.'

'You'll ring me every other day? No matter how things are going?'

'Mm.'

'Oh, Rosemary.' The whine in her mother's voice intensified. 'I'd never have let you go at all without that mobile. It's *very* unique. You'll have to be very, very careful with it.'

'I promise. I promise.'

'And ring me the *minute* you land.'

'Oh, don't cry, Mum. Please don't cry.'

Rosemary's trip to Paris with two girlfriends had been only the summer before. She'd been a full seventeen years old then, and even so her mother had fretted for weeks beforehand. She'd gone to Lake Geneva and Berlin on school trips, and her mother had fretted even though there'd been a busload of other children with her. But Rosemary had never been abroad all by herself. Nor had she left with less than twenty-four hours' notice. The fretting this time was of a whole different order.

'There it is!' Rosemary cried, leaping to her feet.

The departures board read: 'Aeroflot AE 273 for Minsk. Gate 12'.

Rosemary disentangled herself from her mother's embrace and raced towards the departure area, not even looking back to wave. She fizzed with excitement: boarding pass check, passport check, X-ray machine, body check, departure lounge, long moving side-walks, boarding pass and passport again, tube into the plane, buckle the seat belt, take off, incomprehensible announcements in exotic rounded syllables, England down below, then clouds and more clouds: throughout it all Rosemary was Alka-Seltzer tossed into a glass of water.

Four hours later, still fizzing, she landed in Minsk and followed the other passengers to passport control. The line inched forward. She gazed around, enchanted by this place. Signs in the Cyrillic alphabet, a babushka in a headscarf — granny dress with slip showing beneath it, face like a withered tangerine out of a Russian fairytale book — pushing a mop and a bucket. This place couldn't really exist. It was out of a movie. Rosemary kept expecting it to disappear in a puff of smoke. When she finally faced the stiffly uniformed officer herself, he eyed her up and down, opened her passport, scanned every page meticulously even though nothing was written there, eyed her up and down again and then started in on her visa.

'You are work Minsk?' he said in a guttural accent, face stern and impassive, voice tinged with contempt.

'No,' she said, 'I'm going to Dubiczewo.' The slight shift in his eyebrows told her he didn't believe her. There were very few lone women travellers in Belarus. 'I'm with the Follaton Foundation,' she added, a little primly.

'What you say?'

'The Follaton Medical Foundation.' He opened her passport again and again began at page one.

'You ought to at least know the name,' she said, more primly still. 'The Foundation does important work in your country.'

'Is penalty for lie,' he said without looking up.

'Why would I lie?'

He glared at her then. 'Is penalty!' She didn't flinch. 'Wait,' he said, stepping down from his perch.

'What for?'

'Wait!'

He took her passport with him to a glassed-in room way across the open space of passport control; she could see him in conversation with another uniformed officer. Ten minutes passed. Fifteen. But when he returned, his face was wreathed in smiles.

'Come,' he said.

'Pardon?'

'Come.' He took her arm.

'Where?'

'Come!'

At customs, other passengers shifted from foot to foot in front of open suitcases, contents spread wide, officials picking through shirts and ties and toiletries. Rosemary's escort ushered her past all this — nobody queried him, not even a glance — and brought her out to the public section of the airport, where there were herds of people as there are in every airport — except that here lots of them were squatting down, some in groups, some alone, bags and baskets beside them like beggars in the street. Rosemary was so preoccupied with them that she hardly noticed the man who bumped into her hard enough to knock her to her knees.

'Okay?' said her escort, helping her back onto her feet.

'Of course I'm okay,' she said as she brushed down her dress.

He led her to a plump, black-haired woman, who dismissed him with a few curt words in Russian and then turned to Rosemary. 'I am Kamilla Sapega,' she said. 'I take charge of volunteers. You come with me.'

'I don't know where my luggage is.'

'Come. Come.'

'But what about my bags?' Rosemary insisted.

'All is taken care of.'

Rosemary followed Kamilla out to a shiny, new Lada that stood alone in front of the airport. It was only as the engine started up that she remembered her promise to call her mother as soon as she landed; the ‘very unique’ mobile was a satellite extension which could reach home from anywhere in the world. Rosemary rummaged in her bag.

The phone was gone.

# 32

## DARTMOUTH, DEVON

Helen wasn't remotely prepared to let Charles come between her and the ritual of lunches with Zoya on alternate Sundays, and yet she'd had to miss one already because of her trip to the Lescaze house; she hadn't seen Zoya since the engagement. The two of them usually met at the restaurant of the Dart Marina Hotel, which overlooked the Dart River and the sailing boats, across to the green West Country hills. Zoya was there when Helen arrived.

'Oh, Helen!' she said, folding away a copy of the *Dartmouth Chronicle*. 'You're here at last!' She got out of her chair and kissed Helen's cheeks. Not just one cheek. Not even two. But three: Christ, Christos, Christi is a Russian blessing at Easter. Zoya used it the whole year around.

The likelihood that Helen's phone was tapped meant she hadn't had a chance to explain about the engagement which wasn't an engagement. She was so busy trying to get the complications across that she barely noticed Zoya's beautifully cut tan suit, its elegance only slightly upset by the bright red spots on her cheeks. In the old days, Russian dancers used lipstick instead of blusher; she wasn't about to relinquish a romantic piece of theatrical lore just because her eyesight was so bad that she couldn't see how much she'd put on.

'Oh, that *is* a pity,' Zoya said when Helen finished. 'I do wish it weren't pretend, but it's tremendously exciting even so. Let me see the ring.' Helen held out her hand even though she knew Zoya couldn't see what was on it. Zoya ran her fingers over it and sighed. 'You'll have to give it back, I suppose. That's a pity too. Wine,' she demanded then. 'We need wine. Where is it?' She looked around her with the blank face of someone who knows perfectly well she isn't going to find what she wants. 'The bottle is supposed to be here somewhere. I've already had a glass.'

Helen pulled the bottle out of the ice bucket beside the table and poured for them both.

'*Santé*,' Zoya said, raising her glass and clicking Helen's.

'*Santé*,' Helen replied.

'Imagine marrying a lord *and* being able to talk about science!'

'Zoya! I've just told you that nobody's going to — '

'*I* am going to pretend a little longer,' Zoya interrupted. 'You look so happy, just like a bride-to-be ought to look.'

Helen shook her head — a wry combination of despair and indulgence — and picked up the menu; Zoya could just about make it out with her thick glasses on, but she'd rather have dropped dead than wear them in the Dart Marina Hotel. The cream of Dartmouth society lunched there. She'd only been pretending to read the newspaper when Helen arrived.

'Now let's see,' Helen said. 'They've got . . . there's no melon but the chicken sounds like you.'

'What are you going to have?'

'Chicken is fine.'

'You don't care what you eat, do you?'

'Not particularly.'

Zoya laughed, turning to appeal to the waitress who was standing beside the table with her order pad. 'What are we going to do with her, Jennie?'

'Hi, Dr Freyl, congratulations!' the waitress said. 'When's the wedding? Are you going to get married in Westminster Abbey?'

'Oh, don't talk about it,' Helen said irritably. 'The whole thing makes me squirm.'

Jennie bit her lip, gave Zoya a sheepish smile, looked around for something else to focus on and settled for Zoya's elegant tan suit. 'You *do* look lovely today, Miss Bezukhova. Is that a Versace? A real one?'

'Aren't you a clever girl, Jennie.' Zoya opened her jacket to show off its lining, and her neatly folded newspaper slipped off her lap. Helen reached under the table to retrieve it, then caught a glimpse of the headline.

The earth stopped spinning on its axis. She jolted so abruptly that the wine glasses toppled over.

* * *

One glass went rolling across the table towards Zoya's Versace; only the waitress's speed with a napkin saved the suit. Two other waitresses came running. There was a flurry of towels, then of napery — fresh tablecloth, fresh napkins — silverware and clean glasses.

'Zoya, your paper . . . ' Helen said, finding her voice at last. 'Zoya, the headline says 'Death of Local Russian Teacher'. It says, 'Feodor Mussinov, teacher of calculus and French at Dartmouth Naval College, died some time during the night of Friday.''

'Oh,' said Zoya with a sad shrug.

'You *knew* about it. How did it happen? All it says is that he's dead. Was it an accident?'

'Well, not . . . er, not really.'

''Not really'? What's that supposed to mean?'

Zoya turned away to stare through the window at the Dart river and the boats. Not that she could see them all that much better than she could see the newspaper. Out in the middle of the water a ketch with three red canvas sails tilted. Its rigging swung in the wind. 'One of the college cleaners says he hanged himself. She found him, poor dear.'

Helen opened her mouth. She shut it again. 'Hanged himself?' she said in a hush. 'Feodor? *Why*?'

Zoya knitted her brows — grief, not puzzlement — covered her chin with her hand to hide its tremor, turned away. 'I don't know anything about it, Helen.'

'Of course you do.' Zoya only shook her head. 'Please, Zoya. You've got to tell me. I saw him only a couple of days ago. He was upset, but I certainly didn't get the impression that he might have anything like *this* on his mind.'

Zoya gave another shrug, then straightened her shoulders. 'He wanted a canterbury.'

'A what?'

'You've seen mine. It belonged to my mother. It's made out of special mahogany. I keep forgetting the name. Sort of like 'sweet tenant' — but that isn't it. Helen, you *know* what I mean. You've seen it a million times. It holds magazines.'

'Magazines?'

'He wanted one exactly like it. He couldn't possibly find one exactly the same. I told him that, but he was absolutely — '

'Zoya!'

'Helen, it should be perfectly clear to anybody with any wits at all that a man who wants a canterbury isn't a man who's going to kill himself.'

Zoya often saw bizarre connections between things; usually the sheer surprise of her logic made Helen laugh despite herself and whatever the circumstances. Not today. Today, any doubt cast on Feodor's suicide only increased the abrupt distress that had enveloped Helen when she saw the headline in the *Dartmouth Chronicle*.

'What *do* you think happened?' she pressed.

Zoya was shaking her head. 'I don't believe a word of it. Not a single word.'

'Are you suggesting — ?' Helen stopped short and studied her friend. 'You're not trying to tell me you think somebody killed him, are you?'

'I owe him loyalty. He deserves at least that, don't you think?'

'You *do* think somebody killed him. Who would do that?'

'Helen, please.'

'What's loyalty got to do with it? He's dead.'

'He was my friend, Helen.' Real distress showed in Zoya's voice and on her face. 'I've already said too much.'

Helen had known Zoya long enough to know she'd get nothing more, no matter how hard she pressed, but her upset tightened into fear while lunch dragged on through talk of the wedding that was not to be: chicken came and went, then chocolate ice cream sundaes, then coffee. Helen shifted impatiently from foot to foot while Zoya patted her hair in front of a lobby window, unaware that it wasn't a mirror, cocked her head, decided that whatever she saw — or didn't see — met her satisfaction, then took Helen's arm.

'Back to London now?' Zoya said.

Helen nodded absently. 'I hope so.'

''I hope so' doesn't make sense, Helen.'

'Doesn't it?'

But Zoya wasn't steady on her feet, and negotiating the steps outside the hotel took so much concentration that she didn't pursue the subject. She'd forgotten it altogether by the time Helen helped manoeuvre her into the taxi that delivered her back to her apartment, then took Helen on to the train station.

* * *

The scenery on the trip from Dartmouth to London can be glorious if the tide is in. On this day though, the tide was out, and the river was nothing but mud flats squeezing water into rivulets that trickled down to a crooked sluice. They even *looked* like the anxieties Helen felt.

How could Zoya's skewed logic about magazine holders have made her so certain that Feodor's death was murder? He himself had failed to frighten her. So had Leslie Bloeden. Yet the more she thought about it, the surer she was that if she'd listened to either of them, Feodor would be alive. Which made his death her fault.

But the scariest part was that nothing quite added up.

Only this morning, a bugged telephone had seemed part of an exciting game more than anything else. Now she could only think that if somebody was listening in on the phone, why not the house? He might have said something before they'd left the building. She strained to remember. Had he mentioned the bees in that frightened voice of his? Or the venom? Or the patents? But why would UCAI kill him merely because he'd guessed what they wanted from her? And assumed they'd have before the year was out?

Perhaps Feodor knew something that he didn't even know he knew. If so, she might know it too. But *what*?

And yet UCAI was less frightening than Charles, who'd never really seemed threatening — except in Becky's mind — until Helen knew that Feodor was dead.

'Charles Hay isn't what he seems,' Leslie Bloeden had said to her.

'Who of us is?'

'I don't mean that, Dr Freyl. He's different. He's a dangerous man.'

She'd been thoroughly irritated by that time, certain Leslie would tell her anything that came into his head. There'd been an infuriating condescension in his manner. Galleas's offer of $10 million for the rights to Joshua's venom was an insult to her intelligence; he'd never have made it if she'd been a man.

He hadn't borne her irritation well. 'What *is* the matter with you? Charles Hay killed his own brother to get at the family gold. You don't think he's going to stop at a nice American girl, do you?'

And that was before Feodor had repeated the warning, and Feodor had wanted only to help.

She could even see how Charles might have worked it. A shrewd assessment of her as a woman pining for a dead lover and a dead father, a person adrift, a little unstable. It wouldn't have been difficult to become in her eyes a man as upright as her father, a devoted suitor who listened hard, sympathized with her troubles, flattered her skilfully, amused her and — most important — let her feel she was calling the shots.

If Leslie had been right and Charles *had* killed his own brother, her father might have suspected something but been unable to prove it. Or he might have known it was true but didn't feel he could expose somebody he'd been close to for so very long. Suppose then that Charles had wanted to find out if he'd told tales about it: what better way than to have Feodor sound her out?

She had no idea of the state of Charles's finances. If he was as ruthless as his reputation, he wouldn't balk at playing the rich man whether he had money or not. For all she knew, he was bankrupt. If he'd killed his brother for the family money, he'd more than likely be willing to kill his fiancée for the fortune her bees represented. If he killed her, he'd be killing Becky at the same time; the trip to Springfield would have told him that. Then he could go after Joshua, who could be easily manipulated by a threat to his family.

As the train crawled its way towards London — Sunday trains are slow — Helen began to see that she had no choice. Go back to the house, pick up her passport, taxi to Heathrow, standby to Chicago. Turn Joshua's patents over to UCAI. Just get out before she ended up dead like Feodor.

# 33

## LONDON

The train lurched to a halt in the suburb of Ealing Broadway, sat half an hour, then inched through the dirty brickwork, desolate graffiti and criss-cross of railway lines that announce London. At the great glasshouse of Paddington station, it spewed out its load of passengers. Helen was pressing her way through the crowds towards the underground for a dash to Notting Hill and her passport when it occurred to her that if they were after her — whoever *they* were: UCAI? Follaton? Charles? — *they* were all too likely to be following her.

The street where she lived was quiet. She'd be isolated there: an easy target to pick off. A taxi would be safer. But the moment she got into the taxi line she realized all they had to do was make sure she got into a cab, then follow that. She glanced around at the others in line. There were probably fifty people waiting, most with luggage and that dishevelled end-of-a-weekend-in-the-country look to them. It could be almost any one of them. That man, for example, the one in glasses and a duffel jacket. Was he avoiding her eye? Or the one with his hands thrust deep in the pockets of his trench coat? Or how about . . . ?

She turned away from the taxi line and set out on foot.

London traffic is heavy on Sundays. The streets were clogged with cars, buses, people. She struggled to keep her pace slow, to be just another one of the multitude glancing at the windows of the down-at-heel stores that cluster around the station: shoe repairs, dark drug stores and dry cleaners, fast-food joints with rotisseries of meat dripping fat. At dusk, windows become shadowy mirrors. She found herself studying them in search of an elusive follower, checking each group behind her for someone who stopped when she did. She was pretending to look at a display of cheap pine furniture when she noticed a woman who seemed to be waiting outside a small supermarket. She had the vague feeling that she'd seen that knitted cap before, the woollen scarf and the jeans too.

Helen walked rapidly away, then turned back as though remembering something, waited a few minutes, saw nothing untoward, glanced at her watch — it was nearly 7.30 — and decided to steel herself to flag a taxi and take that trip to her house for the passport. The taxi driver could go with her to get it or maybe go alone while she waited in the taxi or maybe . . . She glanced at the window again.

Off to one side, deep in shadows, was that knitted cap.

Despite herself, Helen spun around, her heart pounding in her chest. But reflections in a window can be confusing. A moment of indecision, a moment of getting her bearings, and the knitted cap was gone. Helen stood there, staring at the spot where it had been. Half of her insisted that the whole business — including that knitted cap — was imagination. Pure imagination. Nothing else. The other half was terrified.

What are people supposed to do in situations like this? In the movies there's a convenient store with a back way out or a subway entrance or a partner in a nearby car with the engine running. The only oasis Helen could see was a small café with steamed-up windows. She crossed the street to it, went in, sat at a table.

'What can I get you?' said the waitress, a thin, tired-looking woman with a few straggles of dyed-blonde hair in her eyes.

Helen didn't want anything except to be in off the street. 'Just coffee, I guess,' she said.

'Anything else?'

Helen shook her head. She sat rigidly, waiting — but without any idea whatever what she was waiting *for*.

The waitress set a cup of pale coffee in front of her. 'Milk?' she said. Helen shook her head. 'You okay?' asked the waitress.

'Well, I . . . ' Helen began. But despite herself she ended in a sigh.

'You're *not* okay, are you, darling?'

'I can't even get his ring off me.' There was a sob in Helen's voice as she held out her hand. 'I've pulled and pulled, and it won't come. The bastard's never going to let me go, is he?'

'Bloody men.'

'How could I have got myself into this?'

'We'll see about that ring,' the waitress said.

'Come on. Through here.' Helen followed her into the kitchen. The stove was aluminium streaked with grease. Piles of dirty dishes waited by the sink. The waitress soaped Helen's hand in the dishwater and tugged gently. The ring wouldn't budge. 'Bloody men,' she muttered again. 'Not to worry, love. Not to worry.' She reached behind a fraying curtain, pulled out a bottle of window cleaner and sprayed Helen's finger.

The ring slipped off at once.

This small act of defiance — this claiming back of a corner of control over her life — brought Leslie Bloeden to mind again. Why hadn't she thought of him before? If anybody was far removed from the interests of UCAI, the Follaton Foundation and Charles, it was Leslie Bloeden of Galleas International. He'd help her. Of course he would. Helen rummaged in her purse for the card he'd given her at the book festival, found it, got out her mobile, only to hear a message transferring her to Leslie's voicemail. She started talking, then hung up abruptly. *Now* what stupid thing did she think she was doing? Leaving a message? Letting him see her desperation? She could feel the burn of Becky's contempt from all the way across the Atlantic: 'How can you expect a man to accept your terms when it is painfully clear that you need his help?' Besides, what did she know about him? Maybe he didn't represent Galleas at all. If he was right about Charles, maybe Charles was right about him: maybe she'd got herself caught up in a game of espionage. Leslie might even belong to UCAI.

'I need a drink,' she said to the waitress.

'Sorry, love. Try the hotel next door.'

Next door was small, dark, intimate, a curved bar in mahogany, a few tables and a few red plush chairs, the old song 'Black Velvet' grinding away in the background as Helen walked in:

*A new religion that'll bring ya to your knees*
*Black velvet if you please*

Helen's father had liked that song. Or at least he used to pretend he did. Maybe he hadn't liked it at all. On the other hand, maybe he had. Helen knew she'd never understood him.

'A Black Velvet, if you please,' she said to the bartender, who had frazzled hair and a pug nose.

She'd never had the drink before. It turned out to be a vicious combination of stout and champagne, but it seemed precisely right. Helen swallowed it, ordered another, leaned back against the red plush — and sure enough, her mind became a comfortable blank. She drank another Black Velvet. Then another.

That's when the panic set in again. She tried to stifle it with yet another Black Velvet. No use. 'You don't have an internet connection, do you?' she said to the bartender on impulse.

The bartender had to help her into the hotel's office, had to help her get into the chair too. She wavered drunkenly in front of the screen before she could get her eyes to focus on it, then she spilled out her terrors to Lillian, to whom she'd always turned when life seemed to be closing in on her.

Lillian, what am I going to do? Somebody's trying to kill me. I don't know who. I don't know why. I had everything under control. Except maybe . . . Don't tell Grandma. She'd be furious. I want David Marion. I need him. How can the bastard be dead? How can he do that to me?

# 34

## DUBICZEWO, MOGILEV REGION, BELARUS

The heat of this summer was still killing people throughout the Mogilev region just as it was in Illinois. At night women covered their children in wet sheets — as Midwestern mothers had done a century ago and were doing again this year — and laid them at open doorways to catch what breeze was stirring. The official forecast predicted a cold and early autumn. Belarusians prayed the government would get it right for once, but they weren't surprised when the heat stretched right on to October 1st.

Rosemary didn't know about any of that. For her, the weather only added a glow to the fairytale world that she'd glimpsed at the airport and that kept on surprising her during the drive from Minsk to Mogilev. Everything was so clean, so neat, so tidy. The trees were so tall. The land was so flat. There were so many lakes and rivers. Tiny clapboard villages appeared out of nowhere. So did the occasional sugar-candy castle where an ogre or a princess might live.

It was evening when she reached the Mobile Clinic outside Dubiczewo. The site looked to her like military encampments she'd seen on TV. Kamilla gave her a quick tour of canvas-covered trucks that carried equipment, tunnel-shaped tents where volunteers and staff slept and worked, the two vast bus-like units that were the consulting rooms and test lab. In the biggest of the tents, local women were serving dinner — soup, cheese, cold meats and black bread — to volunteers and staff. The chatter was in a variety of languages; the work of Follaton Medical Foundation attracted people from all over the world.

Dr Tatiana got up from her meal, embraced Rosemary and said, 'Welcome to our clinic. It is very good to have you here. You have experience in chemistry, yes? At school? This is wonderful for us. Sit, sit. You must be hungry. How was your journey?'

The others clamoured to introduce themselves in a pidgin English that seemed all the more friendly because it took so much effort. An hour later, Rosemary fell into a happy, exhausted sleep in a tent with seven other women, and the next morning her work began in another tent. She prepared her first slide of blood film and carried out her first blood count. By lunchtime, she'd identified leukaemia cells and picked out a squamous cell carcinoma from a tissue sample even though she'd never seen either before except in books. She was exhilarated. At long last, she was helping, making a contribution.

And then — even though it seemed as though nothing could improve on this experience — she found James working right next to her.

It was his first day too. He'd arrived that very morning from London to help collate the

Clinic's statistics. His hair was gold, and his shirt was unbuttoned halfway down because of the heat. Even at home, he'd have interested Rosemary. Here? Well, here the curve of his back made her feel giddy. She pretended indifference. During that first day, the work so absorbed her that the pretence wasn't too difficult. On her second day, distraction came in the form of a harvest festival. A priest held mass outdoors. A little girl presented a wreath of rowan berries and meadow flowers to Dr Tatiana, who was playing the role of the local squire in a top hat. For the celebration feast, the Clinic supplied meat, vegetables, fruit, wine, vodka, beer, all shipped from Minsk. The real reason for this generosity was that the volunteers weren't allowed to eat local produce because the radiation levels in it were too high. The Belarusians didn't care; by evening tables were piled high with boiled pork hocks, potatoes and buckwheat groats, apples, pears, plums. A band of fiddles and a squeeze box played.

Rosemary danced with James but left him — like Cinderella — as soon as the music ended. Early the next morning when they were at work in the research tent, she whispered to him, 'You want to go to bed?' Her head was bowed over her microscope.

'What?'

'You heard me.' Still she didn't look up, but she let him catch a smile playing about her mouth.

'Now?'

She laughed her husky laugh, shaking her

head. The elderly Japanese in charge of the Geiger counter glanced up with a smile.

'When? Where?'

'That's a problem,' she said. 'I'll think about it.'

* * *

The morning was a long and hard one for Dr Tatiana; she began it by reviewing patients she'd examined in the spring. Her last case before lunch was a man with a growth behind his eye that she guessed must by now be as large as a tennis ball — only a scan could tell for sure — and her stomach grumbled throughout the entire half hour.

A volunteer led the man off to the test lab vehicle. Dr Tatiana finished her notes on him, then left her consulting room, smiled reassurance at the paramedic who was manning the front desk; the staff changed almost as frequently as the volunteers, and he'd been with the Clinic only a week. She climbed down the metal steps outside and started towards the mess tent. The healthy patients greeted her as she passed by their awning.

'God give you many children, Dr Tatiana,' cried a toothless old man.

She was past fifty. Not even God was going to give her another child to go with her beloved 20-year-old son. 'May He do the same for you, Georgi,' she laughed. She had a general's memory for names; she knew all her patients, their families too. But she didn't recognize the one who jumped to his feet, ran up to her, kissed her on both cheeks, hugged her impetuously, then dropped his arms and stepped back in disappointment.

'Dr Tatiana, are you not glad to see me so healthy?'

He was a strapping lad, tall, blue-eyed, an open-necked tunic revealing a ruddy neck. 'I'm very sorry, my boy, but I don't . . . ' She paused. 'Boris?' she said tentatively. Could it be? Could this really be the leukaemia patient she'd seen only six months ago? The boy whose kneecaps were the largest things on his emaciated body?

'You *do* remember.' He smiled happily.

'How could I forget you, Boris? It's just that you . . . ' She paused again, shook her head. 'You young people keep growing and changing. It's most annoying. How do you expect us old folk to keep up? How's the hockey?'

'They say I may not be quite fast enough to compete until February,' he said, 'but I will prove them wrong.'

She put her arm around his shoulders. 'Come and have lunch with me,' she said. 'I need to know who's going to play centre while they're keeping you on the sidelines.'

They sat at a trestle table in the mess tent to eat a meal of pork, turnips and puréed beans. Dr Tatiana introduced Boris to the volunteers and staff, then listened transfixed to his tale of ice hockey practice on dry ground even though she'd always thought that pushing around a chunk of something — on ice or anywhere else — was a silly waste of time and energy.

But imagine *Boris* being alive at all, much less

sitting here with animated gestures, pink cheeks and games to play in the future.

Until quite recently, she'd have said that spontaneous remission had to be the cause of his recovery. It *does* happen; she'd have put him down as one of the rare lucky ones. But now? She'd begun seeing unexpected improvements in her patients for some time before she'd first examined him. She'd duly noted details in her reports, but she'd thought of them as an anomaly rather than a trend.

Early in summer, she'd realized there had to be more to it than that. Possibly much more. The reduction in headaches, stomach aches and gum disease — so prevalent among radiation victims — was significant. The severity of colds, flu, bronchitis and the standard childhood ailments that come with radiation-compromised immune systems: nearly a full half of these had eased well beyond any margin of error.

But most exciting were the leukaemia patients, the girls as well as boys like Boris. All of them should have been dead or dying. Just under half of them were unaccountably better. Not just *better* either: they were well.

Dr Tatiana was very devout, and she believed with all her soul that God was merciful. It troubled her deeply that He could allow so much pain, especially in children. She'd prayed for a miracle that would help reduce the damage Chernobyl had done to them. The doctor in her sometimes scoffed at her faith, but with the glowing young hockey star in front of her, she wasn't so sure any more.

* * *

Usually Dr Tatiana kept an eye on the Clinic's volunteers. She had to write a report on each of them; the Follaton Foundation kept careful watch over all its foreign helpers. But Boris so preoccupied her that she didn't notice the two young English people slip out of the mess tent, first the girl, then the boy.

'The woods, of course,' Rosemary said to James as soon as they were far enough away so that nobody else could hear. His hair shone in the sun, and he had her hand in his. He gave it a gentle tug, smiling at her. She could see he was still worried that he might have misread her.

'I bet that's how Gretel tempted Hansel,' he said. 'Supposing we get caught?'

'What do we know? We're two silly kids. Irradiated air went to our heads. We were looking for mushrooms and got lost. Oh, James, isn't it wonderful to actually be here? I *still* can't believe it.'

The Clinic's accommodation emphasized communal living. People wandered in and out of the sleeping tents. Showers were outdoors. Toilet facilities were a cramped and smelly two-holer in a portable shed off by itself with wood shavings in the crêpe-like toilet paper. On the pretence of a visit to it, James had scoured the village of Dubiczewo as well as the rest of the encampment. There had to be a quiet nook or cranny, somewhere — anywhere — where people could be alone together for half an hour. He found nothing. How did these Belarusians reproduce?

An hour later while he was busy eating pork and turnips, Rosemary had come up behind him, touched his arm, tilted her head towards the tent's opening. A few minutes after that he'd followed her out of the tent.

They half-walked, half-ran through the smattering of cottages that made up Dubiczewo; babushkas in flowered scarves squatted in open doorways, sorting apples from last year's crop, and watched the couple hurry past. The two of them crossed a field that had been solid blue with flax only a month or so ago. A lone figure in a tunic, possibly a farmer surveying next year's prospects, watched them disappear — stumbling in their eagerness — into the silver beech and pine that made up the outer edges of the Lowieza Woods.

⋆ ⋆ ⋆

Their bed beneath the trees was soft with moss and leaf mould. Beside them, ferns swayed in an unexpectedly cool breeze. A stream tumbled over rocks nearby. Not that Rosemary and James paid attention to these charms of nature, not even to the audience of birds and squirrels that watched their struggling reach a quick crescendo amid delighted gasps and cries.

They slipped back from each other and lay, fingers entwined, eyes staring blankly up into the elaborate tracery of branches above them. 'What'd I do with my jeans?' Rosemary said lazily. Half their clothes lay strewn out across the small clearing. They were still wearing the rest.

'You can't be cold.'

'No way.'

He reached across and ran a proprietary hand over the fabric that covered the top half of her body. 'What do you suppose is beneath this pretty blouse you've got on?'

She rolled up on her elbow. 'Think you're the only insatiable one?'

'I might make you prove me wrong.' He sat up, pushed her back gently and set to work. She watched him with a smile; there must have been a dozen tiny buttons between the rows of ruffle that ran from neck to waist, and by the time he'd undone half of them his body trembled with anticipation.

She pulled away as her blouse fell open. 'James!'

'You can't go prudish on me *now*.'

'That noise!' There'd been a sudden rustle from the trees. 'What is it?'

He cupped his hands — greedy rather than protective — over the flesh he'd revealed. 'The sight of you startled the wildlife.'

She swung around just as figures emerged from the trees.

It happened so quickly she wasn't even sure how many were there. Three? Five? Robots? Men from the moon? All of them crashing towards her at once, bubbles of black glass where their faces should be, yellow hoods, shiny yellow uniforms head to foot, white oxygen tanks on their backs.

Ether causes a choking sensation. Not that either Rosemary or James knew it was ether.

They knew only that they kicked, fought, tried to scream — and couldn't breathe.

* * *

Dr Tatiana never did notice they were missing. She was on her third patient after lunch when she got the message that her son had been badly hurt in a motorcycle crash on his way to Poland. She left as soon as her replacement arrived a couple of hours later.

# PART 3

# 35

## SPRINGFIELD, ILLINOIS

'A leg of lamb is just exactly right' was Lillian's first thought on waking. She'd gone to sleep with the idea of roast turkey — oyster stuffing and crackled brown skin — and rejected it in her dreams; the weather was too hot. Before dawn, rib eye beef seemed perfect, but she fell asleep again before the idea could take hold.

Tonight was going to be very important. Tonight she was making dinner for the children of Joshua's new girlfriend Palassia. It wasn't going to be easy. Palassia's children didn't like him; they didn't seem to realize how special he was. A horse that had never had a saddle? It let Joshua ride it the first time around. Cranky dogs? They knelt down so he could pet them. Women were the same. It didn't hurt that at sixty-five he was still good looking enough to turn heads in the street. He'd married five times, had children all over the place, mostly with his wives.

'The thing I *can't* figure' — Lillian had said to Helen more than once — 'is how come a woman marries a tom cat 'less of which she expects anything but a tom cat.'

This new Palassia was a sweetheart, a nurse at Memorial Hospital and just the kind of person sick people want around them; things went calm the moment she walked into a room. The courting had been different too. Joshua's other wives had chased him. This time he was the one doing the work. Lillian had laughed when he told her he'd tried to go to church for Palassia; he'd certainly never done that for any of the others. They planned to get married around Christmas, but her children — a boy and a girl — wanted no part of this substitute for their dead father. They were both lawyers, and they lived in white neighbourhoods, which is saying something in Springfield. They wore designer shoes. They went to private viewings at the Rebecca Freyl Museum of Art. They even belonged to the Sangamo Club.

And Joshua? What they saw in him was no more than a dirt poor bee farmer from Alabama. Lillian was going to have to work very hard tonight to convince them that he was good enough for their mother.

She went to Schaum's for the leg of lamb even though it cost half again as much as at the mall. Potatoes, carrots, apples, broccoli all came from the Old Capitol farmers' market downtown. For coffee and half-and-half she stopped on her way home at the Shop 'n Save on East Monroe. She parked at the back of the store and walked towards the entrance, a little tense when she realized she'd have to pass a whole group of the homeless to get there.

They were clustered around a skip, maybe a dozen of them, while a waif of a girl danced, banging on a tambourine, and a skinny guy in dreadlocks whined, ''This is where you messed up . . . Whoa oh ooh whoa oh . . . ''

Lillian wasn't more than twenty feet away when a can spewing beer came clattering across the macadam towards her and a tussle broke out.

'You don't know jack shit,' shouted a bag of dirty laundry at a much bigger guy with fingernails as long as talons. 'You the most dumb-ass nigger I ever did lay my eyes on.'

'' — talk smack behind my back'' — Dreadlocks' voice skidded into a screech — ''mmmm, hmmm, mmmm, don't hate me baby . . . ''

Lillian glanced uneasily back at her car, then glanced over at the group again.

That's when she saw him.

He was leaning against the skip, right at the back, bearded, hair reaching to his shoulders, baseball cap shielding his eyes, cigarette dangling from his lips. 'David?' she said in wonder. Despite herself she plunged into the group. Dreadlocks shut up at once. So did the others. The waif stopped dancing. 'David Marion! It *is* you-un. What in tarnation are you doing here, boy? We all thought you was dead. How come you ain't?' Her only reply was a scowl. 'How come you acting like this? *Talk* to me.'

'Hey, lady, please,' said Dreadlocks. 'You don't want to . . . This here's Canada, and he be kinda new around here, know what I mean? He just *look* like somebody you met once or something. That's it, ain't it?'

Lillian scanned the face. Well, she *could* be wrong. She'd never been all that good at white faces, and there wasn't a flicker of recognition on this one. Besides, a beard changes a man completely. She backed away. 'I'm real sorry, mister. I guess I just kinda miss my dead friend. You understand, don't you?'

She turned then and headed for the big front doors of Shop 'n Save.

* * *

She was upset as she peeled the apples back home in her kitchen; the more she thought, the more that bearded man seemed like David. His age was right, maybe thirty-five. There'd been a meticulousness about the clothing despite its threadbare state, no obvious dirt, no tears or rips in jacket or jeans, shoelaces tied. That was right too. So was the angry glint in the eyes.

Refusing to speak to her was *not* like him. Nor was a beard and long hair and homelessness. Unless of course, he was in some kind of trouble. Which certainly made sense since he was supposed to be dead. She puzzled the matter for a while, wishing she had the time to go back and check him out, let him know she'd help if he needed it. On the other hand, if he really didn't want to talk to her, she had no right to meddle.

She was about to clear her laptop off the dining table when she first noticed the email from Helen in London. She bent over the screen and read it, drew back with a frown, read it again, more amazed the second time around than the first. But how could the timing of the thing be worse? There was so much cooking to do. There were napkins to iron and the table to lay.

But she hesitated only long enough to take off her apron before she rushed out to her car and back to the Shop 'n Save.

* * *

David had arrived in town that morning and headed towards the homeless shelter on Washington Street. He'd reached it as the first inhabitant emerged: an old man with shaggy hair, an even shaggier beard and a plastic supermarket bag.

'Hey, you,' David said.

'Top of the morning to you, my dear sir,' said the old man, putting down his bag to concentrate on David.

'Any ex-cons around here? Insiders maybe?' The steady exchange between the prisons and the homeless meant that South Hams gangs were well known on Springfield streets.

'Are you an Englishman, may I ask?'

'None of your business.'

'Oh, really? Now let me see.' The old man cocked his head to the other side and smiled gently as he scanned David's face. 'You will most likely find a couple of fellows of interest to you in the parking lot at Shop 'n Save round about eleven, maybe noon.'

David had arrived at ten to find Dreadlocks and the odd collection Lillian saw him with, but no Insiders — at least not yet. He knew

Dreadlocks, though. Dreadlocks had spent maybe ten years in South Hams as a hanger-on of the Black Guerrilla family. David had accepted the offer of a beer and leaned against the skip to wait.

Instead of a fellow Insider, he'd found himself face to face with Lillian.

* * *

The moment EJ Dowd had crouched down at the mushroom festival, David had recognized army training; which meant to him that EJ was a second attempt to fulfil the contract on him. The poster his rescuer in Colorado had shown him — he'd thought about it for the weeks it took him to recover his strength — looked all too much like the opening shot in a third. Some pittance from his grandmother was hardly bait, but including Helen Freyl as one of her heirs: what could it mean? Why *her*?

He remembered his grandmother as a screaming witch with a white-coated mouth and blood clots for eyes. Not likely to be an accurate portrait, but enough to make it easy for him to avoid her when she'd surfaced briefly while he was in prison. He'd assumed she was long dead now. If she really was alive, old prison colleagues would be in a better position than he was to take a look at her; they'd also know his reputation well enough to think twice about collecting a reward without talking to him first.

But the contract on him emanated from UCAI, and executives at UCAI were people who dined at country clubs and sat on boards with people like Becky Freyl. They were the kind of people Lillian worked for, the kind of people who owned her, who could easily put pressure on her.

And the woman comes back for him less than an hour after she's spotted him for the first time.

* * *

'Go home, mother!' Dreadlocks cried, his arms flapping. 'Go home afore you gets yourself hurt.'

'You be quiet!' Lillian said. She didn't shout but the command in her voice was absolute. 'I ain't here to do him no harm, and he ain't — '

'He be waiting for someone.'

' — gonna do me no harm. And I ain't going nowhere lessun he talks to me first.'

'You don't know what you be — '

'I ain't afraid of you, boy, and I ain't afraid of him.' She peered into David's face, scanned the eyes, then smiled and patted his shoulder. 'David, I got to talk to you alone — not with this riff-raff about. And don't you scowl at me no more. I don't like it. Go on, shoo!' She waved dismissal at the others with the magisterial authority of a woman who'd raised seven children and fought for them every inch of the way. 'You heard me. Shoo!'

The group withdrew in disarray towards the other side of the parking lot.

'It's about a email,' she said to David.

'Who'd you tell about seeing me?' he said irritably.

'Didn't tell nobody. Why should I? Miss Helen and I been writing emails. Right out of the blue she sends me one saying she needs you. Not nobody else. *You*. How could you . . . '

David lost track of the words. This new piece of information shifted the boundaries. It hadn't occurred to him that Helen might be an active part of the trap.

' . . . you ain't eaten nothing today at all,' Lillian was saying. 'You come back to the house. I'll make you some breakfast. How come you ain't dead?'

'Get to the point.'

'I done told you the point. I got this here email.'

'Let's see it.'

'I don't got a copy *with* me. This here's a emergency, and Miss Helen done asked for you special — even thinking you was dead. You gots to come back to my house.'

'Why would I do that?'

' 'Cause I asked you to. That's why. And 'cause from the looks of you, you ain't got nothing better to do with your life.'

Lillian lived in one of the better black neighbourhoods on the east side; the lawn was mowed and the last of the dahlias were still blooming. But a respectable black neighbourhood in Springfield is a place where the housing is cheap and cheesy, where it looks old and haggard after only a few years of occupation. The structure settles. Windows let in draughts. Walls crack. Doors stick. She'd battled the shortcomings with paint and bright colours, carpets, family photographs on tables.

She sat David down at her kitchen table and gave him a glass of orange juice while she made him coffee, eggs, hash browns, bacon, toast.

'You going to tell me about this email or not?' he said as she set a vast plate of food in front of him.

She wiped her hands on her apron and went into the living room for her laptop.

'You eat too fast,' she said, setting it down on the kitchen table across from him. 'I got plenty more here. Want some?'

David shook his head, turned the laptop, scanned the short paragraph.

Lillian, what am I going to do? Somebody's trying to kill me. I don't know who. I don't know why. I had everything under control. Except maybe . . . Don't tell Grandma. She'd be furious. I want David Marion. I need him. How can the bastard be dead? How can he do that to me?

* * *

There were times when David hungered for the simplicities of prison life. The workings are harsh, but they're finite, graspable. Outside, there's only anarchy. He'd hated the idea of Lillian and Helen as participants in the trap set for him, but with the cynicism of an ex-con, he'd entertained it. On the other hand, he knew Helen's style. He'd read her letters and her essays — high school and college both — when he'd broken into Hugh's files in the search for somebody to pin Hugh's murder on. He'd read her article in *Nature*. He'd even ploughed through her thesis on collision theory. And this thing — this email — came across as a genuine cry for help.

'Sounds nuts,' he said to Lillian.

'Sounds *scared* to me.'

'You shown it to old Mrs Freyl?'

'You just listen here at me, Mister David Marion. Miss Helen is not a flibberty-gibbet. If she says she's in trouble, she's in trouble. If she says she wants *you*, then she wants *you* — not her grandma. You gots to go over there and help her.'

'I can't even get out of the country. You know that. I'm a convicted felon.'

Lillian put her fists on her hips. 'You trying to tell me you spent eighteen years in prison and still can't get around a little regulation like a passport?'

He glanced over the email again. 'I need money.'

'I don't got no money, David.'

'No savings?'

'Well, yeah, but . . . How I know you ain't gonna just take it and run away?'

'You don't.'

'David, you got to help me out here.'

He swivelled the laptop away from him. 'I came here to look for somebody who's claiming to be my grandmother. I'll give you the information I have. You agree to find out what you can about her and you got yourself a deal.'

Lillian always kept money in a wall safe behind

the photograph of her father's grave. Sometimes cops in Springfield needed cash; her Little Andy had been in trouble all his life, and his house was one of the first places they stopped. They'd pull him in even if she asked them to wait while she went to the ATM machine down-town. She brought David $500.

'That all?' he said. 'Not going to get me very far, is it?'

She emptied out her purse on the table. He scooped up bills and change, took his jacket off the back of the chair and started out the door.

'Hey, where you going?' Lillian said, taking hold of his arm.

He turned a baffled look on her. 'London.'

'Ain't you even gonna say goodbye?'

Not even Sunday lunches with the Freyls could wash away all those years behind bars. His bafflement increased. 'What for?'

''Cause folks like it.' She patted his arm to reinforce her point. 'And anyhow,' she went on, 'you can't go to England looking like a mangy old bear or something. I got to cut that hair, and you got to shave off that beard. You go on and get started. There's Little Andy's shaving stuff in the bathroom upstairs.'

'What about this fancy meal of yours?' On the way back from the Shop 'n Save, she'd told him about Joshua, Palassia and the two lawyer children coming to dinner this night.

'I'll get your ticket online,' she said, 'then you can help me.'

But by the time he'd shaved, she'd found that all flights to London were full. He'd have to opt for a walk-on ticket. She sat him down, brought out her scissors and went to work on his hair.

'Now look at you,' she said half an hour later, standing back to survey her handiwork. 'You look practically respectable. Not *real* respectable, mind you, but *practically*. 'Cepting for that jacket and them shoes. Them pants is okay, I guess.'

She called Hiram, her oldest son, who used to chauffeur for Mrs Freyl. He wasn't anywhere near as tall or heavily muscled as David, but he was fat. He offered to donate shoes and a denim jacket. After work, by which time two apple pies were ready, the lamb in the oven, the vegetables prepared, the glasses polished, the table set — everything in order for the guests due at six o'clock — Hiram drove David 200 miles to O'Hare airport in Chicago.

# 36

## SPRINGFIELD, ILLINOIS

Lillian's dinner party didn't start well. When the doorbell rang, there stood the two lawyers alone.

'Where's your mama?' Lillian said.

'I'm afraid she couldn't make it,' said Palassia's daughter with one of those half smiles people use when they're lying and want you to know it. 'She caught the emergency evening shift at Memorial Hospital. She sends her apologies.'

Lillian was angry at once — God knows what elaborate story they'd made up to keep their mother at home — but Joshua only laughed. 'Well, well, well,' he said, 'now ain't that something? Gimme your coats.'

There was talk of the weather, the state of the roads, the morning's headlines, the sale out at White Oaks Mall. But there were too many pauses. Fortunately the lamb was so good that nobody was willing to introduce the wedding until the meat was off the table.

As soon as Lillian began to clear away the plates, Joshua leaned back in his chair. 'Well, I figure we'd better get this show on the road,' he said. His tone was amused, teasing. 'You kids don't like me much, do you?'

'Oh dear,' said the daughter with her half smile. 'I can't imagine what gave you that idea. I can assure you our likes and dislikes have nothing to do with the matter.'

'You can, huh?'

The daughter clearly hadn't expected him to take the initiative. She frowned, paused, regrouped. 'Look, we're both sorry if coming alone seemed rude, but we have to have some guarantee that our mother isn't going to end up scratching out a living on a *bee* farm. It's not just the money. They're disagreeable things. They *sting*.'

'Not if you treat 'em right,' said Joshua, thinking of the intruder who'd sent a high voltage through one of his hives.

'I see.'

'That's a start, ain't it?'

The son snorted irritably. 'You don't even own that farm, do you?'

'Nope.' The amusement in Joshua's voice deepened.

'The Freyls do.'

'Yep.'

'You work it for them.'

'Yep.'

The son shook his head. 'You see what concerns us? You're clearly an intelligent man, and you probably could have done anything you wanted with your life. But you didn't. You kept right on playing Uncle Tom to the Massa Freyls of Ilinois. Now you expect our mother to do the same.'

Joshua only chuckled, but Lillian was furious. 'Don't you dare say Joshua is no Uncle Tom,' she burst out. 'When he was fifteen years old — '

'Come on, Sister,' Joshua interrupted. 'That ain't got nothing to do about nothing. Where's that pie you promised me?'

'Well, they're gonna hear about it whether they likes it or not.'

Lillian had told the story many times. She started talking while she brought in the dessert and portioned it out. This happened in Alabama, back before Martin Luther King; schools were segregated, even drinking fountains were segregated. Joshua was in his biology class when a couple of big white cops with guns and billy sticks knocked open the door in the middle of a lesson and started shouting at the teacher. Nobody had any idea what it was about. *White* cops? In a black school? The kids were so scared they couldn't have understood even if the words had made sense.

Then the biology teacher pointed the two big white cops straight at Joshua.

They grabbed him, marched him out of the classroom, out of the school and down the street to where a group of firemen in shiny yellow suits stood around a fire engine. But they weren't doing anything except standing with hoses and nozzles and axes at the ready — and no fire in sight, not even any smoke. There were a couple of squad cars too, and some cops standing around looking as fidgety and aimless as the firemen.

Joshua was so scared, the cop had to say it twice. 'What we gonna *do* about these fuckers, boy?'

All over the road were bees. Nothing but bees.

A thick carpet of them buzzing and milling around all over each other. In the middle, there was an odd-looking hive — an off-green in colour — that had fallen down out of the tree above.

'Your teacher says you got a nigger way with animals.'

Joshua had been so sure they were going to lynch him that it took him a moment to catch his breath. 'What you want me to do?'

'Well, how the fuck am I supposed to know, kid? Get 'em back in the hive, I guess.'

Young as he was, Joshua had kept a swarm for years. His family had farmed bees ever since the Emancipation; several Brewsters owned small-holdings around Caton. He'd known all the species since he was five — *cerana, dorsata, florae, mellifera* — but his interest had gone well beyond the family business. When he was ten, he'd started ordering books on apiary from the library. He'd learned the flight patterns and dances of dozens of varieties. But he'd never seen any like these before.

'Don't make no sudden movements, huh?' he said.

'Yeah?' The cop wasn't putting on any pressure. Joshua could see that he was scared too.

Joshua took a deep breath, then gingerly, going slow, easy, steady, he walked right into the carpet. The bees pulled back to let him pass like Moses and the parting of the Red Sea. When he reached about the middle, he bent down, put a finger in front of the one giant bee in the swarm

— the queen herself — gently urged her forward into the palm of his hand, then put her into the hive.

There was a moment of dead silence, everybody absolutely still, bees included. Then a whoosh — and they all swarmed back inside after her.

'Well, fuck me,' said the cop in wonder.

'What you gonna do now?' Joshua asked him.

'Douse that fucking thing with gas and burn it.'

Joshua couldn't keep his mouth shut. He knew better. Of course he did. 'You really got to do that?' he said. 'They's special bees. I *know* it. They's something . . . I don't know. They's *different*. Let me take 'em home with me.'

'Now you *are* kidding.' Joshua shook his head. The cop burst out laughing. So did all the other cops and the firemen. Joshua stood there until they finally calmed down. 'Okay, kid,' the first cop said, 'but I'm telling you, just one of them fuckers flies out and we gonna have us a nigger roast as well as a bee roast. Ain't that right, boys?'

But not one bee did fly out, and Joshua had farmed those bees ever since.

* * *

'It's a very impressive story,' said Palassia's daughter. 'But I want my mother to be able to retire and be comfortable. I'd like her to have some money to spend.'

This time Lillian really lost her temper. She

had to clench her teeth to keep herself from asking why they didn't give their mother some of their big salaries if they were so worried about her welfare, but instead she blurted out: 'Miss Helen, the way she figures it — she's real smart — she'll make Joshua rich. Real soon too. They got UCAI sniffing around the farm.'

The son laughed. 'UCAI?' he said. 'At a *bee* farm. Tell me another.'

'Why not? Honey's good business.'

'UCAI owns oil fields and uranium mines, my dear lady. They make materials for Stealth bombers.' The son laughed again. 'What would possibly induce them to stoop to jars of *honey*?'

'You got no respect, know that?' said Lillian. 'You just listen here at me. A bunch of fancy lawyers from St Louis made an offer for that there farm. Miss Helen turned them down. Then they wants to buy exclusive rights to the venom, and they's gonna pay just as much for it than they's tossed on the table for the farm. Her grandma says, 'We gots to find out who these people is', and she tracks it down. It's UCAI. Miss Helen turns 'em down again.'

'She wants a higher price,' said the lawyer son. Lillian kept her mouth shut and watched him finish off his last bite of pie. 'Now we know where we stand. She's getting ready to sell the farm. Joshua will be out of a job, and my mother will be on the streets. I'm very glad we had this conversation.' He got up from the table. 'I think we're done here.' His sister got up too.

By now Lillian was fit to be tied. She could have cut her tongue out afterwards; Helen had sworn her to secrecy, and Lillian had never told one of her secrets before. 'Ain't nobody can handle them bees except Joshua. Miss Helen made us all sign a paper saying if'n there's a sale, he keeps working the bees hisself,' she said furiously. '*And* he gets half the money. We done it in a lawyer's office, so it's all right and legal. I don't know what Miss Helen's got in her head, but whatever it is, it don't include nothing UCAI done offered yet.'

'How long ago was that?'

'The letters done come straight to the farm last spring.'

'Nothing since?'

'She don't tell me *all* her business.'

'She's just plain stupid,' said the son. 'She's lost her chance. You get a good offer, you take it. Where'd you put our coats, Joshua?'

Lillian exploded. 'You're the one that's stupid. Mrs Freyl's got appointments next month with Pfizer, Ciba-Geigy — even Wal-Mart. They's gonna have a bidding war, and one of 'em's already put $50 million on the table for them bees. Joshua's gonna be the richest man your momma's ever gonna hope to snag.'

# 37

## LONDON

The drifting awake began okay, then reached an odd, empty plateau. One more layer and Helen knew she'd be lucky if she made it to the washroom in time. She bolted out of bed — hand pressed over her mouth — and scrambled across to it. When the gagging finally eased, she sat back, breathless, faint, hanging on to the toilet bowl, steeling herself for the return to the bed.

Even Becky teased her about how badly she held her liquor, but she'd never been like this before. How long had she stayed at that hotel bar next to the café where she'd taken refuge? How many of those Black Velvets had she drunk when she got there? She had no idea on either point. All she could be sure of was that champagne and stout make a deadly mixture.

She pulled the covers over her pulsating ache of a head and mapped out the day's programme. Lie still. As soon as a mouthful of water stays down, try to sleep until the next one. And then? The long term? The solution that had seemed next to impossible last night was the obvious one. Forget all the overexcited nonsense about followers sneaking around after her. Go back to the house in Notting Hill as soon as her stomach permitted, get her passport, fly home to Springfield. Turn the negotiations over to Becky. Entirely. All of them. To hell with it. Helen was trained in physics, not business.

She'd never been so ashamed in all her life. What weird hysteria had gripped her last night anyhow? Feodor couldn't have been murdered. Of course not. This was England. He was a teacher of calculus at a naval college. Nobody murdered people like that. Nobody was chasing her either. How could she have convinced herself of all that stuff?

On the other hand . . . No, she wasn't going to think that way. It was too stupid. She'd let herself get so scared and so drunk she'd emailed all her nonsense to Lillian, and there wasn't a damn thing Lillian could do even if there'd been any truth to it. Whereas, Emilia did make some kind of sense. She was deep enough in conspiracy theory to believe what Helen was saying, and nobody would look for her here even if there were something to her fears.

'Which there isn't,' she said to herself firmly.

Most of the inhabitants of this east London area were gone — Belarusians like Emilia along with the city's other cast-offs — and the battalion of machinery across the street would have soon completed demolishing the factory that had once turned out 100 million bricks a year and employed so many. Emilia and her neighbour were the last residents left in this building; they'd both been looking frantically for somewhere else they could afford to live. In a few years, duplex apartments for the rich would replace the eerie fairyland of straw mobiles Helen lay in.

Emilia had done the decorating, but this was her neighbour's apartment. Emilia lived next door; that's where the straw unicorn shared a table with the tea urn. The two neighbours had welcomed Helen last night as though she were a sister even though she was drunk and disgusting. They'd helped her undress, put her to bed in the neighbour's apartment and gone to sleep at Emilia's so that Helen could make her ignominious recovery in private.

Work on the old factory site began before dawn with the bleeping that vast machines make when they go backward. Demolition started a few minutes later; Helen barely heard Emilia and her neighbour making breakfast and leaving for work. The day passed in a haze of banging and drilling, her water intake increasing to a quarter of a glass, then half. By the time the racket stopped and she heard Emilia return, she could keep down a full glass.

The rain began then; she must have gone to sleep to pattering on the window because it was night when she heard movement from Emilia's apartment again. She was starving and much, much better, but she felt dirty, soiled more by drunkenness and shame than a day without a bath. This apartment had only the washroom; Emilia's shower served both her and her neighbour. Helen tossed on her raincoat as a robe over the nightdress Emilia had loaned her, stuck her feet in her shoes and crossed the hall. The door to Emilia's apartment was slightly ajar.

Helen assumed it had been left open for her and gave it a gentle push.

The man's back stopped her cold.

She gaped at him for a second before she realized that his trousers were part way down his body, his white, muscular buttocks thrust forward and clenched so tight the cheeks were hollow. He was pumping away with his hands, head thrown back, right on the verge of his ecstatic grunt-sigh. Helen was not a screamer. Which was fortunate because Emilia's face was staring out at her from between his feet, eyes protruding like billiard balls, swollen tongue stuck out through purple lips.

The body to one side of him must have belonged to her neighbour.

Helen spun around and ran down the stairs. They were too rickety for silence, and Emilia lived on the top floor. As she reached the bottom, she heard Bare Ass start down after her. The street was empty, deserted, not a person, not a car, nothing but boarded-over storefronts and the entrance to the demolition site with a crane blocking the way. She ran across to it, squeezed past and stumbled into the wasteland of churned-up ground where brick kilns used to burn at 1000°C all day and all night. The machinery she'd heard from Emilia's stood there, glistening orange from arc lights and the day's heavy rain. Puddles shone in tyre tracks. The remains of a hangar-like building loomed ahead of her, windowless, roofless, steel support rods dangling from it like shreds of muscle from a ripped-off arm.

Mud sucked at her shoes as she ran towards the ruin. She slipped down an incline to its side and clambered up a debris-covered slope beyond. A huge amorphous shape between it and another wrecked building turned into a hillock of cast-off tyres, thousands and thousands of them. She crawled up the rubbery mass, but lost her footing and slid down in among them, started to struggle out, then shimmied further down, pulling her body into a foetal position and praying the mountain wouldn't collapse inward.

There was a moment of stillness before she felt the tyres tremble under Bare Ass's feet. Another moment and she could see the beam of his flashlight scanning back and forth across her view of the sky.

'C'mon, c'mon, c'mon.' His voice was high-pitched even though he spoke through his teeth. 'Where are you, lass? C'mon, c'mon.'

He stood there awhile, flashlight beam strafing back and forth, then she felt him half-slide, half-fall down the other side of the heap.

Faint sounds in the night are so hard to gauge. Was that his breathing? Or was it hers? Was he waiting to see what she might do? Did he think she'd managed to get herself to the far side of this barrier? Could those be footsteps going away? Or was it just the sound of rain starting up again?

She'd left her watch behind at Emilia's along with her clothes and her handbag, but she carried her mobile in an inside pocket of her raincoat. She eased it out. She didn't dare use it — he'd hear — but at least she knew what time it was: 11.30. The clouds broke long enough to reveal the moon edging into view on one side of her burrow, then closed over as before. Rain fell harder. She buttoned her coat and pulled the collar up around her neck, but water still dribbled down her back, soaking Emilia's nightdress, and into her shoes. The time was 11.34. Her nose ran. Her knees began to ache. The time was 11.36.

She watched the minutes creep by. At 12.13, she eased up through the tyres far enough to see across the top of them. No flashlight. She eased up further and waited again, sniffing the air like some rabbit at the door of its hutch. The rain grew heavier. She slipped and slid her way down the tyres, then ran back towards the debris-covered slope, up to the front of the ruin and past the crane that blocked the entrance to the demolition site.

As she reached a desolate street, a taxi was rounding a corner only a block away. She flapped her arms with all her might. It pulled up, and the window rolled down.

'You okay?' said the driver, leaning out to take a better look at her. He was grizzled, pale-skinned, pouchy beneath the eyes and around the jowls.

Helen opened her mouth. Nothing came out.

'You'd best get in,' he said. 'Try to keep the mud off the seat, okay? Want to go to the station?'

She was terrified, wet, dirty, shivering. 'Are you nuts? Do I look like I'm on my way to the Lake District or something?'

'You want to make a complaint to the police or don't you?'

What was left of her composure snapped, and her voice slid off on a tangent. 'What the fuck do you care?'

He slammed on the brakes. 'Get out.'

'What?'

'There's no call for that kind of language.'

'Language?' Only then did she realize what she'd been saying to him. 'Oh, God, I'm sorry. I didn't think . . . I'm just . . . well, you can see, can't you? I'm truly sorry. I'll be good. I promise.'

He turned around. 'You're American, aren't you?' Helen nodded. 'On holiday?' She nodded again. 'Lost your way? Got into trouble?'

'Couldn't you take me to the centre of London?'

He turned back to the wheel. When the meter reached £30, he turned once more. 'I don't want to be rude or nothing,' he said, 'but won't you be wanting to go somewhere? I mean, it's late.'

Helen's knees and hands burned from the debris-covered slope she'd climbed. Her heels burned too. Blisters probably. But she could hardly go to her own house. If Bare Ass had gone back to Emilia's, he'd have found her handbag. He'd know where she lived.

'The Basil Street Hotel,' she said.

The Basil's entrance was a small foyer. A few steps led up to the desk with a big brass bell that brought a concierge during the day and a night porter at an hour such as this. Opposite the desk a few steps more took her to the glass enclosure of reception. She opened the door. The manager, a small, pin-striped, black-haired man, sat at work over accounts.

'Ah, dear Dr Freyl!' he said, looking up from the ledger in front of him. 'What a pleasure to see you again.' He rushed from behind the counter, completely unfazed by a client showing up at night unannounced, filthy, soaking wet, a threadbare nightdress straggling out from beneath her raincoat. 'Have you come to stay with us? Wonderful. Wonderful. But you do not look well, Dr Freyl.' The British are known for their cool, but the Poles — and the manager was a Pole — outdo them every time. 'Do your shoes, er, need a polish?'

Helen was carrying them in one hand, holding them out from her like dead rats. 'I have no money,' she said, 'and I have a taxi outside waiting to be paid.'

He picked up the intercom at once. 'Joseph,' he said to the night porter, 'take care of Dr Freyl's taxi.' He set down the receiver. 'You need a room for tonight, Dr Freyl?' She nodded gratefully. 'And — please forgive me for asking — do you perhaps need to consult a medical person?'

'Do I? Why? I don't think so.'

'I believe it would be best, Dr Freyl. You are bleeding.'

'Am I?' Helen put her hand to her forehead, felt something damp, was puzzled to see the red on her fingers when she took them away. 'Look, this may sound crazy,' she said, letting out a sigh that even she could hear was dangerously close to a sob, 'but I not only need a room, I have to make sure nobody knows I'm here.'

'Ah, you wish privacy.'

'And there are people I don't want to see.'

'If you give me their names . . . ' But Helen was shaking her head. 'You are not entirely sure who they are? Ah, I understand perfectly. Perfectly.'

The 'medical person' turned out to be an unflappable doctor in a three-piece suit, who cleaned and treated the blisters on her heels as well as cuts, scratches, grazes on arms, legs, hands, face; he gave her some Valium to help her sleep. A chambermaid took away the filthy raincoat and exchanged it for nightgown, robe, toothbrush, comb and bowl of soup. Helen ate, bathed, took a couple of the doctor's tablets and went to bed. Useless. She only tossed and turned. The rest of the Valium shut her away in a land of bare-assed men, mountains of tyres and that terrible face of Emilia's.

By four in the morning, she was wide awake again despite the pills. She shook the Valium bottle. Empty. Why are English doctors so stingy?

She pulled the telephone off the bedside table and dialled Lillian's number.

'I'm so sorry I sent you that email,' she began before Lillian had a chance to speak. 'I wanted you to know I'm okay.'

'I been trying to call you — '

'God, it's good to hear your voice.'

' — all day. Last night too. Miss Helen, I got

something real important to say. You setting down?'

'Is it Grandma? Don't tell me you showed her that email.'

'Don't you worry none. What I got to — '

'She's okay, isn't she? She's got to be all right. What am I going to do if — '

'Miss Helen, will you shush up? You ain't letting me get a word in edgeways. I'm talking about David.'

'David?'

'I done found him.'

'You know where he's buried?'

'Miss Helen, you ain't listening. I just had David Marion setting right here beside me only yesterday. He ain't dead at all. He's as alive as you and me.'

# 38

## DUBICZEWO, BELARUS

The strange weather patterns of the summer ended in an abrupt collapse of the heat all over Europe. The Mobile Clinic's thermometer dropped to 15°C not long after lunch. By evening, it plummeted to zero. Frosty ground crunched under Kamilla Sapega's feet as she crossed the encampment to the tent where the female volunteers slept.

There were seven women inside. 'Roll call,' Kamilla cried. She spoke the pidgin English that was the only common language at the Clinic, and twice-daily headcounts were part of the Follaton Medical Foundation's careful watch on its foreign helpers.

A glance was all it took for her to see that she was not going to be able to check every name off her list.

'Rosemary?' she said.

A burst of giggles was her only reply.

'Is not funny. Say where.'

The volunteers shook their heads, giggling still.

'Nobody sees her?'

'She go with James,' said a Greek woman.

'James? You see her?'

'Yes,' said an Italian.

'When?'

'Lunchtime.' The Italian held up her blanket and gestured at it. 'She take-a dee . . . '

Well, that certainly clarified matters. Rosemary, that good-looking James and a blanket. Kamilla frowned. Why couldn't these English girls keep their legs together? Kamilla was plump and dark, with the beginnings of a moustache, perhaps forty-five years old. The first time she'd seen Rosemary, she'd felt a pang of envy near her heart. Red hair and deep brown eyes, a come-hither laugh and peaches and cream for skin. It wasn't fair.

'I go check men,' Kamilla said.

But Rosemary wasn't in the men's tent either. Nor was James. The mess tent was empty. So were the research tents and the portable toilet.

Kamilla dawdled on her way to tell Dr Tatiana's replacement about the missing English couple. Dr Zukim tended to giggle as happily as the volunteers at antics like these, and Kamilla didn't approve. But she needn't have worried. He was stern-faced as he listened to her report. He seemed weary, tense, angry. He told her to leave it in his hands; to her surprise, he said he'd inform the Foundation in London at once. As she left, he added that perhaps Rosemary and James would turn up for breakfast in the morning, but there was little conviction in his voice.

They didn't turn up. When they weren't back by noon, he called the mayor of Dubiczewo. A search party formed. As it approached the Lowieza Woods, Rosemary and James came stumbling out of the trees.

* * *

Back in London, Jeffrey Hardcastle had ordered Dr Tatiana's replacement as soon as the report came through of Rosemary's disappearance into the woods. He'd spent a restless night worrying that Dr Zukim would make a mess of his very simple duties — call the mayor, form a search party, report the return of the two missing teenagers — before Gabriel Walker took over.

Gabriel was already in Belarus; he'd arrived the morning after Rosemary had. When the go-ahead came through from Jeffrey, a government car picked him up and took him to an army heliport in Minsk. He landed late in the evening on a cleared stretch of road just beyond the Mobile Clinic's tents in Dubiczewo.

Dr Zukim ran out to meet him. 'Ah, Mr Walker,' said the doctor in stilted English. 'Is good you here.'

'Let's get this over with,' Gabriel said.

'Refreshment? Glass of tea with lemon?'

'I have work to do first.'

'Please?'

'Take me to the goddamn patients.'

Any of the Mobile Clinic's tents could be pressed into service if they were needed for an outbreak of flu or mumps or scarlet fever. The director led him to the research tent where Rosemary and James had been working only the day before. The research tent's equipment — microscopes, computers, Geiger counters — stood on the floor. Two trestle tables, topped with air mattresses, served as beds.

'Leave us,' Gabriel said.

'Please?'

'Go! Scram! Beat it!'

Dr Zukim scurried away.

Rosemary and James were not a pretty sight. Their bodies were swollen beneath thin coverlets. Water-filled blisters hid cheeks and ears. Skin peeled away from raw flesh beneath. They moaned, too weak to scream any more, and the plea in their eyes was only for relief from pain. Gabriel scanned the dark red hair spread out across white linen bedclothing. How could it have intrigued him so? It looked like an animal's pelt tossed down on the pillow beside the eviscerated beast itself.

Gabriel was good with his hands, well trained, quick: the fascinating transition from alive to dead was as delicate as the snapping of strands in a spider's web. He stood there for a minute to ensure that his work was done, then closed their eyes in tribute to it.

He washed the debris from their burns off his hands at the portable basin that Rosemary had used herself only the day before in preparing slides for her microscope.

* * *

The following morning, Gabriel made his way back across the compound to Dr Zukim's office in the Mobile Clinic. Kamilla awaited him there, her ankles primly crossed, her arms held close to her plump body.

This was the office where Dr Tatiana had first

treated the young leukaemia patient Boris, but it had been orderly then; she'd kept tight control over the paperwork. Not so Dr Zukim. He was well known among the villagers for losing records even when they were on the desk in front of him, and the desk was always spotted with lunch, yesterday's if not today's. Gabriel wiped it off in disgust. The lack of squeamishness he exhibited in his killing didn't extend to driblets of soup on his work surface.

'Gregor Mihailovich Buznov,' the volunteer paramedic called out from beyond the door.

A farmer in a tattered tunic scuttled into the room, clutching a bag of cabbages and glancing nervously out the window. An empty road stretched into the distance under an inch or so of snow, as straight as any of the roads in Illinois, not a vehicle in sight. A straggle of villagers squatted in the middle of it, one with a basket of potato pancakes, another with a pig leashed on a rope, a third with a pouch of home-cured tobacco. They were waiting for a bus to Ludnigrad, where a market was held once a month. The farmer wanted to be on that bus. More than that: he *had* to be on it.

'Sit!' Gabriel said, opening a spiral-bound book.

Kamilla translated.

The farmer sat, then grunted answers to questions, a wary eye on that road outside. Yes, he'd been a member of the search party that found the two young English people. Yes, they had both seemed sick. How? The farmer spoke slow. He spoke loud. He said what he'd already said several times in several ways — and *still* the foreigner couldn't get it.

'Is only ignorant peasant' — Kamilla's cheeks were burning — 'is use very coarse language.'

'I can take it.'

'He, er, he mean, 'They are not well.''

'How?'

The farmer belted out his words in a staccato shout. Kamilla steeled herself. 'Much, er, being vomit.'

'Did they say anything?'

The farmer shrugged and got up from his chair.

'Tell him to sit *down*,' Gabriel said. 'Ask him if they seemed to know what'd happened to them.'

'I ask this before. He have no answer.'

'Ask again.'

The farmer edged towards the door, shouting louder. ''They funny in head,'' Kamilla translated. ''They say, 'Raid, raid, raid.' And they say, 'Shun, shun, shun.' Is stupid boy and girl. Like all foreign peoples.'' Kamilla enjoyed delivering that last shot — and noticed Gabriel did not write it down.

The next interviewee was an ancient woman with no teeth and a stare as hostile as the farmer's. She had jars of last year's rowanberry jelly to sell at Ludnigrad, and she was certain she could see the bus on the horizon.

''Vomit? Is no vomit,'' Kamilla translated. ''Skin for faces is'' — Kamilla struggled to find an appropriate word — ''not *well*. Boy's skin. Girl's skin. Very' — how you say? — 'with burn?

Much burn. Skin all big. Like jelly bag. No words.''

Then came a rake of a man with a wisp of a beard.

''Boy and girl talk, talk, talk,'' Kamilla translated. ''Say many things. Many secrets. For $100 American I tell everything.''

'You speak English?' Gabriel asked. The blank look was enough of an answer. 'So you're saying both the boy and the girl spoke to you in Belarusian?'

The man nodded vigorously. ''Good Belarusian,'' Kamilla translated. ''*Very* good. *Many* secrets. For $50 American, I tell everything.''

Dr Zukim was the last interviewee. He arrived with an English/Russian dictionary, and Kamilla left.

Gabriel closed his notebook and put it away. 'What's the story going around the Clinic?' he said.

'Rosemary, James: they went into woods for . . . ' The doctor giggled. 'She pretty girl. He pretty boy. Is natural.'

'Any letters home since they met?' Gabriel asked.

The doctor shook his head. 'In woods, alone, they do — ' He opened his dictionary and bent over it.

'Never mind the word. Get on with it.'

The doctor looked up, somewhat peeved. 'I like improve my English.'

'Practise on somebody else,' Gabriel said.

'Please?'

'Just give me the story.'

'Rosemary say that men come. They hold her down. I examine. She have bruises, cuts. James too. Clothes smell of ether.'

'Jesus. Anybody else in on this?'

'I tell everybody Rosemary hal . . . ooo . . . sin — '

'*Everybody*? Who the fuck is everybody?'

'In Clinic only I and Kamilla Sapega speak English good.'

'Weren't we clear enough for you? You didn't write any of this down in some kind of report, did you?'

'No. Never.' The doctor looked horrified at the thought.

'The Sapega woman heard all this? Saw the kids?'

The doctor nodded. 'Is not very intelligent lady. She think smell is English cleaning fluid. She say, 'Weather is cold.' She say, 'Rosemary and James find boxes, get close so can stay warm and do business. Business get' — how you say? — 'maybe little bit strong.''

''Strong'? You mean rough?'

'Yes. 'Fall asleep after'.'

'Think she told anybody about the other stuff? The men?'

'Nobody to tell. She is sad lady. She have no friend.'

Gabriel sighed irritably. 'What about the boy?'

'Too much pain to speak.'

'Even when you got him back here?'

'Please?'

'Did he say anything later?'

'Little bit speak, not much. He say men wear

radiation suits. Kamilla Sapega does not hear this.'

'You sure?'

The doctor nodded. 'She must talk to other volunteers. They are scared.'

'Who found the boxes?'

'Is not *boxes*. Is' — a flutter through the pages of his dictionary — 'Ah: kar . . . nist . . . ter. This is correct. Is canisters. Six canisters.'

'You're going to hear from English reporters. What are you going to say about them?'

'Canisters are warm. Frost melts in big circle all around. Is interesting for me. I read about in books, but not *see* this symptoms before.'

'They might well ask you for a diagnosis.'

The doctor nodded. 'Acute radiation poisoning. Very high dose. *Very* high.'

* * *

Dr Zukim led Gabriel out the front doors to the government helicopter that still awaited him.

'You will see parents in England?' the doctor asked.

'Not my job, thank God.'

'You wish me to . . . ?' The doctor trailed off.

'What?'

'Facilities in Dubiczewo: very limited, Mr Walker.'

'Jesus, do what has to be done.'

'I not have instructions.'

'Just get rid of the bodies, for Christ's sake.'

# 39

## LONDON

At eight in the morning, the chambermaid at the Basil Street Hotel arrived with a box that contained underwear, cosmetics and as pretty a dress as Helen had seen in ages, a ruffle at the neck, lightweight, a clinging material like crêpe.

'How did you do this?' Helen said to her in amazement, checking it out in the bedroom's mirrored closet. The fit was perfect. 'What is it? 1930s? Is it real?'

The chambermaid lowered her eyes. 'I can tell ladies' sizes.'

She'd brought back the raincoat too, washed, cleaned, pressed. She'd even recharged Helen's mobile. Lillian had said she couldn't be sure what plane David had caught, but he'd get to Helen as soon as he landed. At 8.30 her mobile signalled a message:

Where??????????????????????

That's all. Only a number as the sender.

Helen knew those question marks. Mobile phone technology all too often goes screwy outside its country of origin, and David's would be American. Her own had done that exact same thing; she'd tossed it out and bought an English model.

She texted back at once:

Basil street hotel knightsbridge

She figured twenty minutes for him to get out of the airport — he'd have no luggage (she was certain of it) — twenty minutes for the Heathrow Express to Paddington station, twenty minutes to find the hotel, maybe twenty more of waiting around in between. By nine — just to be on the safe side — she was sitting in the upstairs reception room.

She ordered toast and two pots of coffee, all too aware that however lousy last night's Valium had been in getting her to sleep before her talk with Lillian, it was clogging her brain now. Helen couldn't even remember saying goodbye to her.

But that had to be excitement as much as anything else.

David alive! How could such a miracle happen? Helen was going to see David again. How could she have waited until morning? How could she wait another twenty minutes now? She tried to reconstruct his face in her mind, but the harder she concentrated, the further his features slipped away from her. Why couldn't she remember faces like normal people? How could she be so dim-witted? The cheekbones: how high were they? How widespread were the eyes? Did the mouth curl at the corners? She watched the hands of a clock across the room jump sluggishly from one minute to the next — and began to worry that she wouldn't recognize him at all.

On the other hand he was something like six feet five. That should be enough of a clue even for her.

Clients of the Basil read *The Times* or the *Daily Telegraph*, most certainly not the *Daily Mail*. But a Fellowship that involves the public face of science — especially when it concentrates on a prominent medical foundation — involves knowing what the papers say. She'd got used to skimming them all. They sat in a heap beside her, and she began going through them systematically in an attempt to bully time into speeding up. The *Daily Mail* was the third she came to. Its front page was no more than an uglier slant on the Cabinet shuffle that preoccupied the others, but a headline on the next page stopped her piece of toast midway to her mouth.

**Two young Britons die in Belarus**

> Rosemary Figgis 18 and James Smith 19 died yesterday in Belarus . . .

Rosemary? Dead? In Belarus? What was she doing in Belarus? What *could* she be doing there? Helen had seen her only last week, working the Foundation's front desk as usual. Despite suspicions about the Foundation, Rosemary's heart had remained set on going to Belarus. That was the most puzzling part. Why hadn't she been bubbling over with it? The very fact that she hadn't been, meant they must have sent her there on some kind of emergency basis.

An 18-year-old? With no experience? Sent on an emergency basis? To Belarus?

Helen didn't hear the waiter approaching her, and she jumped at his voice. 'Excuse me, madam,' he said. 'Oh, dear, did I startle you? I do apologize.' He was Portuguese, mid-thirties, as punctilious as Wooster's Jeeves; she knew him from her stay of last spring. 'May I ask, madam, might you be awaiting a visitor? I believe — '

But she was running down the stairs to the lobby before he could finish his sentence.

In other circumstances such a double-take would have been funny. Not in this one. It was Charles who strode towards her with his arms stretched out.

'Helen, my dear girl,' he said.

* * *

The shock of seeing him made Helen's skin go prickly. All she could think of was Emilia's face with its billiard ball eyes and black tongue protruding.

'What have you done to yourself?' he said. 'Have you had some sort of accident? Have you seen a doctor?' Helen opened her mouth to speak but could think of nothing to say. 'I came as quickly as I could,' he went on. 'The traffic is horrendous. I tried everything yesterday, your mobile, landline, email, because — '

'Because of Rosemary?'

'Such a terrible, terrible thing, Helen. I didn't want you to read about it in the papers, and clearly you have. Yesterday I had Jeffrey combing the streets for — '

'Jeffrey?' She could almost see that warning shake of Emilia's head at the boardroom lunch on her first day in London, right back at the beginning.

'He's usually good at finding people. Not you, though. Then I thought, 'Why not try a text?' It took me ages to compose one, and then some idiot button erased most of it. Never mind. You have no idea how relieved I was to get your answer. That silly little manager insisted you weren't here at all.'

'I want to go home.'

'Of course you do. I'll take you there at once.' He put a protective arm around her shoulders.

'No, no. I want . . . I need some air. I want to walk.'

'I'll walk with you.' He turned to see the Basil's manager hovering, hands clasped in front of him. 'Is there something you want?' he said.

'Is everything all right, Dr Freyl?' asked the manager.

She gave him a quick but fearful glance. 'I left my purse and my coat upstairs.'

'I'll fetch them at once,' said Charles.

'This morning is ladies only on the first floor, sir.' The manager was polite but firm. 'I cannot allow a gentleman. I would fetch Dr Freyl's coat myself, but not even I am allowed.'

'Rubbish. I saw several men going up myself.'

Helen had been sitting across from a whole table of them — to say nothing of her waiter. But the manager's patience took on a steely edge.

'Michael will help you flag a taxi, while Dr Freyl fetches her coat. Michael! Henry!' He clapped his hands. Two large porters appeared at once.

Charles's moment of consternation gave her the chance to pull away from him and run up the stairs to the lounge. She'd go back to her room. Call Springfield from there. Becky could pull some strings. She was good at that, an emergency passport, a flight home on a private jet. Or something. Helen grabbed her coat and turned towards the lift only to bump into a denim jacket.

'Excuse me,' she said.

That's when she caught sight of the face — and sat down abruptly on the table that still held her coffee cup, the remains of her toast and jam, the jug of cream.

'David?' Her voice wavered uncertainly.

How could she have thought she might not recognize him? That young but deeply etched face? The eyes like a child's awakened from sleep? The scar on the cheek? She had the feeling, thinking about it later, that they'd stared at each other for an hour before he spoke, but it couldn't have been more than a few seconds.

'I bet you have jam all over your backside,' he said. She'd heard the rasp in that voice in her dreams.

'David, I've got to get out of here. Right now.'

'Stairs?'

'No!'

'Even joints like this have back doors, don't they?'

* * *

Of course there was a back door. Helen knew it well. She even knew the service stairs that went to it. When she'd first arrived in London, she'd gone to Harvey Nichols to get her hair cut — out the Basil's front door and down the street — but a mix-up in appointments had resulted in her marching off in a huff and into the first place that looked like it might do the job. She'd become a regular; her last appointment was what had made her late to Emilia's party.

The Revelation beauty salon was only 200 yards from the Basil's service entrance. A bell jangled when she opened the door. David followed her into the mirrored room with its hairdryer on wheels and mobile basin. A transvestite with shocking pink hair was sitting at a manicure table; a woman bent over his huge hands, painting his nails as shocking a pink as his hair.

'Hiya, Helen, we aren't seeing you today, are we?' she said looking up. She wore her usual badge: 'I'm Francine'. She was about Helen's age, tip-tilt nose, still pretty, but the strain of running a one-person business showed in dark circles under her eyes.

'I need your help, Francine,' Helen gasped.

'There was a bloke in here yesterday looking for you.'

'Skinny little guy? Hawk nose? Slight accent?'

'That's the one.'

Over dinner at Epidaurus Helen had often entertained Charles with tales about Francine's eccentric clientele; it was one of the first places he'd send Jeffrey to look. It was probably the first place he'd look for her today.

'He gave you them bruises?' Francine asked.

Pink Hair clucked angrily. So did the other customer, a woman with a plaster of Paris ice cream cone upside down on her head. 'I got nobody in the treatment room,' Francine went on. 'I'll put you in there. Okay?'

'What about them?' David said, tilting his head at the customers.

Pink Hair drew himself up. 'We are not blokes — at least not today. We know how to stick together.'

The treatment room was small: high, padded couch, straight chair, aluminium trolley with several angry-looking machines stacked on it, each with dials and gauges. A shoulder-height window separated it from the main area.

'You scrunch down below the window,' Francine said to Helen. 'Anybody opens the door, you're hid behind the trolley. You' — she turned to David — 'up on the couch. Come on. Up you go. Chop, chop. So what's it going to be?'

'What's what going to be?' David said, settling back.

'Acid skin peel, tinting, microdermabrasion, Botox, leg thread veins. You name it, I do it. You can't just lie here, can you?'

' 'Tinting'?' It was the one thing that didn't sound painful.

'Make your eyelashes look a treat.'

'Let's do it.'

Helen ached to touch him, hold him, breathe in the scent of him. All she could do was look; at least the mirror on the ceiling above the treatment table let her do that. She watched a puzzled expression cross his face while Francine mixed: clack of brush against aluminium bowl.

'I've never seen an ocean before,' he said.

'What did you think of it?'

The puzzlement increased. 'A lot of water.'

'The Pacific's even — ' Helen stopped short. 'How did you know where to find me?'

'You did tell Lillian you were staying at the Basil Street Hotel.'

'Did I? Really? Last night?'

''Up a flight of stairs drinking coffee,' you said. She said you sounded pretty bleary.'

'But you weren't on the stairs.'

'Elevator,' he said. His features gentled into a hint of a smile. 'I like elevators.'

Francine spread dye on his lower lashes, then the upper lashes; she gave Helen a reassuring glance and left to attend to her other customers.

'Why aren't you dead?' Helen burst out as soon as the door shut behind Francine. 'How could you do that to me?'

'Do what?'

'Disappear without a word. Just up and go. What was I supposed to think?'

The puzzled expression brought on by the Atlantic deepened to bafflement. 'I have no claim on your thoughts.'

'Yes, you do, dammit. How could you tell me to go away? I ran after you in the street, and that's what you said, 'Go away.' How could you *do* that?'

She could hear the hurt in her own voice, and she studied his face for some kind of response. Any kind of response. Could that be a flicker of concern between his brows? Was that tension in his jaw?

'You going to tell me how you got yourself all beat up?' he said.

'That's it? That's all you're going to say?'

'What more do you want?'

'An explanation. Something I can get hold of. Don't you have any feeling for me at all?'

She could see that he wasn't going to answer the question, but this time the colour in his cheeks did heighten, and she could see tension in the jaw. The trouble was, she couldn't be sure he wasn't just irritated with her. 'Look at it this way,' he said. 'You sounded like you could use some help, and I'm here. Tell me what's going on, huh?'

* * *

Helen spoke as quickly as she could, and she started quite well, she thought, explaining that her Fellowship had taken on aspects of a Public Relations job, but the next moment she found herself babbling about Emilia's black tongue and protruding eyes, the half-naked pursuer, the hill of tyres in the old brick factory site. And now this morning: Rosemary.

'I don't see why they'd send any girl that young all the way to Belarus without any notice.

She must have stumbled across something . . . something here in London. They must have . . . I can't figure out . . . It doesn't make sense. I've got myself mixed up in something way over my head. And for what? Jesus. Just to get out of Springfield for a while. How stupid can you get?' Helen took in her breath, let it out, looked at David.

His eyes in the ceiling mirror were nothing but white cotton pads. 'Who'd you say the dead woman was?'

'Rosemary was only a girl, David. She couldn't have been more than eighteen.'

'The one you saw in that apartment.'

'Follaton's cook. Her neighbour too. I don't know where she worked.'

'Now you're saying there were two dead women?'

'I think so. I barely got a glimpse of the neighbour.'

'How'd you manage to email Lillian while all this was going on?'

'Email Lillian? I didn't — No, no, I mean, none of the Emilia stuff had happened yet. She was supposed to be — '

The jangle of the door bell stopped her cold, and from the other side of the wall, she heard Francine say, 'Hiya, can I help?'

The words weren't clear, but Helen knew Charles's voice as well as she knew David's. 'Dr Freyl?' Francine went on. 'You mean Helen? Not today. There was a bloke in here yesterday looking for her too. What's going on? She win the Lottery or something?' Charles's words were still inaudible, but Helen could sense the arrogance in them. Francine wasn't interested. 'You could be the Queen Mother for all I care,' she said. 'Do all the snooping you want. Go on. Take a look. Oi, you missed out the till. She might be hiding in there, you know.'

'Helen!' Charles's shout easily penetrated the treatment room. 'Come out. This is silliness. Now you're really scaring me.'

He moved like a man half his age, and before she'd taken in a breath he'd opened the door to the treatment room. 'I'm looking for a girl,' he said, plainly disconcerted to find a man on the table.

'Give me time,' said David. 'I just may make it yet.'

Charles paused a moment, then slammed the door behind him.

Helen was still shaking five minutes later — still scrunched down beside the trolley — as Francine finished clearing the smudges away from David's eyes.

'I've got a bottle of gin under the counter,' Francine said. 'Think it might help?' She brought coffee in paper cups and a bowl of sugar sachets.

'How about getting up off the floor?' David said. Helen shook her head. He sat on the chair beside the trolley and poured a slug of gin into her coffee. 'That's the guy who killed the cook, right?'

Helen shook her head again.

'Where is this dead cook?'

'What difference does it make?'

'Humour me.'

'Stratford. East London. There are mobiles hanging from the ceiling, all made out of straw.'

'A house?'

'No, no. Charwell Lane is all apartment blocks.'

'What number?'

'I can't see — '

'Just give me the number.'

'It's 273. Have you ever seen a mobile made out of straw? They're beautiful, David.'

This time she knew it was irritation she was seeing on his face.

'If that guy didn't kill her, how come he's chasing you?'

She swallowed some of the gin-laced coffee, almost gagged on it, swallowed some more, then told him as quickly as she could about the compound synthesized from Joshua's venom, the drug that depended on it, the Foundation's failure to secure the patent and the game she and Becky had taken on before they realized any of this.

'Venom doesn't sound to me like good news for sick people,' David said.

'I know. I know. But it isn't just one chemical. It's a 'lead compound' in industry-speak.' She was beginning to feel dizzy even though she still sat scrunched down beside Francine's treatment table; she held herself rigid as she talked. 'Chemists tease out the bits they want and toss the rest away. Bee stings swell, hurt, itch because of the histamines. So you dump them. That leaves the useful stuff — powerful antioxidants, some protein compounds, that kind of thing.'

'How do you know yours is so much better than anybody else's? Maybe they used it for a while and discarded it. Maybe they've found some other compound to play with.'

'Oh, Christ, if that's so, how come they offered way too much for Joshua's farm? How come they — ?'

'Hey, Helen' — Francine stuck her head around the door — 'I hate to tell you this, but my ten-thirty full-body wax is waiting outside. Think you're okay to leave here now?'

Helen pulled herself up off the floor, but somehow she couldn't get her legs to work.

* * *

The next she knew she was lying in a bed — terrified again — in a room she'd never seen before, nothing familiar, not even the smells. And no David.

# 40

## SPRINGFIELD, ILLINOIS

'It came in this morning?' Becky said to Lillian, holding up Helen's email. 'It says it was sent two days ago.'

'Every once in a while,' Lillian said, 'my server starts putting things in my bulk folder and thinking it's spam.' Not *strictly* true. This email hadn't found its way to Lillian's bulk folder, even if one of its predecessors had. Lillian's loyalty to the Freyls was real but complex. Becky had rescued Joshua from ruin when she'd bought the farm for Helen. She'd helped keep Little Andy out of jail more than once. Even so, Helen's interests came first in Lillian's mind, whether serving them took a slight shift in the facts or not. 'I didn't check till this morning.'

'Why didn't you forward it to me?'

'I figured it might give you a shock. I wanted to be here.'

Becky nodded and turned back to the email. ''Somebody's trying to kill me,'' she read, then set the email down with a sharp exhale of breath that was half fear, half exasperation. 'I *warned* her, Lillian. I told her that she could *not* get too close to people *and* play them along. I fear she doesn't heed me when she should, and somehow things have got out of hand.'

'Wait till she gets older.'

Becky looked up. 'You think so?' People in town said Becky was hard as nails. Mostly it was true; she had a terrifying hold on what she thought was right and wrong, but Lillian was one of a very few who knew that her love of her family often caused her great distress.

'All young folks is like that,' Lillian said. 'My oldest — he's forty-three and all grown up now — he finally talks to me as if I'm a human — '

'Have you answered this?' Becky interrupted.

'Yes, ma'am. I asked her if she was okay.'

'Forward the reply to me at once. How can she think I'd be upset with her?'

'You *is* upset with her.'

'I dislike this reference to David Marion.'

Becky had hated every minute of his presence at her table on Sundays. She should have acted on her feelings. That was the hardest part of all. She hadn't been tough enough. The way she saw it, if she'd forced that savage out of Springfield, her only son would be alive to this day.

'Sometimes people ain't what they seem,' Lillian said. She knew Becky's feelings only too well. 'Sometimes *things* ain't what they seem.'

But Becky had work to do. 'That will be all, Lillian,' she said.

* * *

A single telephone call resulted in Googie standing on the other side of Becky's desk.

'Allandale is a very . . . well-known name in Springfield,' she said to him. A nod of acknowledgement. 'You're related to the Sheriff?'

'He's my father.'

'Law enforcement is in the blood, is it?'

'That's what my mother used to say.'

Becky had served on committees with Sheriff Allandale, a pedestrian man to her way of thinking, prim and grey; she'd never liked him, and his younger son's conviction on charges of police brutality had done Springfield no favours. Her consideration of his transgressions took a full minute of silence — she knew the power of mental elbowing — and to her annoyance, Googie began to hum.

She pursed her lips. 'Your father *wasn't* an aggressive man,' she said.

'Well, you know, I'd say that kinda depends on how you define aggression.'

'*I* define it as a man who hums into the empty spaces of a conversation.'

But she was impressed by Googie as well as annoyed. She had the feeling that if she closed her eyes she'd be unable to reconstruct him in her mind. He was perhaps late forties, average height and build. There was nothing to make any one of his features stand out in her mind or anybody else's: a store manager maybe, the kind of man few people would remember.

'I need someone discreet, efficient and highly professional,' she'd said to Jimmy Zemanski. Like her son, Jimmy knew people with what one might call 'interesting' backgrounds.

'What's it about?' Jimmy had said to her.

'I need someone *discreet*, Jimmy, because the matter is delicate, and I don't wish to discuss it with you or with anybody but this man. I require a fully qualified professional.'

He'd called Googie the moment he got off the phone with her. Googie had arrived an hour later.

'I'm prepared to pay you $2,000 a day plus expenses, Mr Allandale,' she said to him. 'I trust this is acceptable.' Jimmy had suggested she open negotiations at $5,000 a day, but Becky sensed more than professional courtesy in the speed of this arrival. She wanted to know what it was.

'Small change, huh?'

'I am entirely serious.'

'Maybe you'd better tell me what you want me to do.'

'I want you to protect my granddaughter. I want her out of danger. I want her home and safe.'

Googie was amused. 'Tell me something, Mrs Freyl, are we talking kidnapping here?'

'Whatever it takes.'

' 'Whatever it takes', huh?'

'Do you accept my terms or not?'

'I can tell you that when I've seen her email.'

Becky handed it to him and watched him carefully as he read it. Why that sudden squinting of the eyes? What could it mean?

'This is deeply distressing,' she said. 'I have tried to reach her, and I cannot. She does not answer.'

Googie handed back the email. 'It's a shame you didn't get hold of it earlier.'

'Lillian said it came in only this morning.'

'That the maid? Came in to her, did it? Well, well, what do you know.'

'Lillian would not say it had if it had not.'

'All we know for sure is that the bottom of the page says she printed out this particular copy this morning. Maybe she saw it sooner than that. Maybe she didn't. What's your granddaughter's relationship with the David guy she mentions?'

The question caught Becky off guard. 'He has no bearing on the matter.'

'Your granddaughter doesn't seem to agree.'

'Don't try to tell me my business, young man. I believe Mr Marion's present condition is 'missing, presumed dead'. Do you accept my terms or don't you?'

'Yeah, why not?'

Becky studied him a moment — and knew she'd been right to bargain hard. 'There *is* something you're not telling me, isn't there?'

Googie smiled. She could see at once why he kept his face expressionless most of the time; the smile was almost shockingly sweet — and distinctly memorable. 'Well, now, ma'am,' he said, 'I got something of a personal interest in David Marion myself. My brother ended up dead in South Hams.'

'Young Allandale? The torturer? You think David Marion was responsible.' She tapped her pencil again. 'I can't say I'd be overly surprised if you were right.'

'No, Mrs Freyl, I don't imagine you would be. But I can tell you something that might surprise you.'

Googie rocked back on his heels. Delivering

bad news is such a pleasure in life; he could only hope it shocked her as much as it had Jimmy and Clotilde before her. 'What if I told you the man himself was walking around Springfield only yesterday morning?'

The blood drained from her face. 'Fiddlesticks,' she said, but there was little conviction in her voice.

Googie gave her a moment to recover before he went on. 'I didn't have to study Marion long to figure a way to smoke him out of hiding and back to Springfield.'

Becky closed her eyes, took in her breath, opened them again. 'You've *seen* him?'

'I've had an operative at a homeless shelter on Washington Street for a while now, and he hit pay dirt: saw Marion coming, met him in front of the hostel, sent him to see some people at the Shop 'n Save on East Monroe and then called me. Trouble is, I was in Bloomington, finishing up a property deal, and by the time I got to Springfield, Marion was gone.'

'Where?'

'Dunno.' Googie rocked back on his heels as he had before. 'Not without the help of a very insistent woman, though,' he said.

'My granddaughter?' There was an abrupt urgency in Becky's voice. She leaned forward on her desk. 'What did this woman look like? Helen is back here? Is that what you're saying? She's *safe*?'

'I'm afraid not, Mrs Freyl,' Googie said. 'This woman was sixties, greying hair, an African American, medium to dark skin. Know what I think? I think it sounds like your maid. The moment I saw her at the door, I thought to myself, 'Bingo!' I figure Marion wants your maid to do some sniffing around for him. But your granddaughter's email shifts the boundaries. Now . . . ' Googie chewed the inside of his cheek. 'Well, now I'm not sure what's going on.'

Becky opened the doors of the red lacquer secretary that sat on her desk, shut them again, turned the latch. 'If you are right, Mr Allandale — if this man is indeed alive — then the situation may be even more serious than I feared. I would not be at all surprised to find that he has already gone to England to find her.'

⋆ ⋆ ⋆

Lillian knocked before she entered Becky's study. It was a house rule.

'Yes?' Becky said.

'You done rung your bell,' said Lillian, opening the door.

Becky sat at her desk as usual, the bronze bell still in her hands. 'We must have a talk.'

'You having people in this Sunday?'

Becky dismissed Sunday lunch with a wave of the hand. 'Did you pay a recent visit to the Shop 'n Save on East Monroe?'

'Yes, ma'am. I was having guests, and I needed some half-and-half.'

Becky pursed her lips. 'Did you or did you not meet David Marion in the parking lot of the Shop 'n Save?'

Lillian paused. 'I seen him.'

'But you did not see fit to tell me about this encounter.'

'You didn't ask me.'

'I am asking you now.'

'Yes, ma'am, I met him. I ain't ashamed of it neither.'

'You took this . . . this supposedly *dead* murderer somewhere' — Becky sighed and shook her head — 'and you did not see fit to mention it to me?'

'Miz Freyl, you didn't ask me nothing about it, and I didn't tell you no lies about it. I done took him to my house and give him something to eat. I got *some* business that's my own.'

'And then?'

'And then nothing. He went away, and I ain't seen him since.'

Becky shook her head as she had before. 'Did you show him Helen's email?'

'Why'd I do something like that?' Lillian was unable to hide the defiance in her voice. 'Ain't no business of mine.'

'I don't know why, Lillian. I assume you have informed her that Mr Marion is still alive?'

'No, ma'am, I ain't.' In more than thirty years of service to the Freyl family Lillian had tried to keep their interests foremost in her mind. She never told them out-and-out lies unless she had no choice.

'Mr Allandale has agreed to go to London and give Helen whatever help she needs. Perhaps you can manage to tell him the truth that for some reason it pleases you to deny me. You may go.'

Becky lifted a ledger off the neat pile on her

desk, opened it and began adding a column of figures. Lillian stayed put. A minute ticked by. Another minute. Becky looked up. '*Now* what?'

'I ain't gonna talk to no Mr Allandale.'

A pale pink tinged the grey crêpe of Becky's cheeks. 'I *beg* your pardon?'

'I ain't talking to nobody no more about *nobody*.'

'That is your final word on the matter?'

'Yes, ma'am, it is.'

Becky shut the ledger, replaced it on the pile, opened the doors of the secretary on her desk, took out a pen and her chequebook, filled out a cheque and handed it to Lillian.

'Here is a month's severance pay,' she said. 'Leave this house. Do not come back again.'

# 41

## LONDON

David had ridden on subways in DC and Chicago, but England's computer-simulated litany — 'Mind the gap. *Mind* the gap' — took him by surprise. There *were* gaps too. On his way to east London he stood at the car's doorway to check them out. Sometimes they were big enough to swallow a child whole or snap an adult's shin if a foot slipped through. What a country: why not design trains and platforms to fit each other?

David had never been out of the US before, and yet the strangeness of London unsettled him far less than Helen did. He'd expected seeing her to be difficult — but not as hard as this. He'd been certain the months away would have eased the intensity those startling green eyes provoked in him, and he didn't know how to deal with what he felt. He had to assume that any show of warmth was only a matter of shrewd business practice. She was a Freyl. Emotional manipulation came with the territory. She couldn't have helped it if she'd wanted to, and why would she want to? But it meant that she'd turn her back on him as soon as the job was done, as soon as she was safe. He just hadn't expected the assumption to hurt so much. The closest he could come to deadening it was the old prison maxim, 'Never let them see you bleed.'

Next to her, London was nothing.

He didn't even bother to open the map that had cost him all but the last £5 of Lillian's money until he'd got off the underground and climbed the stairs into the light. Orienting himself was something of a problem, but once he knew where he was, he found his way easily to the dejected block of apartments where Emilia had lived. Opposite it, machinery crawled around the demolition site. He waited while a couple of men in fluorescent yellow jackets directed an empty dump truck into it. The manoeuvres were elaborate, difficult; the street that ran between site entrance and apartment blocks was very narrow, and if a double murder had taken place here only a day ago, there should be evidence of cops milling around. There should be crime scene tapes, barriers, forensics teams with flashlights and sample bags. The entrance to the demolition site would be closed. And yet there was no sign of anything unusual.

A road sweeper appeared, lights flashing, bleeper bleeping; its brushes stirred up the layer of dust into a cloud all around it. David stepped into the entrance to the demolition site to give it room to inch its way down the street. On the other hand, if the cook and her neighbour were the last residents in the neighbourhood, it might be quite a while before anybody discovered the bodies. He crossed over to the apartment building. The lock on the door itself was a simple swipe of the laminated social insurance card

Samuel had given him, as quick a way to get in as any key.

The stairs inside certainly *felt* deserted. No voices, however muted, came from beyond the doors that were closed, no music either, no radio, no TV. No cooking smells in the hallways. Open doors revealed only empty rooms and the standard detritus people leave behind them when they move house, empty boxes, crumpled newspaper, tattered curtains at the windows. The two doors at the top of the rickety flight were shut. He knocked on one and waited. Nothing. He knocked on the other. Just as quiet. This time the lock took a heavy-duty paper clip and a few minutes' time.

He edged the door open.

The room beyond was empty. Completely empty, not even the standard stuff he'd seen in the other apartments, much less a straw mobile. Pale rectangles on the walls showed where pictures had hung. The wood-plank floor was scrubbed clean. He walked across to the window and looked out over the demolition site but didn't see any pile of tyres. The apartment's only other room was as desolate as the first had been. So were the kitchen and bathroom. The cupboards were bare too, not so much as a spare bottle cap or a loose hairpin.

There wasn't a single indication that anybody had lived here recently.

But the smell of some strong household cleaner hung over everything. And this made it likely that somebody had died here: death spews out a body's contents. Unless preparations are thorough, cleaning up afterwards can be a formidable job.

The apartment across the hall was even smaller, but a broken chair leaned against a wall and a black bag of refuse stood in front of the kitchen sink. David went through it item by item: plastic supermarket bags, a newspaper in a strange alphabet, empty cartons, a few bottles. He checked the cupboards in the washroom and kitchen.

Caught at the back of one of them was what looked like a rat's nest or the remains of a broom. He pulled it out. A few delicate triangles of straw remained intact. They'd been tied with knots he'd never seen before.

* * *

By the time David got back to the street, the men in fluorescent yellow jackets were directing the dump truck — now piled high with rubble — out of the demolition site, an even more elaborate manoeuvre than getting it in. He watched until they had it turned and safely on its way.

'That's quite an operation in a street like this,' he said to the one who had the friendliest face.

The man laughed. 'It's not exactly rocket science.'

'Could I ask you something?'

'My pleasure.'

'What do you know about those apartments over there?' David tilted his head at number 273.

'Not much.'

David hesitated. 'You didn't happen to see an ambulance or anything?'

The man shook his head, but his concern was immediate. 'You think someone's ill in there?'

David hesitated again. 'My stepmother said she'd meet me here today. Top floor. She's lived here for ages. But there's nobody around.'

'I think all these flats are for the chop.'

'She *really* didn't want to move.'

'People never do.'

David paused, glanced at the building, then launched into a detailed if somewhat disjointed story about how he'd visited this fictional stepmother only the week before and helped her knot some straw for one of the mobiles she made.

'Hang on a minute,' the demolition man said. 'I know who you mean. One of the Belarusian ladies, right? Dumpling smile? She gave me a bowl of soup — best soup I ever ate.'

'That's my stepmom.' David had had many stepmothers when he was a boy; none of them was anything other than standard American mongrel, and the state took him away from the only one who'd have brought a bowl of soup to a workman — or to a foster child for that matter.

'You try her friends? Where she works?'

'The thing is,' David said, 'you go up there, and it looks like nobody *ever* lived in those rooms.'

'You mean her *things* are gone? I saw her

myself only yesterday. No, no, I tell a lie. It was the day before.'

David brought out a pack of cigarettes, offered one to the demolition worker — who took it gratefully — took one himself and lit them both. 'Could she have had some kind of eviction notice? She never told me her problems. You didn't happen to see somebody taking stuff out or anything, did you?'

The man drew on his cigarette. 'There were a couple of blokes here yesterday — in my way for hours, they were — loading all sorts into a van. One of them was a big, fat bugger with curly hair — fancied himself something rotten. Could have been bailiffs, I guess. Never had anything to do with bailiffs myself. Never occurred to me they were after *her*.'

'How would I find out?'

The man shook his head again. 'I wouldn't even know where to start. Citizens Advice Bureau maybe? Try them.'

'I don't suppose there was a name on this van.'

'Abbey You-Drive-It. Cheap place down the road.'

* * *

The office of Abbey You-Drive-It was up a flight in a building almost as desolate as the apartments on Charwell Lane but far enough away from the site to be safe from demolition. A dirty glass door opened into a small room. The desk was a couple of planks of melamine balanced across a two-drawer filing cabinet and a saw-horse. A kid with an earring sat at it, mobile glued to the side of his head. He didn't glance up.

'Yeah. Right,' he was saying. He giggled at the response, added a growl to his voice and raised it to make sure David didn't miss a word. 'I'm in a hurry, baby. You have them knickers off by the time I — Hey you!' David had squatted down beside him and was pulling open the top drawer of the filing cabinet. 'You can't do that!'

'I need a name,' David said.

'I don't give out no fucking names.'

'Perhaps I can persuade you.'

'Who the fuck do you think you are?' The kid's fingernails were dirty. There was a pustule on his neck. But he was a pretty boy, square-jawed, brown hair with a blond-streak job on it, used to getting his way. 'Get out of my fucking drawer.'

David stood up, took the mobile out of the kid's hand and clicked it shut. 'Van rental yesterday. Fat guy. Needed something big enough to handle the contents of two small apartments.'

The kid stared at his hand where the mobile had been and then looked at David. 'Are you half-witted or something? How many times to I have to tell you I don't give out no fucking names.'

David glanced down at the file drawer. It was less than half full. He kicked it shut and pulled open the bottom drawer with his foot. Empty. 'Let's keep this civil, shall we?' he said. 'You can tell me how to find the guy, or I can cut your balls off. The choice is yours.'

* * *

The remains of Lillian's money went on a bus trip that dropped David a mile away from the Bel Aire Residential Caravan Park not far from Dagenham on the far eastern fringe of London. The trailer at the number 11 spot on Sanderson Drive was pale blue. At least it had been pale blue when it was young. These days it sagged at the axles, and its colour sagged with it. Years of mud and rain hadn't helped, but it fitted in well with the weed-infested macadam, the litter of beer bottles and waste paper, the overloaded skips and the distant skyline of wind turbines.

The front door to the trailer was open. In front of it sat a hugely fat man with curly hair, once black, now streaked grey and reaching to his shoulders. He had a newspaper open in front of him.

'Pimmson?' David asked.

The fat man lowered his paper. 'Who wants to know?'

'A friend of mine needed a delicate moving job yesterday.'

'You don't say.'

'Straw artefacts.'

'You got me, mate.'

'They hung from the ceiling,' David said. 'Ring a bell?'

'Nope.'

'There were also a couple of cumbersome

items. Needed special handling. Valuable. Not the kind of thing you'd want a lot of people to know about.' David paused. 'Or so I'm told. I could ask further.'

Pimmson put his hands on his knees. 'What *do* you want?'

'A specialty item.'

'I don't do specialty items.'

'There's money in it.'

A generation ago, Pimmson had been as good-looking as the Abbey You-Drive-It kid, and he was beginning to realize it was all gone. The laugh he let out was loud but forced. 'Well, now, I do like money. I have to admit it. What sort of thing do you have in mind?'

'I was kind of thinking a 9mm Glock. Maybe a Smith & Wesson.'

People tend to assume that practically the only variety of hand weapon prisoners can't learn how to wield inside is a firearm. But what is a gun anyhow? A tube with a controlled explosion of gas in it. Any kid can make one. So can an inmate at South Hams State Prison. Roll up a copy of *Time* magazine, soak it in Elmer's glue and you have a barrel. Granulate match heads for gunpowder. Chip off pieces of a tin can for bullets.

But the thing's unreliable. It can explode instead of firing. A real gun is a much safer proposition.

'I'll need maybe a dozen rounds,' David said. 'Not much. I'll take more if you can get it. If not, a dozen will do.'

'Look at me' — Pimmson spread his arms

— 'I'm a peaceable man, sitting in my garden, reading my newspaper. I don't know one end of a gun from another.'

'I'll pick it up tomorrow. Say five o'clock? That suit you?'

Pimmson sighed, folded his newspaper, set it on his knee. 'What are you? American or something? You don't sound American.'

'Canadian.'

'You sure as fuck don't sound Canadian either. Been here five minutes and lost your accent already? It's going to cost you.'

'How much?'

'Thousand quid.'

'Too much.'

Pimmson opened his newspaper again. 'No skin off my nose. You can take it or leave it.'

'I'll pay you five hundred.'

Pimmson shook his newspaper and went back to reading. David waited. A few minutes passed. Pimmson put the paper aside with a sigh. 'You *still* here?'

'I just offered you five hundred pounds.'

'You can't be serious.'

'Can't I?'

'Five hundred is a joke.'

'Not to me, it isn't.'

'Suppose I tell you to go fuck yourself.'

David shrugged. 'I'll have to tell my friend that you weren't polite.'

Pimmson let out his forced laugh again. 'London isn't like back home, mate. You'll have to take what *I* can get, and five hundred will only get me rubbish.'

'Seven fifty, but I want the real thing.'
'Give me a week, okay?'
'I said I want it tomorrow. I mean tomorrow. That your truck? I need a ride back to London.'

# 42

## SPRINGFIELD, ILLINOIS

It wasn't by any means the first time Lillian had been fired. Becky liked flexing muscle; it usually took her less than a week to offer a salary increase in lieu of an apology. Lillian had come to think of 'severance pay' as a synonym for 'bonus'. But this time as she stood there staring at Becky's lowered head, she was thinking maybe she wouldn't come back.

She'd always wanted to run a business of her own like Joshua, and she was the best cook for miles around. She knew it. So did everybody else. She'd spend the final batch of 'severance pay' on some of those nice pots she'd seen out at the mall. She could prepare meals in them — stews, ragouts, pot roast, entrées people couldn't hurt much if they overcooked them — and deliver them to the customer's door. She'd bring tossed salad, dressing, bread in a basket, maybe apple crumble or prune whip for dessert. All the customer would have to do was heat the pot and put dinner straight on the table.

Meals for two would be a specialty. She knew her daughter's friends in the Capitol complex liked the idea of entertaining gentlemen friends at home, but they worked nine to five — some of them far longer than that. Their lives were too busy for cooking. Her younger daughters were always complaining about it. Lillian could run up a few posters on her computer, print out some cards, pass them around.

But first, she'd go and find out about David's grandmother. She'd been shocked when he'd mentioned it. David? A family? She'd assumed there was nobody. She couldn't fit the idea of a grandmother in with what she knew of him, and she was fascinated.

'Sure, I'll look her up for you,' Lillian had said. 'If'n I can, that is. You didn't have to do no bargaining for that, boy. Any idea where she's at?'

He'd handed her the poster advertising for information about him. 'Heaven's Acre,' he'd said.

Lillian had laughed. 'Naw!'

'That's what it says.'

The drive to Heaven's Acre took Lillian through sunny countryside, trees still in leaf, an autumn chill in the air at last, the beeches a clear yellow, the maples a brilliant red. Lillian had always loved this time of year. Maybe it was the start of a new life for her. Maybe this final getting fired couldn't have happened at a better time. A few years more, and she'd be ready for a nursing home herself. But certainly nothing on the scale of Heaven's Acre.

Heaven's Acre had been around for nearly two centuries. A German family with a fortune in liquor built the estate and named it in honour of the promised lands of the Middle West. Generation after generation lived there. Becky used to ask the last of them to Sunday lunch every once in a while; he was a withered-up old man with a copper ear trumpet, and he used to accept her invitations even though he never went anywhere else. When he died, he left his money to turn Heaven's Acre into a home for old rich people like him. Lillian was certain the information on David's poster was wrong. How could *his* grandmother have got herself into a place like that? Either the woman wasn't there at all or she wasn't David's grandmother. Marion wasn't all that uncommon a name, and so many people lose family to homelessness.

The driveway to Heaven's Acre went long and straight through a double row of ancient trees to a great pile of a house, three storeys high with turrets at the corners and gargoyles staring down. A big porch ran front and sides; a couple of frail people sat on it wrapped in cashmere blankets. A wide flight of stairs led to a front door with a brass knocker and a brass bell.

'Please ring,' said a small sign.

Lillian rang.

The woman who opened the door had brown lipstick and dyed blonde hair waving up into a bun at the back of her head. 'Hello,' she said. To Lillian's surprise the voice was friendly and the smile full-blooded. 'May I help you? I'm Mrs Braithwaite.'

'I'm looking for Mrs Clotilde Marion,' Lillian said, 'but I kinda think I'm at the wrong place. You got somebody here named that?'

'Clotilde? Yes. Yes, of course we do. Have you come to visit? Oh, how very kind.'

'She been here long?'

'Less than a month. She'll be so pleased to see you. Come in.' The lobby was more elegant than any hotel's; a huge, polished table with a vase full of fresh flowers stood in the middle of it. 'She has to be lonely, although I'm beginning to realize she's something of a loner too.' The woman chattered on as she led Lillian past a huge living room with overstuffed chairs — several of them occupied by old people — and up a sweeping staircase. 'Not that I can blame her. So many of our clients aren't, well, you know what I mean.'

'No, ma'am, I don't.'

Mrs Braithwaite turned and smiled again. 'I'm afraid some of them are not quite right in the head. The only thing wrong with Clotilde is that she's in pain all the time, poor dear. No wonder she's not always sweet-tempered.'

'What's the matter with her?'

'Rheumatoid arthritis. You don't know her well?' Lillian shook her head. 'This is her room.' Mrs Braithwaite tapped on a panelled door.

'What do you want?' Behind that Illinois twang Lillian could hear the sound of her Creole friends back in Alabama.

'It's only me, Clotilde,' said Mrs Braithwaite, opening the door. 'I've brought you a visitor.'

'I don't want to see nobody.'

'Come, come, Clotilde. Enjoy yourself.' Mrs Braithwaite withdrew and shut the door behind her.

The woman in the wheelchair was certainly tall enough to be David's grandmother, Lillian thought. She had the right kind of strength in her face too. The withered skin and the wart-hog fingers — they stuck out in all directions — spoke of the pain Mrs Braithwaite had mentioned. Lillian wasn't quite sure what to do, how to establish the woman's identity. She stood there uncertainly, then caught sight of the photograph of the angry little David that Googie too had recognized at once. She walked to a chair and sat down.

'My name's Lillian Draper,' she said. 'I come about David.'

All the wrinkles on Clotilde's face jumped together. 'David? You talking about *my* David?'

'Yes, ma'am.'

Clotilde reached one misshapen finger out towards her other photograph. 'This here's my baby,' she said. 'My Fleurette, little flower of my life. How come I let her work in that rich people's kitchen? How could I a done that?'

'You don't got to tell me nothing 'cepting how come you got Miss Helen in your will.'

That had been the real shock in David's request.

'Miss Helen?' Lillian had cried when she'd read the poster he'd given her. 'What's she got to do with your grandma?'

'That's what I want you to find out.'

Before Clotilde began to talk, Mrs Braithwaite tapped on the door with an array of pills. The order of swallowing was a military procedure, and Clotilde needed to rest for a few minutes after it was over. Only then did she start.

* * *

At thirteen Fleurette was beginning the transformation: first bra, first period, long legs and arms, black hair, high forehead, full mouth. With her hair put up and a sock in each cup of that new bra, she could pass for fifteen, and a friend of Clotilde's managed to finagle her a job washing dishes at the Country Club. Hugh Freyl's twenty-fifth birthday party was the season's big event: the whole Club rented out, 200 guests, a full orchestra, a cake four feet tall. One of the waitresses got sick, and Fleurette took her place.

Hugh Freyl was a good-looking kid, but it was his cousin that caught Fleurette's eye. Frank Hogg was a Junior at Florida State and a halfback on the university football team, a big guy, so tall she wouldn't tower over him even in high heels. The first time he saw her (she was no more than a yard from him, carrying a platter of scalloped potatoes), he said, 'Jesus, Hugh, you got some awful pretty girls out here in the cornfields. Where you been hiding them all this time?'

Fleurette blushed and turned away, but she could feel him watching her. She peeked at him more openly after that, and twice they locked glances. After the second time, he got up from the table, ran after her, caught her before she pushed through the door to the kitchen.

'Hey,' he said to her, 'I bet you like the movies, don't you? I can see it in your eyes.' His cheeks were flushed, teeth white, some serious muscle on him.

'Sure,' Fleurette said.

'They're opening a wide screen out at Sangamon State tomorrow. In the new theatre. You know.' Her eyes were a pure, deep brown that glistened in the lights from the dining room, and as for the rest of her — just ripening up like that — he was barely able to keep his gaze where it belonged. 'It's real new. Hugh told me.' He stumbled in his eagerness. 'Could you come? Think so? Really?'

Fleurette was enchanted. He wasn't just a halfback, he was a Freyl. Her mind was racing. She wasn't allowed to go on dates with anybody over fourteen. She wasn't allowed to stay out later than nine, but Debbie would give her an alibi. Debbie's mother let her do whatever she wanted.

'How come you get all the breaks?' Debbie said to her. 'I suppose you want my heels and my make-up, don't you? And that black dress: you could be sixteen years old in that. Almost anyhow.'

Frank borrowed Hugh's car, picked Fleurette up at Debbie's house and headed out of town. Back then, Sangamon State University — the name of the University of Illinois at Springfield in its early days — wasn't much more than a couple of low brick buildings, miles from town, out in the middle of acres of corn higher than a man's head. Frank was telling Fleurette about Florida State, and she was so fascinated that he'd got part way down a rutted lane off the main road before she noticed he'd gone wrong.

'You don't want to go down here,' she said.

'Oh, yeah?' said Frank.

'We ain't going to find no movie theatre going out this way.'

Frank stopped the car, glanced around him at the tall corn, turned off the engine, then turned to face her. 'I think I got all the action I want right here,' he said.

'But you said — '

The slap across her face was so sudden, so hard, so unexpected; it threw her off guard so badly that she didn't even resist when he hooked his hand into the low neckline of Debbie's black dress, ripped the fabric open all the way down to the hemline, then forced his body over hers, pinning her down with his weight while he yanked her legs apart. She was a big girl, a strong one for her age, and she fought with everything she had. But he had her trapped against the car door, and the torn dress hampered her.

She didn't have a chance.

* * *

Frank returned to the Freyl house at about ten that evening.

'Good Lord, what happened to you?' Hugh said. 'Have you been in a fight?'

'You could say that.' Frank threw himself into a chair.

'Who were you fighting? A cat? Looks to me as though you got the rough end of it. Need some iodine?'

'Shut up, Hugh. I'm great.'

Hugh and Frank had been vacation companions from the time they were small boys. Becky and her brother — Frank's father — were close. Even though the boys were so different, they'd arrived at a family toleration of each other. They'd even enjoyed themselves in Chicago once with the same high-booted exotic dancer. There'd been a bit of rough stuff between Frank and her. Hugh hadn't trusted him since.

'She couldn't fight you off, could she?' Hugh stared at his cousin in disgust. 'Who was she? Not that girl you were ogling at the Club. Frank, she's only a child. What's the matter with you? She can't be fourteen years old.'

Frank shrugged. 'She's trash.'

Hugh got up from his chair, paced across the room, paced back. 'Okay,' he said. 'Here's the plan. I drive you to the airport and blame your sudden disappearance on a broken heart. We'll send your belongings later.'

Frank bolted upright in surprise. 'Hey, Hugh, come on. What do you care? It's none of your fucking business anyhow.'

'I'll find the girl and do what I can for her,' Hugh went on. 'I will urge her to go to the police and help her make a statement. You'll be safe in Florida, but if I ever so much as suspect that you've approached her again or molested somebody else, I'll make sure you're put behind bars where you belong.'

The Country Club was happy to tell the Freyl heir anything he wanted to know about anybody. He drove to the east side address they gave him and knocked on the door.

Clotilde answered. She was in her thirties back then, tall and striking like her daughter but already beginning to show the effects of years on the night shift as an office cleaner, too much liquor, too many cigarettes, too many drugs, too little sleep.

She was also very angry. 'What the fuck do you want?' she demanded. 'Ain't you rich assholes done enough?'

* * *

Clotilde shut her eyes and clenched her teeth.

Lillian waited.

When Clotilde opened her eyes again, she almost spat the words out. 'My darling come back to me bleeding like a pig. Both eyes black. Bruises all over her. I wasn't no virgin at thirteen, but she was. She spent about a week laying in bed, then one day she wasn't there when I got home. I didn't see hide nor hair of her again for nine months. Nine months! Fuck it, woman, nine months to the day, and she shows up at the door with a kid in her arms. Said he'd got born under some bridge in Cincinnati while she was high on something. Shit knows what. One day she's big as a house, and the next, she's got this kid at her tits. She don't remember nothing but pain in between.'

'The lil child was David?'

Clotilde nodded. 'Poor little fucker.'

# 43

## LONDON

A penniless foreigner in a strange city needs all the information he can get.

David had glanced over *The Times* and the *Guardian* on his way across the Atlantic; they gave him some sense of the place he was wandering around in when Pimmson dropped him in central London. But it was British Airways' in-flight magazine that told him what he needed to know. He'd read it cover to cover. He'd taken notes and reread sections to make sure he'd understood them. There were listings of museums, festivals, exhibitions, theatre-land and club-land, palaces, parks, hotels. There were articles too. One gave tips on living and travelling in England, the currency, the prices, the banking facilities. Another joked that there was no fool on earth like the British public schoolboy who's brought up to think he owns the world.

David hadn't expected the opulence of London's ancient structures to oppress him as much as the richness of Samuel's life had. But they did. The detail was so elaborate, so unnecessary, and there was so much of it. He wouldn't have been tempted to go inside any of the buildings even if he had the money for entrance fees. The people made him uncomfortable too. He avoided crowds even in Springfield, but couldn't do that here. A couple of years as an ex-con wasn't enough to erase his initial reaction to them as swarms of maggots on a corpse. He tried to concentrate on what the in-flight magazine had referred to as the city's 'extraordinary diversity': men with table cloths on their heads, men in dresses, veiled women, flocks of Japanese in blue and yellow uniforms, people feathered, beaded, parasolled. But he wasn't looking for anybody like that. He wanted to see a bowler hat on a man who owned the world, and there wasn't a bowler hat anywhere.

He wasn't in any hurry though; the dark of a night in October lasts far longer than he needed. Around eleven he wandered into Hyde Park. He walked beside the long, thin lake, then turned into one of the paths that took him towards trees and shrubbery. He emerged from a copse to see a glasshouse bursting with light in the distance ahead of him. The Serpentine Gallery? He knew from the in-flight magazine that receptions were held there. He'd plainly got his directions mixed up though because he was sure it should be on the other side of the lake, and there was no glimmer of water in front of it.

He stood watching the light for a few minutes, trying to get his bearings, and that's when his opportunity came. It nearly stumbled into him.

'Oh, I do beg your pardon,' this opportunity said to David's darkened outline. 'You *are* a big boy, aren't you?'

He never got the chance to see David's face.

He had only the sense of being roughly bundled behind some bushes, then bent double with both arms pinned to his back, the chocolate marquise — it had ended a very fine dinner — welling up in his throat. His suit was pin-striped. His tie was silk. He carried an umbrella like a cane.

David was pleased. If Englishmen refuse to wear bowlers these days, they should always carry long umbrellas. A quick pat of the pockets with his free hand revealed a mobile, a wallet, a good wad of cash, some credit cards.

'PIN numbers,' David said. The in-flight magazine had been specific; all credit cards in England needed PIN numbers.

'What?'

'Give me the PIN numbers.' David had had pen and paper ready since nightfall. 'Start with the Mastercard.'

'Two . . . no, three . . . one, two, three, four.'

'Come on, friend, is it worth it for a few hundred pounds? I don't want to hurt you if I don't have to.'

The man gave an uneven sigh. 'One, nine, ninety-five.'

'That the truth?'

'It's the year my boyfriend was born.'

'Kind of young for you, isn't he?'

'He's a sweet, free spirit of a child.'

'Now the Visa card.'

There were five in all. 'You're not going to hurt me, are you?' the man said. 'You *promised*.'

Pressure on the carotid artery renders a

person unconscious, but only for a minute or so. David worked quickly. He removed the man's coat — leaving the mobile in it — shirt, pants, underpants, shoes. He didn't bother with the socks; he'd never seen anybody wearing garters before, and he quite liked the effect. He didn't bother with the expensive watch either, and he carefully replaced the man's glasses on his nose. The umbrella caused him only a moment's hesitation, but it was cover — might give the guy an easier time of it — and those garters provided more humour than anybody could ask for.

The man was waking up as David left with clothes, mobile and umbrella in a bundle that he deposited in a skip after he'd left the park behind him.

There was probably at least an hour's grace. It was already close to twelve, and Hyde Park closes at midnight — another detail David owed to the in-flight magazine. Even if a naked man in garters manages to get through the gates before that, he's hardly likely to be in a position to call his credit card protection company at once.

The wallet turned out to have just under £200 in it. David pocketed it along with the credit cards and slipped the wallet through the bars of a street drain. Then he found an all-night store near Paddington station.

The camera in a cashpoint machine works on a direct line of sight. Approach it from the side and it doesn't see you coming. It's at the top of the machine; if a customer is wearing a sweatshirt with a hood that goes well over his head — and if he keeps his head bowed — it can't register his face. One not far from Piccadilly Circus photographed a tall, hooded man as he withdrew the maximum £300 on each of the four cards.

The machine ran short of money on the fifth.

# 44

## LONDON

Helen didn't faint. She'd never fainted, and yet the first time she came to her senses in this strange room, she bolted out of bed only to pass out again. She must have slept after that. God knows how long.

She woke to a knock on a door that opened before she'd had a chance to locate it.

'Helen?'

She twisted around to look.

'You've woken up at last! I'm Francine's mother. You know, your hairdresser. Feeling better?'

Francine's mother didn't look all that much older than Francine, but her close-cropped hair showed Francine's sure touch. The room was small, cramped, single bed, darkened, draped window with daylight at its edges.

'Is this your house?' Helen said, pulling herself up on her elbows.

'It's a hotel. I don't own it — just the manageress. Your friend brought you here yesterday. You think maybe you could — '

'Yesterday?'

Francine's mother smiled. 'I gave you something to help you sleep. You looked like you needed it.'

'You said my friend? You mean David?' Helen described him quickly.

Francine's mother sighed appreciatively. 'That's the one. He left me a telephone number to give you — '

'What is it?' Helen interrupted again.

'I've written it down for you. There's a phone by the bed. I'll get your clothes. There's coffee and toast downstairs. Think you can manage it?'

But Helen was already dialling the number. 'David?' she cried.

'Yes.' The rasp in the voice was all she needed to hear.

'It's me. Helen.'

'Yes.'

'Where are you? How are you? When can I see you?' She could hear herself babbling on, but somehow she couldn't stop. 'I'm so sorry about . . . Could it really have been yesterday? Have I lost a whole day? The collapsing I mean. I must have collapsed. I did, didn't I? I don't know what came over me. I'm not usually that . . . ' she trailed off. 'David? Are you there?'

'We need to talk.'

'I know. I know. Where do I find you?'

'The hotel has a side entrance. I'll meet you there in half an hour.'

His back was to her as she emerged from the door, and somehow the sight of it — a man's back is vulnerable — was more exhilarating than her first view of his face in the Basil's upstairs lounge. And yet now that she had the chance, she didn't dare touch him.

'David?'

She watched the sun catch his features as he turned. 'There's no trace of your Belarusian friends,' he said.

'You went to Charwell Lane?'

'Yes.'

'How could you bear it? You found my purse? My clothes?'

'No.'

'That bare-assed bastard did go back and get them.'

'There wasn't *anything* there.'

Helen gaped at him. 'Nothing?' she said stupidly.

'No.'

'What about Emilia? What about her neighbour?'

'Like I say, there's no trace. None. Your friends might as well never have existed. Were they here illegally?'

'Emilia was. I'm not sure about the neighbour. Probably her too. How can there be no trace of them? What's that supposed to mean?'

He told her that he'd gone to Emilia's apartment, found only empty rooms and a scrubbed-clean floor.

They walked away from the hotel and into a residential area: sculpted door knockers on neat town houses and window boxes with ivy drooping down from them. Helen searched David's face. There was no expression on it.

'Why did you take me to that funny little hotel?' she said.

'You weren't going anywhere on your own.'

'You weren't worried about leaving me alone?'

He looked baffled. 'Why would I be?'

'I didn't even have money.'

'I took care of it.'

Helen stopped, her hand over her mouth. 'Jesus, I haven't told you about UCAI, have I?'

David said nothing. He couldn't have spoken if he'd wanted to; it was all he could do to control his breathing.

She watched him, could make no sense of his reaction, feared she'd offended him somehow. 'You've heard of UCAI, David,' she said at last. '*Everybody's* heard of them. They're the hidden buyers. You know, behind the offers for Joshua's farm. But why would they chase around after somebody like me? Why not talk about our conditions like normal — ?'

'What did you say the conditions were?' he interrupted.

'Percentage of the profits and a non-branded supply to the Chernobyl victims.'

Again he said nothing, and they walked in silence until they emerged into the vast open spaces of Trafalgar Square: lions, fountains, tourists.

'What do you think I should do?' Helen said at last.

'You want to play games' — he let her hear the anger in his voice — 'find somebody else.'

She literally gasped. 'Jesus, you think this is a game? I'm scared out of my wits. I don't know what the hell to do.'

But he only turned away from her and started across Trafalgar Square towards the great gates of the Mall. She watched him go for a minute, then rushed after him. 'Is there something you don't approve of in how we're going about this?' she demanded. 'Is that it?'

He turned. 'Following me around, are you?'

'Who the hell are you to disapprove of what I do or how I go about it?'

'You're lying to me. Makes me nervous.'

She was abruptly righteous, indignant. 'How can you be so stupid? Why would I do a dumb thing like that? There's no point in lying to you.'

'Isn't there?'

'David, goddamn you, what *possible* point can there be — ?'

'You told me about those offers to purchase,' he interrupted again, 'but they were back at the beginning. Right? Now suddenly I find out that you've upped the ante to a percentage and a non-branded supply. Meantime, the only hint you've given of formal negotiations to get you from the one to the other is that UCAI doesn't seem willing to talk at all. I figure that means you and your old grandma haven't approached them direct in all this time, and *that* has to mean you're talking to somebody else to get the terms where you want them before you approach UCAI with them. If I were UCAI management, I wouldn't be pleased. You've set up a battlefield where they're going to have to fight for something they assumed belonged to them. I hate it when people lie to me. We'd better talk about fees for services.'

'Fees? David, I wasn't lying. I swear to you.'

He nodded. 'I don't come cheap.'

'Oh?'

'Not long after I got out of South Hams, your grandmother offered me $100,000 just to leave Springfield.'

'She didn't!'

'Not such a hard job. All I had to do was get away from the Freyl family and stay away. A year later, she actually wanted me to do something, and the price had doubled.'

'I don't believe you,' Helen said. 'I don't believe either story. She's a wicked old woman in many ways — I know that perfectly well — but she doesn't pay people to get out of town. And she doesn't hire murderers to work for her.'

David shrugged. 'Whatever you say.'

She stood there staring up at him, caught in his gaze, unaware that he was as caught as she was. 'I was afraid you'd . . . I wasn't *lying*, David. I swear it. I thought you might think I was greedy if I told you all of it — I mean right away — and I didn't want you to think such a . . . I'll pay you whatever you ask. I need you.'

'You *are* greedy, and there's a condition.'

'Christ almighty, I'm beginning to think you have Freyl blood in you. What's the condition?'

'Don't lie to me again.'

'David, dammit, I wasn't *lying*.'

'You were holding back. Don't do it again.'

* * *

The day was balmy, the heat of the summer at last humbled in England, if not broken as in Belarus. Helen led David into Green Park; they'd walked most of the way through it when she said, 'I'm starving. I didn't have any breakfast.'

'I want fish and chips,' he said at once.

She laughed. 'I've never even tried it. It sounds dreadful.'

'I want a scone too. What is a scone?'

'A kind of teatime thing. Like in strawberry shortcake.'

'Where do we start?'

'Fish and chip shop.'

They found a café just opening and walked away with fish and chips in greasy paper and smelling of vinegar. They sat on the grass of a tree-shaded square and unwrapped their booty. Helen watched him test it.

'What do you think?'

He nodded approval, and they ate in silence for a moment. 'Let's hear about the other contenders,' he said then.

'My grandmother and I approached Galleas not long after I got here. One of their representatives tracked me down. Their first offer was, well, insulting. Their second wasn't all that much better, and Grandma decided on an auction.'

'When?'

'Next month. One of them has already offered a flat $50 million.'

He raised his eyebrows. 'That's it?'

'Oh, come on, David, why would I lie to you about something like that?'

'Beats me. You let Hay in on any of this?'

'Only as much as we wanted UCAI to hear. You know, I still can't see where it all went wrong. Truly I can't.' She smiled uncertainly.

'I met one of their people because of your father,' he said.

'One of whose people? UCAI? Galleas?'

'Galleas.'

'You didn't!' she said. 'Really?'

He glanced away from her, then glanced back. 'What do you make of the players?'

Helen shrugged. 'I don't know what to make of Charles, but the Foundation seems to have a heart of pure gold. My grandmother craves the role of Lady Bountiful, and I can see that supplying the drug at an unbranded cost to Chernobyl victims is fantastic publicity. Maybe UCAI will have to have its arm twisted, but they'd have to see it too. If Galleas or one of the others takes over, it's the steal of the century.'

David glanced away again. 'No wonder you got people chasing around after you. When'd you last hear from the Galleas representative?'

'Maybe ten days ago.' Then she said, 'I never did tell Charles that Zoya was with me at that book festival.'

'Who's Zoya?'

'An exotic old lady I know. I want you to meet her as soon as possible.' She gave him a quick, nervous glance. 'There seem to be things she alone knows but won't tell me. Oh, how she loves men though. I bet you she'll tell you anything you ask her. We could drive down this afternoon.'

'How far away is she?'

'A little over four hours. We could rent a car, have tea with her. She'll give you that scone you want. She always has scones for tea. I could call her right now.'

He picked up a chip, had it almost to his mouth, then shook it at her instead. 'Won't work. I'm meeting somebody at five.'

'You're not! Who? Why? You don't know anybody here.'

'Who says so? Suppose I call this Galleas guy.'

'What for?' She scanned his face quickly but found no room for manoeuvre in it. 'If you do, I get to listen. He's a condescending shit.'

'Afraid not.'

'David, I have to know.'

'No, you don't. What's his name?'

She scanned his face again and handed over the card Leslie Bloeden had given her. She watched David pace back and forth on the other side of a bed of chrysanthemums as the conversation took place. Fifteen minutes later — she'd finished the last of the chips and lain back on the grass — he squatted beside her.

'Okay,' he said. 'Now the lying really stops. Right here. Right now.'

She bolted upright. 'I'm not lying. I promise. Damn you, David. I said I wouldn't. And I'm not.'

'Call it what you want. Just tell me the rest of the story.'

'The rest? What rest?'

'How about starting with what you and Charles Hay have cooked up.'

' 'Cooked up'? Me? With Charles?'

'Bloeden says you're into something deep with him. He doesn't know what.'

'*Into* something . . . What could he . . . ? You haven't seen the papers?'

'What papers?'

Helen dropped her head back in her hands and rocked it there. 'Okay. I guess . . . I guess it is kind of deep. But I wasn't holding it back. We got engaged. I assumed you knew.' A glance at David's face showed it was as expressionless as before.

'To be *married*?' he said.

'David, it was only part of the . . . charade. Only pretend. Not real. I never 'cooked up' anything with Charles. Not a thing. You've got to believe me.'

She looked up again to see the faint softening of his face that was probably as close to a smile as she would ever see him come. 'Now why would I do a thing like that?' he said.

# 45

## LONDON

Merlin Googe Allandale's plane landed in late morning. He knew the bustle of Heathrow airport well. He'd been through it again and again just as he'd been through most of the major airports of the world. He caught a taxi to the CIA-owned house in Ganton Place, a handsome three-storey building on a quiet street in Notting Hill where he'd stayed several times before. The refrigerator downstairs was stocked with eggs, Florida orange juice and American bacon for tomorrow morning. A saucepan of his favourite chilli was ready to heat on the stove for lunch. Upstairs in the living room, a bowl of Frititatas ('the taste of Mexico with the heart of Illinois') stood on the coffee table beside a bottle of Mountain Dew — his favourite soft drink — and bucket of ice.

He called his wife while he poured himself a glass. She didn't like airplanes. She didn't like the English either.

* * *

It could hardly have been the Mountain Dew, but Googie collapsed into a coma-like sleep for a couple of hours after it. When he woke, he had a head that ached like crazy and a fog in his brain. True, he'd been up all night. He couldn't sleep on planes; it had never bothered him before, and last time around was only, what, two years ago? Getting old was bad enough, but doing it this fast was a disgrace.

He was glad of the fresh air and the walk to Mowbray Square.

'Merlin Allandale to see Sir Charles Hay,' he said to the receptionist at Follaton House, a middle-aged woman with frizzy white hair, a long, narrow face and a string of pearls. She sat at the Victorian mahogany desk that Rosemary had guarded so recently.

'You have an appointment, Mr Allandale?'

'I was kind of thinking I wouldn't need one.'

'Oh, I'm afraid you will. Sir Charles is a busy man.'

'Tell you what. Being as I'm kind of busy myself, why don't you call him up on that phone of yours there and tell him I represent Mrs Rebecca Freyl?'

Googie was shown upstairs at once, past the outer room and into Charles's office, where Charles sat at his desk, intent on a file of papers in front of him.

'Mr Allandale?' he said, looking up.

'That's me,' said Googie.

'You represent Helen's grandmother?'

'Right.'

'Take a seat, please. I won't be long.' Googie sat and waited, not at all displeased at the opportunity to study the man in his subtly ostentatious surroundings. Minimalism takes money, and arrogance — even towards someone on a mission from his prospective grandmother-in-law — amused Googie but did not surprise him.

'Now how can I help you?' Charles said five minutes later.

'I wasn't exactly looking at it like that, Sir Charles. I was more thinking like we could help each other.'

'Oh? How might that be?'

Googie shifted in his chair. It was a comfortable chair, but there wasn't much support for the back. His doctor had diagnosed a curvature of the spine, and it called for painkillers after the long flight. 'I got something that's gonna interest you, and you got something that's gonna lead me to what I want. I'm figuring it might be a good idea for us to work together.'

'I have no idea what you're talking about,' Charles said irritably. 'Has Mrs Freyl sent you here to work out some sort of deal?'

'Nope.' Googie allowed himself a chuckle. 'I'm kinda talking for myself at the moment. You want to marry Helen Freyl, and I have some business to conduct with a man called David Marion.'

'Who?'

'David Marion.'

'Never heard of him.'

'I don't suppose you have. He's got something of a reputation out where I come from, and they go back a long way.'

'Who goes back a long way? Wait a minute. Isn't David Marion the man they held awhile for Hugh Freyl's murder?'

'The very same.'

'I see.' But Charles shook his head. 'No, I don't. What do you mean by 'talking for' yourself? I thought you represented Mrs Freyl.'

'I figure the truth of the matter is, I do and I don't.' Googie got up, suppressing a grimace at the pain it caused him, extracted a copy of Helen's email from his wallet and handed it to Charles, who took it and scanned it.

> Lillian, what am I going to do? Somebody's trying to kill me. I don't know who. I don't know why. I had everything under control. Except maybe . . . Don't tell Grandma. She'd be furious. I want David Marion. I need him. How can the bastard be dead? How can he do that to me?

Charles frowned. 'Mrs Freyl gave you this?'

'I can't tell you how happy I was to see it.'

'Really? It says your David Marion is dead.'

'We got an old Illinois saying: don't believe everything you read.'

Charles read the email again, carefully this time. 'He isn't by any remote chance someone Helen once fancied, is he? Is that what you're telling me?'

'Local scuttlebutt says as much.'

'He's *alive*?'

'Yep.'

'In England?'

'That's how I figure it.'

'And Mrs Freyl suggested you come to me with this?'

Googie chuckled again. 'Now I got to admit that was kinda my idea.'

Charles got up from his desk, walked around it, smiled, offered Googie his hand. 'I'm so sorry,' he said, 'what did you say your name was again?'

# 46

## DAGENHAM

It was about three in the afternoon when David left Helen at the hotel run by her hairdresser's mother with strict instructions to stay inside; he said he'd pick her up in the morning. From there, he took the underground as far east as it went, then a bus to the outer fringes of town. He ran the mile to the Bel Aire Residential Caravan Park.

The door was open to Pimmson's sagging trailer; David rapped at the panel beside it and walked in. Pimmson was at a table, eating pizza. His face was flushed, his mouth too full to greet a visitor. He acknowledged David with a nod in the direction of a bench that ran along the far side of the trailer.

The ceiling was too low for David to stand up. As he crouched his way across to the bench, a woman emerged from the kitchen area with a serving bowl of Angel Delight and whipped cream. She gave David a weary smile and set the bowl on the table next to the pizza.

'Here's your trifle,' she said.

Pimmson swallowed and waved her away. 'Out, out.'

'You got something for me,' David said when she'd gone.

'Yes, sir, I do.' Pimmson opened the door to a cabinet, pulled out a gun and handed it over. 'I'm a man of my word.'

David took it, turned it in his hands, glanced at the barrel, then tossed it on the table beside the trifle.

'Now get me the other one.'

Pimmson frowned. ' 'The other one'?'

'Come on, come on, we're wasting time here. Get me the piece I paid for.'

'That's it, mate.'

'No, it isn't.'

Pimmson laughed, looked David up and down, laughed again. 'You Canadians,' he said, still chuckling. 'It isn't like home here, you know. This is going to do the job for you — whatever the job is — and then some. Cost me a fucking fortune, it did. You got yourself a bargain.'

'It's a piece of junk.'

Pimmson's face flushed with anger. He stared hard at David. 'What are you trying to say?'

'You heard me.'

'You don't know what you're talking about.' Pimmson picked up a quarter of the pizza and folded it into his mouth.

David's knowledge of weaponry came from a few handguns he'd played with as a kid, a couple he'd made in prison and a rifle he'd stolen from one of his foster fathers. Pimmson's offering was an automatic; it said so on the barrel. The stock had 'Union' printed on it. There were a few scratches here and there. Beyond that? David had read that automatics were less powerful than revolvers and more likely to jam, but that was about it. Pimmson was right. David didn't know what he was talking about.

What he did know was that Pimmson was lying.

'One of the hardest things about negotiating with a stupid man,' David said, 'is that he doesn't know when he's lost. I suggest you give your kid brother back his toy and deliver something along the lines of the 9 millimetre I paid for.'

'I don't get you, mate' — Pimmson pushed the pizza to one side of his mouth to speak — 'I know this market, and I'm telling you this little bugger is better than anything I expected for your fucking £750.'

David sighed irritably. 'See what I mean about stupid men?' He ran an eye over Pimmson's gross body. 'I bet you I can tell you something you don't know.'

Pimmson shrugged his shoulders and continued chewing.

'I spent some time making coffins once, and we used to hate seeing corpses as big as you. We didn't have specifications large enough, and we had to — I'm afraid there's no way to put this delicately — hack off slabs of fat until we could squeeze the body in.'

Pimmson's face grew redder. He swallowed the mass in his mouth. 'You wouldn't be trying to frighten me, would you?'

David raised his eyebrows. 'Surely that's not necessary.'

'What are we talking about here?'

'The sale of a weapon.'

'I did exactly what — '

'Don't,' David interrupted, holding up his hand. 'I got no objection to a guy trying to gouge a buck out of somebody as long as that somebody isn't me.'

'Now you listen — '

This time David only held up his hand as interruption.

Pimmson took a swig of his tea, made an attempt at his hard stare, abandoned it, shrugged again, then reached as before into the cabinet beside him. This time, he took out a revolver and handed it over with a grunt. 'Now you're going to tell me what you actually wanted was a .45.'

'I don't plan to shoot out any windshields,' David said.

* * *

This handgun had 'ME 38 magnum' etched into the barrel. Pimmson explained that it had started out life as a replica sold by the German firm of Cuno Melcher. An engineer in Manchester imported several models on a regular basis, drilled through partial obstructions in the barrel and installed new cylinders. Sometimes the aim wasn't perfect, but there was no paper trail.

And the penetrating power was as great as any 9mm Glock or Smith & Wesson on sale in America.

# 47

## THE *Daily Mail*

That day's edition featured a follow-up story on James and Rosemary. A fetching picture of her in a bathing suit ran down the whole of the right side of the page. On the left was one of James that had appeared in a local paper when he'd played for his school cricket team.

**EXCLUSIVE INTERVIEW WITH DEAD GIRL'S MOTHER**

Rosemary Figgis 18 and James Smith 19, who died in Belarus of acute radiation poisoning, had gone there to help radiation victims from the Chernobyl meltdown in 1986.

They were working for Victim Support (Belarus), a charity attached to the Follaton Medical Foundation, and were seriously injured when exposed to high levels of radiation while out for a walk in the woods.

Sir Charles Hay, Director of the Foundation said, 'I'm devastated. I knew Rosemary, a lovely girl, passionate about her work.'

'They are heroes, wonderful examples of the often maligned young people of today. They gave their lives to help others, and I'd give my soul to have them back. My heart goes out to their parents.'

James's parents were too distraught to comment. An interview with Tracy Figgis, 42, appears exclusive to the *Mail*.

The exclusive was short and dull. There was a picture of Tracy with Rosemary as a baby, another of the two of them on a winter beach in Brighton, a third of Tracy alone, bravely showing a tear-stained face. She'd said to the reporter, 'Rosemary could be a bit silly sometimes. You know how girls are today. It's just like her to go off on a walk in a strange place and not think ahead. Oh, why didn't she phone me? Why did she go there at all? She's my little girl, my only child.' Tracy broke down at this point — the journalist described her pain as 'terrible to watch' — then launched into the usual clichés about Rosemary's sunny, happy nature, how everybody loved her. 'The only good thing about it,' she said, 'is that it was an accident. Nobody is to blame. Everybody has been so kind.'

Osama bin Laden, robed, bearded, armed, alien, stared out opposite the smiling youngsters and the grieving mother:

**My suicide bombers don't need bombs**

Al Qaeda pays premium prices for the lethal radioactive substance that killed Rosemary Figgis and James Smith. A new black market is thriving.

The old Soviet Union had no comprehensive programme for the disposal of nuclear waste. Thousands of highly radioactive sources such as generator parts, rifle scopes, X-ray machines lie hidden in bunkers, caves, forests, lakes. Sometimes the innocent stumble across them, as Rosemary Figgis and James Smith did.

Black marketeers scour the countryside for them. A single canister is worth a fortune.

Caesium-137, the deadliest radioactive by-product and the one responsible for the deaths of the young Britons, is a terrorist's dream come true. It is a powder that looks like flour or talc. All a suicide bomber has to do is fill his pockets with it and sprinkle it in an office or a playground. No explosion necessary. He will die, but so will many others.

As yet there is nothing medical science can do to save them.

An accompanying article featured Sir Charles explaining that a forensic task force from the UK had been organized immediately and sent to Belarus to cooperate with local authorities in an official investigation. Inquiries would continue for several weeks, but the facts of the case seemed to reveal themselves within the first few hours. The explanation was brutally simple. Rosemary and James had gone for a walk, penetrated perhaps too deeply into the woods, lost their way as it was getting dark and found themselves near the warm canisters. It got very cold in Belarus that night. What would be more natural than to snuggle up to something warm until morning? They'd woken feeling ill, struggled for several hours to find their way out of the woods and into the arms of a local search party.

They had died at the clinic less than a day later.

The story closed with Sir Charles saying:

> 'The Follaton Medical Foundation continues to work night and day to find a cure for the terrible consequences of exposure to radioactive materials. Perhaps one day soon we will be able to prevent this happening to anybody ever again.'
>
> 'We can only pray that the public will continue to contribute generously to our efforts.'

Pledges of money for Follaton Medical Foundation began pouring in as early as six in the morning. By noon they threatened to clog the Foundation's computer system.

# 48

## LONDON

'David!' Helen cried, jumping out of a sad green chair in the lobby of the hotel Francine's mother managed. 'I thought you weren't coming until tomorrow.'

He tossed a copy of the *Daily Mail* down on the table. 'I got to know more about this girl.'

'What girl?'

'Read the paper.'

'The *Daily Mail*?'

'Read it.' He'd picked up the paper on his trip back from Dagenham.

She took it from him and skimmed the stories while he stood over her watching; then she shook her head and handed it back. 'I don't think this makes an awful lot of sense.'

'Why not?'

'Rosemary wouldn't go snuggling up to a canister of caesium-137. She was smart. She'd done a lot of reading. I used to run into her in the Foundation library at least once a week, and I know damn well she'd realize some can of junk could be radioactive if she felt heat coming from it.'

'Maybe she got caught with some of that powdered stuff.'

'What'd she do? Open up a rusty can of

strontium? Inhale just for fun? Or swallow it? They'd have to force her or trick her to do that. If she and this other kid had wandered into a contaminated underground bunker or something, the press releases would have said so.'

David frowned. 'Do reporters rely on them much?'

'Press releases? Jesus, a lot of stories are lifted word for word, and the Foundation must have been spewing them out all over the place. Do you want some coffee?'

He shook his head, sat down opposite her, pulled out a cigarette, lit it. 'You're saying the information comes direct from Follaton.'

'Maybe not everything, but certainly most of it. You don't think some *Mail* reporter went to Belarus, do you? A couple of Foundation press releases, a couple of telephone calls to some English-speaking person connected with the clinic where Rosemary was: there hasn't been time for much more than that.'

'She talked to you before she went.'

Helen shook her head. 'I didn't even know she'd gone, David. I told you that.'

'I mean generally. She must have said something.'

'Not really.'

''Not really.' I see. What did she say?'

'David, she had an overactive imagination: the only flaw in a good mind. She had vague suspicions of one kind and another. She herself didn't think they made much sense.'

'How about you tell me what these 'vague suspicions' were.'

A haze of smoke from David's cigarettes hung over the chair covers of the hotel lobby by the time Helen had finished describing the party at Emilia's and Rosemary's intention to investigate the basement at the Foundation. 'What was down there?' he asked.

'Down where? The basement?'

'Didn't you ask her?'

'Oh, I kidded her about it a couple of times. Made her mad as hell. If she'd had any luck she'd *certainly* have said something, but she was her usual self when I saw her last, and the next I heard was that story in the *Mail* saying she was dead.' They sat for a few minutes in silence. 'You going to offer me a cigarette?' she asked.

He took the pack from his pocket, shook out a cigarette for her, gave her his to light it from. 'Okay,' he said. 'Here's what we do.'

# PART 4

# 49

## ISLE OF DOGS

Nobody knows how this area of London came to have its name. Perhaps because the gallows were here. Or perhaps because it was a kennel for Henry VIII's dogs. For generations it served as the city's dockyards, notorious for gangsters, crumbling tenements, twisting streets, drugs, whores, muggers, pickpockets. Policemen were too terrified to set foot in it alone. Then the docks closed. There was no work. The rich moved in with fortified skyscrapers that tower over an explosive population of ex-dockers with no money and no prospects, their community dying around them, nothing left except anger, grudges, pit bull terriers and Nazi salutes.

It was nearly seven by the time David opened the door to a pub in the shadow of one of the silver skyscrapers but hidden from it by a Berlin wall of brick. A young woman stood behind the bar polishing glasses. Only three tables were occupied.

'Evening,' the young woman said, turning to greet him with a smile. David had never seen female bartenders before arriving in London, and this one was a pink-cheeked, polished penny of Englishness with eyes that sloped down at the corners, perhaps twenty-five years old.

'Nice one, isn't it?' she went on.

'Nice one?' David said, lost already in the intricacies of small talk.

The girl's smile deepened. 'It's a nice *evening*.'

David sat on a stool at the wraparound bar and leaned forward on his elbows. 'I wouldn't know,' he said.

'You're a Yank, yeah?'

'That's right.'

'So what're you drinking?'

'Beer,' he said.

She bent down behind the bar, opened a refrigerator there, brought out a bottle. 'First trip to England?' she said. He nodded. 'Seeing the sights?'

'I'm waiting for somebody.'

'Anybody I know?'

'You might. What's your name?'

'Martha.'

* * *

The pub was called Grendel and the Harpist. A sign outside showed a half-boar, half-man monster transfixed by the harp that dangled from his clawed hand. But before David had even caught sight of it, he'd been stopped in his tracks by a sandwich board that proudly announced:

**TONIGHT!**
**TUESDAY STRIPPERS AT TEN**
*brings you*
**THE LOVERS OF LESBOS**
**Butch-Ella and her special friend**
**The Sunbeam Kid**

As he drank his beer, Martha bubbled with enthusiasm telling him that the originally billed strippers had called in sick and suggested the Lesbians as substitutes. She predicted a full house tonight, and by 8.30 the pub was boisterous and smoke-filled despite England's ban on smoking in public places — customers three deep at the bar, three barmaids working flat out. Men in suits and respectable couples from the other side of the brick wall manoeuvred their way with glasses of white wine past grizzled ex-dockers with pints of bitter and skinheaded football fans, drunk already and laughing too loud.

Martha took full charge of the proceedings, keeping order among the customers as well as the staff, and she glowed in that room. David couldn't repress a pang when she seemed to listen all-too-attentively to a dark-haired man while she poured out his Scotch on the rocks. But she caught David's eye over the guy's shoulder, the tilt of her head telling him that this was the man he'd come to meet; she pointed him in David's direction.

'David Marion?' the man said, holding out his hand. David only gestured at the seat opposite him. The newcomer looked down at his own hand, closed it into a fist and let it fall by his side. 'You didn't sound friendly on the phone either,' he said. 'Okay. It's up to me, is it? Right. As you've probably guessed, I'm Leslie Bloeden.' He sat down with a swish of his coat.

'Get to the point.'

'You're the one who suggested we meet, Mr Marion. Or do I call you David?'

'Get to the point,' David repeated.

'How can I be certain you represent Helen Freyl?'

'You can't.'

'Well, yeah, I guess it's proof enough that you're the one who knew where she was' — Leslie took a sip of his Scotch — 'when her Follaton tails lost her as assuredly as I did.'

'She has *two* sets of guys following her?'

'He gave a short laugh. 'The Follaton contingent have been bugging both house and landline since before she signed the lease.'

'Before? Sounds unlikely.'

'Your little girlfriend let the Foundation find her a place to live. What did she expect? Anyhow, as I was trying to tell you when you hung up on me yesterday, all that's kid stuff. What *is* important is that it looks like nobody who has a glimmering of what actually goes on at Follaton Medical Foundation gets out of there in one piece.'

'You telling me Galleas International has developed a sudden interest in the health of a medical foundation's employees?' David said.

'I'm sure you appreciate that we're anxious to ensure Helen Freyl's heath.'

'From what she tells me, you haven't shown all that much concern.'

'I'm only the messenger, Mr Marion. But I can assure you that the concern is real. Did she tell you anything about a guy called Warren Collcutt?'

David had never heard the name. 'What about him?'

'He's the first dead man. Or at least, he's the first we know about because he was the first to come to us with an offer. UCAI hired him back in St Louis to help with the statistics coming out of Belarus. Thing is, the figures seemed to show trends that didn't make sense unless something pretty strange was going on. He told us he knew what it was, but before we could finalise the deal, Follaton threw an anniversary party for the staff. Collcutt drove home to clean himself up for the champagne, got in his car to go back, turned on the ignition and — Boom! No more friendly statistician. Local cops plumped for 'accidental vapour explosion' and closed the case.'

'Any proof it was anything else?'

'His wife insisted on an investigation, but the entire file on him had pulled a vanishing act.' David shrugged. In his experience, files conveniently lost were almost as common as ones that stuck around. 'That's when we started approaching people,' Leslie went on. 'We managed to turn another statistician called Jane Littlejohn. She was strangled. Simple as that. A couple of young cops saw her killer leave her house and got a good enough look at him for a forensic artist to draw a picture of — '

'*Two* statisticians?' David interrupted.

Leslie nodded. 'They both worked for a guy called Martin Goldsmith: UCAI's scientific adviser. His specialty — in case you're interested — is statistics. Anyhow, UCAI managed to see the forensic drawing, and the cops were put on paid leave. Both of them retired early with bank accounts at a Bahamas branch of the Royal Trust Company of Canada. Now they're living the good life in — '

'How'd UCAI get to see the drawing?' David interrupted again.

Leslie shrugged. 'Got inside contacts, wouldn't you say?'

'What about you? How come you know about it?'

Leslie shrugged again. 'We've got inside contacts too. Who doesn't?'

David lit yet another a cigarette, drew deep on it, kept it in his mouth as he spoke. 'Two dead guys doesn't convince me of anything,' he said. Of course, he had to add them to Helen's list — the cook, the cook's neighbour, Feodor Mussinov, Rosemary Figgis, James Smith — even if she had no idea why they'd been killed.

Leslie shook his head. 'As of eighteen months ago we were certain about five murders. Then a prospective number six showed up.'

'The cook?'

'What cook?' Leslie said, his face blank as he gave the ice in his glass a shake.

'At Follaton. Emilia Somebody. Youdin, I think.'

'Nope.'

'How about a girl named Rosemary?'

'The kid in the paper?' David nodded. 'I don't know,' Leslie went on. 'It's possible. Anything's possible. But the guy I'm talking about is an administrative assistant called Gwinner. He told us he could get hold of some of the material the blown-up statistician had been working on. Over the next couple of months he stashed it in a safe deposit box in a London branch of Barclays Bank until he had enough to make a deal. He wouldn't come through with anything more than a teaser until he had money in a numbered account in the Caymans. Meantime, he went ice fishing in Norway. On his second day there, he fell through the ice and drowned. When his executor opened up the safe deposit box, there was nothing inside.'

'But the teaser got you going.' It wasn't a question. 'Any idea how deep this goes into UCAI?'

A burst of laughter erupted at the football fans' table. The ex-dockers joined in. The respectable couples and the suits glanced at them in alarm.

'UCAI tossed millions at the Foundation's Belarus project,' Leslie said. 'Research into radiation levels in soil, long-term effects on the inhabitants. It was one hell of a package. On top of the survey, they supplied fertiliser, combine harvesters, agricultural expertise. They set up a chain of health care clinics. Belarus didn't have to do a damn thing but sit there and soak it up. The press blathered on about 'God's work'. Money rolled in: private donors, other foundations, trusts, faith groups, the British and American governments, the Russians, assorted European countries — practically everybody you can think of. Published results aren't what you'd call exciting, but they're solid enough: crop yields up, public health measures in place

— hygiene and vaccination standards up, that kind of thing.'

'So what's the catch?'

'What's barely hinted at in the papers' — Leslie's fingers beat out a tattoo on the table — 'is that UCAI offered Belarus a hefty 'investment in infrastructure' to allow Follaton to carry out 'God's work'. Not only that, they promised a generous chunk of the profit from any drugs that might develop out of the study. Curious, don't you think? I mean, how come UCAI is going so saintly all of a sudden? And why so shy about it? Nobody but Christ Himself is going to offer a second handout to persuade somebody to accept an incredibly generous first one.' Leslie swallowed back his drink. 'Another beer?' he said, getting to his feet.

David ignored the question. 'You going to tell me what the catch is or not?'

'How about that drink first?' David's gaze didn't change. 'I don't know what I've done to bug you like this.' Leslie sighed and sat down again. 'The best information we have on the 'catch', as you call it, is the drowned guy's teaser.'

'Go on.'

'He sent us four pages about four villages on the outside edges of the Chernobyl zone. Page one reported ground radiation levels in the first village of more or less 0.05 megabecquerels per square metre. Page two — '

'Mega — *what*?'

'Megabecquerels per square metre: it's a way of measuring how much radioactive stuff there is on the ground. Page two recorded a shipment of fertiliser to the second village. Page three charted fall tests in the third village. They showed radiation levels in the range of 2 megabecquerels per square metre.' Leslie paused. 'Get what I'm saying? Well, 2 megabecquerels is a *bizarre* result, especially way out at the edge of the zone. It's the kind of level they found in villages that had to be evacuated after Chernobyl blew. The question is, why would Gwinner think we might be interested?'

David's glass was nearly empty. He tipped it back and forth; the shallow pool ebbed and flowed. 'Low radiation levels in one village, a delivery of fertiliser in a second village, high levels in a third? An accident? Something radioactive in the fertiliser? Is that what the guy was hinting at? People have killed for less.'

Leslie's grimace was a lopsided dissent. 'So near to the truth — and yet so far,' he said.

'What are you saying? That somebody deliberately added radiation to the fertiliser?'

'You see that story in the *Mail* beside your Rosemary's death? The one that talked about a guy filling his pockets with caesium? A dirty bomb without a bomb. Powdered thorium looks like flour. Same with all kinds of radioactive substances. You can do practically anything you want with them. The Russians caught a guy last week with a kilo of powdered uranium and radium in his briefcase. He could have got a hell of a good price for that. This stuff is so easy to come by that some politician or other — Cheney? — said massive civilian casualties are a matter of 'when' not 'if'. Tell you what: if you won't let me buy you a drink, why don't you get me one?' He held out his empty glass to David.

David paid no attention to the gesture. 'Why are you telling me all this?'

'The word from on high is that Galleas might have a use for your, er, services.' David said nothing. 'We'll send word.' David made no response. 'Martha's a good sort, you know.' Leslie was still holding out his glass, watching David watch him. Then he went on, 'Galleas owns this chain of pubs. Anything you need, you ask her.'

'Didn't you say four pages? What was on the fourth?'

Leslie wavered, then sighed as he had before and set his glass down. 'Chernobyl exploded a long time ago,' he said. 'It doesn't matter if you accept the official figures for fallout or the much higher ones that Follaton uses to cover itself with. In either case, the spread in radiation levels is gradual. It's a slow, slow process. This fourth page starts out with the fourth village a couple of years later. Radiation levels are normal in the winter. A shipment of fertiliser arrives in the spring. A soil test is run soon after the tractor spreads the stuff. The radiation level now? It's shot up to 2 megabecquerels per square metre. The village should have been evacuated at once. Does that happen? Nope. Instead, there are statistics recording symptoms experienced by two groups of people in the village. One group is treated with the Follaton radio-protectant masquerading as a vitamin/antioxidant supplement. The other group gets a placebo. Both groups are tested after a week, a month, three months, six months.'

David tapped a fresh cigarette out of the package on the table and lit it from the butt of the old one. 'That's a lot of information to cram into one page. Is it some kind of summary or something?'

'It's all in Gwinner's handwriting.'

'He could have made up the data just to keep you interested. You got any way of knowing if it's any more than imagination?'

'Would you kill a guy for phoneying some statistics? Why bother? It's too easy to discredit him. As for your accident idea, I can't really see a couple of identical fuck-ups with contaminated fertiliser separated by a two-year gap, both times resulting in soil levels that measure exactly the same. But just for the hell of it, let's suppose that's what happened. I can see killing a guy to avoid the real bad publicity that might follow if he leaked something, even though a press release, a grovelling apology and a handout would probably do the trick. But doesn't *six* dead bodies seem a tad out of proportion?'

'On the other hand,' Leslie went on, 'take a village with plain folks in it, spread a load of thorium or caesium or something on their vegetable plots, feed half of them the new drug so you can see if it works better than a placebo does on the other half of them. When you finally get your radioprotectant right — and doctor your results so your methods aren't visible

— you'll have more than enough data to satisfy FDA guidelines for clinical trials. They're what costs serious money. Research is cheap. Those results are pure gold dust. Well worth killing for.'

David wasn't easily taken aback, but he frowned, stubbed out his newly lit cigarette, lit another, stubbed it out too. 'How many villages are involved? Could we be talking *hundreds* of people?'

'Could be thousands for all I know. Maybe millions. Belarus is a fairly sizeable place.'

David frowned again, shook his head. 'Contaminate a whole *country*? Just to test a drug?'

'Welcome to the real world, Mr Marion.'

# 50

## SPRINGFIELD, ILLINOIS

Becky lay in an elegant private room at Springfield Memorial Hospital, pale and wan, a huge bruise on her forehead, an IV in her arm, a bag of electrolyte solution suspended from a tall rack beside her bed.

It had all happened suddenly. She threw up everywhere, all over her desk, her papers, the carpet. She fell to the floor in a faint, hitting her head on the chair. The 'new girl' — a grandmother of fifty-three on emergency duty from the Maid for You Employment Agency — came in with the mail a few minutes later. If she hadn't, Becky might have died. Choked on her own vomit.

'Disgusting,' Becky thought, her mind on the frailties of decrepit old people like herself. 'Absolutely disgusting.'

The indignity of it made her furious at Lillian all over again. If Lillian hadn't betrayed a lifetime's trust, none of this would have happened. It was the strawberries. Becky knew it. That dim-witted 'new girl' had served them for breakfast. Nearly thirty years ago — only months after Lillian came to work for her — strawberries had had exactly the same effect. Becky was allergic to so many things:

peas, kiwi fruit, dogs, shellfish, oranges, detergent. Not that she could remember them all. Only Lillian knew the list for sure.

Becky hated being dependent on people. The need for parents had made her childhood hard, and a husband had made marriage close to impossible. But dependence on Lillian! The shame of it! It wasn't just allergies either. A single day without Lillian, and her bathroom basin showed water spots. The pictures on the wall were crooked.

She must have dozed off then because she opened her eyes to find Lillian seated beside her bed.

'Just look at you,' Lillian said. 'What you gone and done to yourself?'

'*I* didn't do anything. What took you so long?'

'I'd a got here sooner, but I was out when the nurse done call me. I come the minute I got the message. Didn't even take off my coat. How you feeling? Any better?'

Becky clenched her thin fists. 'I have no pep.' Her face showed that extreme vulnerability that only Lillian knew. 'It was strawberries. I have no *pep*.'

'Strawberries? You can't eat no strawberries. 'Course you ain't got no pep. Who you got working for you anyhow? Don't she know no better? You want me to have a talk with her? That it? I can make out some lists: allergies, things you like, things you doesn't, which is the right pills for what. Maybe talk to her some?' But Becky was moving her head side to side (she was too tired to shake it). 'That ain't it? Then what you want? Huh?'

'Take me home,' Becky said.

* * *

Lillian organized the operation like a general orchestrating the evacuation of a besieged town. Within a couple of hours, Becky was installed in her own bedroom, albeit in a fully functional hospital bed with an intravenous drip in place, oxygen mask at the ready, fearsome array of pills in the bathroom cabinet. The hospital had said a nurse might be important; Becky sent the woman to watch TV in the living room. Nobody but Lillian was to come near her. She felt hot: only Lillian could remove a blanket. She felt uncomfortable: only Lillian could fluff her pillows. She even allowed Lillian to bring her some chicken broth.

When it came to sleep, the dark and the emptiness of this room in her old age brought back the night horrors she'd had as a child — that Helen had suffered too — and only an exhausted Lillian drowsing in a chair beside her could restore a sense of calm and control.

Despite all this Lillian tried to get through to either Helen or David. Both numbers yielded up only an English robot voice saying, 'I'm sorry but the person you called is unavailable.' Lillian wasn't overly concerned. She'd heard the response on Helen's mobile before; hearing it on David's at least indicated that he'd arrived. If he had, Helen had one of the protectors she'd asked for.

If he hadn't, there was Googie Allandale. Lillian didn't like him, but on reflection she was glad that Becky had hired him. With him in England, Helen had *two* allies, one of them a professional.

One way or another, she was safe.

# 51

## LONDON SUBURBS

Weather forecasters predicted heavy rains throughout the whole of England, but the morning was bright and snappishly cold as David emerged from Grendel and the Harpist. He'd spent the night in one of their rooms, surprised all over again that the great city of London had quietened like a baby and gone to sleep around him even in this hard-nosed area of it.

He didn't have to wait long. The car that drew up at the curb was big, black, old, and Helen sat at the wheel.

'Where'd you get this beautiful beast?' he asked her, getting into it. The door opened the wrong way around: hinged at the mid-struts of the body.

'I found a classic car company in west London,' she said. 'I thought you'd like a gangster car. Can't you just see Al Capone at the wheel?'

He ran an appreciative hand over the rosewood dashboard. 'What year?'

'Nineteen fifty-two. A two and a half litre. Rileys were racing cars once. You said rent a car, so I combed the net for a suitable one. I'm bored out of my skull at that hotel Francine's mother manages. You think I'll have to go back?'

'I don't know.'

'How did the meeting with Bloeden go?'

'He can't be trusted.'

'That's certainly what Charles thought. Me too.'

'He said CIA, didn't he?'

'Either that or FBI.'

David fell silent, stared out the window, watched the area change around him from the angry mix of the disgruntled poor and the silver towers to middle-class suburb. He preferred the Isle of Dogs. On these suburban streets at the city's fringe, innocent signs like 'ladies hairdresser', 'greengrocer,' 'chemist' made him feel as though he'd entered some parallel universe where details were *almost* right — but not quite. Helen stopped at a light, tapped her fingers on the wheel, struggled to match his silence, then could bear it no longer.

'Bloeden must have said *something*.'

'Yeah.'

'Well, what, dammit?'

David glanced at her, then back at the streets.

'He tells me six guys got dead so far over this thing — none of them in the cook's apartment or in Belarus or in Devon.'

Helen felt abruptly unsteady. '*Six*?' she said. 'You mean, six *more*? Not including Emilia or her neighbour?'

'Nor your little Rosemary or Mussinov. He figures that anybody who has an idea what's really going on doesn't stay alive very long.' David paused. 'He says your house is bugged as well as the phone.'

Helen frowned. 'Did he? My *house*?' She nodded. 'I was afraid that might have . . . I mean Grandma insisted we act as if the phone was, but if it was the whole *house* . . . ' She trailed off. 'He also says you're being followed.'

That's when it hit her. She slammed her foot on the brake, and the tyres skidded on the macadam. 'Oh, Jesus, I really *am* next. That's what he's saying, isn't it?'

When provoked — especially if there's a woman at the wheel — England's polite drivers turn into New York madmen, hands jammed on horns. People on the street turned to look.

'Somebody's going to . . . I can't believe this is happening to me,' Helen went on, oblivious to the commotion she was creating. 'I hired you to protect me. *Do* something.'

David twisted around to see the outraged face in the Range Rover behind them. 'Think a riot is going to help?'

'Oh, fuck it,' she said, starting the Riley with a jerk, but her hands shook so badly that the car began to weave.

'Pull over,' he said. She obeyed without thinking. 'Get out.'

'Why?'

'I'll drive. Get out.' David slid over and adjusted the driver's seat. 'You have to double declutch this thing?' he asked as she climbed into the passenger's side.

'What's that?'

'Guess not.' He eased the Riley into first and pulled out into the street. 'Know where we're going?'

'Why not just go? You always end up *somewhere* if you keep going, don't you? Of course, you have to end up somewhere even if you veer off to — '

'You got a map?' he interrupted.

'I'm scared out of my wits, David.'

'I know.'

'What the fuck do you care? You're not scared, so what does it matter? Is that it?'

'No, it isn't,' he said softly. 'I've been scared every single day of my life as far back as I can remember.'

Helen was so shocked by this unexpected insight into his past that she pulled out the map the rental agent had given her, unfolded it over her lap and forced herself to concentrate on it. 'What do you know?' she said a few moments later. 'It turns out I was right. Keep going for another couple of blocks.'

'You were able to fix up something?' David's plan of yesterday included Helen's arranging for a visit to Tracy Figgis, Rosemary's mother, as well as a car to take them to her.

'No trouble at all.' Helen's spirits began to ease a little. 'I said we were reporters for the *Chicago Tribune*' — David had left the details to her — 'and our friend Tracy seemed almost too willing. Francine's mother loaned me a camera.'

David nodded. 'I see a problem with that.'

'With the camera?'

'That exclusive interview.'

'Oh, Lord, all she did was weep all over the *Daily Mail*. She didn't even mention it to me.'

'She's likely to have thought about it since.

Maybe they paid her something.'

'I doubt it. I mean, why would they? She's eager to talk. What else did Bloeden say?'

'There's some standard industrial espionage going on. More or less what you'd expect. Where do we go from here?' he said as they reached a crossroads. 'Right or left?'

He didn't want to risk telling her that UCAI seemed to have turned the entirety of Belarus into a testing ground for the radio-protectant that needed Joshua's venom. She hadn't coped all that well with what he'd told her so far, and he needed her in control of herself. He kept asking for directions to distract her; she concentrated on the map spread out across her knees.

London's suburbs straggled to an end. The landscape bloomed into scenery out of a Disney cartoon, a peaceable valley of rolling hills, green grass, wildflowers alongside the road, sheep, a stream twisting in the distance, hardly the kind of place where girls grow up to die of radiation poisoning in faraway dictatorships.

# 52

## SHAW MILLS, SURREY

The small town of Shaw Mills wasn't pretty by English standards, but it had women in stout shoes chatting to each other on the High Street, one with a shopping basket over her arm, another with a scarf tied under her chin. Then came a park with schoolgirls in uniform skipping rope and boys in short pants playing soccer, an old church, a row of white cottages with geraniums in boxes beneath the windows.

Rosemary's mother Tracy lived in a cheap 1960s development at the far edge of the town. David parked in front of her gate.

'You're Miss Bezukhova,' she said as she opened the door to Helen, who'd borrowed Zoya's surname for the occasion. Tracy's face was as tear-stained as it had been in the *Daily Mail* picture of her, eyes red-lined and puffy, nose red and sniffling, Kleenex clasped in her hand. She was a tired dust-and-mop of a woman. A lively daughter like Rosemary must have left her gasping at the end of every day. 'Oh, dear, I'm afraid you've come all this way for nothing,' she went on. 'I'm so very sorry. I can't talk to any other newspaper. I promised.'

'You needn't worry,' Helen said, putting an arm around her.

‘The *Tribune* is American. The *Mail’s* exclusive covers only newspapers on this side of the Atlantic.’

‘Oh,’ said Tracy. ‘Well, in that . . . Are you *certain*?’

‘I’ve worked on newspapers in several countries,’ said Helen, who’d never worked on a single newspaper in any country; she had no idea what the *Mail’s* rules on exclusives were. ‘They’re all the same. It’s a kind of international agreement, you know, like the United Nations. Exclusives apply only to the country the newspaper is based in.’

‘This is Reverend Joliet,’ she went on, introducing David without a flicker of a smile. ‘He’s the colleague I mentioned on the phone.’

‘*Reverend* Joliet?’ Tracy’s suspicions dropped away at once. ‘Oh, I see.’

The tiny, ugly living room was much colder than the day outside. Three overstuffed chairs squashed up against each other between dank walls. Helen stared balefully at an elderly electric heater standing unlit in a fireplace while Tracy clattered in her kitchen and returned with a teapot under a tea cosy.

‘Do forgive the temperature in here,’ she said as she filled the cups. ‘The weather is so peculiar these days. Milk? Sugar? I’m afraid the fire broke last night. Rosemary was good at fixing things like that. Her dad taught her, you know. I’m hopeless.’

‘Let me take a look,’ David said, getting up.

‘Oh, please don’t trouble yourself, Reverend.’

‘No trouble.’ He squatted beside the old

heater, checked the strange outlet that had its own on-off switch, flicked it — no response — and examined the huge plug attached to the heater's lead. 'Got a screwdriver?'

Tracy brought him a cardboard box with a few tools in it. 'Belarus is a long way from home,' he said, unscrewing the back of the heater's plug.

She suppressed a sob. 'Rosemary was meant to be coming back on Saturday week. We were meant to be talking on the phone every day from the day she left until then. We were given a special mobile — it was just the luckiest chance that I got it in time — but I never heard her voice, not even once, after I left her at the airport.'

'A job that far from home can be so exciting you forget everything else,' Helen said, getting out a notepad and a pencil.

'That's just what the lady from the *Mail* said.'

'Your daughter must have got quite a kick out of working at a place like the Follaton Foundation,' said David.

Tracy smiled sadly. 'Sir Charles said she was the most reliable person in the organization. She was ever so chuffed.'

'First job?' He kept his head bent over his work. Helen hadn't expected such gentle inquiry. She could easily imagine him beating information out of someone, but coaxing it out? It was only then that she realized how well he'd managed to get a coherent story out of her.

'Oh, no. Rosemary loved her pocket money: paper rounds, trainee at an estate agent's, checkout at Somerfield, filing at the job centre, all sorts. Not a holiday went by without a pay cheque.'

'She was going on to college, wasn't she?' Helen said.

The mother nodded. 'Manchester University: she wanted to do something called radiation biology. That sounds very grand for such a young girl, doesn't it? I was so proud of her.'

'Pretty smart, wasn't she?'

'She *was* a clever girl, even more so than her dad. She certainly pulled the wool over Sir Charles's eyes. I mean, imagine him calling her the most reliable person around.' David plugged in the heater and switched on the wall socket. The electric bar began to glow. 'Oh, Reverend,' she cried, 'aren't *you* the clever one. Thank you *so* much.'

'You don't think Rosemary was reliable?' he said.

'Oh, she *could* be, but she was always a bit nosy. She listened in on their conversations, opened some of their letters, read some of their memos. She even got caught prowling around in a basement that belonged to the building next door. They told her off for that — and she went back again. If that's the most reliable person around . . . well, you see what I mean. You look pleased, Reverend.'

'I'd have gone back too.'

'That's just what James's father said but he — '

'You talked to James's father?'

'He rang almost as soon as we' — she caught

her breath to steady herself — 'found out what had happened.'

'Rosemary *did* go back to that basement?' Helen looked up from her notepad.

'Oh, yes. She told me about it at the airport.'

'What kind of trouble did she get into this time?'

Tracy shook her head. 'I don't think they knew. I mean, they wouldn't have chosen her to go to Belarus, would they? At least the first time she went there she had an excuse: she only wanted to use it to store some of the hallway clutter. The second time was just nosiness.'

Helen leaned forward urgently. 'Maybe she found something interesting down there.'

'Oh, I'm sure not. I mean, it was a basement.'

'She didn't say anything?'

'Not to me.'

'But they chose her to go to Belarus? Any idea why her particularly? Our readers would love to know why they picked her above the others.'

Tracy shook her head again. 'I'm not quite certain, to be honest. She was keen, and she *was* clever. It was all so sudden, though. She came home on the Wednesday night and told me she was leaving the very next day. They arranged everything, visas, tickets, everything.'

'I see.' Helen duly made a note on her notepad, frowned, prepared herself. 'Are you *sure* she didn't find anything interesting in that basement? We'd love to be able to give our readers a glimpse into how such an important organization works, well, er, you know, at the simplest level.'

David looked at Helen askance, but Tracy didn't seem to find anything odd in a request that couldn't possibly reveal anything about the way an organization worked. She shook her head again. 'She didn't say so. Oh dear, I really shouldn't have told James's father about that, should I? It made him even angrier. How I wish . . . ' She suppressed yet another sob, took in her breath again, went on. 'Sir Charles himself rang me to say how sorry he was. I told him I couldn't understand it. He said accidents like that have been known to happen in the former Soviet Union, and it was just terrible, terrible luck. At least she didn't suffer. He said the clinic was specially good at pain relief, and he'd personally got the doctor's word that she'd been comfortable. I couldn't bear to think of my girl in pain. I just *couldn't*. He did his best to explain *everything* to me.' She made a helpless little gesture. 'I had to stop him. I couldn't understand a single word, Reverend, but he's the sweetest man. He truly is. He arranged for that interview in the *Daily Mail*. They paid me so much I can pay off my mortgage now.'

'Did they?' Helen said in surprise. '*Really*?'

Tracy nodded. 'I only wish I could see my girl one more time. But they say she's contaminated or something. When she finally comes home I'll scatter her ashes around the Harlequin rose. She'll help it grow. She'd like that, I think.'

'She's going to be *cremated*?' Helen was more surprised than before. 'Are you *sure*?'

'Oh, dear, I know a lot of people don't approve of cremation. But we talked about it once. It's what she wanted. She did have a strange side — didn't she? — thinking about such things at her age. Is your tea getting cold, Miss Bezukhova? Can I hot it up for you?'

Helen shook her head. 'You know, we'd kind of like to talk to James's father while we're at it,' she went on. 'Any idea how we get hold of him? A guy called Smith is hardly easy to find in the phone book.'

'I don't think . . . Hang on a minute, I wrote it down somewhere.' Tracy went to the kitchen but came back almost at once. 'Sorry. I threw it out. I remember now. It wasn't a long chat. He was so angry, you see.'

Helen and David took several photographs of Tracy — seated staring out the window, holding the cup Rosemary had won in a cross-country race — and she came outside to see them off. David had already turned the key in the ignition when she tapped on the window. He rolled it down.

'It just came to me,' she said. 'Beaston Court. That's the address. Beaston Court, Peckham Rye.'

* * *

The morning's bright sun had paled to a few weak rays as Helen and David drove back past the town park. A ladies' bowls team — pleated skirts, white socks and tam o'shanters — had replaced the schoolkids.

'Reverend Joliet, huh?' David said.

Helen laughed. 'I considered Professor Sing

Sing and Dr Alcatraz, but somehow neither seemed to suit you quite so well. I thought you seemed every inch a reverend gentleman with Tracy.'

David glanced at her with his hint of a smile. 'What was all that about cremation?' he said.

Helen shrugged. 'The woman's an idiot. Where are they going to do it? Belarus? It's Orthodox. Orthodoxy prohibits cremation outright. Besides, if Rosemary actually did die of radiation poisoning, her body's not contaminated, it's irradiated. To put it crudely, she's nuclear waste.'

'So?'

'You can't *burn* nuclear waste, David. You'd contaminate the air for God knows how many miles around. You have to bury it and bury it deep. She's probably just misunderstood. Or maybe they'll cremate a couple of chickens in a coffin and hand her the ashes in an urn. She'll never know the difference. Nor will her Harlequin rose. Keep going towards London,' Helen said as they reached signs for a criss-cross of roads ahead. 'What *is* the matter with people like that?' she went on irritably. 'She can't even be bothered to find out how her daughter died. The poor girl went through agony. That's a hard way to die. And anyhow, what's other than plain weird about an English boy and girl coming down with acute radiation sickness in Belarus?'

'People believe what they want to believe.'

'A paper like the *Mail* doesn't. It's as ruthless as they come. I still can't see them paying a lot of money for a boring exclusive with a boring woman no other paper would bother with. I know Charles has strong connections there, so he must have handed over the cash. Why? What's he doing? Paying her off? Why would he need to — ' She broke off and turned a face of enchanted discovery on David. 'David Marion, who the hell are *you* to set conditions for *me*?'

'What's that supposed to mean?'

'You know exactly what I mean. You *lied* to me. There's more to this than some 'standard corporate espionage' or whatever piece of junk you figured I'd swallow. People don't run around killing English teenagers for that. So what gives? Come on. Bloeden told you more than that. I can *feel* it.'

'You don't want to know.'

'Yes, I do, goddammit. I not only want to know, I *need* to know.'

He did his best to minimise the significance of the research snippets that seemed to show Follaton was seeding the ground of Belarus with radiation and turning villagers into guinea pigs for the radioprotectant's human trials. But minimising such an operation wasn't easy.

'Emilia was *right*?' she said aghast. 'They couldn't really get away with that, could they? Nobody could.'

'Like I say, people believe what they want to believe.'

'My father used to tell me that we are none of us very nice, but how could anybody do something like *this*? I mean, somebody must have *planned* it.' She shivered, sighed, stared fixedly through the window at the outskirts of London. 'To think I dismissed what Emilia said. No wonder they killed her.'

'Now where?' he said.

'Straight ahead. David, it wouldn't work.'

'What wouldn't?'

'These guys are based in England, right? The ones who've turned over the research material?' David nodded. 'The data's all on paper all right, but it's stored in government archives in Belarus,' she went on. 'I can't tell you how many times I wanted to use some of the . . . Unless — ' she broke off.

'Unless those files in the basement aren't so innocent after all,' he finished for her. 'One trip down there, and they give the girl a job with a good salary so they can keep an eye on her. A second trip down, and she's sent off to Belarus before she can tell anybody what she's seen.' He handed her his mobile. 'Get the number for James's father. We'd better let him know we're coming.'

She began rummaging in her purse. 'My own is in here somewhere.'

'You've got your *cell phone* on you? It's off, isn't it?'

'Of course it isn't. Why should it be?'

'How can somebody so smart be so stupid?'

His voice was harsh, and she'd already taken in her breath for an angry retort when she realized what he was saying. 'Oh, shit, they've been picking up the signal, haven't they?'

* * *

In the US it's 'cell phone tower triangulation'. In Europe it's the 'global system for mobile communication'. Mobiles communicate via a base station or tower; the strength of the signal tells a tower how far away any active phone is but gives no direction for it. In open country or near built-up areas like London, a phone can easily be in communication with two or three towers at the same time. Measure the distance between the phone and each tower, and you can 'triangulate' the phone's position in much the same way astronomers plot an asteroid's path through the solar system.

Helen had been wearing an electronic tag. Before David could stop her, she'd thrown the phone out the window. It hit the road and broke into pieces.

Anybody watching would have seen the trace go dead.

* * *

Helen wasn't the only one under surveillance.

The day before Rosemary left for Belarus, a representative from an up-and-coming outlet, Fones of the Future, appeared at her mother's door, a polite, nervous young man, who'd said he was a student at Christ Church, Oxford. He'd opened his heart to Tracy about his love life over several cups of tea. She'd had to lead him back to telephones herself; rather shamefacedly, he explained that the company he represented had developed a new model and that she'd been randomly selected for a trial of it. It did many things her old telephone did not. It could receive email. It came with three months of free calls to any landline or mobile phone in the UK. It even had a satellite extension phone which could reach it from anywhere in the world. She could stay in touch with her daughter every minute of the day. All she had to do was wait for the base unit to ring once, then go quiet, and all the phone's new functions would be activated.

How could she know that a whistle blown down the receiver after that single ring had opened the line for a sophisticated German device called a 'built-in infinity transmitter'? Everything said in her living room since had been beamed back to UniCom Intelligence Associates, the UCAI subsidiary that provided high-level security for Follaton Medical Foundation.

# 53

## MOWBRAY SQUARE

Charles was shocked to the core of his being. He sat frozen behind his desk, unable to bring himself to speak. He'd been listening for forty minutes without a single word.

' . . . yes, yes,' came Helen's voice on the recording. 'That's good, Tracy. That's really good. Now turn your face to the left. That's your better side, you know.'

'Oh, is it?' came Tracy Figgis's whine. 'We could do one photo with me and Rosemary's picture. What do you think, Reverend?'

'Sounds right to me.'

The pity of it was that Charles had grown fond of Helen, and he'd been certain — absolutely certain — she was close to falling in love with him. He'd even thought that perhaps she might turn over the patents as a wedding present if he handled his end of it precisely right.

'This 'Reverend' ' — he spat the word out at Googie, who sat listening too — 'he *can't* be your David Marion. He sounds like a pussy cat.'

'That's Marion all right.'

'How can you say that? He doesn't sound like any villain I ever heard before.'

'Notice that growly sound when he talks? Some nerves got damaged in a prison brawl.

That English accent comes from her father.'

'I want him dead,' Charles said. 'I want them both dead. Do you understand me?'

He got up abruptly and paced the room, wounded, angry, not just humiliated but humiliated in front of Googie and Jeffrey, two underlings, two hirelings, two nobodies. He'd never been jilted before. There was a pain where his heart was. There was a weight, an ache.

He stopped, swung around to Jeffrey. 'Where are they now?'

'I imagine your Mr Marion became aware of Dr Freyl's mobile. Or should I call her Miss Bezukhova? He seems to be rather clever that way. The trace went dead shortly after they — '

'You *lost* them?' Charles interrupted. Now he was outraged. 'How could you lose them, you idiot?'

'Calm yourself, Sir Charles. Mrs Figgis knew nothing. Perhaps we may pick them up at James's parents' house.'

'You bugged *his* parents? When? Why? I never authorized it. That woman had lost the address.'

'Mr Smith is a Labour Councillor and a person of strong opinion. It is a pity that young Rosemary could not have found herself a male related to someone, er, less likely to express outspoken views. As it was, we felt it necessary to take the precaution as soon as we identified the young man. I do not imagine it will take Dr Freyl and Mr Marion long to track the Smith parents down, perhaps a couple of hours, perhaps a day.'

* * *

Fones of the Future had appeared at Beaston Court in Peckham Rye on the same day James and Rosemary disappeared with their blanket into the Lowieza Woods outside Dubiczewo. Neither had been missing yet, at least not officially. James's parents couldn't possibly have known that anything was wrong. They were as pleased as Tracy Figgis to have such a fine, modern device in their home — especially when it came with three months of free telephone calls.

And back at Mowbray Square, the receiver for the infinity transmitter in it began recording in the basement of the Foundation while Jeffrey and Googie were still upstairs in Charles's office trying to reassure him that they had plenty of time.

# 54

## LONDON SUBURBS

'I would not have agreed to see you if my wife was here,' James's father said, leading David and Helen through a hall dominated by a tapestry of a small boy with 'James' written on his tee shirt. James's father was thin, balding, jumpy, his movements erratic, his manner both querulous and tormented. 'You said you were family. They didn't mention you in the paper. I checked.'

'I wasn't *real* family,' Helen said, 'only a cousin — but I guess I kind of thought of Rosemary as a little sister.' Helen had become fond of Rosemary, but not any more than that. Even so, she launched into this second elaborate lie of the morning as though her imaginary job at the *Chicago Tribune* were mere preparation. 'I took care of her for about a year while her mother was . . . Her mother wouldn't have mentioned the time she spent being, well, she's had some pretty severe depressive episodes.'

'We have lost everything, Miss Bezukhova. James was our life.'

'I'm so sorry,' Helen said, and David knew that however fake the story she was telling, the warmth in her voice was real.

The Peckham house wasn't oppressively

child-oriented, but the sense of the boy who'd grown up here wasn't limited to the tapestry. A collage on one wall documented his progress from babyhood (wrapped in a blanket, playing on the grass), to primary school (a series in school cap and scarf), then secondary school with holidays in between (rowing one year, sliding down ropes another). Marks up another wall charted his growth. His father opened a marquetry cabinet and brought out a decanter and glasses with gold rims.

'Sherry?' he said.

The sense of grief and anger about him didn't ease as Helen and David dutifully sipped Harvey's Bristol Cream, and Helen elaborated on her relationship with Rosemary, leading him to volunteer work in Belarus.

'You didn't want to speak to the newspapers?' she asked.

'The *Daily Mail*!' His contempt was absolute. 'They have no exclusive with *me*, and I'll tell my story *my* way at *my* convenience to a paper of *my* choice.'

'Did Sir Charles talk to you about the accident?'

'He smarmed his way around it while I tried to find the truth.'

'I'm anxious to know too. Tracy was vague on the details.'

James's father bristled with hurt and indignation. 'I doubt you'd understand it.'

'She has a PhD in physics,' David said.

James's father gave her an angry glance. 'Sir Charles said the causes of it date back to

Soviet days. Exactly like that story in the ghastly *Mail* said.'

Helen knew what the *Daily Mail* reporter had been talking about. The Soviets really did toss their nuclear waste away like candy wrappers. Radioactive relics really do litter Russia, Lithuania, the Ukraine, Georgia, Belarus in the form of decommissioned generators, radiation therapy machines, reactor coolants, abandoned military equipment from rifle scopes to enriched uranium for gun-type bombs. Sources of caesium-137 — such as the *Mail* described — are everywhere. So are technetium-99, tritium, cobalt-60 as well as uranium, radium, thorium and many others. Some of this junk lies buried deep in mine shafts, bunkers, caves, but lots of it is just lying around, ready to be carted away by whoever runs across it first. Most of it is called 'trivial' because it contains only small amounts of dangerous material.

Some of it is far, far from that.

* * *

As soon as the go-ahead had come through from Jeffrey Hardcastle of the Foundation — just as Rosemary and James reappeared from the woods but before anybody was supposed to know what had happened to them — Dr Zukim of the Mobile Clinic had sent for rad rangers from Minsk. These internationally funded teams hunt down the cast-offs that, as the *Mail* said, can be made into a terrorist's dream: the heart of a dirty bomb as well as a tool for a new breed of suicide bombers who don't need explosives to wreak havoc.

The team had discovered metal canisters the size of paint pails. Instruments had indicated that the contents were in fact strontium-90 — not the caesium the *Daily Mail* talked about — in a form so concentrated that forty seconds at a time was the maximum exposure a person dared risk.

That's why the old men had taken over the operation. They always do when the source is as hot as this: the young ones have families to raise. It took two days, twenty-five old men and one stopwatch to get the canisters and their contents inside lead-lined drums.

An unexpected oddity of this case was that the canisters weren't rusty; they looked almost as though they'd been placed there within the last few days. Impossible, of course — which explains why it wasn't mentioned in the official report.

* * *

'This junk was within walking distance into the trees?' David said to James's father. 'How come nobody else had stumbled across it?'

'Sir Charles told me the canisters had been found a month ago,' said James's father. 'He said bureaucratic delays in clearing away such things are endemic and that all volunteers were told about them and warned away from the wood. I do not believe him. James would have told us about it. He liked a good story. But what's the point in dwelling on that? I know that if I went over there to investigate, I'd find exactly what they describe.'

James's father clenched his teeth, but he couldn't hold back his anger any longer. 'They should have protected my son. They have no *right* to cover up their failure to do so. A letter goes off to my MP tomorrow. A copy will go to the newspapers, the BBC, Radio 4, all the local London stations I can think of. I have become friendly with a number of editors over the years. People will hear about this.' He shut his eyes, breathed in and out unevenly, recovered his balance. 'You can see why I won't speak about James when my wife is here. She's very broken-up, and there *will* be publicity. I won't rest until I get it.'

Helen found herself struggling with her own emotions, seeing sets of patterns — just as he was — where there shouldn't be any. 'There isn't anything that can compensate us for what happened,' she said, 'but a public airing is what I want too.'

James's father scanned her face, and his anger suddenly collapsed. 'I'm so sorry, Miss Bezukhova, Reverend.' Helen had gleefully introduced David to him with this new alias. 'I do hope you'll forgive me. You've both been very patient, and I've been unconscionably rude. Let me show you the garden. James was good with flowers. More sherry? No? Have half a glass. Please.'

He took them through the kitchen out to a walled yard filled with bloom, a mound of deep blue caryopteris, Japanese anemones in white and pink, a reddening Virginia creeper that spilled itself over one entire wall.

Helen was impressed. David, taking his cue from her, praised the flowers too.

'Look,' Helen said to James's father, 'as to your MP and all, James didn't by any chance tell you anything about the statistics he worked with at the Clinic, did he?' Where there are traces of one new pattern, there are likely to be others. A smart kid might have seen something suspicious — or inconsistent — in the research carried out by the Clinic. 'You know, to give you some idea what he was doing all day. Tracy isn't interested in details like that. Maybe he talked about research methods or data storage or something?'

James's father shook his head. 'Mainly he told us amusing anecdotes. Pathetic, isn't it? My information I mean. The only new thing I can add is the drawings. I doubt they'll make much of a stir on their own, but they can provide me with an opening. Are you chilly, Miss Bezukhova? Would you like to go in?'

'What kind of drawings?' said David before she had a chance to answer. 'Patients? The Mobile Clinic?'

'No, no. I'm afraid they're only architectural plans of the Follaton building in Mowbray Square. It was talking to Rosemary's mother that made me think of it. I don't have high security clearance but — '

'*Security* clearance?' Helen interrupted. 'To see blueprints for a *charity*?'

'I was looking around for something to catch

them out on. So I checked the Council files and found a reference stating there was no public access to the plans. I'm a director of London City Cleaning Services. We have contracts for many local government offices.' He smiled for the first time since they'd arrived at his house. 'I felt it was my duty personally to check on the dusting of the architects' filing cabinets.'

'Good for you,' Helen said. 'Find anything interesting?'

'Not really. Follaton Medical Foundation replaced the glass in the basement windows with stone and failed to notify English Heritage — not much, but it is against the law to alter architecturally valuable buildings without permission, and this one is Grade 1 listed.'

She frowned. 'You're saying that basement *does* belong to the Foundation?'

'Oh, yes,' he said. 'The Foundation owns it. Most definitely. I studied the plans. Let me get them for you. You can see for yourself that the basement is an integral part of the property. There's no access to or from *any* other building.'

⋆ ⋆ ⋆

'How can people drink that stuff?' David said as they drove away.

'God only knows. The second half of mine went in the ivy.'

'I saw that.'

'Where'd yours go?'

'Lawn.'

She studied his profile. What was it about him

that appealed to her so? The nose had clearly been broken. The ears were, well, just ears. But how could she work her mind around the power in the body and the glisten of the skin in the sunlight that had broken again through the clouds. 'You know something?' she said softly. 'We've made a good team this morning.'

'How come no other newspaper has tried to talk to James's father? He plainly wasn't going to give any exclusive to the *Daily Mail*.'

'Guys like Charles — to say nothing of mammoths like UCAI — can put a lid on practically anything unless somebody really starts screaming. No newspaper lawyers are going to let James's father say everything he wants to, but he's certainly the kind of person who can give Follaton a red face. There's also the chance that some journalist — maybe somebody like Emilia's nephew — might start snooping, and that might show up something important. Jesus, I hate grief. That poor guy — ' She stopped short. 'David, they *did* kill those kids.'

He was pulling up at a pedestrian crossing. 'How do you figure that?'

'Let's assume Rosemary and James did get a dose of radiation from some radioactive relic. Okay. Fine. If the dose was high enough to kill them as quickly as the time scheme dictates — even before the parents can be notified that they've been injured — they'd be far too sick to find their way out of any forest. If the dose was low enough to allow them to walk out of the forest as Charles says they did, it was low enough so that they'd still be alive. Which means that if they actually did get out of the forest alive, they were murdered not long after they hit that clinic.'

'Why so elaborate? Why not run them over with a truck? Drown them in a lake?'

She shook her head. 'No idea. Turn left here.'

'On the other hand,' David said. 'Those newspaper stories were pretty impressive. I bet you couldn't buy that kind of publicity for any amount of money.'

'Jesus,' Helen gasped. 'You *are* a cold bastard, aren't you? You think they planned it like that?'

'Why not? Sounds good to me. A diagnosis of radiation poisoning in a couple of nice-looking English kids. Osama bin Laden looking scary. A story saying he can come and get you right in your own home, and you're going to die if he does. Then Hay tells you that his Foundation is fighting tooth-and-nail to make you all better if that happens. The money must have come pouring in.'

Helen's shoulders slumped. 'Oh, God, if you're right, maybe it's a blessing that they had to have died some other way. At least they didn't suffer long.'

* * *

James's mother had been making the final arrangements for her son's funeral. She dreaded going home, went for a long walk near the undertakers to put it off, had a cup of tea, filled the car with petrol.

The marriage wasn't good — hadn't been for years. James was the only reason it still existed, and her husband's rage at Follaton was the final straw. The way she saw it, he was flailing around, desperate to hide the truth from himself. James had died because of him. He hadn't just been the one who suggested Belarus, he'd insisted on it — 'about time you learned how other people live' — and she loathed him for it. She was hugely relieved when he didn't seem to be at home. She sat in the living room, listening to a steady drip, drip from upstairs, didn't know what it was, didn't care, went up to the bathroom only for a pee.

Her husband's bony knees poked out of pure red water that was dribbling over the rim of the tub. His hands floated on the surface, but the rest of his body was no more than a shadow beneath it.

* * *

The police were kind. They were comforting. They assured her there'd be no publicity for the simple reason that suicides in London were more frequent than fires in fish and chip shops.

She didn't protest even though she knew perfectly well that her husband hadn't slit his own wrists. The simple fact was that she couldn't help feeling grateful to whoever had relieved her of the turmoil of divorce.

The only question in her mind — it didn't disturb her much — was why anybody would bother to kill a nonentity like him.

# 55

## DARTMOUTH, DEVON

Helen and David stopped at a motorway service area for a late lunch on their way to Devon and an even later tea with Zoya. That's part of the reason the drive took more than five hours. The rest of the reason was that David kept the Riley at seventy miles an hour.

'For Christ's sake, can't you go any faster?' she complained. 'I mean, like I said, this is supposed to be a *racing* car. The guy told me it floats along at a hundred. Come on, try it. I bet you didn't even know an old British car could go that fast.'

'What's the hurry?' David said.

'Here I am thinking of you as a wild man, and it turns out you're a respectable, law-abiding citizen.'

'That's me.'

David liked speed. He got a serious kick out of it, and he'd have loved to see what this old car could do. But an ex-con with any sense at all is paranoid about cops and unnecessary questions. The licence David carried was the one that Samuel had given him months ago. He had no idea if it was valid in England, and getting pulled over for speeding without a licence at a time like this sounded like a really stupid idea to him.

Helen sighed in resignation and leaned her head against the Riley's passenger window. 'Jesus, if I hadn't whined about the boxes in the hallway and then taunted Rosemary into going back for a second look, she wouldn't have ended up in Belarus at all, would she? If she hadn't gone, that James Smith wouldn't have met her. It's all my fault, isn't it?' Helen could hear pleading in her voice; she looked at David for reassurance but found none.

'I don't know,' he said.

'How could I have been so stupid?'

David only glanced at her. 'Where to now?'

'I have no idea whatever.' Her sigh came out as a sob.

'I'm talking about your friend's apartment. The sign for Dartmouth was just back there.'

'Through the roundabout and down the hill toward the river.' Helen directed him past the imposing structure of the Royal Naval College that rules the town and into one of the narrow streets that layer the hill beneath. 'We'll be going down there.' She pointed to a long, crooked flight of steps that joined this street to the street below. He pulled the car to a stop.

'You can't park here, David. There's a place in the middle of town.'

'They going to tow it away?'

Helen shook her head. 'You'll get a ticket.'

'Not me,' he said, getting out. 'You're the one who rented the car.'

* * *

Zoya ushered Helen and David into a dining room that combined tsarist theatrical, a dash of Paris and a good measure of Old South femininity.

'Oh, Helen,' Zoya was saying, 'you didn't tell me he was *so* good-looking. You don't want tea, do you, Mr Marion?' She gestured dismissal at her table with its frilly placemats, flowered teapot, platter of scones. 'Of course you don't. You *couldn't*. It's too late for tea anyway. May I call you David? *Such* a nice name. American men want whisky. Just *look* at the muscle on him, Helen! Oh, damn! I haven't got any whisky. We could go to the Royal Castle. They'd be open, wouldn't they, Helen?'

'I like tea,' said a bemused David. He couldn't have said why the compliments were so pleasing, especially since he knew Zoya was legally blind — Helen had told him so — and wouldn't even recognize him the next time she encountered him.

Zoya laughed happily. 'You *do* like tea? Are you *sure*? How amazing. Helen hates it. It's so funny watching her try to — '

'Do shut up, Zoya,' Helen interrupted.

Zoya felt carefully for each cup to verify its position on the table, peered into it as she poured, handed one to Helen, one to David, then passed the platter. 'Take two, David,' she insisted. 'Have you really never had a scone before?'

'We've come to talk about Feodor,' Helen said.

Zoya looked away at once. 'Oh, no, Helen. I couldn't. Do have another scone, David,' she said, although he hadn't touched the ones she'd just given him.

'Listen to me, Zoya,' Helen said. 'It begins to look like Feodor was murdered. Maybe some other people too. I'm scared. I could be next on somebody's agenda, and I think — *we* think — that Charles could be that somebody.'

'Oh, no. Surely not, Helen. He's a *lord*.' Zoya set down the plate and appealed to David. 'You do understand, don't you, David? Feodor was my friend. He'd be mortified. I can't tell a friend's innermost secrets just because he's dead. Charles couldn't possibly hurt Helen, could he?'

'He might try,' David said.

* * *

The telephone call had wakened Zoya after midnight.

'Feodor,' she said, slurring his name a little (she needed heavy sedation to sleep), 'do you know what time it is?'

'They do not tell me the time.' His voice was high-pitched. She could hear a struggle against tears in it. 'They have taken my tie and my shoelaces. They have taken my belt with the Mussinov buckle. What am I to do without my Mussinov buckle?'

'What *are* you talking about? Who's taken your shoes?'

'Zoya, they give me one telephone call only, and I make it to you. I cannot face my wife. I cannot face my children. I shall *never* be able to face them. Not ever again. I decide to telephone you because — '

'Feodor!' Zoya interrupted. '*Who* has taken your shoes?'

'Not my shoes, Zoya. My shoe*laces*. I have never done anything wrong. Not in all my life. How can they say these things of me? I have *never* — '

'Feodor!'

He began to sob. 'Zoya, I will spend this night in a cell in Torquay police station, and I am cold. I am a thief. This is how they charge me.'

'I'll be there at once.'

But she knew that Feodor needed a lawyer more than warm clothes and a shoulder to cry on. As she dressed, she called Mr Higham, who'd drawn up her will a year ago; he met her at the station. His interview with Feodor was long because Feodor kept bursting into tears. He dispatched the custody officer in five minutes and led the weeping Feodor — wrapped in a red cashmere Armani coat from Zoya's closet, his belt restored to his waist, his shoelaces and tie in place — out of the station and into Zoya's care.

She took Feodor back to her apartment, sat him down on the sofa with a box of Kleenex, brought out a bottle of brandy, poured him a glass, waited for it to calm him.

'I must become a monk,' he said then, his lower lip quivering. 'I must never venture out in the world again.'

'Don't be ridiculous, Feodor. You haven't done anything wrong. Mr Higham said so. You heard him yourself. All you did was take your daughter to Brighton. That's not a crime.'

That morning, Feodor's daughter had insisted on returning to her university in Sussex even though she'd barely recovered from a long bout of glandular fever. Feodor's wife fretted. He fretted too: a five-hour train journey with several changes, a suitcase and books is very taxing. His daughter finally consented to let him drive her back in one of the Naval College's cars. He'd done so many times before, ferrying her luggage to and fro at the beginning and end of term. A member of staff at the College didn't need a car of his own; he could borrow one with no more than the okay of the Duty Officer.

When Feodor returned that evening, the Duty Officer collected the keys, took note of the petrol tank, then told him that the Commander wanted to see him. Feodor was delighted; the Commander didn't ask for members of staff except to commend them or inform them of a salary increase. And imagine! He'd clearly stayed late — it was already past eight o'clock — to deliver this special piece of news.

Feodor knocked timidly on the solid oak door with 'COMMANDER' across it in gold letters.

'Come!' This was what the Commander always said. So had the Commander before him.

Feodor opened the door, a smile of anticipation playing about his mouth. 'Good evening, Commander,' he said.

But the Commander's face was grim. He cocked his head at Feodor — not so much as a 'Hello' — and two police constables stepped forward.

'Is this the man?' one of them said, addressing the Commander.

'It is,' he replied.

The constable spun Feodor around, yanked his hands behind his back, handcuffed him. 'You have the right to remain silent . . . ' The American Miranda is based on the British caution — the two are much the same — but Feodor was too horrified to make out the words.

'What have I done?' he cried.

Nobody answered. The constables bundled him out the door and into the midst of the cadets, who turned to stare, then giggle, then jeer. Feodor had once seen wolves tear into a rabbit, and he could almost feel his flesh rip open with the shame of it.

At the police station, they took away his belt, his tie, his shoelaces. 'Can't have you hanging yourself and cheating justice, can we?' said the constable as he shoved Feodor into the station's single cell with its two other occupants. A terrible hour followed. Feodor wept. One of his fellow prisoners hit him on the side of the head to shut him up. The other prisoner woke and threw up over the floor. Feodor gagged at the smell, then was sick himself. Nobody came to clean up the vomit.

At about ten o'clock he was handcuffed again, taken out of the cell, escorted to a small room in the station, where he sat alone, not knowing what to expect. Perhaps ten minutes later a man in a suit appeared.

'Oh, God, these guys stink,' he said, catching a whiff of Feodor.

'What *have* I done?' This time Feodor was pleading.

'You stole a car. Not for — '

'What car?' cried Feodor, shocked to the depth of his being. But the man in the suit kept on talking.

' — for the first time either. The college has — '

'How could I steal a car?'

' — ignored your behaviour so far — '

'I do not know *how* to do such things.'

' — in the hopes that you would give up your illegal activities,' the man went on relentlessly. 'But no. You kept at it. Couldn't you hire a car like an ordinary person? Your salary must be high enough.'

* * *

'Then it *isn't* my fault that he's dead,' Helen said when Zoya finished her story. 'It had nothing to do with me.'

'Of course it's not your fault,' Zoya said. 'How could you think such a thing?'

Helen took in her breath. The last few hours had been very hard for her, and the thought that she might not bear so heavy a burden of guilt was exhilarating. 'I suppose a man can die of shame. It's possible, isn't it? I sometimes feel as though I could.'

'I don't buy it,' said David.

'You wouldn't!' Helen said, abruptly angry.

'Nor do I,' Zoya said. 'Not for two seconds. David is right. Feodor was a happy man. That college killed him. They set him up. He'd been born in Paris. His family were Russian aristocrats. He did not fit in.'

'I don't buy that either,' David said.

This time Helen shook her head too. 'I have nothing against conspiracy theories but — ' She stopped short, put her hand over her mouth. 'Wait a minute. Zoya's got the wrong conspiracy, that's all. When I realized UCAI was backing Follaton as well as making offers for Joshua's venom, I looked into them pretty thoroughly, and I remember noticing — only because of Zoya living here — that the beneficiaries of one of their endowment funds included Dartmouth Naval College. I forgot all about it, didn't even remember it when I was wondering why Follaton got *Feodor* up to London to do the translating. London must have hundreds of Russian and Belarusian speakers. But no, they get this guy all the way up from Devon. On the other hand, what's more natural if they're shovelling money at the college? It's not the college that killed him. It's UCAI. They *did* overhear him at my house.'

'It's no big deal to hang a guy,' David said then.

'Done it yourself, have you?' said Helen.

He only shrugged.

* * *

Feodor had slept for a few hours on Zoya's floor, snuggled in her Armani coat, but woke before dawn, too restless to stay where he was. He wasn't at all sure what he was going to do, but the desire to see the Royal Naval College was overwhelming. Oh, how proud he'd been to work there.

He walked up the hill to the long, powerful buildings overlooking town and river, then sought sanctuary in the old chapel. He loved the damp smell of ancient stone and the stained-glass window that showed the Archangel Gabriel, Messenger of God, Supreme Leader of the Host, with halo and huge wings, hand raised in greeting. The pews had rotted away years ago. Two long wooden tables now took their place. The chapel was supposed to serve as an alternative study room, but the cadets preferred the warmth of the library in the main building.

Feodor sat at one of the long tables and dropped his head into his hands in the prayer written by St Mardarios, who was tortured and martyred for Christendom. 'Oh, Master and God . . . have mercy on me a sinner, and save me, your unworthy servant, in any way you know, for you are blessed unto — '

A sudden chill along the spine told him he wasn't alone. He looked up to find Gabriel Walker watching him from the other side of the table. 'Oh, Gabriel,' he said, knowing as any good Catholic does, that the Archangel Gabriel who adorned the stained glass as God's messenger is also the Angel of Death, 'Have you come for me? Can what I have done be so terrible a sin?'

'Let's get this over with,' Gabriel said.

'I am an innocent man in the eyes of the law. Mr Higham says so. He says I am unjustly accused.' And yet Feodor knew full well that the saint whose prayer he'd been saying was also a man unjustly accused.

'You think we can't improve on car theft? Where were you a week ago today in the afternoon?'

Feodor had to think. 'Right here in the chapel. I like it. It is quiet. It is peaceful. I can write poetry here.'

'Alone?'

'Yes.'

'What a good place to lure an innocent young boy.'

'A cadet? Why would I do that? They prefer the library.'

Gabriel laughed. 'Haven't you ever heard the old proverb, 'A woman for duty, a boy for pleasure, a melon for ecstasy.' The melons in this country are crap. You had to make do with second best.'

Feodor was too shocked to speak for a moment. 'You mean they'd have me arrested for — ' He couldn't bring himself to say the words out loud.

'Slip a hundred quid in a cadet's pocket, and he'll swear to anything.'

Gabriel took a length of rope out of his briefcase, secured it to the beam, helped Feodor get his head through the noose, knocked the chair away from beneath his feet and watched the death struggle with the satisfaction of a job well done.

* * *

That was in the early hours of Friday morning. Rosemary had left for Belarus only hours before; Gabriel had had to rush back to London to board the UCAI jet to get there himself. Jeffrey wanted him there with plenty of time to make sure the 'Rosemary situation' guaranteed positive publicity for the Follaton Medical Foundation.

# 56

## THE BACKROADS OF SURREY

It was ten o'clock when Helen and David set out from Dartmouth for London. The sky was clear. The moon was full.

The fast route between the capital and the West Country is the motorway they'd taken on the way down. The secondary highway is slower, but it goes past Stonehenge, and Helen liked the idea of Stonehenge in the moonlight. She drove. 'I promise I'll keep to the speed limit,' she said as they pulled out of town.

He seemed puzzled. 'Why?'

'You don't care if I get caught?'

'No concern of mine.'

Rebellion is so difficult in permissive society. Helen revved the Riley up to over 100 miles an hour for a ten-mile stretch in the hopes of annoying him. So far as she could tell, he actively enjoyed it. So she slowed down to below the speed limit. He didn't seem to mind that either.

Clouds gathered even before they reached the open downland of Salisbury Plain. Rain began to fall. By the time they passed the brooding, primeval stage set of Stonehenge, it might as well not have been there. The rain fell heavier. Forty miles out of London, the traffic increased, then clogged into a jam, the two city-bound lanes making a Christmas string of red tail lights as far ahead of her as she could see through the slish-slosh of the Riley's wipers. Cars closed in behind.

The other side of the road was completely empty.

'What's this about?' David said.

'Making you nervous?'

'I don't like being hemmed in.'

'Me neither.' Helen shoved the Riley into first, gunned the engine, made a sharp right turn. A jolt and a clank of the Riley's heavy body, and it mounted the grass barrier. Another jolt and clank brought it down and completed the U-turn. She took the first side road she came to.

'Feel better?' she said, turning to him with a smile.

'Much.'

But rural roads in this part of the country — as in so much of England — are narrow, poorly marked, twisting; she quickly lost all sense of where they were or in what direction they were heading.

The clank in the Riley's engine returned and turned almost at once into a screech. 'We're going to have to stop,' David said.

'Like hell we are.'

'It sounds like the water pump.'

'So what? That's the car's problem, not mine.'

'The metal melts, the pistons seize, the engine blows. You're going to stop whether you like it or not.'

The road was narrow, overhung with trees. As soon as she switched off the lights, the dark was absolute. David got out his mobile. No signal. 'You stay here,' he said, opening the door. But by now, the rain was belting down in sheets. He shut the door again.

'Better give it a few minutes,' she said.

She wasn't aware of falling asleep, and she awoke slowly as the first rays of the sun dappled through the trees, her head on David's shoulder, his arm protectively around her, the morning bright through an overhang of trees. She nestled against him a few minutes, basking in the animal warmth of his body, then shifted so she could see his profile above her, forehead, cheekbones, mouth, curl of hair at the neck. The temptation was too great; she reached up to kiss him on the lips, paused a moment, pulled away, studied him a minute.

'David!' she cried in alarm.

The blow caught her completely unawares, his awakening so abrupt and so violent that at once he had her pinned against the far side of the car, elbow poised above her throat. A moment of pure bafflement clouded his face. Then he let her go and fell back against the Riley's leather seat.

She settled herself gingerly in the driver's side, massaging her jaw where the uppercut with the palm of his hand had hit. 'Goodness,' she said, 'you do wake up cheery.'

He looked away; she could see the clenching of his teeth in the muscles of his cheeks. 'I can't explain.' The words sounded ground out of him.

'It's okay, David. I'm okay.'

'It's *not* okay.' A little pressure where the chin

meets the neck and the larynx crushes: death by asphyxiation.

But what did Helen know of such things? 'I'm going to consider that an apology, and I never heard you apologize before. I can't say my headmistress would accept the tone. Me? I kind of like it. That some trick of the old prison warrior?' He let out his breath irritably. 'You sleep so quietly, I thought you were dead,' she went on. 'It's terrifying. Don't you even dream?'

'We need a phone,' he said, getting out of the car.

No more than 300 yards up a narrow lane, they found a farmhouse, called a taxi, sat silent all the way to London, as far apart as the seat would allow, neither knowing how to break this new addition to the tension between them.

# 57

## ISLE OF DOGS

As soon as David and Helen's taxi pulled up in front of Grendel and the Harpist, Martha ran out of the pub.

'Stay where you are, David,' she said.

'Who the hell are you?' Helen demanded.

'None of your fucking business.'

But Martha's smile was disarming, and as she slid into the back seat, she forced them together. They held themselves rigid against the abrupt intensity of arm against arm, leg against leg; they'd left the Isle of Dogs behind them and reached the highway known as Limehouse Link before Helen could distance herself enough from the touch to speak.

'Where are we going?' she said.

'Edgware Road.'

'Is there a reason?'

Martha cocked her head at David, then gave Helen an amused and knowing grin. 'Looks to me like somebody important wants to see him.' She handed him a card.

A simple business card, nothing more.

**Galleas International**
**Office of the Chief Executive**

On the opposite side, in a fluid upright hand was written,

*Kent Mansions. Edgware Road. This morning.*

David cleared his throat. 'How'd you get this?' he asked.

'Special courier.'

'You believe everything a special courier tells you?'

Martha made a face. 'My dad saw some spook in the pub last night.'

'What's this all about, David?' Helen asked.

He dared not look at her. 'Cop maybe?' he asked Martha.

'My dad knows a copper when he sees one. He says spook, he means spook. Then this special courier comes around with a business card from my boss's boss, and I'm thinking, 'Edgware Road's got to be a better place for this lot than the Isle of Dogs.''

The ride to Edgware Road was worse than the trip to the Isle of Dogs had been. Even Martha seemed tense, and London traffic is terrible despite charges levied against everybody who drives in the city. On top of that, today happened to be the first of a two-day strike by signalmen on London's underground — it had been threatened for weeks — and it meant that the city's roads clogged to a standstill again and again. The taxi finally pulled up behind a stretch Hummer with its boot open and propped wide to accommodate three figures in burkas, gesticulating at each other in what seemed to be an animated discussion. Just beyond them, a store called Al-Karam's displayed chests of drawers encrusted with gold leaf and seashells. To one side, Babylon Travel advertised trips to Cairo from £320. Under the awning to the other side, ornamented tables supported hookahs; a clear plastic enclosure sheltered patrons in colourful keffiyehs from the chill of the air.

'*This* is Kent Mansions?' David said.

Martha shrugged. 'They call it 'Little Beirut' around here. You're going to have to walk the rest of the way.'

'I'm coming too,' Helen said.

'No.' David didn't even glance at her.

But she couldn't bear the idea of letting him out of her sight. 'What's that supposed to mean? I go where I goddamn please.'

'Not this time.'

'Let 'im go,' Martha intervened. 'The boss's boss asked for him, not you, and I've got to find somewhere for you two to stay tonight. No way he can come back to the pub.' She turned to David. 'Give her your mobile. Ring her when you're done here. I'll ring her when I find a place.'

# 58

## MOWBRAY SQUARE

Charles paced back and forth in his office. 'You *said* she'd ring.' He pointed an accusing finger at Googie, who sat — rather more comfortably than before — on a straight-backed chair: just the right support for the lumbar spine. Jeffrey looked on with a wary and appraising eye.

Googie shrugged. 'I ain't clairvoyant, you know. The old lady knows I can't keep track of her granddaughter without a cell phone number. She'll keep at it until she's located the girl. It's only a matter of time.'

Charles paced some more. 'Suppose she doesn't ring? Suppose Marion keeps his mobile turned off? Or won't let her ring Grandmama on it? Or she uses a pay phone?'

Charles had already decided how to move ahead. Helen's death would destroy Becky, perhaps kill the old woman outright. He'd seen for himself that her angina was advanced. If her heart didn't do the trick, Jeffrey would have to arrange something suitable. A fall down the stairs perhaps. With all the Freyls in the grave, the bee farm would revert to Joshua Brewster, and negotiations would be much simpler. Joshua had a large, close family. He was newly married. People like that are easy to pressure.

'Oh, for crying out loud,' Googie said, 'stop worrying. We'll find them. Kind of convenient, them being together. I'm thinking car accident.' He paused, considered. 'Marion likes cars. Sooner or later we'll get him.'

'Sooner or later?' Charles was abruptly angry. 'What good is 'sooner or later' to me? They could be in France for all we know.'

'Do not distress yourself, Sir Charles,' said Jeffrey. 'I believe the situation is rather better controlled than that.'

'Not by me it isn't.'

'We know Dr Freyl is with Mr Marion because we have overheard their visits to both Shaw Mills and Peckham Rye. Mobile numbers would of course pinpoint their position as of now, but you have established your man's general whereabouts, have you not, Mr Allandale?'

Googie nodded. 'An hour ago he and the girl picked up a passenger outside a pub in the Isle of Dogs.'

Charles glared at him. 'I see. So now you're telling me you've lost them *again*.'

'Get a hold on yourself, Charlie.' Googie rolled his eyes. 'If the old lady doesn't call by this afternoon, I'll call her. She's already scared. All I got to do is put the wind up her a little.'

# 59

## EDGWARE ROAD

Kent Mansions was a once-grand Victorian façade that stretched from side street to side street. It rose in four floors of grey stone above a run of Little Beirut shops two blocks away from where the taxi dropped David. He rang the bell; a guard in an olive-drab army uniform answered a few minutes later.

'Yes?' he said.

David showed him the Galleas business card.

'Identification?'

David handed over the Canadian passport in the name of Richard François Gwendolyn.

A second guard arrived, frisked him, escorted him up a stairwell and into an anteroom with a window overlooking a dark courtyard. A third guard appeared at once.

'This way, sir,' he said.

The room beyond was larger. Its gable windows framed the view of a matching building on the other side of Edgware Road, but this might have been the office of a Springfield pro bono lawyer or an elderly doctor in nearby Petersburg. Degrees in thin brown frames hung on the walls. A few manilla folders lay open on a chunky, battered desk. Behind it sat a woman.

She got up, her hand held out. 'Mr Marion.

I'm glad you came.'

'Me too,' David said, and he meant it.

Christina Haggarty, CEO of Galleas International, was about his age, and she made no effort to look younger. No trace of makeup prettified her gamine face with its short upper lip and almond eyes; she dressed severely in a black suit. She'd run Galleas International for almost a decade, ever since her father died. He'd been a legend in the financial world, and she was Queen Elizabeth to his Henry VIII. Her reputation as a leader of men — ruthless, ambitious, imaginative — easily outstripped his.

David had met her in New York during that period when he was looking for somebody to pin Hugh Freyl's murder on. Their discussion had concerned Hugh's involvement with UCAI and Galleas — the Freyl firm had dealt with both corporations — and the venue had been one of New York's most exclusive restaurants. David had had to rent the clothes he wore there; here, the denim jacket he'd borrowed from Lillian's son was very much at home.

'My mother grew up in this building,' Christina said, guessing his thoughts and gesturing at the room. 'I consider you a valuable man and, as you can see, I've given your safety some thought.'

'I'm touched by the concern.'

She studied him as he sat on an elderly sofa off to one side of her desk. 'You know,' she said, 'I'm not sure whether you understand what this meeting is about or not.'

Her doubt was addressed more to herself than

to him. The Galleas dossier on him — it was in one of the folders on her desk — showed that he wasn't without negotiating skills. The South Hams Prison drug ring had gone from success to success for more than a decade until its abrupt collapse a month after Hugh got him out. Which meant he'd had to cut deals with prison administration as well as guards and prisoners. And then an ex-con who disappeared and was presumed dead only to show up alive, well and travelling on a passport that had all the earmarks of the genuine article *despite* being in the wrong name and from the wrong country: this she hadn't expected.

'I fully understand Dr Freyl's position,' Christina said. 'There's little sense in selling an essential ingredient outright when the serious money lies in the future of the finished product. The amusing part of all this is that the UCAI executive assume they settled terms and price with her long ago.'

'They're scaring people for fun, huh?'

'I don't think so, Mr Marion. Why would they frighten Dr Freyl? They'd know it would only get them into the mess they're in right now. They're going to have to work out a treaty with an enemy instead of a contract with a desirable potential ally. Worse, they stand to lose their ingredient altogether — and with it, the entirety of a massive investment in a long-term project. No, no. I'm certain they know nothing about it.'

'*Some*body's been handing out phoney information,' he said, 'bugging apartments, getting people on the run, having guys like your Bloeden make threats and offer lousy deals.'

'You don't like him much, do you?'

'No.'

'My belief is that most of the pressure on Dr Freyl is personal.'

'How much of it comes from you beyond Bloeden?'

'He is the full extent of our contribution.'

David took out a cigarette, tapped it on the table in front of him, lit it. 'If UCAI thinks negotiations with the Freyls are all sewed up, you're saying . . . what? Hay wants the venom for himself?'

'No doubt he does, but that's not his immediate concern. He's the man who secured UCAI funding on the basis of experiments with animals. He oversaw the research and development programme in Belarus, the early submissions to governmental review boards, the annual follow-up reports and the clinical trials that are nearing completion. This has been a huge undertaking. It isn't altogether a surprise that he failed to attend to all the minutiae of the situation as it developed.'

David held smoke in his lungs a moment, then let it go. 'You're kidding me. You're saying he *forgot* to get the patent on the venom?'

'He *delegated* it, Mr Marion. Law is not his field, and it hardly seems a difficult job: buying a property from a small-time farmer in Alabama. He turned it over to Follaton's lawyers.' She laughed. 'Apparently there are a number of Brewsters farming bees around Caton, and Sir Charles ended up with the wrong one. This leaves him running hard to get what his masters assume they own already before they realize what's happened.' She handed him one of the folders on her desk. 'I assume that his hopes for a wedding are no longer viable. You may find this useful even so.'

He took it from her, opened it. The title page read, 'Randolph Gerald Maurice Hay (deceased)'. The contents included an autopsy, a report of the inquest into the death of Charles Hay's brother, medical records and signed witness statements. Every page bore the round CIA seal.

David closed the folder, handed it back to her. 'I've seen guys put away on a lot less than this.'

'Only a few years earlier, and they might have hanged Sir Charles Hay because of it. I imagine Dr Freyl's father had some views on the subject.'

'Oh, yeah?'

'I'm told the friendship was never quite the same afterwards, and I would certainly say this material is sufficient to provoke a reopening of the case — under the right circumstances of course. Please inform Dr Freyl,' Christina went on, 'that Galleas International is prepared to offer her everything she wants — including a fully subsidised product and a fully subsidised distribution system throughout the Chernobyl regions. We are also prepared to help both of you out of your present difficulties.'

Three pigeons landed — an anxious flutter of wings — on the window sill behind her. David shook his head. 'I'm not buying it.'

'Not buying what?'

'You want Hay out of the picture, you kill him. You're willing to write the Freyls a contract they're happy with, you send your errand boy to say so. Somebody as powerful as you doesn't go to all this trouble just to negotiate for rights to a drug.'

Christina made a note on one of the folders in front of her, then looked up at him. 'My father used to say that sex and food are good, but the real fun in life comes from battling over spoils. I'd add only that the spoils must be worthy of the fight. You're right not to let yourself get caught up in a sideshow.'

'A sideshow?' David kept the cigarette in his mouth as he spoke. 'Your competitors poison a whole country — and you call it a sideshow?'

'Casualties are inevitable in the development of a radical new product, Mr Marion.'

'Sure. And the guys who try to let *you* in on the details get dead too. Now are you going to tell me what this is all about or do I go back and tell the Freyls to do a deal with Roche or Bayer or somebody? Anybody but Galleas or UCAI?'

'Are you going to pretend you don't know what I'm talking about?'

'No idea,' he said. He'd always been amazed how often the simple truth sounded like evasion.

'Uranium, Mr Marion. The energy of the future — when all eyes will be on Belarus.'

* * *

Molten rock crawls up from the centre of the Earth and explodes across the surface in a process that repeats again and again as the millennia pass. Uranium seeds itself along cracks in the layers, some of it right out on top where it can be scraped off with a knife. But the higher-grade deposits are deep down, hard to find, harder to get at. The best lie buried in ancient sedimentary basins like the McArthur River in Canada or the Northern Territory of Australia.

Sink shafts up to a kilometre deep with two horizontal levels branching out, one above the seam and one below it. Drill a pilot hole straight through the ore from upper level to lower level. When the drill pokes out at the bottom, attach a rotating head like an egg beater to it and pull it up again, whizzing away. Crush what falls to a powder, dissolve in water, add ammonia. The result is called 'yellowcake' because when people first made it, it came out a bright canary yellow.

That's the end of Phase One.

Next, dissolve the yellowcake in nitric acid. Heat and evaporate to make a gas. Filter until you get an extra whack of the extremely rare and highly unstable isotope U-235 that bombs and nuclear reactors hunger for. Press solid. Bake into ceramic pellets and — *voilá* — you have the most valuable and most dangerous man-made material the world has ever known.

These pellets, packed in tubes of metal alloy, are the fuel rods that make up the core of a reactor. Even all this time later, nobody knows for sure what went wrong at Chernobyl — human error? design flaw? — but whatever it was, it took place right here among these pellets in the reactor's core.

Back in the days when Chernobyl blew — and for decades before that — the Soviet Union wasn't telling anybody anything about *any*thing. The secrets of the meltdown — just what happened, just how many died — are mirrored to this day in the secrets of how much uranium is mined and worked in the old Soviet territories. It's amazing really. All our restrictions on who can explore for uranium and who can't, who can manufacture yellowcake and who can't, who can buy the stuff and who can't — which countries we'll bomb if they don't follow our orders — and no government in the West knows what the old Soviet states are doing in *any* of those categories. Production? Maybe 8,000 tonnes a year, maybe more, maybe less. How much do they process? How much do they sell? We can only guess.

At the time David was talking to Christina about it, probably the only people who *did* know were the espionage departments of the uranium giants: Canada's Cameco, the Commonwealth's Rio Tinto Zinc, the French-based conglomerate Areva, KazAtomProm, which operates out of Kazakhstan. Maybe UCAI and Galleas knew too, although their holdings weren't in the same league. At least not yet.

As for the deposits of the great sedimentary basins in Belarus — yet one more secretive ex-Soviet state — they were so deeply buried that nobody had had any idea how to get at them when they were first located.

The numerous surveys of the area had lain dusty and forgotten at the bottom of a file in the

Institute of Geology in Minsk until only a few years ago.

* * *

'What's uranium got to do with the Freyls' venom?' David asked Christina.

'Let me start with Leslie Bloeden. He's something of a geologist. Did you know that?'

'*That* guy did the Belarus research?'

'I'm afraid not. The work belonged to a friend of his. Rather touching really, one of those internet romances. She wrote him that her father was in the diplomatic service, stationed in Moscow, that she'd spent two summers at the National Academy of Sciences in Minsk, where she'd made her remarkable discovery.'

'And gone to UCAI with it?'

Christina nodded. 'A pity she didn't come to us. On the other hand, Mr Bloeden had neglected to tell her that he was employed by the Central Intelligence Agency and assigned to us. It was his duty to pass the information on. Nuclear energy will soon overtake oil and coal combined as the world's major energy source, Mr Marion.'

'I never liked the idea.'

This time her smile revealed the charm she must have had as a child. 'You have an old-fashioned approach to the realities of life,' she said. 'It's one of the things I like about you. The programme does have snags. On the other hand, what programme doesn't? It's true that man-made machines break down, and nuclear reactors are only man-made machines. It's true that flawed human beings remain flawed — and will continue to make mistakes as they always have. It is also true that we can't possibly build up levels of sufficiently trained staff to man the reactors by the time they go into production.'

'You don't even have the manpower?' He was genuinely surprised.

'Our youngest technicians tend to be in their forties. This is not an area of science that attracts recruits. It lacks' — she cast about for a word — 'sex-appeal. We've worked on the assumption that people will believe anything if they hear it often enough. Over the years, governments have fronted our campaigns to persuade the public that reactors are the first fail-safe design in human history: the single exception to the rule that has no exceptions. They've bought scientists and scientific foundations to support us. They've forced most of the media onto our side. But the public remains unconvinced. Despite all these reassurances, people worry about nuclear waste. They worry about dirty bombs and terrorists. Most of all, they worry about power plant accidents.'

A goose-necked lamp arched across her desk. She altered its angle, studied it a moment, then changed it back. 'The US alone averages one nuclear accident every year. Of course that doesn't cover disposal accidents — they're easy to keep secret — and fortunately, most of these incidents do little damage. I fear we must view an increase in this rate, a doubling perhaps — or even a trebling given the lack of trained staff

— as the price of doing business. What we want to avoid is another Three Mile Island or another Chernobyl.'

'There's got to be a reason why you're telling me this.'

'Mr Marion, you can see how important the radioprotectant is in real terms. If we can't avoid catastrophe, we must be prepared to deal with it. Worries about radiation poisoning become manageable the moment an effective treatment hits the market. Our negotiations with Economic Development in Minsk are well advanced, and the radioprotectant is within perhaps eighteen months of being cleared for marketing by the Federal Drug Administration. As a product, it's unstoppable. This is the moment. Expose the scandal of the Follaton research, and UCAI will have to pull out of the Belarusian uranium fields. We are poised to take over.'

David gazed out at the pigeons. One of them had no toes. Another had a misshapen club where its claw should have been; London's corrosive mix of limestone and pigeon shit eats away at the flesh. 'You haven't told me what I'm doing here.'

'Haven't I?' The intensity in her voice died out. 'Oh, yes, of course. Helen Freyl needs the protection of someone she can trust. I don't want anything to happen to her, and you seem to be the person who fits the bill.'

'Going all kind-hearted, are you?'

'Oh, no. *She* will be the whistleblower.'

* * *

An hour later, David stubbed out his last cigarette.

Christina put several of the folders on her desk into an envelope and handed it to him. 'The jet for Springfield will be waiting at Gatwick whenever Dr Freyl is ready. Leave a message if there are any changes in the plan. The number to call is clipped to the material.'

'You expect changes?'

'There are always changes, Mr Marion.'

He turned towards the door, paused a moment. Lillian had said that he should say goodbye when he left to go somewhere. He wasn't altogether sure whether this was such an occasion or not.

'Mr Marion?'

'Goodbye.'

She laughed. 'You're supposed to look at me when you say that.'

'Am I?' He turned back.

She laughed outright at the consternation in his face — and made what seemed to be a rare spur-of-the-moment decision. 'The contract on you has gone to a CIA agent. I'm afraid I don't know precisely which one, but I can tell you that there's a new occupant in one of the CIA-owned houses in London: 22 Ganton Place.'

# 60

## HAMILTON STREET

Helen had confessed to Martha that she was terrified to stay on London streets by herself and that she needed somewhere safe behind doors until David was finished with his meeting. Martha had nodded, then directed the taxi to a vast pile not far from Hyde Park.

'This doesn't look like the front door,' Helen had said to her.

'Servants' entrance.'

'The *servants*' entrance?'

'Pay the taxi,' Martha said.

She led Helen through a bare foyer, down a narrow flight of stairs to a darkened hallway. A door at the end of it opened onto an airy room. A brightly painted rocking horse stood off to one side and a waist-high dolls' house off to the other. French doors looked out into a garden of lawn and trees where a young man and two small girls were playing catch.

Martha opened the doors. 'Willard!' she called. 'Willard's me brother,' she said to Helen. He turned and waved. He had a Union Jack tattooed over the back of his neck; it extended up onto his jaw. His head was shaven.

Helen gave her a wry smile. 'I'm scared to stay

on the streets and you deliver me to the Fourth Reich,' she said.

'The Carmarths leave him in charge when they're away.' Martha's voice was proud. 'He's the nanny. Got a diploma and everything.'

The only chairs in the room were for small children. Helen sat cross-legged on the floor. The girls were identical twins, four years old; their shrill voices bit into her like mosquitoes. A game of tag followed the game of catch. Half an hour of lessons came next and were quieter. Afterwards came a snack and a story read out loud. Only then did Helen decide she could risk getting Becky out of bed in Springfield.

But David's meeting had to be nearly finished. Helen didn't dare tie up his mobile; she asked Willard if she could use the house landline.

'Sorry,' he said. 'The Carmarths wouldn't like it.'

'I can reverse the charges. They'll never even know.'

He took a mobile out of his pocket and tossed it to her. 'Be my guest,' he said. 'Use it and keep it.'

'I only need to make the one call,' she laughed.

'I get them in India for £20 a hundred. I got the bloody things coming out of my ears.'

Helen dialled the number.

'Lillian?' she said, surprised. 'What are *you* doing there?'

'I done spent the night, Miss Helen. Now afore you goes and gets yourself all upset, your grandma's fine — excepting she's been right worried about you.'

'Oh,' said Helen in a small voice.

'Why didn't you call her, girl?'

The simple fact was, Helen hadn't given a thought to how her silence might have affected her grandmother. 'I don't know,' she said in the same voice.

'Miss Helen, you been saying that to me since you was two years old.'

'My cell phone broke.' That much was the truth after all. Kind of anyhow. 'Is she up yet?'

'Why didn't you get yourself to a hotel or something?'

'I don't know,' Helen repeated.

Lillian sighed. 'I just got her into her bath. You're okay?'

'I'm fine. Fine. Tell her something really interesting is about to happen. She must wait for a call from me. I *know* how we should move ahead next.'

# 61

## SPRINGFIELD, ILLINOIS

For the first time since her allergic reaction to strawberries, Becky felt almost human. But a bath can be tiring; Lillian had waited until she'd been lying on her bed to give her the news that Helen was safe and well. Becky hid the intensity of her relief by placing a call to Merlin Googe Allandale.

After all, what possible use could the man be now? Especially at $2,000 a day plus expenses?

'I shall no longer be needing your services, Mr Allandale,' she said when he answered. 'I will of course pay your flight back to Springfield provided your return is not too delayed. Is that clear?'

'You found your granddaughter, huh?'

'I have, yes.'

'She's okay?'

'She is.'

'Well, now, Mrs Freyl, I'm real glad to hear that. But where's she been at all this time? Where's she at right *now*?'

Becky realized irritably that Lillian hadn't said where Helen was. 'The question is no longer relevant, Mr Allandale. She's safe. That's all that matters.'

'How long ago did she call?'

‘Perhaps ten minutes. I didn’t speak to her myself.’

‘What about Marion? Don’t tell me it was the maid what spoke to her.’

‘Mr Marion is not relevant either, Mr Allandale.’ Becky’s voice was tart, but the point worried her. He could hear it.

‘Tell you what,’ Googie said. ‘Let me have her number. I’d kind of like to talk to her myself. For my own satisfaction. You know what I mean.’

# 62

## LONDON

Helen heard from David at almost precisely one o'clock.

'How did it go?' she asked him.

'Too complicated. I'll tell you when I see you.'

Helen was outside waiting for him when Martha called with directions to a flat in Mile End, not far from the pub in the Isle of Dogs. The signalmen's strike cut off travel by underground. The buses were likely to be crammed and taxis unobtainable. But they could walk it if they took their time.

Helen saw him as he turned the corner into the mews behind Carmarth House. 'David!' she cried, running towards him. 'What did she say? What went on? My grandmother's been a fan of Christina Haggarty's for years.'

'Only this morning you didn't seem to know the name.'

'You didn't ask.'

'She tells me you've got quite a part to play in all this.'

Helen flushed with pleasure. 'Did she really? She'll give us what we want? Have we won? Oh, my God, have we really done it? Tell me everything.'

They walked along crowded London streets

and into St James's Park while he recapped his meeting.

'So I was right!' Helen said, interrupting him mid-sentence. 'Uranium! Jesus. I was right, dammit. I was *right*.' She bit her lip. 'I mean, it *had* to be something like that, didn't it? I was figuring maybe, you know, oil supply to Europe. UCAI has big petroleum holdings in some of the old Soviet states. Teams of workers gathering data could cover for pipeline construction or rerouting or exploration — even drilling.' She rattled on happily until David's silence became oppressive. '*Now* what have I done wrong?' she said.

He spread his hands.

'Come on. Tell me,' she pressed.

'You ought to carry a warning sign, know that? 'Never enter into a contract here'.'

'David, what *are* you talking about?'

'My price was $200,000 and a condition. Remember? No more lies.'

'I didn't *lie* to you. I just didn't tell you everything I was thinking. I couldn't be sure there were interests beyond the radioprotectant. I didn't *know*.'

'Another sin of omission, huh?'

She stared down at her feet for a moment, took in a breath, then turned to face him. 'It wasn't a *mortal* sin, David. Venial at best — or at worst. The idea that somebody might hurt me because of something I figured out scares me stupid. But you? What would I do if they hurt *you*? I couldn't bear it. I thought you were dead. I've just found you again. I thought the less you knew about the possibilities, the better.'

'What's a venial sin?' he said.

She smiled sadly. 'A sin that God will pardon.'

Her concern for David, her fear that she'd offended him, was not at all what he'd expected. He'd been certain a minor power struggle was coming up, and he knew how to handle power struggles. But this? He was out of his depth. And yet his face was impassive, expressionless. She watched him tensely, as uncertain of her ground as he was of his, fearful that she'd gone too far, said too much, revealed more feeling for him than he wanted to see.

Which was exactly what she had done. He could manage himself in her presence — just about — as long as he could convince himself that what seemed to be warmth was no more than the skilful manipulation all Freyls were born with. But now? His need for an escape route was abrupt and visceral, and all he could find was a window taken up by an open barbecue. A man in a striped shirt stood behind it grilling chicken.

His question was no more than a raising of the eyebrows.

'Absolutely!' she said, turning into the restaurant.

The lunch crowd was thinning out. They had a table to themselves. The service was quick, the chicken crisp and black, the wine harsh but plentiful.

'Do you see, David?' Helen was holding a drumstick in her hand. 'We got Galleas to commit to producing *and* distributing for nothing, so Grandma's going to be happy. And they'll have to let us write our own terms because *we* know the uranium deposits exist and — ' A sudden doubt hit her. 'But why did Christina . . . ?'

' . . . hand over information she doesn't have to?' David had no intention of telling Helen about the CIA house in London and the contract out on him, but Christina volunteering that address nagged at him more than the uranium deposits. 'She's hard to make out, but I'd put my money on a bribe.'

'A *bribe*? What for?'

'She wants more from you than just venom.'

David pushed his plate away and told her that in exchange for the information — and a jet home from Gatwick — Christina had cast her as the whistleblower in the Follaton scandal that would oust UCAI from the uranium fields of Belarus. He gave her the envelope Christina had given him. Helen licked grease off her fingers, and her hair fell over her face as she read. She caught her breath over the material on Charles, but set it aside as soon as she'd scanned it. She set aside a cache of newspaper clippings almost at once too. Leslie Bloeden's information on Belarus took longer. She ran her finger down the columns of figures, knitted her brows in concentration, read each page twice.

When she was finished, she handed him the envelope with an angry shrug. 'What the fuck is the matter with God? How *dare* He allow people to do something like this? Poisoning a whole population . . . and the statistics . . . they're so'

— she struggled for a word — 'so *numb*.' She took in another breath. 'You know what's almost as bad? We can't do anything with this material, David. Not a goddamn thing.'

'How do you figure that?'

'Partly because it's *so* terrible. Even with accusations hundreds of times less awful, the proof has to be rock solid. We have to have documentation. Lots of it. This isn't it. It's not a quarter of what we need. Not a tenth.'

'What if we get that journalist who wants a story on Follaton? The kid with steel teeth? You told me he's been trying to get something on them for more than a year.'

'You're not hearing me, David. All Kastus Youdin had was his aunt Emilia's suspicions, a few rumours and maybe Feodor's translations of the orders for lead-lined tractors. David, look, I spend weeks at a time trying to figure out what stories will sell to newspapers, and if I've learned nothing else, I've learned what a newspaper's legal department will buy into. This isn't it. Not *any* of it. Kastus would love this stuff. Of course he would. But his editor would kill it even before the legal guys got to it, and if UCAI got wind of it, they'd add Kastus to their death list.'

'He's probably already on it.'

A waiter cleared the plates away. 'There's got to be more,' Helen said. 'When are you seeing her again? When can *I* see her?'

'She'll have left for New York by now.'

'That's all? She's finished?' He only shrugged. 'This *can't* be all, David. She *can't* be that näive. I mean, just look at this stuff she's given us.

We've got reports of a couple of fertiliser shipments and analyses of radiation levels that might — stress that 'might' — indicate something in the fertiliser raised them. The increase in radiation victims *could* reflect that, but it's far more likely to reflect better medical records. Charles insists that the official fallout figures are way too low anyhow, and he has some powerful backing. Kastus knows all about that. We even talked about it. Or maybe some locals found a briefcase full of strontium-90. Maybe they're getting sick selling it at cut rates to the Taliban. Who knows?'

'We've got to think of something,' he said.

'What? What is there? David, it's *so* easy to make statistics look like anything including the precise reverse of what they really mean. It's even easier to fabricate them altogether. Take this page copied out by hand. It's the only straightforward indication that Follaton was deliberately raising radiation levels in Belarus, and if somebody handed it to me I'd toss it in the garbage as a figment of a nasty screwball's imagination.'

He nodded. It was precisely the point he'd made to Leslie Bloeden.

'Then we've got a batch of obituaries,' she went on, picking up the newspaper clippings. 'The screwball who supplied our information went fishing and got dead. How? The inquest said an accident. Too bad, especially since without him there isn't even the possibility of some kind of human interest story. The obits for the other guys aren't any more helpful. One's an unsolved murder, sure, but the rest are officially accidents — just like Rosemary and James. Feodor's officially a suicide. Emilia and her neighbour have disappeared off the face of the earth. It's a bad record for a short period in a medical foundation. No doubt about it. But we have no *proof* that it's anything else. Even if we had something to convince Kastus's editor that Follaton — or UCAI or Charles — had a hand in the deaths, no editor is going to get the story past the newspaper's lawyers. The drawbridge would bang shut at once. Risk a defamation suit from some Croesus of a company? Forget it. Even if they knew they could win, they'd also know that cases like this can be made to drag on for years. Fighting it would wipe them out before they ever got to court.

'That leaves us with Charles killing his brother. We have records showing he had a drug problem as a kid, and his brother didn't. We have an autopsy report from nearly forty years ago that somehow didn't make it to the inquest and a couple of damaging statements that didn't make it either. My father probably knew the whole story — he may well even have had first-hand knowledge of it — but he's as dead as Charles's brother. The *Mail* might pick up on the drugs angle, but the rest of it? Not even *their* legal department would implicate a lord in a murder this old unless he were already in trouble over Belarus and the radioprotectant. But he isn't.' She sighed. 'We could turn the file over to the cops, I guess.'

'They'd only bury it,' David said.

The waiter brought the bill. Helen stood and brushed crumbs from her dress. 'David, I'm really sorry. Haggarty may be a genius, but even a genius can have a dumb idea.'

He glanced up at her and nodded. 'Yes.'

'You agree?' she said in relief.

'I took her too literally.'

Helen sat down again. 'Oh, God help me, what have you got in mind *now*?'

'What makes the best kind of story?'

'You talking generally?'

'I guess so.'

'Money, sex, corruption. Movie stars and royals — *any* kind of celebrity. Heroes and villains. Wars, earthquakes, murders, assassinations. Stuff that could come straight out of a kid's comic book.'

'Yeah?'

'I'm afraid so.'

A fleeting expression — pain? pleasure? both? — crossed his face. 'I figure we can hold off on your journalist until tomorrow. Then I'll give you a story for him.'

# 63

## MOWBRAY SQUARE

The weather did another abrupt U-turn that afternoon and became Indian summer, balmy, with the pleasantest kind of breeze. Windows that people had shut for the winter were open again all along the street except at the one house where David stopped. When he was a kid, he'd always looked for shut windows when it was warm. He always rang the doorbell to make sure of course — asked for a glass of water if some guy really had locked himself away from good weather.

The front door had a huge brass knocker. He banged it, then bent down to examine the lock, frowned, looked again — and walked away without waiting to see if anybody answered or not. Who could have guessed he'd find one of those things in use? He'd never even seen one up close, although a professional locksmith he'd known in prison told him it remained as close as man could come to an unpickable design.

David carried the architectural plans from James's father in a shoulder bag that he and Helen had bought as soon as they'd finished their lunch. The house he'd just left — it stood behind the Foundation — looked perfect on the site plan: direct access through a yard at the back. Now Follaton's street was going to have to do.

The Foundation stood mid-block among façades that melded together to make an elegant sweep of cream-coloured stucco, iron railings at street level, iron-railed terrace running along the entire length of the next floor, tall windows overlooking the trees and flowers of Mowbray Square. Only the red and yellow alarm boxes marred the sense of calm and unity. To one side of the Foundation, the houses had been converted to offices with discreet brass plates; on the other, they seemed to be privately owned. David strolled back and forth; Follaton closed at four on Fridays, and there was no traffic in or out. He opened his shoulder bag from time to time to consult a paperback on English buildings.

When he'd loitered as long as he dared, he knocked on the door of the corner house. It opened to reveal a middle-aged woman with the hectic-pink cheeks of someone who takes long walks in the cold, probably to exercise the dog. David sincerely hoped not. Dogs bite. The woman looked worried at the size of him but smiled bravely.

'Can I help you?'

'I'm real sorry to bother you, ma'am,' he stammered, broadening his accent as far as he could and sticking close to his childhood technique, 'but could you tell me if this here is a Georgian terrace?'

'Actually it is, yes.'

'See, I promised my mom I'd bring her a picture of a real Georgian house in London. I don't suppose you'd know who the architect was?'

He paused awkwardly; he'd been much better at this when he was a kid. He'd even got a real kick out of the country-boy manners; now they grated. But she smiled again and took pity on him. 'It's Capability Brown's only known terrace in London. People don't usually think of him as an architect. There aren't many buildings of his around.'

'Ma'am?'

'The man who designed the Blenheim Palace gardens. Your mum should be very impressed. What part of the States are you from?'

'Springfield, ma'am.'

'Massachusetts?'

'Illinois, ma'am.'

A few more exchanges and she asked him in for a cup of tea. By the time he left, she'd shown him around; he knew her dog had died only weeks ago — a Jack Russell called Matilda — and he had a good idea of how houses all along the row were laid out. She'd even helped him take some shots with the camera Helen had borrowed for the interview with Rosemary's mother. He spent the next few hours wandering London streets.

By ten o'clock several houses around the square were bright with the lights and laughter of Friday-night guests. Others had the sense of quiet about them that tells a housebreaker they're empty for the evening. The house belonging to David's new friend was half-and-half: top floors somnolent and dimly lit but a heavy beat at high volume booming out through windows in the basement. The woman had despaired of her teenage son: 'The silly child wants to run a club in Soho instead of going to university,' she'd said. Partly drawn shades revealed assorted sets of expensive shoes at the ends of jeans-clad legs, probably something interesting being smoked or snorted while mama and papa were across town drinking Chardonnay. David was relieved: no one upstairs, only kids off in some dreamy drug-land downstairs.

He'd been afraid he might have to wait until the whole family went to bed.

His shoulder bag held a fluorescent yellow jacket with broad aluminium strips on it; the surplus shop had called it a 'high visibility traffic jacket'. He put it on. The job of opening the door of the corner house on Mowbray Square was going to be slow, but nobody notices workmen in fluorescent colours, not even at this hour of the night. One of the locks was the burglar's friend, a standard Yale pin-and-tumbler. A square cut from a plastic milk bottle, slipped in and over, and you're through. The other lock was a deadbolt, much better for the householder, although as far as David was concerned, the main obstacle was that his tools weren't machined. The hours between shopping and the trip back to central London had gone into making a set of picks from a design he'd improvised all those years ago when he was ringing doorbells in search of TVs to steal for pocket money.

A recessed contact switch between door and door frame is a home security system's first defence. It triggers the alarm after a few seconds' delay so the owners have time to disable the system when they come into the house. David stepped inside quietly despite the deafening blast of music from the basement and shut the door behind him. The door to the kitchen was open. This afternoon, he'd carried his hostess' tea tray from there — he could see the silver milk jug still unwashed beside the sink — across the hallway carpet where he'd nearly tripped, up the curved staircase to the living room with its antique furniture and its pair of windows looking out across the terrace onto the square. He'd already reached the windows when he realized the burglar alarm hadn't gone off. He paused uncertainly, then went back downstairs to the hallway and the master control box.

Not much of a problem: remove the cover and trip the alarm switch manually.

A shrill, pulsating screech swallowed up the music a few seconds later. Why people bother to fit burglar alarms was as much a mystery to David as their faith in Yale locks. Cops don't pay any attention. Why should they? Ninety-nine out of a hundred call-outs are false. The windows in this house were no more carefully thought out. His teatime survey had revealed that his hostess, like most of the rest of the world, left the key to the window locks lying on one of the sills. He checked the street — still and dark, none of the neighbours out yet to complain about the racket — opened the window, replaced the key on the sill, crawled out, shut the window behind him. If anybody noticed it wasn't locked, they'd blame the kid downstairs.

He strolled along the terrace, peeking into windows that were lit, waving at a teenage girl — just another repairman, this time in search of the electrical fault that was causing all the noise. He might have needed a more elaborate story to explain changing his shoes in front of the windows to Charles's office, but nobody showed any more interest in him or his high visibility jacket than before.

The shoes had been an after thought. He wasn't used to covering his traces. But run a security business as he had, and you have to know a little about the forensics of burglary. Fingerprints didn't worry him much. Lifting a print from a surface touched by one person is about the extent of the technology; in a busy office like this one, his would blend into the unintelligible stew made by all the others. But wear shoes for a while, and they develop identifiable characteristics. He'd had only the one pair with him — Lillian's son's shoes — and unlikely though it was, some eager young detective or some thorough security expert might be able to tie shoeprints left at a Mowbray Square break-in to prints left by a fake preacher at Rosemary's house and James's house or even a legitimate visit to Zoya's apartment: which could lead to trouble.

The rest of the fancy stuff on TV is more

sleight-of-hand than science.

Helen had assured him that the windows in Charles's office weren't double-glazed. A sharp elbow swing, his arm protected by his coat, broke the glass — its noise completely inaudible with that alarm screaming. He crossed Charles's office and was halfway down the stairs to the ground floor when the Follaton alarm exploded into its own ear-splitting clamour.

The Victorian mahogany desk with its old video console — the desk that had once been Rosemary's — stood in the ground-floor lobby facing the front doors to the square. The boiler room was at the back of the building, down a dark hallway and behind a fire door with a one-way lock: no handle, no doorplate. Fire doors have to conform to regulations; part of David's business had been adapting them for maximum security. He ran his hands over the casing that surrounded it, found a button, pressed. The door made a sighing sound — locks like this operate on pneumatic pressure — and eased open.

Boiler and hot-water tank stood entangled in the usual mesh of electrical wires and plumbing pipes. The walls around them were blue tiles divided into panels by aluminium strips. David paced off a two-metre distance from the far corner of the room and could easily see the join where the tiles met at the top of a concealed door. There had to be another manual override somewhere, but he didn't have time to locate it. A prybar from his bag, staple of the carpenter's trade, peeled off the aluminium trim to reveal the edges of the door. He used it to wedge open the door itself. He knew he'd find CCTV coverage of some kind in the basement; he slipped on a mask of plastic leaves and greenery that he'd bought in a London side street.

The stairs beyond the door led down to the large room that Rosemary had found in her search for a place to store the clutter from Follaton's entryway. David flipped a switch, and neon panels on the ceiling spluttered into life. The dark blue filing cabinets still lined the walls as they had when she'd seen them. The computer cubicle holding screens, keyboards, processor and memory bank still glowed pale blue.

But from above, the bald, black eye of a camera followed his every move. Rosemary must have really scared people; a glance told him the roving eye was newly installed. Some broken plaster around it hadn't yet been repaired. There was no new burst of alarm to add to the two that blared away outside. Top-level, mission security installations like this one are silent, wireless, often feeding information straight to private police forces. The response to his presence here was likely to be swift, professional, thorough.

He photographed almost at random. He dared not take longer than a few minutes, then ran back up the stairs to the broken window in Charles's office and crawled through it. By this time the parties around the square had emptied into the street to protest the deafening screams of two burglar alarms. Dinner guests milled about, agitated but aimless, some with hands clasped over their ears. One or two looked up as David climbed over the iron terrace, lowered himself towards the ground and jumped the rest of the way to the street.

'Any luck up there?' a woman in an evening dress shouted at him.

'Can't find where to turn it off,' David shouted back.

'Why do the police *never* come when you need them?'

'I'm on my way to the station right now.'

'Good man,' she said as he jogged away from her towards a pedestrian-only side street where a thick cement post barred the way to cars.

He heard sirens even before he reached it. But two audible alarms and one visual one going off in a single street are much more likely to be an electrical fault than anything else; the few minutes distraction they caused would give him the chance he needed.

# 64

## SPRINGFIELD, ILLINOIS

Becky slept for an hour after lunch. At about the time David was buying his mask of greenery in London, Lillian came into her bedroom with the handset of the house telephone.

'It's Miss Helen,' Lillian said. 'She says she gots everything ready.'

Lillian fluffed Becky's pillows, helped her to lean back on them, gave her the handset.

'Helen, my dear?' Becky listened a moment. Then she pulled herself up further in bed and waved Lillian away.

A few minutes later, the fragile old woman was as good as new, as vigorous and demanding as ever. She went to her study and said nobody was to disturb her — *especially* if she was on the phone. She sent Lillian out for the *Wall Street Journal* and the *New York Times*.

That's when Lillian suddenly realized she hadn't found out what David had asked her to find out. Her trip to his grandmother at Heaven's Acre Nursing Home had revealed that Hugh Freyl's cousin Frank was probably his father, and the information had so shocked her that she'd forgotten to ask why Helen Freyl was listed as an heir in the will of someone she'd never known. The more Lillian thought about it the less sense it made. Why would Clotilde leave money to a member of a rapist's family? Where had the money come from in the first place?

She picked up Becky's newspapers on her way out to the nursing home.

'I don't got no more to say,' Clotilde said as Lillian entered her room.

'Now you listen here at me, Mrs Clotilde Marion' — Lillian didn't have much time to spare — 'You ain't told me nothing about why you got Miss Helen down in your will. That's how come I'm here.'

'I'm tired.'

'That ain't no concern of mine. You gone too far to stop. Now you gonna explain.'

* * *

All those years ago, Hugh Freyl had arrived at Clotilde Marion's house to find Fleurette huddled in a dirty blanket, looking even younger than her mere thirteen years, hair in pigtails, Barbie doll clutched in her arms, all pretence of being a sophisticated fifteen wiped away. Her eyes were swollen shut, both of them a deep blue-purple. Blood oozed from beneath a Band-Aid on her chin and a cut on her lower lip.

'Why aren't these wounds dressed?' he said, kneeling beside her.

'None of your goddamned business,' Clotilde said. She'd let him in only so he could see for himself what his fat-cat cousin had done to her daughter. 'Now get out.'

But Hugh's almost mesmerising sincerity — it

was to become a byword in Illinois courts — made its first full-blown appearance at that very moment. In the end, the Freyl family doctor accompanied the three of them to the police station, and the Freyl family lawyer met them there. Which is to say, Fleurette's experience was by no means the usual one for a rape victim at the time — or any other time for that matter. Afterwards, Hugh arranged for a course of treatment, then took her and her mother home.

* * *

Clotilde broke into a prolonged fit of coughing. Lillian brought her water, helped her drink it — her gnarled hands were too painful to hold the glass — and waited until she could breathe easily again.

'So that's it, huh?' Lillian said then. 'Miss Helen's in your will because her daddy been good to your girl back then?'

Clotilde shook her head. 'My baby was sick when she showed up at the door all them months later with her own kid in her arms. She got sicker. I give up my job and started thieving and whoring and dealing to pay for the doctor. That doctor, he stuck her full of this. He stuck her full of that. She got worse. She needed to go to the hospital, but I couldn't thieve and whore fast enough to make that kind of money. I couldn't even deal fast enough for that. Then one morning I came back and — ' Clotilde broke off with a sob. 'My baby's dead.'

Lillian let her calm herself, then she said, 'What happened to David?'

'I don't know.'

'Come on, woman, you don't expect me to believe that.'

Clotilde leaned forward in her wheelchair. 'I don't know what happened to *me* after that. I must have started doing much, much worse than what I was doing already — and I was doing bad enough — because I don't remember nothing of him after that. They told me they took him away from me when he was six years old. They said he had fleas and bruises on him and sores on his face. I didn't believe them. I thought he was dead too until they showed me his picture. I done some bad things in my time, but I'd never do that to a child. Not of my own free will. Not ever.'

Clotilde went on to explain that a representative of the American Bank of Chicago had tracked her down because Hugh Freyl had set up a trust fund in her name.

'So the trust fund is why you got Miss Helen in your will?' Lillian pressed.

All the wrinkles in Clotilde's face jumped together. 'I want to see my grandson. I want to tell him I'm sorry. I want him to know I didn't mean it. I'm not like that. Mr Allandale said if I — '

'Allandale?' Lillian interrupted. 'You *sure* his name was Allandale? Medium height? Looks like some kind of identikit on TV?'

'He does a little, don't he? He's an awful nice man. It was his idea: putting Helen Freyl in the will. He figured that if it's only David, I might never see him.'

'Wills ain't public. How's he supposed to find out about it?'

'Mr Allandale said my David is out on the streets. He said he was going to put ads in homeless places telling about the will. He was certain sure that if David knew Hugh Freyl's girl was in my will, he'd want to know why.'

# 65

## MILE END

'All that stuff just sitting there, and they don't even have a security guard,' Helen said, shaking her head. It was nearly midnight.

'Charities aren't supposed to need security guards, are they?'

'A street full of Americans would never have let you get away like that.'

'I wouldn't bet on it if I were you.'

They sat at a rickety kitchen table with a checked oilcloth over it, a largely drunk bottle of wine open, plastic glasses, a plate of cheese and bread all but devoured. The flat Martha had found for them belonged to a friend of a friend of her father's; it was in a slum tossed up in the 1860s for workers in a Mile End rope factory, and it was theirs for a night or two. It smelled of bug spray. The sofa in the alcove of a living room was lumpy and as unsteady as a see-saw. The bathroom hid at the far end of a creaking, threadbare hallway; an array of mould in greens, blues and blacks thrived in the shower.

Helen and David had seen the place for the first time a couple of hours before he left for Mowbray Square. 'Oh, this is so deliciously awful,' Helen had said as she dumped packages in the kitchen.

They'd done their shopping in a daze — supermarket, hardware shop — aching to get here, to be alone together, a sheer physical pain of separation that threatened at any moment to blank out the mind entirely. They'd raced up the two flights of stairs. Helen had fumbled for the key — hidden in an alcove a yard from the door — almost dropping a bag of groceries, dropping the key instead, kicking it accidentally as she reached for it so that it fell down the stairs, setting her packages on the floor to run after it while David — too impatient to wait — used his trick of sliding his plastic social insurance card along the lock to get it open at once.

'You're pretty good at that, aren't you?' Helen said, laughing.

But as soon as the door shut behind them, neither knew what to do — not Helen despite her sophistication, nor David despite his propensity for direct action — except unpack what they'd bought, hardly able to breathe when they brushed against each other in the cramped space.

This was not a situation David understood at all. Prison sex: barter or violence. However you look at it, that's poor preparation for the courtship rituals of the world beyond bars. His one deep entanglement after he got out had made him fear what was happening with Helen the way a rabid dog fears water. He'd hidden his confusion in the next few hours by making a set of lock-picks that dated from a childhood where breaking in and stealing promised adrenaline rushes and momentary escapes from uncertainty.

Helen wandered about the tiny flat as confused as he was. She wasn't used to this kind of thing. If she wanted a man in her bed, she took him and kicked him out when he disgusted her — which had always been sooner, not later. Why the hell couldn't she do it this time? She'd gone into the kitchen intent on her purpose only to be stopped dead the moment she caught sight of the tension in the muscles of David's back, wholly unaware that the sense of her behind him was the cause of it.

In the end, she'd persuaded herself to fall into a fitful sleep on the bed that was as lumpy as the sofa.

He was gone when she woke.

'This is crazy, David,' she said to him now across the rickety kitchen table. He only tilted his plastic glass at her and drank the last swallow of his wine. 'Absolutely nuts. You do know that, don't you? So you have pictures of a roomful of filing cabinets. So what? Just *saying* they're in the Follaton basement doesn't mean a damn thing. Besides, what's in them? Personnel files? You don't have the slightest idea. Kastus is so eager to get something on the Foundation that he'll probably invest some time in this stuff you've put together, but it could be months — years — before he comes up with saleable goods. If they don't kill him first, that is.'

'He'll have to take his chances.'

She laughed abruptly. 'You know, buying all that junk — prybars, metal saws, vices, yellow traffic jacket — and helping a real, live burglar plan a real, live break-in: I haven't had so much fun since — I don't know — maybe when I was eight and painted the toilet seats white at school.'

'That was *fun*?'

'Oh, it was lovely. Every single girl who sat down, jumped up at once with a white ring around her ass. You want more wine?'

But the bottle was empty. A second bottle stood on the cabinet beside them. They both got up at the same moment to open it, bumped into each other and sprang apart as though they'd been stung — so slapstick a reaction that Helen giggled, then reached up impulsively and kissed him, a light kiss, a bare breathing of a kiss, the kind of kiss a child might give a co-conspirator after a successful prank. He touched his lips with the tips of his fingers, his face that mixture of bafflement and pain that so enchanted her, and pulled her roughly to him.

* * *

She woke suddenly an hour later in that lumpy bed and shook him awake, wholly forgetting the dangers of it.

'Something the matter?' he said, waking at once but only to reach out for her this time, to run his hand over her shoulder, just to make sure she was real, not some figment of his imagination. He'd never awakened to a sense of peace before, a sense of comfort, of belonging where he was.

'You're *doing* it again,' she said.

'Doing what?'

'Sleeping like that. Don't you breathe when

you sleep? All that quiet scares me. It really does. I hate it.'

'Yeah? Well, you snore a little.'

'I don't!' she said, pulling back.

'I kind of like it.'

'I worried about you this afternoon, David.'

He pushed her hair away from her forehead to reveal the pale blue vein in her temple that he'd studied so intently while she was reading the Bloeden papers. 'Why would you do that?'

'You could have got caught.'

'Me? Naw.'

'Why didn't you call me?'

He'd left his mobile with her in case she needed it. 'I didn't know you wanted me to.'

'Oh, I did. I did. I waited and waited. Will you show me how to do that thing with the credit card someday?'

'What 'thing'?'

'You know. Open a door with it. You did it so fast. I'd love to know how to do that.'

'Why?'

'I'd like to be able to do . . . ' She hesitated. 'While you were telling me about the basement, I kept trying to see it as *you* saw it, through your eyes, to think what *you* were thinking even as you thought it. I kept trying — ' She broke off. 'That sounds screwy, doesn't it? Of course it does. I can't do anything like that. But I *can* learn to do some of the things you do.'

'Like picking locks?' He was quizzical, puzzled, unsure if she was teasing despite her apparent sincerity.

'If that's the closest I can get, I'll take it.'

He searched her face for the catch that half of him was certain had to be there, that the other half so passionately hoped wasn't there, and found only a brow knitted with the intensity of what she felt and the colour of cheeks heightened with it.

'Don't you ever shut up?' he said, both hands on her shoulders now to bring her body down over his.

* * *

Helen's second awakening was more luxurious, but this time he wasn't there. The grey light of dawn showed through nylon net over the windows.

'David!'

'Kitchen,' came the response.

'What time is it?'

'Just before six.'

'Jesus, I forgot. You're supposed to call Lillian.' Helen had found all the games wiped off his mobile. She'd got out the one Martha's brother had given her and spent a frantic few seconds locating David's when it rang.

'Where is it?'

'What?'

'Cell phone.'

'Side table in the living room. You going to call her *now*?'

Helen's answer was the sound of the door closing behind him.

* * *

'David? That you?' Lillian said.

'Yes.'

'You think I keep the kind of hours you do?'

'She said it was urgent,' he said.

'When was that?'

'Just now.'

'Well, now lemme see. 'She' is got to be Miss Helen 'cause I done talked to her on your phone only about noon, and it's getting near enough to eleven at night here. So it's got to be pretty early in the morning in England. I bet that girl's laying in the bed right next to you, ain't she?'

He didn't answer.

'You ain't gonna tell me nothing, is you? Well, I'm going to tell *you* something, boy. *I* know the name of the guy what's after you. I figure I know how he done set you up, and I got a real good idea how come he's probably getting close.'

* * *

But what Lillian couldn't possibly have guessed was that she'd given Sir Charles Hay a stay of execution.

# 66

## LONDON RETURN

David made a hurried call to the private Galleas number Christina had given him to arrange a courier service for their whistle-blower's information and a private jet from Gatwick to Springfield for the whistleblower herself. Then he sprinted back to the slum of a building, up the stairs, not even shutting the door behind him in his rush to get there.

Only twenty minutes later did Helen think to ask, rolling over lazily to face him, 'What was that all about?'

She'd never seen David so much as really smiling, but he laughed out loud.

'David!' she cried, sitting up. 'You have dimples just like me. You've got to laugh more. It's the only thing that brings them out.' Then she said, 'I was talking about the call from Lillian. What does she want?'

'Nothing important.'

'You ran out of here fast enough.'

'I needed some air.'

'The hell you did.' He didn't answer. 'Talk to me, dammit.'

'This steel-teethed guy you know on the Sunday paper.'

'Kastus? What about him?'

'You got to write him a letter.'

She sat at the rickety kitchen table and wrote while David dictated.

*Kastus: My grandmother hired a man called Merlin Googe Allandale to do a little looking into the Foundation and its Belarus connection. Yesterday he gave me this envelope . . .*

Helen paused, looked up at David, smiled.

'What?' he said.

'This is hardly the truthful Helen you keep insisting on.' But before he had a chance to answer, she remembered what he'd said at that second lunch at her grandmother's table. 'I know, I know,' she said. 'I'm following your directions 'too slavishly', aren't I?'

He smiled back at her. 'Something like that.'

'I suppose we couldn't really claim that Galleas was the source of all this nonsense, could we? It *is* nonsense, you know, my dearest David. Complete nonsense.'

'Sure about that, are you?'

'Absolutely.'

'Where were we?'

' 'Yesterday he gave me this envelope . . . ' '

David continued dictating.

*. . . and told me to hand it over to somebody like you if I didn't hear from him by this afternoon. What's here should be enough to get you a start on your story. Helen.*

‘Don’t you think we should at least tell him about Emilia?’ Helen said.

David shook his head. ‘He’ll find out.’

‘She’s his aunt, David. He might not even know she’s missing, much less dead.’

‘All the better. We want him focused.’

Helen glanced down at the note. ‘What did my grandmother really hire this Allandale guy for?’

‘You don’t think Lillian kept that email of yours to herself, do you?’

‘Oh, God, of course she didn’t,’ Helen said with a sigh. ‘What’s he supposed to do? Fly all the way over just to see if I’m okay? Jesus. Or . . . Did she hire him at all? *Is* he here?’

‘I don’t know.’

‘I wouldn’t be at all surprised if you’d made him up.’ She laughed, and despite her worldly sophistication her eyes were the naughty eyes of that child who’d painted the toilet seats white at school.

He pushed the hair away from her face as he had before, as he’d longed to do for as far back — or so it seemed to him — as he could remember. ‘We’ve got to get out of here,’ he said. ‘Meet me in front in twenty minutes.’

* * *

David delivered Helen’s package to the courier Galleas had arranged for him, an assured delivery to the *Sunday Times* before noon, then drove back to the crumbling tenement. He leaned across, opened the door for her, hadn’t expected anything like the kiss he got, came away from it breathless, fumbled as he shifted the somewhat elderly Ford Fiesta into first.

'I have to admit I can hardly wait to get out of here,' she said, watching his every move. 'I hate being frightened, David. You're sure Galleas can finagle a passport for me?'

'So they say.'

'You'll follow soon?'

'Yes.'

'How soon?'

'I don't know.'

'Why'd you wipe the games off your cell phone?' she said, abruptly curious.

'I get started playing those things, I can't stop.'

'You don't have *anything* on that phone, David, not other people's numbers, not messages, not anything.'

'Snooping, were you?'

'Mm.'

His eyes stayed on her long enough for him to clip the bumper of the car parked in front of him as he drew out into the road. 'This has got to stop too,' he said.

'Oh, please, no.' She'd had no idea one person's skin could hunger for another's like this, especially after a night such as she'd spent, and she needed air. She pressed the window opener on her door. Nothing happened. 'Open my window, will you?'

'Mine's open. Won't that do?'

'The *windows* don't work?'

'Nope.'

'How can they get away with renting such junk?'

But she suddenly caught his scent on the air. At first she'd thought cumin and mustard seed. Now she wasn't sure. There's a somewhat musky smell to the azaleas that bloom in England in the spring: could that be it? Or some exotic combination of all three? She failed to get herself back under any meaningful control even when he stopped at a service station a few miles along the motorway that encircles London. She watched him fill the tank, pay for the gas, get back into the car, bend down to reach under the dashboard. Only then did she realize what he was doing.

'David Marion!' she said. 'You *stole* this car. You broke the driver's window and stole it.' He glanced up at her, then shrugged. She watched him pull out two wires and cross them. The car started as readily as if he'd turned the key in the ignition. 'Can you do that with any car?' she said then.

'Only old ones.'

'What about new ones?'

'You have to punch the ignition.'

'What does that mean?'

'Cut a hole in the dash.'

'First you have me aiding and abetting an illegal entry. Now you've got me escaping in a hot car.' She settled herself happily on the seat. 'What do we get to do next? Run smack to Austria? Kidnap a banker in Marrakech?'

Helen was so bewitched with the excitement of it all that she only noticed the sign announcing the Gatwick exit as they sped past it.

'Hey, where do you think you're going?' She

twisted to look behind her. 'We aren't kidnapping *me*, are we?' The idea didn't seem at all unattractive, but then everything he did pleased her; and yet she sensed a sudden preoccupation in him, something new, unfamiliar, not friendly.

'We got a problem,' he said.

'Do we?'

'What's the matter with you? Can't you *see*?'

His voice was impatient, irritable, as though he'd just dropped what had happened between them, tossed it out the window like an empty Coke can, turned his attention to some new game with the car instead. He began criss-crossing the highway, veering from the outside lane to the inside and back again. She was hurt and confused, all the more so since she'd been enchanted only moments before. Usually her defence mechanisms snapped to her aid whenever she needed them. Not this time. They seemed as distant and preoccupied as David himself.

'What *is* it, David? Don't scare me any more. I can't take it.'

A Ford Fiesta may be a favourite with car thieves like David because of its poor security system, but it's seriously limited in other respects. It's underpowered. It's slow. A good modern car can run it down easily. Of course the modern car has to keep it in sight first. David couldn't have said why the maroon Porsche had made him nervous as soon as he'd caught a glimpse of it in the rear-view mirror. Maybe just paranoia. But weave the Fiesta in and out of lanes on a congested highway, and if the Porsche sticks tight, paranoia becomes a less likely explanation. This one was one of those sporty models with fat frog lips that stretch from ear to ear where its jaw ought to be. David figured it had been following them since they entered the motorway heading west towards Gatwick. Maybe even longer.

The exit to Redhill loomed. David kept up his speed, drove a couple of hundred yards past the exit, then swung so abruptly onto the hard shoulder that Helen's body flew against him, only to be jerked towards the windscreen by the screeching stop that followed. He reversed back to the exit, swerved into the slip road and headed down it.

The slip road at that junction is unusually long — more than a mile — and made slower this day by a parade of roadworks lorries. At the end of it, David followed the circular road that brought him up over the bridge across the motorway he'd just left, then down again to the motorway itself, now heading east though, back towards the Gatwick exit that he'd sped past a few minutes earlier.

He and his pal Tony had jacked their first cars when they were so little that one of them had to work the pedals while the other steered. As soon as they grew up enough to handle both ends of driving alone, they'd started jacking two cars so they could play TV cops and learn how to spot a Porsche on a tailing job — like the one tailing him now — and reverse into a slip road as he'd done.

But a ragdoll pummelling like this isn't easy

on anybody. Helen's heart pounded. Her hands trembled. She hurt all over, her chest where the seat belt had yanked into her, her shoulders where she'd hit his body, her neck from the recoil.

She held her side as they entered the motorway traffic again. 'Goddammit, David, *what* problem? I don't see a problem. I don't see anything.'

He sighed, half exasperation, half something close to a fond indulgence. 'It doesn't matter. I think I've lost him.'

'Somebody's following us?'

'A maroon Porsche, just like — ' David broke off.

' — that one?' she finished for him.

He leaned forward to peer ahead. The car that had stuck so tight until the Redhill exit seemed to have somehow got itself in front. Perhaps three cars away, and travelling in the fast lane. He had to be wrong. He *had* to be. He slowed, just testing. The Porsche slowed too. It moved into the middle lane.

'He knows where we're going,' David said.

'Oh, David, come on. Even if he did know, why would he be making it obvious?'

'He wants us to know he knows.'

Her father had told her there'd been several psychotic episodes while David was in prison. The excuse had been that South Hams Prison used chemical restraints on its violent prisoners — thioridazine, haloperidol, chlorpromazine — and that paranoid episodes were one of the common side effects. She'd never doubted it until now.

'Don't you think you might be letting your imagination run away with you?' she said.

David glanced at her. 'Roadworks. Beyond the Redhill exit.'

'Roadworks?' She'd paid little attention to the signs waving traffic to the other side of the road. Single lanes of vehicles moved in opposite directions there, separated only by temporary barriers and traffic cones. She could see that perhaps — just perhaps — a hypothetical pursuer might have made a U-turn through all that so he could stay on the motorway while the Fiesta was still on the roundabout trying to get back there. It was *possible*.

But she didn't believe a word of it. 'He knew about those roadworks too, huh?' She didn't try to keep the scepticism out of her voice.

'The only people who know where we're going are your friends at Galleas.'

'David, David. That doesn't make sense either. I mean, why would they? What's the point? As of yesterday in New York, our deal with them was public. We're their partners, bearers of the goose *and* the golden eggs. Running me down couldn't interest UCAI any more either. Or Follaton. Or Charles. Grandma notified all of them — a lot of the financial pages too. Everybody knows about it. *Everybody*.'

The Porsche hit the brakes, dropped back, crossed into the slow lane, only following now, nothing aggressive.

'David?' She studied his angry profile. 'Have I done something wrong *again*?'

'*Everybody* knows about the Galleas deal — except me.'

'Oh,' she said in that small voice she used when Lillian was scolding. 'Things got so . . . complicated.'

'Sure they did.'

'When you came back safe last night, I was so relieved — so happy to see you that it kind of . . . made all this other stuff unimportant. We drank the wine and then . . . well, you know what happened then. I didn't think of anything else. I didn't *want* to think about anything else.'

'What did smart old grandma do anyhow? Email all those guys?'

'Um.'

'You think everybody heads for their email the moment they get up on a Saturday morning? It ever occur to you that maybe they set something in motion yesterday and can't stop it?'

Helen shrank into her seat.

The exit to Gatwick appeared. David slowed to take it. After all, what was there to lose? Now that both he and the Porsche knew what was going on, the motorway to the airport offered some scope for defensive driving. David was good at that. He started to ease into the slip road.

But one of the Fiesta's limitations is that its acceleration is no match for a Porsche. The German car shot forward on David's left, rammed the Fiesta's bumper, forced it back into the heavy traffic of the motorway. The Fiesta veered. It swung. Steadying it took all David's attention. By the time he had it under control, the Porsche was behind him again.

'Convinced?' he said to Helen.

The impact had thrown her against the door. She felt another, heavier pain in her chest. But it was the shock that silenced her.

'I only got one trick for this set-up,' he went on. 'Brace yourself this time, okay?'

The exit for East Grinstead approached — no roadworks here — and he sped past it, then swung onto the hard shoulder as before, reversed into the slip road. He took the first country lane he came to, then turned again after a couple of miles.

Helen eased her body from its rigid position. 'Is he gone?'

'Looks like it.'

South Fairleigh and Clayhill dominated the sign at the first major crossroads they came to. David pulled off to one side, reached across Helen, took a map out of the glove compartment, unfolded it over the steering wheel.

'We can go south, then west,' he said. 'Gatwick isn't far.' He put the map away and turned the car towards South Fairleigh.

In his childhood games of chase with stolen cars and his friend Tony, losing the first car either ended it altogether or brought out the backup, some new car that had to be spotted all over again. Which meant the flash of maroon he'd just caught in the rear-view mirror shouldn't be there. He hit the accelerator hard, skidded out into the road, swung towards Clayhill instead. But the Porsche reappeared at the first set of traffic lights on outskirts important enough to include a supermarket, garden centre and morning shoppers from miles around. It edged closer to the Fiesta with every block until the town square blossomed ahead with market stalls starting up, trucks delivering vegetables, meat, fish, flowers, clothes. A red light at the crossroads there brought the Porsche directly behind the Fiesta, the driver clearly visible in the rear-view mirror.

He nudged the Fiesta, a gentle tap, then another, then a sharp jolt.

'Jesus,' Helen said, twisting around to look. 'What *does* he want?'

'You ever seen him before?'

She shook her head.

The light changed. Cars began to move. David moved with them as far as the centre of the crossroads, then turned abruptly into the stream of traffic from the opposite direction. The blare of horns and screech of tyres drowned out a pick-up truck's thud into the Fiesta's rear bumper. The Fiesta skidded and swerved into a side street, swerved again, then straightened. This time a glance in the rear-view mirror showed an assorted tangle of vehicles but no Porsche.

Signs pointed to 'All Routes', one of them apparently leading to a forest. Trees should be good. David and his friend Tony had played out the scenario a couple of times around Lake Springfield. Drive straight into a wooded area. Get out and run. Your follower is going to have to come after you. He can't see you to shoot you, and you get to plan your own ambush.

The converted 38 magnum that David had bought from Pimmson was fastened beneath the dashboard. The trouble was, there didn't seem to be any trees showing up here.

'Where *is* this forest?' David said. 'We're supposed to be in the middle of it.'

Helen laughed, then grabbed at her side. The pain was sharp, deep, unexpected. 'British Petroleum got rid of most of the trees years ago.'

'*Now* she tells me.' But the warmth in his voice disappeared: the rear view mirror showed a maroon car in the distance, just turning into the road. 'How long have you had it on?' he said.

'Had *what* on?'

'Tell me how long.'

Keeping an eye on the mirror he reached across, took her handbag, shook its contents out onto her lap, picked up the mobile Martha's brother Willard had given her.

Towns, villages and mobile phone masts surround the open plain of Ashdown Forest. Maybe on the way to see James's father she hadn't thought about triangulation turning a mobile into an electronic tag. But this time? After he'd explained it in detail?

The Porsche was gaining on them steadily.

'Oh, Christ,' she said. 'You've got this all wrong.'

'Who is he?'

'I have no idea, David. None.'

'Oh, yeah?'

By now, the Porsche was no more than a hundred yards away.

'I didn't dare tie up your phone, David. You

were going to call any minute. Willard gets hundreds of cells for nothing in India. He gave me one, and told me to keep it. How could I possibly — ' She broke off, then began again, her voice urgent as the Porsche closed the gap between them. 'You have to understand that I wouldn't put you at risk. Not in *this* car. You wouldn't have a chance.'

'Neither would you.'

The Porsche caught the bumper on the left. David swerved again. The Porsche slammed into the right. Helen gritted her teeth — the pain in her chest racked her by now — and twisted around once more to see. The unknown driver's face was as intense as David's. He swerved back and forth, connected to the Fiesta as though with a tow rope.

Then he dropped back abruptly and gunned the engine.

'Face the front!' David shouted at her. 'You'll break your neck.'

But she wasn't prepared for the impact when the Porsche rammed into them full force: the sledgehammer on the heart that she'd felt when her mother's car had hit a tree head-on nearly twenty years ago. She was barely aware of the Fiesta careering across the road, into the ditch beside it, out again.

Swing a car around — back to front — in a single manoeuvre? It's called a bootlegger's turn, staple of TV shows, Tennessee moonshiner's gift to the world. Get off the gas, steering wheel sharp right, hit the handbrake, depress the clutch: all at the same time. The car skids sideways across the road, hub caps flying, clattering away across the macadam. Release the brake, straighten the wheel, let out the clutch, hit the gas with everything you've got.

The Fiesta was already a couple of hundred yards away, going in the opposite direction, before the Porsche had recovered from its own ramming job. It was a few minutes' grace. No more. All David could do when the Porsche recovered was keep swerving and hope for a miracle. As soon as the Porsche pulled alongside, the chase would be over.

He'd told Pimmson that he wasn't going to be shooting out any windows: the converted magnum wasn't powerful enough to penetrate *any* part of the German car.

The Fiesta's tyres screeched as David right-angled into a road that dipped, rounded a hillock, rose a little, rounded another hillock. The sun was blinding. He squinted into it — then slowed down and came to a gentle halt.

No more than fifty yards away, a tall, thin woman was marching ahead of a crowd that filled the road. A man balancing a shoulder camera bigger than a vacuum cleaner walked in front of her. His jacket read 'Meridian TV South East'. David's first thought was a convention of circus freaks. Then he saw that they were just extremely old: wheelchairs, canes, walking frames; white hair, bent heads, bowed legs. A seven-seater Mitsubishi crawled alongside. The banner across its radiator read, 'Walk for Help the Aged'.

David drew closer, leaned out the window. 'Can you tell me what the next town is?' he said to the tall woman.

'Hildenbridge,' she said. Her face was long, the jaw prominent. 'You wouldn't want to contribute a pound or two to our fundraiser, would you? Everybody here is at least ninety. Except for me and Angela, of course.' She indicated the driver of the Mitsubishi. 'They've come from all over England to march.'

David pulled out his wallet. 'How far are you going?'

'Ten miles.' She gave him a determined smile.

'I wish you luck.' He handed her a bill.

She glanced at it. 'Oh, dear, you've made a mistake.' She held it out to him. 'This is a £50 note.'

A glance in the rear-view mirror showed that the Porsche had stopped a couple of hundred yards back and was turning around. 'Seeing you has made my day,' David said. 'I mean it. It's not anywhere near enough.'

'Are you sure? Absolutely? You *are* kind. Thank you so much.' She turned to her parade and waved the note. 'Everybody! Look! This nice man has given us a whole £50.'

She turned back to thank David again, then peered into the car. 'Oh, dear, I'm so sorry.' He turned to follow her line of sight. 'Is your wife ill? Can we help?'

Helen's eyes were terrified. Her lips were tinged blue. Red foam bubbled from her mouth.

# 67

## HILDENBRIDGE

The tall woman issued some quick instructions to the cameraman, then got into the back seat. David's calm hadn't deserted him through the entire chase with the Porsche, but his hands trembled as he crossed the wires beneath the dash.

His new passenger wasn't interested in the details of car ignition; she murmured gently to Helen as the engine started up and the car eased its way past the crowd. 'Not to worry. It'll all come right. You just wait and see.' Then to David, 'Sharp right here. What did you say your name was? Richard Gwendolyn? I'm Eugenia Wynne. Now sharp left. Two miles straight ahead down this road.' She turned back to Helen. 'There, there, Mrs Gwendolyn. Breathe in and out. That's it. Slowly in. Slowly out. We're proud of our doctors in Hildenbridge. You'll be right as rain in no time. Sharp left after the roundabout, Mr Gwendolyn. That's it. Pull up here.'

'This isn't a hospital.' David was furious. The building was red brick, Victorian, gabled; they'd pulled into a walled court in front of it. 'We need a hospital. Where's the hospital?'

'You stay *here*, Mr Gwendolyn.' Eugenia's voice took full command. 'This *is* a hospital, however it may look to a tourist's eyes.'

Helen's skin was very pale. Her eyes were shut. Her breathing came in gasps. David had told himself that nothing moved him any more, that he was dead at the core, but he cleared the hair away from Helen's face yet once more — and was terrified.

'Helen?' he said.

She opened her eyes. A flicker of a smile played about her lips. 'You've never . . . called me by . . . my name before. Can you . . . ' But she lost consciousness before she could finish.

'Do something!' he shouted at the middle-aged man who appeared at her side, grey hair rising in a halo around his head. A nurse stood behind him in a blue uniform. 'For the love of God, *do* something!'

The doctor took out a stethoscope, listened to Helen's chest, gave orders to the nurse, who ran back inside.

'You were hit by somebody?' he asked David.

'Rammed.'

The nurse appeared with a companion, a neck brace and a stretcher. David stood back, helpless, while the two of them and the doctor lifted Helen out of the car and onto the stretcher. He followed as they bore her away through heavy oak doors, down a corridor, into a room that seemed to be half office, half operating room, and transferred her to a high table there. A sudden flurry of activity — David's brain couldn't make sense of the words — resulted in a ventilator tube going down her throat. He gagged as though it were his own throat, and was hardly aware of the nurse as she led him away to a public room, sat him down there, brought him a cup of tea.

'She's going to be okay?' he said, not even trying to hide the panic in his voice.

'Oh, yes. Not to worry. Of course she will be.'

David knew the nurse was lying. He knew it. He got up, sat down, got up again. The upholstery of his chair was frayed. A man whose face was yellow from disease slumped in a matching chair opposite him. David couldn't bear it a minute longer. He went outside and called the number Christina had given him. The conversation was brief and to the point.

Then he called Martha. 'I want a boy.'

'A *what*?'

'Maybe ten years old. Maybe eleven. No older.'

'What *for*?'

'I also need a big plastic bottle of Coke or Pepsi — or anything else the kid likes — and a large bag of packing peanuts.'

'What if I can't get a boy?'

'Boy, girl, it doesn't matter.'

'This doesn't sound like a nice night in front of the telly even with them peanuts.'

'*Packing* peanuts. Styrofoam. Like you use for shipping fragile things. One last item. One of those hose clips. The kind you can adjust. Metal. You know what I mean. Got that?'

'Not really.'

'Meet me somewhere near the Notting Hill area. Pick a place. I don't know London.'

'How about Kensington Gardens? Speke's Monument.'

'Where's that?'

'Great big tall thing. You can't miss it.'

David went back into the hospital, explained to the nurse that a private ambulance would pick Helen up and take her to a larger facility, then he got back in the car and drove to London. He dumped the car on a residential street and walked towards the centre of town.

# 68

## LONDON

Martha sat on a bench opposite the monolith celebrating the man who looked for the source of the Nile and found Lake Victoria instead. She wore respectable running shoes instead of her usual clippety-clop heels, and she'd somehow managed to make herself look like a young mother or maybe an au pair — a bit harassed, not a seamless fit into Kensington Gardens, but not altogether wrong either. As though to reinforce the impression, a small boy who'd been skipping around Speke's Monument stopped suddenly, waved at her, skipped over. He wore a bright red tee shirt with a chicken in a top hat on it and the word 'Wombat'.

'I want me lemon squash,' he said.

'This is Kevin,' she said to David, pulling a big bottle out of a plastic bag from Sainsbury's and handing it to the boy. 'You don't mind if he drinks it now, do you?'

'It's all his.'

'You don't want any?'

David shook his head, and Kevin upended the bottle in his mouth.

'Will he do what I tell him?' David said to Martha.

Martha gave him a wry smile. 'He's a lousy

pickpocket, but he'll sell his body to any guy who'll pay the price. Who knows? He might even surprise you.'

* * *

Googie was thoroughly disgruntled by his morning's performance. Not that he could blame himself for *all* of it.

The number Becky gave him had brought him within only a couple of hundred yards of the small cliff that his MI6 ground traffic controller was aiming towards, his every move — as well as David's — monitored from London by satellite. The position was a superb fatal crash scene. Perfect.

Two shots to the chest and one to the head? It's one of those Hollywood fantasies that's been swallowed whole by newspapers, TV producers, the public at large. It's okay for street thugs who take a childish pleasure in showing off their pricks. But the last thing corporate clients want is the possibility of being implicated. The ruling principle of the real professionals like Googie is that if you do it right, nobody will ever know. Accidents happen. If a bereaved relative does suspect something, there is no trail to follow.

The Porsche couldn't have been bettered as a vehicle: reinforced ram bumpers, stainless steel brake lines, heavy duty steering pump. It made David Marion's Fiesta — a *Fiesta*, for crying out loud — almost too easy a target. Googie's UK colleagues had been happy enough to supply both the car and an AR-15 rifle modified to shoot pellets of a compound — it's known in the trade as pseudocosanol — that mimics a high blood alcohol level. The bodies would be badly burned, and post-mortem forensics would reveal another sad case of drunk driving.

It was a technique Googie had used before, very successfully too. But what had so fine an example of international cooperation come to this time? Before he'd had a chance at the kill, he'd had to pull back and run away from a road crammed full of ancients.

And yet it *was* funny. His baby brother Robin would have thought so too — if Marion hadn't killed him first, that is. It was even apt in its way: Robin had loved dressing up as an old man with a long beard. Googie missed his baby brother. He missed his wife and kids. Another Hollywood fantasy is the lone and troubled hit man. Googie was just another civil servant at heart. The excitements he was homesick for were the ones of his back yard on days like this one, kids climbing the jungle gym, dogs barking, rainbow shimmering in the sprinkler's spray, charcoal beginning to catch fire for a barbecue, neighbours arriving with potato salad and blueberry muffins.

At least the afternoon was sunny. The living room of the CIA's Ganton Place house was up a flight of stairs; its floor-to-ceiling windows gave it a full view of the street below. A girl rode a bicycle with her hair floating out behind her. A gaggle of teenagers pranced and flirted. A little boy in a bright red tee shirt worked his way from door to door, his mother hovering anxiously with tonight's dinner in supermarket bags.

Googie was already downstairs to answer the knock when the little boy reached his house. 'What is it, Superman?' he said, opening the door to greet the child. 'Money for the school gym?'

To his surprise, the boy squatted down at once.

Googie barely felt the shot.

* * *

Googie's doorway, like all the doorways in Ganton Place, was set back from the street by a short stone wall and a minute courtyard, the door itself recessed further still to allow for an outside light and protection from the elements while owners fumbled with keys and groceries. David had slipped in beside the little boy Kevin while Googie was on his way downstairs. The kid had glanced up at him for his okay, knocked, waited for the answer, then crouched down.

'Go,' David said to him.

The boy got to his feet. 'Is he dead?'

'Go!'

'Can I ask next door?'

'Yeah. Sure. Now go.'

Googie glanced down at his chest and touched the blood that was spreading out across his shirt. 'Marion,' he said, taking a step backwards into the house. David followed, shutting the door behind him.

The working parts of the 38 magnum were hidden from Googie, but he knew the trick. He'd taught it to Robin. Fill a big plastic bottle with Styrofoam packing peanuts, clip it to the muzzle and maybe it looks weird but it's got to be the quickest, cheapest silencer in the world. Nobody had heard the first shot; he'd barely heard it himself. Nobody would hear the others either.

'I get a final request?' he said to David.

'What?'

'Let's make it look like on TV, huh? You know, like people want. One more to the chest. Last one in the head.'

The press would lap it up. They'd know for absolute certain there'd been a real, live contract killing here. Googie's dying thoughts were of headlines and glory. He could see his picture spread across the front page of the *State Journal-Register*.

**CIA AGENT TAKEN OUT IN LINE OF DUTY**

Maybe they'd ask his wife to Washington to collect a medal.

The joke of it was that he and David were both after precisely the same effect.

# 69

## GATWICK

The kid in the red wombat shirt was the one who called Kastus Youdin from a public pay phone. Nobody could have faulted the performance: too terrified to tell anybody his name or where he was calling from or how he'd got hold of this number at the *Sunday Times* but careful to be very precise about the dead man he'd seen at 22 Ganton Place.

David walked Martha and the kid to the tube station at Queensway, then went back through Kensington Gardens and along the crowded London streets to Victoria. He took the train to Gatwick, where a uniformed chauffeur met him at the central information desk and led him out to a limousine that occupied a reserved space right outside the airport's main entrance.

The ride took twenty minutes through security checks, onto the airfield itself, past hangars and row after row of jets, across acres of runway beyond them to a plane that could hold at least eighty passengers and that stood alone in a huge, open stretch of unmarked macadam.

The words 'SOS International' covered most of the length of the plane's white body. Just under the cockpit, it said 'Air Ambulance'.

A stairway was already in place. David climbed

it to a standard airline door that opened into a standard tight airline corridor. But instead of seats, the corridor continued past two doors and ended in a third with a red light burning above it.

The person who walked forward to meet him wore a name tag that read: 'Zuba'.

'Where is she?' he demanded. 'Let me see her.'

'I do hope you will forgive me, Mr Marion, if I say that this is not a convenient moment. We had presumed we would be in a position to give you a complete report' — Zuba could have stepped out of an American hospital except for the formality of her speech — 'but pneumothorax can present in a rather puzzling fashion, as I am certain you are already aware.'

'Pneumo — ?'

Blood never makes sense. Allandale's blood this afternoon could have belonged to a piece of beef. Nobody on earth could tell the difference between it and Helen's just by looking. But things don't work like that. Pneumo-something: lungs? Were they cutting into Helen's lungs? The thought made him feel sick.

Zuba smiled reassurance. 'Do not distress yourself. The doctor will give you more details soon. We are a top level facility, able to carry out critical care services even mid-flight. Miss Freyl has already undergone surgery of much the kind she would undergo had she remained in an English hospital.'

'*Already*?'

'As I say, pneumothorax can present in a rather — ' She broke off. 'Perhaps it would be best if I found you a place to lie down. Yes?'

He followed her to a bedroom-like cabin, where Martha's hypodermic — another grocery item from those Sainsbury's plastic bags — offered him a few hours of peace.

# 70

## GUILDFORD

Charles spent the quiet of this Saturday waiting for Googie's report and staring moodily across a broad sweep of lawn that led to National Trust land beyond the Hay family estate's boundary. As a child, he'd run along the secret passageway that Lescaze designed for his father. He'd played in the woods as his father had before him; he'd climbed the trees, found his way along the hidden trails. Usually just knowing the Trust land was there soothed him, but today his tension mounted hour by hour; he had to keep telling himself that Googie hadn't been at all sure how the timing might work out. Maybe today. Maybe tomorrow. Monday morning at the latest. He had no doubt that Googie would succeed, whichever day.

He didn't cope well with the feelings that Helen had forced on him: to think he'd allowed himself to grow fond of the woman, that she'd manipulated him — *him*, Charles Hay — that she still had the diamond that had been in the Hay family for generations. His heart flip-flopped in his chest. He could taste bile in his mouth. His fists clenched and unclenched on their own. His only regret right now was that he'd be robbed of watching her die.

When his telephone rang at about five in the afternoon, he leapt to answer it.

'I haven't heard from Allandale yet,' he said irritably as soon as he heard Jeffrey's voice. 'I told you I'd ring you as soon as I had.'

'Have you checked your email?'

'Get a grip, Jeffrey. He said he'd telephone or come to the house. You know that too.'

'I suggest you check your email at once, Sir Charles. I'll be at your home at eight with Martin Goldsmith.'

He hung up before Charles had a chance to object.

Charles scanned his inbox, found nothing, checked the emails he'd deleted. He could see why he'd passed over this one. It was marked 'priority', and the subject line read, 'Important alteration in status of Patent US 005483167A'. Spam for get-rich-quick investments often looks like that. The address of the sender was JZ@HFZ.com — all the more like spam. Since he hadn't opened the email, he didn't see that copies had gone to all UCAI directors and all executive personnel at Follaton Medical Foundation as well as the financial sections of several US newspapers.

Dear Sirs:

The US Patent Office will confirm that the patent for Yeznik (LA)-205.3 has been in the sole ownership of Dr Helen Freyl since its registration 11 years ago. At 4:40 PM New York time, Dr Freyl reached agreement to lease it to Galleas International for an undisclosed sum.

For further information, please contact James Zemanski of Herndon Freyl & Zemanski at this email address.

Yours sincerely,

Rebecca Freyl

Charles's first reaction was panic. That dry-sounding email meant he was a dead man. He bolted into the fresh air outside and rushed unseeing along the forested trails he'd known all his life.

* * *

At about the time Follaton was becoming involved in Belarus, Charles had come across an intriguing reference to some animal experiments in an article buried in the middle of *The Times*: a small lab in Dorset, a brilliant but cautious biologist, some extraordinary-sounding results. He'd taken the lab's reports to the Ministry of the Pharmaceutical Industry in Minsk. Scientists there were as intrigued as he'd been; they suggested he buy out the Dorset lab and contact the up-and-coming American conglomerate UCAI. They set up the meeting themselves. They also proposed that UCAI plan to test the new formulation on the people of Belarus.

The idea in itself wasn't criminal. It's not even unusual. Many US pharmaceuticals are tested in foreign countries. People are more tractable abroad; they don't know they have a choice. The problems began to arise when the UCAI board pressed for uniform background radiation levels to speed up the trial schedule. The only way Charles could think of achieving that was to seed the ground with irradiated fertiliser. They'd agreed. They'd supplied lead-lined tractors, the fertiliser itself and the powdered caesium to go in it. They'd also sent him Martin Goldsmith and a couple of assistants to handle the paperwork. Undertakings like this call for elaborate double bookkeeping: one set of figures for the real situation, another for public consumption. All reports of the real situation had to be hard copy; electronic records are never secure.

Only a year ago, one of these assistants had checked through the files at the US Patent Office just for fun. What she'd found out was that Follaton didn't hold the rights to Yeznik (LA)-205.3 at all; instead they owned only a nineteenth-century remedy composed of venom, honey and bee propolis. Most such quack medicines weren't patented at all, but Joshua Brewster's grandfather had registered this one in 1895. A cousin of Joshua's — also called Joshua Brewster — had been only too happy to sell it. Why not? The patent had run out a hundred years ago.

By this time, UCAI's Birmingham labs had been synthesising Yeznik (LA)-205.3 for several years, and clinical trials in Belarus were nearing completion. Their results excited everybody. Almost every Belarusian treated with the new drug showed marked improvement, even those who'd been exposed to high doses of radiation. Very soon, the corporation, the Foundation and

Charles personally — he'd cut himself an excellent deal — were going to be able to produce a pharmaceutical that every army and government on earth would have to stockpile.

But cancer is big business too. The leukaemia children had been a totally unexpected side effect of the drug. Many young people who should have been dead were very much alive, a medical surprise to rival the introduction of antibiotics. And further research was giving reason to believe that Joshua's venom might be effective against other forms of the disease as well.

Charles was mid-step over a log when he realized that, carefully played, it was the Belarus project itself that could save him.

* * *

Jeffrey was punctilious. He and Martin arrived at the house at precisely eight. Charles wasn't surprised that Martin stank of liquor.

'You look tired, Martin,' he said.

'How can you be so fucking calm?' Martin was close to tears.

'You'd better come in before you collapse.'

Both openings of Lescaze's fireplace in the living room burned as they had when Helen had been a visitor. With the flames reflected on the two-inch-thick plaster walls, the room almost achieved a sense of human warmth.

'Your usual, Martin?' Charles said, sliding open the door to the drinks cabinet. 'Jeffrey?'

'Thank you, no.'

Charles handed Martin a Scotch and poured some for himself. 'I believe I know how to handle this,' he said.

'Thank Christ for that,' said Martin.

'We have time on our side. I'm virtually certain that none of the directors at UCAI will remember enough detail of the formulation to recognize the significance of the email right away. I'd forgotten the patent number myself, and the Slad twins weren't even on the board when the Belarusian deal went through. When people do see what it means, they'll require corporate decisions before they act. I estimate that we have two days — maybe even three — to set things in motion. What *I* am going to do is draft a personal disclaimer of responsibility. The suitably horrified tone will call for care. I'll spend tomorrow on it. Martin, it's not going to be difficult to gather a few pages of documentation, is it? Enough to make clear all major aspects of the project?'

'No problem.'

'I'll lodge the material in three locations. My instructions will be that if I die, the material is to be photocopied and spread throughout the media of Europe and the United States. The first copy of my disclaimer will go to corporate headquarters in St Louis. I do not believe the righteous Slad twins will enjoy the prospect of UCAI becoming a synonym for mass murder.'

Jeffrey nodded. 'I fear blackmail is the only avenue open to us.'

'I prefer to think of it as life insurance,' Charles said. 'I merely run a charity. There's no reason for me to have access to the details of a massive UCAI business operation.' Charles took a sip of his whisky. 'After all, UCAI is only one of Follaton's backers.'

'Are there roles for others' — Jeffrey glanced over at Martin — 'in this pretty scenario?'

'The way I see it,' Charles said, 'you're the hero of the tale, Jeffrey. A Belarusian national should be the first to sense that things are not as they ought to be in his home country and the first to dig deeper. You will be the man who brings the atrocity to my attention.'

Martin's eyes had moved sluggishly back and forth between the two of them while they talked. 'What about me?' he said.

'Yours is the more standard story, Martin, which makes it all the more readily believable. You direct a team. You're not always here to supervise them. This makes you subject to the machinations of assistants, *all* of whom come through UCAI. There can't be one of them who isn't aware what the Belarusian figures mean. This means they're all culpable in any case. Are you all right, Martin?' Charles paused a moment. 'Martin? Are you with us?'

Martin's eyes were shut. He began to snore.

Charles watched him a moment. 'He says he sleeps better at my house than anywhere else.'

'That was quick,' Jeffrey said. 'What was it? Rohypnol? GHB?'

'It did work well, didn't it? Very pleasing. How about that drink now?' Charles went to the drinks cupboard, poured out a shot of vodka and handed it to Jeffrey.

‘Martin’s position is rather more problematic than ours,’ Jeffrey said, taking the vodka from Charles. ‘The man in charge of manipulating the statistics is so vulnerable to accusation.’

Charles nodded. ‘Especially when he’s the only member of UCAI’s board in our midst, and even more especially when people who work under him keep dying. He drinks too much, poor fellow. Such people are notoriously unreliable. I’ve already arranged for what might be called’ — a gentle knock at the door barely interrupted his flow — ‘a few ‘financial irregularities’ in his dealings with offshore accounts. Involvement in something like that makes a good starting place.’ The knock at the door repeated. ‘What is it?’ he called.

‘There’s a man to see you, Sir Charles,’ came a voice through the door.

‘An American?’

‘Oh, yes, sir. Very broad accent.’

Charles glanced at Jeffrey. ‘Show Mr Allandale into the library.’

‘Get rid of him,’ Jeffrey said. ‘We don’t need him any more.’

‘Don’t you think an insider at UCAI might prove useful? Somebody wholly unconnected to the scandal? Do pour yourself another vodka while I deal with him.’

The library’s window wall showed only the black of a clouded-over October night, no hint of the National Trust land that had been Charles’s playground. The lighting in the room was diffuse, subtle; it glowed with promise.

But he started when he saw a man he’d never

met leaning back in one of the upholstered chairs designed by Lescaze himself.

'It's not very comfortable, is it?' the man said, patting the chair's mahogany arms. When he spoke the light glinted off steel teeth in his mouth.

'Who are *you*? What are you doing here?'

'Don't let my American accent fool you. My name is Kastus Youdin, born and bred in Pripyat.'

'Go away, Mr Youdin. I'm busy.'

'Yeah, sure, but I got a problem, and I figure you can probably give me some advice. See, I'm one of the Belarusians you've been poisoning for the last few years. Trouble is, that's going to take an awful lot of effort to get across. So I'm thinking your brother's a good place to start. What do you say?'

'What *do* you want?'

'There's some neat new evidence: a couple statements sworn out forty years ago as well as an autopsy report that shows tissues surprisingly clear of any known drug for a guy who's just died of an overdose. Of course, there's also your own record of youthful indiscretion.'

'Get out.'

Kastus frowned, shook his head. 'See, that's what I wanted to ask you about. Smart legal work could overturn that stuff, couldn't it? On the other hand, nobody's smart enough to clear you of what you've been doing in Belarus. I'll stake my reputation on that. Not that I have much of one. Not yet anyhow. You're going to change all that for me. But is Belarus the right place to start? In terms of my career, I mean? Probably Mr Allandale is better, don't you think? He's the most straightforward.'

'Are you actually refusing to leave my house?'

'Why would I leave? I wouldn't miss this for the world.'

Charles picked up the telephone and began to dial.

'Police? Don't bother.' Kastus leaned back in his chair. 'They're already on their way. Of course, that's only one team. You've got the whole of Scotland Yard in an uproar. I suppose one troop of them must be at Mowbray Square right now. Another one should — ' He broke off. 'I think I can hear sirens.'

Charles couldn't hear anything. He knew Kastus couldn't either. But an unease about the man made him abruptly certain that Kastus hadn't been able to wait as long as he was supposed to — thank God for the stupid eagerness of the young — and that there were a few minutes' grace before those sirens would actually become audible.

'Oh, I'm with the *Sunday Times*.' Kastus found himself struggling to hold Charles's attention. 'Sorry, did I neglect to mention that? Hey, where do you think you're going?'

Charles had his hand on the door, 'You will excuse me now, Mr Youdin,' he said. 'I have work to do.'

The passageway Lescaze had built for his father took him to the woods; he knew them well even at night. He called a taxi from the edge of them to take him to Guildford station.

# 71

## THE PRESS

The internet edition of the *Sunday Times* carried Kastus Youdin's first headline story.

**EXCLUSIVE**
**Warrant issued for the arrest of Sir Charles Hay**
**The charge is murder**

Yesterday afternoon, a *Sunday Times* reporter following an anonymous tip found the body of a man who police believe was the victim of a contract killing.

An envelope of evidence given to this reporter suggests a clear connection between the death of this man, American CIA agent Merlin Googe Allandale, and Sir Charles Hay . . .

Sir Charles has not been seen since yesterday evening, and a police search is underway. His solicitors have issued a statement emphatically denying all charges . . .

Within hours, the *Mail on Sunday* felt free to sensationalise the more personal aspects of the story.

**ARISTOCRAT MURDERED HIS OWN BROTHER TO GAIN INHERITANCE**

Sir Charles Hay, already being sought for the murder of an American CIA agent, now faces a second murder charge . . .

The Freyl family of Springfield, Illinois, employed the murdered CIA agent to investigate Sir Charles, whose ultra-respectable life style may have hidden a role in the drug overdose that killed . . .

Sir Charles Hay's solicitors have issued a statement emphatically denying . . .

Kastus Youdin's real news took another week to appear.

**CRIMES AGAINST HUMANITY**
**A British Dr Mengele?**
**Law Lords to decide charges against Sir Charles Hay**

Sir Charles Hay, Director of the Follaton Medical Foundation, supervised a programme that subjected literally millions of human guinea pigs in Belarus to high levels of radiation for medical experiments. Photographs and specimen documents reveal that Merlin Allandale gave his life to expose this modern holocaust mastermind . . .

If a charge of crimes against humanity is brought against Sir Charles, he will be the first human being in history to be prosecuted for mass criminal acts not connected with armed conflict . . .

The deaths of several English citizens are also under investigation, including a young man and woman who had volunteered for what they thought was a worthy cause . . .

Sir Charles Hay is still at large. His solicitors have issued a statement emphatically denying . . .

The *Wall Street Journal* was the first to pick up the energy connection.

**Belarus reveals massive uranium deposits**
**UCAI rejected in bid for exclusive rights to mining and exploration**
**Galleas International takeover**

. . . the American giant's involvement with Sir Charles Hay, charged last night with crimes against humanity, has allowed its rival Galleas International to grab the opportunity and move forward on newly discovered deposits . . .

UCAI has issued a press release emphatically denying . . .

A day later the *Financial Times* ran a small piece on a public body set up in England to help ensure healthy competition in the business world.

**HARDCASTLE & WALKER APPOINTED**

Mr Jeffrey Hardcastle, whose inside information is crucial to the government's case against Sir Charles Hay, will head the Human Resources Department for the Competition Commission . . .

He brings with him his colleague Mr Gabriel Walker.

Becky's piece of the puzzle appeared first as headline news in the *New York Times*:

**NEW MIRACLE DRUG WILL BE FREE TO ALL CHERNOBYL VICTIMS**

But it was only right and proper that the US government honoured Mrs Merlin Allandale's request: the *State Journal-Register* broke a story that was even better than the one Googie had died wishing for. A photograph of him looking stern and important filled the entire front page beneath a headline that read:

**SPRINGFIELD HERO TO RECEIVE CONGRESSIONAL MEDAL OF HONOR**

# 72

## HARROW ON THE HILL

Trains run regularly from Guildford into London, and the underground system stretches all the way to Harrow on the Hill, near where Charles had gone to school with Hugh Freyl half a century before.

The hotel Charles chose had passed from mother to daughter for generations; it was a small, shabby place, with a lucrative sideline in Harrow boys. To this day, many of them lose their virginity there — and return again and again to practise their newly learned skills — just as Charles and Hugh had. They'd done the original deed together: straw Harrow boaters tossed on a battered table and a couple of warm-hearted girls, one of them the proprietor's daughter.

The bored woman at the front desk almost went to sleep on him as he told her he was researching a book about British bus transport, but she did understand that he'd pay well to have his meals brought in and that he didn't want to be disturbed.

The room was not pleasant. The bedstead was iron. The wallpaper bubbled over damp spots, and the walls were thin. Travelling salesmen snored through them. Water pipes clanked.

Harrow boys grunted. Nor was there a radio or a television to drown out the sound. Underneath the bed, Charles found a book of cryptic crosswords. Usually he was good at them, but this time he didn't seem able to grasp the simplest of clues.

Charles had never contemplated suicide; he did not think of himself as contemplating it now. It had never occurred to him that he'd find himself in a situation that he couldn't get out of one way or another. The trouble was, this one didn't seem to be revealing any loopholes. He couldn't stay in this hovel of a place for much longer. Even if he could bear the sheer nastiness of it, the cash he'd had on him was running out. But if he went outside, someone would recognize him. He followed the news on the browser of a mobile he'd bought near Paddington, and he knew his picture was everywhere. The police were watching all airports, trains, roads; they'd traced him as far as London, and their search would bring them to Harrow on the Hill sooner rather than later.

As the days went by, he began to realize that he could not escape.

A drawer beside his bed in the Lescaze house held Valium and barbiturates. A cupboard in the kitchen held a selection of other useful drugs. Opportunities from his garden included yew, laburnum bark, belladonna, roots of the handsome purple hemlock, that bloomed in the spring.

Charles would have preferred such a peaceable end. On the other hand, he'd spent a lifetime going for the jugular; this was hardly the time to stop.

The tool was no problem. On the off-chance that he'd need a weapon of some kind, he'd bought a chef's boning knife — razorsharp — at a supermarket not far from where he'd bought the mobile. The act itself? Not quite as straightforward as one might think. There's a secret to it. A lifetime ago, when he'd been young and so fond of cocaine, he'd overdosed once — only a month or so before he'd managed to rid the world of his brother — and wakened to find himself in an inner-city emergency ward.

An outraged doctor was shouting at a nearby patient swathed in bandages, 'What *is* the matter with you? You *actually* want to cut your throat? Well, next time do it *right*, for Christ's sake. Hold your fucking head back.'

Charles would do as the doctor ordered. He would not bow his head to die. But this entire affair was *wrong*. How dare people expect so much? And having got it, how dare they pretend to shock at the necessities that brought it about? And how dare they force *him* to pay for their hypocrisy? It's so sad — so desperately sad — to take the life of such a brilliant human being, a man reaching his prime, a man with so much to offer.

That was when he noticed drops of water on the blade of the boning knife. He studied them a moment before he realized they were his own tears.

# 73

## SPRINGFIELD, ILLINOIS

The Freyl house stood in a private park in the middle of Springfield. A small stream ran through the lawns and flowerbeds; a grove of big trees hid the road that divided this finest of west side properties from its more lowly neighbours to the east. David drove along the road leading to it in a car loaned him by Lillian's son; he parked in front. The roof of the house was copper, new only a couple of years ago. Since then it had taken on a rich verdigris patina; a row of columns made a portico along the front.

Lillian opened the door as he approached.

'David,' she said, pulling him into her arms. 'She be waiting for you in her study.'

'Any idea how come?'

'She don't tell me nothing.'

Lillian led him to the study door and knocked. 'He's here, ma'am,' she said through it, giving David's shoulder a pat of encouragement.

'Come in, Mr Marion,' Becky said. 'That will be all, Lillian.'

Becky sat behind her desk in the study that had once been her son Hugh's. David had known this room well when computer equipment for the blind dominated it; for months, he'd practised the intricate rituals of life outside prison here: how to buy a tube of toothpaste, how to use a credit card, how to respond to a comment on the weather. Now the frailties of the very old had taken over. A walking frame stood beside Becky. Newly installed red buttons for summoning help dotted the walls even though the old bell that had brought Lillian for thirty years stood on the desk.

Becky scanned David icily. 'First you are responsible for the death of my son, then you try to do the same to my granddaughter.'

'You weren't doing so badly on that front yourself.'

'I *beg* your pardon, Mr Marion. Mr Allandale gave his life to protect her. The newspaper reports make that obvious.'

She hadn't greeted him. She hadn't asked him to sit down. He chose one of the art-nouveau chairs opposite her desk, leaned back in it, stretched out his arms and waited. Becky's customary sense of superiority was in a state of acute confusion. This man — this murderous protégé of Hugh's, this bane of her life — had suddenly turned into a blood relative, son of her own brother's boy. At the same time, her granddaughter's fiancé had been exposed as a person so villainous that Belarus — the last country in Europe with the death penalty still in place — had petitioned the British government to have him extradited. What would have awaited him there, so the *State Journal-Register* said, was a show trial and summary execution by firing squad.

The petition had come through about the time

Charles cut his throat. The body was cold by the time the police were called in, and Becky was profoundly grateful for the death. It prevented a lengthy court investigation into his relationship with Helen. But it was David's connection to her own family that particularly upset balances in the scheme of things. Levels of authority had to be re-established, order to be restored.

'I assume you want money to keep this quiet,' she said.

'You do, huh?'

'Well, do you or don't you?'

'Depends on what you want kept quiet.'

Becky wasn't sure whether she was seeing insolence or stupidity. 'You and Helen are second cousins. The disgrace would be too much to ask her to bear.'

'Sounds like there hasn't been a family conference yet.'

'Most certainly not. What do you take me for? She knows nothing. This is as it must remain.'

'At all costs?'

'At a *reasonable* cost, Mr Marion. At a reasonable cost. Well?'

He was amused. 'I have to admit I kind of like the idea of sharing a secret with you.'

'How *much*?'

He got up, took a card from his wallet and tossed it on her desk. 'Why don't you work out the details with my lawyer?'

She pushed the card to one side without looking at it. 'I do not deal with intermediaries.' But he was already on his way out the door. 'A moment please, Mr Marion. There is another issue I wish to raise with you.'

He didn't turn. Nor did he shut the door behind him.

'Mr Marion!' She heard only his footsteps going away and the murmur of his voice and Lillian's from the entrance hall.

She stared after him a moment, then gave the bell on her desk an angry shake. 'Lillian!' she called out. 'Lillian, come here at once.'

* * *

Memorial Hospital stood in the middle of Springfield's notorious east side. David's drive there took him through streets where he'd played stick ball as a child, past stores he'd stolen from and houses he'd broken into. As a young teenager he'd mugged unwary patients leaving the hospital alone — the street price for pharmacopoeia drugs is wonderfully high — but he'd never been inside the hospital itself.

The reception hall was a vast, glassed-in structure with full-size trees in pots and groupings of comfortable chairs. A suite of stores — gifts, flowers, hot soup — lined the back of it. He hesitated in front of a display of Peruvian lilies and again in front of some chocolate but walked away from both. An elevator took him to the top floor and a nurses' station.

'Helen Freyl,' he said to a nurse behind the desk there. She had a frizz of red hair and a rosebud mouth.

'I'm sorry, sir, Miss Freyl isn't receiving any — '

'*Doctor* Freyl,' David interrupted irritably.

The nurse looked him up and down, and her rosebud mouth eased into a smile. 'It's David, isn't it?'

He gave her a quizzical glance.

'Helen was a little delirious for a while.' The rosebud mouth stretched wider. 'I bet you I know all kinds of things about *you* that practically nobody else does. Turn left, down the hall, last door on your right.'

Helen lay in Memorial's largest private room. The screen of a monitoring unit showed her heartbeat marching ahead at a steady pace. A scaffold on wheels beside her bed sported a bag that fed into a vein in her hand. Her hair straggled. Her face was blotchy. The nasal prongs of her oxygen supply spread out across her cheeks.

'You look awful,' David said.

'David!' she cried, then caught her breath with a gasp.

'Pain?'

She nodded. 'The damn lung collapsed again. They say I've got to give up smoking. Can you credit it? My grandmother hires some nut who practically gets me killed, and *I* have to give up cigarettes.'

'She says you don't remember anything about it.'

'Discussions involving you have never been her strong point.'

'It was my fault.'

'The hell it was. How'd you get her to let you up here anyhow? I thought you'd been banished for good and all.'

'I beat her into it.'

He'd come to tell Helen that this collapsed lung had frightened him more than anything had ever frightened him before, that even before it happened, she'd turned his thoughts into a tangle they'd never recover from, that he couldn't bear to let her out of his sight.

And yet all he could find to say was, 'How come you have a clothes pin on your finger?'

'It measures oxygen levels or something. David, I was so afraid you weren't . . . ' She trailed off.

'What?'

'I mean, I thought maybe you'd be . . . Why haven't you come to see me?' She was abruptly angry, 'I've been here for a whole week without you. I missed you. I needed you. Where've you been all this time?'

'Nowhere special.'

'You're not getting ready to turn your back on me again, are you?'

His face softened. 'Why would I do a thing like that?'

'You ran away from me in the street once.'

'I was scared.'

'Of me?'

'Terrified.'

'Do you think — ' She broke off, bit her lip, her anger gone as abruptly as it had come. 'UCAI aren't going to like your role in all this, you know.'

'I know.'

'People like that can turn nasty, David.'

'I'll bear it in mind.'

'You'd, um . . . You know, they'd have a much harder time being nasty if you were married to me.'

He sat down on the bed. 'Is that a proposal?'

She smiled, traced the puzzlement on his face with the tips of her fingers. 'There's a condition.'

'A condition? You?' He raised his eyebrows.

'You have to teach me how to pick locks.'

*Other titles published by The House of Ulverscroft:*

## LITTLE GIRLS LOST

**J. A. Kerley**

Children are disappearing in Mobile, Alabama; the latest snatched from her own bedroom. There are no clues — and, as yet, no bodies. With public anger reaching dangerous levels, homicide detective Carson Ryder finds a case hopelessly tangled up in murky local politics. Ryder's bosses have one last hope though, in Conner Sandhill, a former cop whose uncanny ability to solve baffling crimes is legendary. But Sandhill left the police in mysterious circumstances and his presence on the case causes uproar. With the hunt ever more urgent, he and Ryder must form an uneasy alliance. At the root of these disappearances is something truly evil — and its source is closer to home than either could have imagined.

**COLD HEARTED**

**Beverly Barton**

Jordan Price doesn't look like your typical serial killer. Young and beautiful, she exudes innocence and vulnerability. But after her latest husband dies in mysterious circumstances, investigator Rick Carson is forced to consider her capable of cold-blooded murder. The deeper he delves into the string of deaths which seem to stalk Jordan, the more dangerous the game of cat-and-mouse becomes. The targets are changing and suddenly no one is safe. If Jordan is as innocent as she claims, Rick may have placed her in a brutal killer's crosshairs. But if she's guilty, Rick will pay in blood . . .

## MERCY STREET

### Mariah Stewart

It's a balmy spring evening when four teenagers meet for the final time — the next morning, two are dead, the others missing. Are the missing kids on the run for murder? Or were they, too, the victims of a ruthless killer? Ex-cop turned PI Mallory Russo is determined to figure out what happened in the park that night. And with the unofficial help of detective Charlie Wanamaker she resolves to find the teenagers and prove their innocence — whether they be dead, or alive. But what Charlie and Mallory discover will take them down a twisted path that leads to an old unsolved murder — and justice for a killer with a heart of stone.

## EMMA'S BABY

### Abbie Taylor

Struggling as a single mother, Emma sometimes wishes that her thirteen-month-old son would just disappear. But when, one quiet Sunday evening, Ritchie is abducted by a stranger from the London Underground, Emma is thrown into a situation worse than she could have ever imagined. But why don't the police seem to fully believe her story? Why would they think that she would want to hurt her own baby? If Emma wants Ritchie back it looks like she'll have to find him herself. With the help of a stranger called Rafe, the one person who seems to believe her, she goes in search of her son. And she is determined to get him back . . . no matter what it takes.

## TRUST ME

### Jeff Abbott

Luke Dantry tragically lost his parents when he was a teenager — his father was murdered by a crazed operative, his mother died in a terrible accident. Brought up by his stepfather, Luke now works with him on his research, monitoring extremist groups on the internet. Yet within the seemingly harmless world of the internet lie untold dangers. And Luke suddenly feels the full force of them when he is kidnapped at gunpoint in an airport car park. He's an ordinary guy who's led a blameless life, so why has he been targeted. He just knows that he must escape — somehow.

## THE LIAR'S DIARY

### Patry Francis

School secretary Jeanne Cross is an ordinary wife and mother with a seemingly perfect life when Ali Mather, the new music teacher, arrives on the scene. Ali is everything Jeanne isn't: flamboyant, reckless and sexy, with a habit of breaking rules and hearts wherever she goes. Despite their differences, the women are drawn to each other and an unlikely friendship develops. But beneath the surface, both of them are troubled. For Ali, it is the suspicion that someone has been breaking into her house — not to steal, but to terrify her. For Jeanne, there are secrets too dark and too brutal to face alone; secrets that will be dragged into the light with devastating results for her family and her friend.